FINAL DEPARTURE

Visit us at www.boldstrokesbooks.com

FINAL DEPARTURE

by

Steve Pickens

A Division of Bold Strokes Books

2016

FINAL DEPARTURE

© 2016 By Steve Pickens. All Rights Reserved.

ISBN 13: 978-1-62639-536-7

This Trade Paperback Original Is Published By
Bold Strokes Books, Inc.
P.O. Box 249
Valley Falls, NY 12185

First Edition: February 2016

Credits
Editor: Jerry L. Wheeler
Production Design: Stacia Seaman
Cover Design by Jeanine Henning

Acknowledgments

They say no one writes a book alone, and I have certainly found that to be true. Without these folks who have helped me shape Jake and Sam in this book (and six others that follow), I'm positive I wouldn't have been able to do it. I am forever in your debt: Ang, Brandon, Debbie, Gloria, Lonnie, and Mom and Dad.

Special thanks to Jerry Wheeler, who made editing a smooth and incredibly easy process, and to everyone at Bold Strokes for helping me fulfill a lifelong ambition.

For my grandmother, Thelma,
the kindest person I have ever known,
and always for B.

CHAPTER ONE

Y ou miserable, black-hearted old tub!" Jake Finnigan muttered as the ferry *Elwha* dropped into a trough. The three-hundred-eighty-two-foot vessel shimmed like a geriatric hula girl, rattling and sending out a sharp *bang!* that reverberated through the hull. He waited for the ferry to return to center, but the *Elwha* hung on the roll instead, leaning to port for a fraction of a second longer than it should have. Grudgingly, she returned to an even keel, and he let out the breath he'd unconsciously been holding.

He was already in his bunk, trying to read and not contemplate the tempest outside as the ferry struggled through the strait on its last trip of the evening headed to Friday Harbor. The ferry gave another lurch, shudder and bang, righting itself quicker. Moments later, the bobbing stopped, and he knew they must have sailed into the protective waters of Thatcher Pass.

Sighing, he glanced at the clock. One hundred fifteen hours, fifty-five minutes, and twenty-eight seconds, and Sam would be home. If he'd realized six months was going to be so long, he'd never have agreed to Sam running off to Australia, even if it did hasten Sam's Retire At Forty plan. The long days apart had been unbearable, the phone bill astronomical, and his generally amiable nature tarnished by what his captain called "a severe case of the crabbies."

"I'll be so glad when Sam gets back and you are your usual self," said Captain Rhoda Trelawney the week prior.

He smiled at this now, setting aside the book and feeling his stomach drop out as the *Elwha* plowed through the heavy seas outside. Crabby, because he hadn't seen his partner of nearly ten years for six months. Many couples would have looked forward to that break. Once again, Jake let the knowledge that he was a lucky man wash over him, and with a contented smile, he shut off the light and went to sleep.

❖

Hours later, Jake gasped, sitting bolt upright. He took a few deep breaths, shivering, his body sheathed in sweat. He threw his sleeping bag open and sat on the edge of the bunk, holding his head in his hands. When he had regained his composure, he glanced over at his clock and saw it was just after four in the morning. No point in trying to get back to sleep now, he knew, as he'd have to be up in forty-five minutes to sail back to Arrow Bay.

He went to the basin and ran the water until it was warm, trying to push the images from his dream out of his head. He'd never seen the crime photos, but his imagination was all too vivid. He visualized the plastic sheeting, the shadowed figure within, the plastic coming unfolded and catching a glimpse of the pale blue lips…

"Knock it off," he said aloud.

He washed his face and brushed his teeth, not wanting to think of it, but the dream had brought it back to him in Technicolor again. He wondered vaguely if it wasn't an ill omen for the day, and he quickly shoved the thought out of his head.

Thirteen years, and still unsolved. The homicide of Christopher Nethercutt Aponte, Jake's best friend from the first grade until his death just before Jake graduated from high school, had gone glacier-cold a decade before. A construction worker on his way to a jobsite had discovered the body, but Jake had read about it and thought about it so often that when he dreamed of Chris, *he* was the one who found his friend dead and wrapped in plastic on the beach near the old Port Jefferson Paper Mill.

An idea flitted through his head like a butterfly in a sunbeam. He quickly pulled out his battered three-ring notebook and pen and flipped through page after page of scribbles until he found a blank sheet. For the next twenty minutes, he wrote frenetically, getting every word and bit of dialog from his head.

Sam had asked him many times why he hadn't gotten a laptop so he could get his ideas down more efficiently.

"By the time the damn thing boots up," Jake had replied, "I'll have forgotten."

"You?" Sam had asked, arching an eyebrow over his glasses,

stroking his bearded chin and looking overtly skeptical and, as ever, like the twin of film director Kevin Smith. "Mr. Eidetic Memory? Forget?"

"I remember what I see and hear, Sam, not what phantom ideas float around in my head," Jake had pointed out.

He looked up from the paper. *Sam.*

Glancing at the calendar, Jake bloomed into a smile. Four days to go.

Four days.

Even now Sam must be making plans for his departure. Jake could hardly wait. Crabby was now being replaced by anticipation, and he knew he'd been walking around the ferry like an idiot the last day, unable to keep from smiling.

Jake finished shaving and made a mental note to stop at the bar for dinner on the way home. He suspected he'd need a drink to wind down after working with Fred Phillips, the homophobic relief mate who barely kept his contempt for Jake in check. In return, Jake barely kept from flattening Phillips's nose, particularly as he suspected Phillips was pilfering his chocolate cupcakes from his lunch each day.

He slipped into his bathrobe and went down the short corridor to the crew bathroom. He took a quick shower and returned to his room, dressing quickly and tidying up his bunk, stowing the sleeping bag in his locker. He made his way up to the wheelhouse to start the coffeepot. Glancing out the windows, he saw the sky lighting up in the east though the sun would not rise for quite some time, close to seven a.m. They would be departing Friday Harbor in the usual gloom, although it looked as if the rain and wind had stopped.

Once the coffee had sputtered to a halt, Jake poured himself a cup and sat down at the computer desk at the back of the wheelhouse, pulling out the latest Kent C. Spievens novel, *The Clock Struck Murder*, wondering if his best friend and fellow Spievens enthusiast, Rachel Parker, had read the book yet.

Jake made a mental note to call Rachel and see if her plans for traveling home to Washington for the holidays had solidified yet. He *knew* something was up with her as she had gotten flakey with her messages and had been difficult to get hold of. Last time that had happened, her most recent relationship had suddenly expired, as she had put it, "like milk just before the pull date. You know, when it sometimes sneakily goes bad the day before it is supposed to and you end up with a mouth full of sour milk before you realize it."

Bitter End, call Rachel, he wrote on the pad in front of him, tearing off the sheet and slipping it into his pocket. He looked up at hearing the sound of footsteps down the corridor; either Captain Trelawney was up or First Mate Fred was. He hoped it was the former and not the latter, as he didn't want his morning brought down just yet. Despite having been awakened by the nightmare, he was feeling quite good.

He shook his head and returned his focus to the task at hand, relieved when he saw Captain Rhoda Trelawney yawning as she climbed the stairs into the wheelhouse.

"Ah, coffee," she said.

"Mind the bite," Jake replied, setting his book down.

"I don't know what plantation in hell this coffee came from, but it's horrible," she said. "Who picked it out?"

"That would be Fred," Jake said. "He likes his coffee's bitterness just slightly under sulfuric acid."

Captain Trelawney, a slender woman of about sixty with thick, brown hair cut in a wedge, shook her head and added copious amounts of dried creamer to her cup before adding the coffee. She took a sip and grimaced. "Yuck. Next time I'm buying."

"Well, we only have to wait until we get back to Arrow Bay. Once the galley crew comes on, we can get some real coffee," Jake said.

"Hmm," Trelawney replied skeptically. "What's our weather like for today?"

"Clear," Jake said. "I haven't checked the forecast today, but as of last night, it was supposed to be okay until the late afternoon," he said, looking out the window, mooning.

"I will be so glad when Sam gets back," Rhoda Trelawney said, shaking her head. "You haven't had your feet on the ground all week."

"Erm," Jake said, shaking his head.

Rhoda chuckled. "It's okay. It's not like you're not doing your job or anything. It's just your usual focus has gone all fuzzy."

"Speaking of not doing a job," Jake said slowly, "I've had another complaint about our favorite ordinary seaman."

"Sean?" Trelawney asked, taking Jake's seat at the computer after he vacated it for her. She brought up NOAA's website to check the weather forecast.

"Yeah," Jake said. "Sally mentioned that the women's head looked like it hadn't been touched all day yesterday."

"She mention this to Fred?" Trelawney asked Jake.

"Twice," Jake confirmed.

"I'll have a word," Captain Trelawney said. She caught Jake's expression and said, "Don't worry; I won't bring you or Sally up."

Jake smiled, and mouthed the words "thank you" just as Fred entered the wheelhouse. As he went to pour himself another cup of coffee, he suddenly realized it was indeed Daphne who'd killed Lord Bettiscomb at Claxton Manor. The Craigganmore Codwallops had always worn their jumpers inside out in the school photo, ever since Giles Gnatworth had been accidentally killed by lightning in the thunderstorm in 1919. It was supposed to have been a way of warding off bad luck...

❖

"Make it one-four-zero, Jake."

"One-four-zero." He made the course correction. "Wind's up a bit. We'll at least avoid it tonight," he said, looking out over Ferryboat Channel as they approached the Arrow Bay ferry terminal. The sky above was flawlessly blue, but heavy clouds were building over Mount Baker. By evening, there would be rain. The temperature was at fifty-six degrees, and the leaves of the vine maples along the rocky shores of Enetai Island were already ablaze in crimson.

"Don't even mention it," said Captain Trelawney. "If we have another run of foul weather like we did last year, I'm bidding off this watch. I've never seen so much green water on the car deck in my life going through Haro Strait."

"And we're stuck with this old top-heavy tub," said Jake.

"You don't care for the *Elwha*, do you Jake?" Trelawney asked.

"No, I do not," Jake readily agreed.

"Get that partner of yours to design us some new boats," Trelawney said, taking the tiller over from Jake as Fred Phillips grunted. "Something you care to say, Fred?"

"Nothing," he spat, looking disgustedly at Jake.

"You can go ahead and clear out, Jake," said Captain Trelawney as they were about to dock.

"Thanks, Captain. See you tomorrow afternoon," Jake said. He looked at Fred and said, "Have a great afternoon, Fred."

Fred said nothing. As soon as Jake slipped down the steps, the *Elwha*'s engines reversed, and she shuddered to a halt. As he made his way down the corridor, he heard Captain Trelawney snap at Fred.

Jake gathered up his bag from the crew quarters and made his way quickly through the ferry and onto the car deck. As they had just returned from Sidney, British Columbia, via Friday Harbor, he quickly cleared Customs and made his way to the staff parking lot, where his electric blue Chrysler PT Cruiser waited for him. Jake pulled out of the lot and sped up the road, heading into Arrow Bay.

❖

Jake turned up Dawson Road toward home after deciding to skip going to the Bitter End. Since the nightmare woke him much earlier than he normally would have gotten up, he was feeling sleep deprived and decided to make an early night out of it. He'd make a quick dinner, then soak in a hot bath before calling it a night.

The narrow road climbed up a steep grade lined with maples and cedar. Dawson Road finally leveled out and High Street, so named because it was at the top of the hill, appeared at his left. The blue and white trimmed house at 100 High Street was one of two anomalies to the neighborhood in terms of architecture. The next-to-last home built on High Street, it was the textbook definition of American Craftsman bungalow: a peaked roof with a gable one story above the front door. A wide porch ran the length of the front of the house, supported by four columns. It was considered a "one and a half story" in true bungalow fashion, with two bedrooms and a full bath upstairs.

Every other house on the block had either Victorian flourishes or, in the case of the Crenshaws across the street, honest-to-goodness Greek-style columns as part of their architecture.

The only other notable exception was the flat, boring ranch-style house that was at number 98 High Street, owned by Leona Weinberg. It had been built in the 1950s and was currently suffering from the sour Mrs. Weinberg's penchant for all things Disney. The latest additions were the red shutters at every window, a big heart cut out of the center of each panel. The lawn was festooned with figurines of the seven dwarves, each on their own little ceramic toadstool, although some lurked in the circle surrounding the old apple tree, buried in the creeping myrtle.

Jake and Sam had bought the house on first look and considered it a rescue; they soon discovered the front porch was full of dry rot and the roof had leaked, ruining the sheetrock in the ceiling of the master bedroom. Had they known about the roof and the prune-faced Mrs. Weinberg, they might have reconsidered, especially when they found out the previous owner had painted over all the oak woodwork in thick coats of pink. Jake and Sam had spent weeks stripping it all off, particularly in the kitchen which had looked as if Pepto-Bismol had been slathered everywhere with great gusto.

The house had become a real home, though, once the work had been completed. They finished out the kitchen with a butcher's block table and uncovered the floor's original hexagonal white ceramic tile. The pink paint had protected the old oak kitchen cabinets, which they refinished. They'd painted the dining room walls sage and pulled up the carpet, restoring the oak hardwood. The table, like all the other furniture in the home, was Mission style.

Upon completion, they'd invited in all the neighbors for an open house, including Mrs. Weinberg, who had refused. They'd been relieved to find that only Mrs. Weinberg seemed to have any kind of an issue with them, and they'd actually formed friendly relationships with everyone on the block, including Mr. and Mrs. Simonton on the other side at 102, who Jake and Sam discovered just before buying the house were aging nudists.

It was *home*, he thought. Nudist neighbors and all. He pulled into the driveway and parked in front of the detached garage, not bothering to put the car in. He got out and slammed the door, looking at the building. He knew it still needed work. The mother-in-law apartment Sam had turned into a makeshift office needed to be restored to a proper guest apartment, and the basement still had to be finished. They'd planned to do the work before Sam left for Australia, but they'd run out of time.

Jake stepped onto the porch and grabbed the mail from the box, rattling the key into the deadbolt, and flipping the tumblers over. He opened the door and kicked it shut behind him just as the answering machine beeped off. A large ginger cat the size of a small dog wrapped itself around his legs, nearly tripping him. Dorothy loved to do that when her food dish was empty. He kneeled down and scratched her ears absently before walking over to the small table near the foot of the stairs and hitting the playback button on the phone and message machine.

"Jake, it's Alex. Give me a call when you can."

I wonder what Alex wants, he thought.

Alexander Blackburn III was an enigmatic figure in Jake and Sam's life. While Jake considered Alex a friend, Sam had always been cool to the man for reasons Jake was not entirely sure of.

Alex was a Blackburn of *the* Blackburn family, the prominent Seattle clan that had roots or, as Alex called them, "tentacles," in the city as far back as the early days of the twentieth century. They had made their fortune in logging and mining in California, Washington, and Oregon, and at one time owned good portions of land in all three states. The family had splintered in recent years over issues on how to manage the company assets, with one side pro-environmental and the other decidedly less so.

Alex, up until he had been in his mid-twenties, had been in the "rape the environment camp," as he put it, until meeting the renowned environmentalist David LeSeur. Much to the chagrin of the elder Alexander Blackburn, Alex had gone back to school to study environmental science and had spent a great deal of time researching the diverse ecosystem in Washington State, culminating with his book *Down the Dark Shaft.* The highly critical study on the history of mining in Washington State and the disastrous aftereffects it had wrought included misdeeds from his own family. They excommunicated Alex as a result.

Jake and Sam had met Alex at a reading of this book they went to one evening as a break from all the overtime Jake had been working. Both had been struck by Blackburn, an incredibly handsome man who always looked like he'd just stepped out of the pages of *GQ.* As he read passionately from his book, he seemed to radiate a smooth sexuality with the slightest of glances and nuances to his melodic voice. The couple had noticed how Blackburn's mere presence in any room turned heads. His undeniable charisma was wrapped up in his lithe movements and open masculinity. It was impossible *not* to be drawn to him. He smiled easily and openly, his blue eyes sparkling with mirth and slight mischievousness. His loose, combed-back curly brown hair and perpetual two weeks of beard growth gave him a rugged quality, though he always dressed in spotless tailored suits of gray, black, or blue.

After the reading, they'd bumped into one another several times, forming an unlikely friendship. Jake found Alex's company enjoyable, as he was thoughtful and intelligent, and Alex for his part seemed to enjoy Jake and Sam's candor and openness, though Jake was far more open than Sam, who still maintained a cool distance years later.

"You don't entirely trust him, do you?" Jake had asked one day as they were walking some trails in the Mount Baker National Forest shortly before Sam left for Australia.

"Not entirely, no."

"Why?"

"Alex is too guarded," Sam had said. "He knows oodles about you, and to some degree about me, but what do we know about him? Other than he's one of *the* Blackburns and that he doesn't get along with dear old Dad too well. Which isn't surprising. I've seen the guy on TV, and he's an asshole."

The assessment of Alexander Blackburn II had surprised Jake. Sam seldom, if ever, swore, and he *never* used an expletive to describe another human being, including the ex-boyfriend who had physically abused him.

Jake made a mental note to call Alex back, flipping through the mail while walking through the dining room and into the kitchen. He snapped on the overhead light and set the mail down on the table, appraising his flock: the gray-haired Sophia sat expectantly next to her bowl while her daughter, the ginger Dorothy, washed her face and pretended to be above the whole issue. Barnaby, the beagle, had just come barreling in from outside through the dog flap and was also sitting next to his food dish, tail thumping on the floor.

"You could have at least said hello," Jake scolded, and the dog tore across the tile floor from the pantry, all but jumping up into Jake's arms. Jake held him for a moment while Barnaby licked his face before he put him down and filled up the food dishes.

The cats and dog fed and ignoring him, Jake left the mail on the table and clomped down the stairs into the basement. Stopping at the laundry room, he stripped off his uniform, tossed it in the laundry basket, and slipped into his workout clothing. Outside of the laundry room section, the finished half of the basement acted as an office for Jake and a makeshift gym. Over the years, he and Sam acquired better equipment than the Arrow Bay YMCA, and he could come down and exercise in the dead of night if he felt like it—which he often did if he was unable to sleep or was particularly stressed about something.

Though tired from his lack of sleep, Jake never missed a workout. For the next two hours he ran through his routine. Soaked through with sweat and feeling exhausted, he went back upstairs to the kitchen and shut the lights off in the basement, cooling down with a Gatorade while finishing flipping through the rest of the mail. He made a face when he saw that his old high school first fling, Tony Graham, had made the cover of *Men's Fitness*, complete in bodybuilder pose and goofy grin.

He looked up at the sound of the rain, which had started in earnest a half hour earlier and was coming down hard now, sounding like popcorn hitting the tin lid of a pan. Hungry, and figuring no one was around to be offended by his sweat-stained clothes, he opened a can of Chunky sirloin burger soup and tipped it into a pot, turning the flame on low under it. He grabbed a bag of Doritos out of the cupboard and popped them open, eating a handful while flipping open the *Seattle Times* that had been in with the mail and pulling out the section for the *New York Times* crossword he hadn't had a chance to get to at work. He had it more than half finished by the time his soup was hot. He ate it right out of the pot, not wanting to dirty a dish, and after chugging down nearly a quart of milk, he finished off his meal with two packages of cupcakes.

Finished with dinner, he went back down to the basement long enough to peel off his workout clothes and toss them into the laundry. He crept back upstairs naked, darted through the house and made his way upstairs to the master bedroom. The bed wasn't made, and the blue comforter was half on the floor. Dorothy was fast asleep in the middle of the bed. Sophia watched him with her large amber eyes from Barnaby's basket in the corner next to the television. Barnaby trotted along behind Jake, ignoring the gray Maine Coon interloper in his basket, instead jumping on the bed and budging up next to Dorothy, who let out a "Murrrph?" and stretched, snuggling up next to the beagle.

"Leave room enough for me, you two," said Jake. "I plan on getting into bed myself soon." Jake stepped back into the hall, headed into the bathroom.

Jake closed the door behind him, reaching over to turn on the porcelain tap and let the water heat up. He dropped the rubber stopper in the claw-foot tub. The tile of the floor was teal and black, cleaned to four-star hotel standard. The tile ran halfway up the wall then broke into crisp white paint. Jake had always felt white conveyed cleanliness in a bathroom, something he figured he'd picked up from his grandmother, a former nurse.

He surveyed himself in the mirror. He needed to shave, as always, but wouldn't worry about it until just before his shift tomorrow afternoon. He had a body many men would kill for—not muscle-bound, but toned, with rock-hard pectorals and a washboard stomach, defined leg and thigh muscles and bulging biceps. He was coated with a fine layer of jet-black hair that ran from chest down to his pubic bone. He shrugged, sticking his tongue out at himself. He suspected anymore he was addicted to working out as much as he was Ho Hos and pizza. As the two had achieved something akin to a Zen balance with one another, he didn't worry about it.

The funny thing was he hadn't set out to get the body he had. It had just *happened* while he worked out the anger and depression over Chris's murder. Three years later, after the workouts and weightlifting had become a habit, he'd caught a look at himself in the mirror one day and had been astonished. He could hardly believe what he had accomplished.

Once established, Jake found he loved the freedom of being able to eat what he wanted. People who didn't know him were aghast at his dietary habits—McDonald's, pizzas, and gallons of chocolate milk. No one knew he worked out for no less than two hours every day, or that he obsessed over his cholesterol. Jake also made sure his blood sugar levels were good, too. His doctor had warned him he would likely have to alter his horrible diet as he moved through his thirties, but for now the workouts were keeping him in balance.

He slipped farther into the hot water, shutting off the taps with his toes. Dorothy pushed open the door and looked at him with some interest for a moment or two, then padded back out. The combo of the workout and the hot water was making him sleepy.

The phone next to the tub rang, making him jump and slosh water out of the tub.

He leaned over the side of the tub and grabbed the receiver. "Hello?"

"Are you in the tub again?"

"Alex," he said drowsily. "I was going to call you back."

"I called you back instead. Rough day at the office? Whatshername bugging you again? The one that never shuts up? June, I think."

"She's on another crew, thank God." He paused. "How'd you know I was in the tub?"

"I heard the slosh when you picked up the phone. And it always sounds like you're calling from a cavern when you're in the bathroom."

"Ah."

"I'm just passing Mount Burlington and was wondering if I could stop by."

"Not tonight, Alex. I'm getting into bed after my bath."

"Nice signal, you right bastard! I hope you get hemorrhoids!"

yelled Alex uncharacteristically. Normally he was the picture of calmness.

"What?" Jake asked, chuckling.

"Oh, some jerk just cut me off. And I just bought this car. That's what I wanted to show you."

"Ah. New car? You mean you finally got rid of that old rust bucket you were driving?" Jake asked, somewhat incuriously. Even with all the money he had, Alex continued to pour money into the first car he'd ever owned, a dowager of a Mercedes Benz.

"Had to. The Mercedes got totaled."

"Alex, why the hell didn't you call me? Were you hurt?"

"It just happened today. That's why I've got the new car. I *am* calling. And no. I wasn't *in* the car at the time."

"Well that's good," Jake said, relieved. "What happened?"

"Oh, a Seattle DOT dump truck rolled into it."

"What?"

"That was what I said. Actually I think I said something like, 'Well, that doesn't happen every day now, does it?' Or something. But yes, it squashed the Black Beauty flat."

"Jesus, Alex, you could have been killed!"

"Oh, I doubt it," he said pausing for a moment. "You sure you don't want to see my car?"

"Tonight, I don't think I could give it the oohs and ahhs it deserves." He thought a moment. "What is it, anyway?"

"Oh, that completely impractical Jaguar I had my eye on."

"Ah. Color?"

"Pacific Blue," he replied. "It had a nice ring to it. Almost poetic. 'Her eyes, Monsignor, / Are so blue that they put lovely little blue reflections / On everything that she looks at / Such as a wall / Or the moon / Or my heart.'"

"Who wrote that?" asked Jake.

"Joyce Kilmer. You know, the fellow who went on about the tree."

"Right. Tell you what, Alex, how about having an early breakfast after I hit the pool? Say about nine, if you're up that early?" said Jake, knowing that Alex tended to be up very late working out of his home office, though exactly what work he did, Jake wasn't entirely sure.

"How about I join you at the pool?" Alex said. "I could use a good swim. Or maybe a steam. The Y still have a steam room?"

"They do."

"Sounds good," he said. Jake heard a pause, followed by the honk of the horn. "There are a bunch of idiots on the road tonight."

"I'm sure," he said, yawning.

"Get out of that tub already before you fall asleep and drown. I'll see you tomorrow morning about seven thirty at the pool. Then be prepared to ooh and ahh. This is the first car I've ever bought, you know."

Jake chuckled. "I know, Alex. See you tomorrow. Good night."

"'Night, kiddo," replied Alex, ringing off.

Jake sighed, replacing the receiver. He slid back into the tub, enjoying the all-encompassing embrace of the hot water around him. He listened to the sound of the wind quicken outside as it swirled over the eaves, creating a restless, nearly inaudible moan that made him slip farther into the water. The furnace kicked on with a dull whoosh. The blind in the window above him began to tap against the frame of the window ever so slightly, an insistent click like a fingernail on a tabletop. The scent of Irish Spring drifted languidly around him, a clean evergreen smell that reminded him of wind blowing through the foothills of the Cascade Mountains.

Spring was a whole season and a half away. It was November now, the Indian summer faded away. The rain wouldn't start in earnest until mid-month. Jake had never liked November. It tended to be very gray and wet, the colors of October long diluted by the incessant tumble of water. He tried to make sure the flower boxes on the front porch constantly had some sort of color in them for the winter, a spark of cheerfulness in an otherwise gray and dreary season in the Pacific Northwest. Usually he waited until November to actually get the dwarf iris, primroses, or winter pansies—anything with a splash of color. He wondered briefly if he'd have time in the morning to run out to Professor Mills's place to get something to brighten the porch up for Sam's arrival.

Jake popped the plug out of the tub with his right big toe and stood up, drying himself off with a soft, fresh terrycloth towel. He tossed the towel into the hamper and padded across the hall into the bedroom, sliding under the chilly cotton sheets of the king-sized bed they had shoehorned into the room. He looked over at Barnaby, who had reclaimed his basket; Dorothy and Sophia had moved to the foot of the bed, curled up into a slate and orange ball.

He hopped out of bed and ran downstairs. He picked up *The Clock*

Struck Murder and ran back up the steps, flopping into bed and earning a disapproving glance from Dorothy. Sophia remained blissfully unaware Jake had even gotten out of bed.

Jake was happy to discover that Claypoole had in fact remembered the infamous 1919 death of Gnatworth, for once outfoxing his intrepid assistant. When confronted with the evidence, Daphne flew into a rage and attacked Claypoole with a tea cozy, which, Claypoole found rather belatedly, still had the teapot in it. He would recover from his concussion by the next book, *The Mysterious Ashtray.* Despite all of Jake's assertions that Spievens was losing his touch, it was already reserved at the Arrow Bay Public Library.

Having finished the book, Jake snapped off the light, listening to the rain on the roof. A few disjointed shadows drifted across the ceiling, cast by the fingers of the street lamp half a block down. Jake listened as the furnace sighed into life again and was thinking about Sam when he drifted off to sleep, where he dreamt not of finding the body of Chris Aponte, but of being chased down a narrow corridor by a gigantic purple tea cozy.

Chapter Two

Y ou look tired," Alex noted as the waitress came by to refill his
coffee cup.

"I didn't sleep particularly well," Jake admitted, thinking back on
the dreams of the giant man-eating tea cozy.

Alex had insisted on having breakfast at Judith Anne's Kitchen,
a hole-in-the-wall establishment housed in a converted Thirties
gable front house just off Central Avenue. Judith Anne specialized
in homemade food and baked goods. Alex had ordered buckwheat
pancakes and a side of fruit; Jake had chicken fried steak, eggs, home
fries and a buttermilk biscuit smothered in gravy which he washed
down with two cups of coffee and a large glass of tomato juice.

"I don't know how you do it," Alex observed for about the ten
thousandth time since meeting Jake years before.

"You know perfectly well how I do it, Alex. I exercise two hours a
day, seven days a week, and weight train four days a week. That's how.
Besides, you're not in such bad shape, you know."

"Not bad for forty-one," he admitted. "But I'm one of the weird
ones that likes to row and bicycle." He took another bite of pancake and
said, "How does Sam like Australia?"

Jake paused for a moment, thinking. "I'm not sure if *loathed* is too
strong a word," Jake said. "He said he was getting up early to get his
walk in before it got too hot. Sam does *not* like heat. His mother sent
him all sorts of tourist stuff to go see, but after finding out how much he
disliked it there, he threw himself into work."

"His mother owns the pottery studio in town, doesn't she?" Alex
asked, adding a drop more maple syrup to his pancakes.

"And teaches at Considine," Jake said, referring to the private
university just outside of Arrow Bay.

Alex grinned. "How does she fit in with the rest of the staff?"

Jake knew what Alex was getting at. Considine had a reputation of being one of the most liberal colleges in the country, known for attracting radical professors. Some of them were very legitimate scholars and some more dubious, like Dr. Pinkie Switcher, a psychologist recognized for her expertise in human sexuality, which included publishing lengthy tomes on her own exploits.

"She's one of the more down-to-earth ones," Jake said, although he knew Evelyn O'Conner *did* have some wild ideas about spirituality and the subject of ghosts.

"You get along with her?"

"Evelyn?" Jake asked. "Like a house on fire. She's considered me a son-in-law since Sam and I first got together."

Alex chuckled. "I've certainly never seen two people more suited to one another."

"Well, we happened to find one another at the right time," Jake admitted.

"I'm an old-fashioned believer in fate. I don't think it was any accident your foot found that patch of ice that day," said Alex, having heard the story of Jake and Sam's first meeting a time or two.

"Does your belief in fate extend to yourself?" Jake asked.

Alex looked at his coffee cup thoughtfully for a moment. He took a sip and said, "I think so. Just not right now. I'm still…well, nursing old wounds a bit, I guess." He shrugged. "I've done enough playing the field in my time. I'm too old to do that now."

"I'm a serial monogamist," Jake admitted. "Before Sam, I can count the number of partners I've had without resorting to counting toes or limbs or other appendages." He thought for a moment. "Okay, *one* toe. There was that Marine I met at a particular low point in my life…"

"Not long after the famous football player abruptly ended your relationship, right?"

"He wasn't famous then," Jake said. "You know far too much about me."

Alex laughed. "Only what you've told me. Although I have noticed you've been out of sorts ever since Sam left for Australia."

"It was like losing my arm," Jake admitted. "Although I think the time apart has been good for us."

"How so?"

"Well, I never want to feel like I'm taking Sam for granted," Jake said thoughtfully. "Since he's been gone, I've appreciated him all the more."

"From anyone else, Jake, I'd say they were being incredibly sappy. You are not sappy in the least, however," he said, taking a bite of pancake. "You're one of the most truthful and sincere people I know. In my line of work, you've no idea how refreshing that is."

"I don't suppose you'll tell me what you're up to?" Jake asked.

Alex flashed him a Mona Lisa smile. "Eventually."

Jake took a sip of his tomato juice, deciding not to push it. "I'm just glad things will be getting back to normal."

"Not too normal, I hope. It's been pretty dull around here lately."

"I dunno," said Jake, taking another bite of the buttermilk biscuit. He stopped. "It has, hasn't it?"

"Not always a bad thing, mind you," Alex pointed out. "How's your writing going?"

"Frustrating," Jake admitted. "I just don't have enough time to stick with it. It's going in fits and starts, and I can't help but feel it's horribly disjointed."

"Aren't you leaving your job when Sam gets back? You must be able to survive off of one income by now."

"That's been the plan all along." He shrugged. "I'm having a hard time adjusting to the idea."

"I'm sorry," Alex said. "It's really none of my business."

"No, I appreciate you asking, really. Sam's not a writer. You are, so you know what it's like."

"One book," Alex quickly pointed out. "And I haven't written anything since."

"You understand about the time, though," Jake said, knowing Alex always had two or three things on the burner at once.

"True," he said, glancing at his watch. "What were you up to the rest of the morning?"

"Running up to Professor Mills's place to get some plants to spruce up the porch for Sam's return," Jake said.

"The old gent who lives up in the hills past Concrete?" Alex said, eyes gleaming.

"Yes," Jake said, not trusting the look in Alex's eye. "Why?"

"How about we drop your car off at your place and I drive," Alex said. "It'll give you a chance to ooh and ahh appropriately."

❖

The clouds had burned away, leaving the wet highway a ribbon of mirror in the sunlight. Highway 22 dropped from four lanes to two as they approached Mount Burlington, causing Alex to downshift. He drummed his fingers on the steering wheel, seeming impatient with having to slow the Jaguar down. They drove in silence for the next few miles, Jake mulling over what Alex had said. Finally he let his thoughts drift away as he saw the sunlight glint off the water-soaked boughs of the evergreens that lined the roadway. The city of Sedro-Woolley breezed past as they worked their way into steadily more rural countryside. Alex sped up as they started up the North Cascades Highway. Jake began clutching his seat.

He was surprised at the way Alex was driving, but he supposed Alex was now appreciating new machinery that didn't require creeping along carefully. Although Jake would have preferred Alex *not* to drive like a bat out of Hades, the tires squealing around corners as they made their way into the hills.

Alex slowed slightly as they reached Glacier Meadows, and Jake relaxed somewhat. A few miles away, tucked in behind the towering evergreens and Big Leaf maples on the sunny slope of a Cascade Range foothill, stood a moderate-sized greenhouse owned by a retired engineer from the University of Washington. Professor Mills, who had once been a teacher of Sam's, now spent his retirement working in his greenhouse. The plants he grew were mainly for his own interest, but he did sell some specialty flowers and plants to friends and former students, the proceeds of which he donated to local food banks.

Professor Mills focused on hybrid orchids and flowering evergreen shrubs but like Jake, he enjoyed keeping flowers and color in the yard year round. Finding plants to brighten up the porch would likely be no challenge.

The blue Jaguar squealed around another corner, making Jake clamp down on the underside of his seat even harder.

"You've been fairly quiet," said Alex.

"Have I been? Sorry. I get quiet when I'm trying to remember the words to the Act of Contrition."

"Act of Contrition?"

"I figure I should have my bases covered for when this bird takes flight," he said.

Alex shot Jake a sideways glance. "Ha ha. I can't help it if you drive like Grandma Moses."

"A much maligned woman," said Jake, closing his eyes as they rounded another hairpin turn. "I also might add that her driving habits led her to live to a ripe old age, whereas speed demons such as you and say, oh, James Dean, tend to end up with the short end of the pretzel."

Alex laughed. "You are just too droll for words this morning."

"Fear of ending up in a twisted mass of metal sharpens my wit," Jake said. "Turn right just past the red mailbox."

Alex turned off the highway and down a narrow paved drive. The trees abruptly fell away, revealing a sun-drenched meadow high up the side of a foothill. To the left, the greenhouse glittered in the light, and directly behind it was a small clapboard farm house.

"How did he end up here?" Alex asked, pulling the Jaguar to a stop.

"Inherited it, I think," Jake replied, hazy on the subject. "His wife passed away or something, and it was her family's property."

"Odd place for a greenhouse," Alex noted as they got out of the car.

"Lots of sun on this slope, though," Jake pointed out. "Faces southeast."

They started down the narrow path to the greenhouse. It curved down a small slope, then went up sharply. Jake breathed in deeply the scent of damp Douglas fir and Western hemlock boughs that drifted in the breeze. The rain of the evening before was rapidly becoming a memory. The sun had completely burned through the clouds, the autumn sky now clear and so flawlessly blue it looked as if it had been painted in.

The rhododendrons lining the path were still draped with evaporating moisture, each droplet of water becoming a glinting jewel in the sunlight before winking out as the leaves dried. Jake took in the scenery, enjoying every breath of mountain air, the scent of moss and distant wood smoke lingering in his palate. A Steller's jay squawked loudly as it flew overhead; the sound of the Skagit River gurgling its way down the valley could be heard in the distance. Jake shunned organized religion. He found spirituality in settings like the deep woods with only the sounds and smells of the natural world around him. If God existed, he felt, surely it was in places like this.

Looking like a Victorian space ship, the greenhouse glinted in the sun. A weathered WELCOME sign hung on the door, indicating that the professor was somewhere inside.

Jake hauled the glass door to the greenhouse open. The building exhaled a warm breath of air, smelling fragrantly of topsoil, copper pipes, and leafy foliage. He breathed deeply again, enjoying the earthy scent. Professor Mills popped out from behind a clump of fragrant hydrangeas wearing his usual neat gray suit with a purple ascot and looking like a frazzled blossom himself.

"Hello, Professor Mills," said Jake, shaking hands with the dapper man.

"Hello, hello, Jake! How are you? And who is this?" he asked in a slightly wheezy voice. Professor Mills had always reminded Jake of an asthmatic seagull.

"I'm fine, and this is my friend, Alex Blackburn."

"Pleased to meet you," Alex said, shaking hands with the man, momentarily taken aback by the strength of the handshake from the seemingly wispy little man.

"Of the Seattle Blackburns?" Professor Mills asked, one eyebrow cocked northward.

"Yes, but don't tell anyone," Alex said with a grin.

"Alexander Blackburn the Third, by any chance?" Mills asked.

"Yes sir," Alex said.

"I read your book," he said with a nod. "I found it very enlightening." He turned his attention back to Jake. "And now that I have deemed your companion suitable, what can I do for you?" he said with a wink.

"Sam is due back in a few days, and I thought I'd spruce up the planter boxes on the front porch. It's looking a bit bedraggled out there."

"Mm, as young Sam will undoubtedly look after that flight from Australia," Professor Mills said knowingly. "I've done that a time or two in my day. Dreadfully long trip."

"Wouldn't know," Jake said, having never been in a plane in his life. "But I'll take your word for it," he said, looking around for Alex, who had disappeared.

"Over here," Professor Mills called.

Jake went around a table covered with row after row of iris and found Alex and Professor Mills standing in front of a small work table where a single plant stood in a large ceramic pot. Alex was staring at the flower intently, receiving pleased looks from Professor Mills.

"That is the latest one I've submitted to the society," Mills said proudly. "It ought to set them on their collective ear."

Jake looked at the delicate flower of the orchid. It was nearly pearlescent, with light touches of lavender and a dark plum center the shape of a starburst.

"It's stunning," Alex said, breathing in its delicate scent.

"The summation of many years' work," Professor Mills said, smiling. "I've decided on calling it Minerva's Slipper, after my housekeeper. Although she says her slippers have been mauled by the dog and don't look anything at all like this."

"This looks like it would complement the shapely foot of a woman nicely," Alex said, smiling.

Jake suspected that Professor Mills and the cleaning lady, a rather elegant looking lady in her mid-fifties, were more than just friends. He'd seen them a time or two on the "pickle fork," or the forward outside deck of one of the ferries on the way to Friday Harbor, holding hands and looking rather chummy.

"Just load up on what you need. There's some winter iris over there and a host of other things in beds six and seven. Take as much as you'd like. I'll be in the back repotting some cuttings."

Twenty minutes later, Jake emerged with a basket full of primroses and blue fescue and some cheerful-looking irises and kales that would make his front porch boxes look livelier than the dead flowers currently residing in them. He would plant the fescues on the patch of lawn in the front yard where he was planning a fountain; the kale, he suspected, would end up along the driveway. Alex picked out some orchids and was loading them into the back of the Jaguar when Professor Mills came out, carrying a pot nearly as large as he was with a scarlet Japanese maple in it.

"Here," he said, handing the pot over to Jake. "That's for Sam," he said, smiling.

Jake was slightly taken aback by the weight and was surprised Mills had been able to lift it.

"Oh dear, I'm not sure it'll fit in your trunk," Mills said.

"Backseat," Alex said. "We'll belt it in."

"Alex, that upholstery is leather, isn't it?" Jake asked.

Alex shrugged. "Yes. No big deal."

"I have a plastic bag we can put on the seat," Professor Mills said, dashing back to the house.

"Wiry little guy, isn't he?" Alex asked as Jake set the pot down. "That must weigh seventy pounds or more."

Professor Mills returned, smiling broadly, and with a black Hefty bag in his hands. Jake carefully lowered the small tree into the bag and they eased it into the backseat of the Jaguar, putting the seat belt around the base of the pot.

"Thank you, Professor, but at least let me pay you for it," said Jake.

"Think nothing of it," he said, smiling, turning wistfully toward the greenhouse. "Besides, I need to get rid of some of this stuff. I've sold the place finally."

"Oh, I'm sorry to hear that," said Alex, genuinely disappointed.

"Well, it was time, I'm afraid. I'm getting on, and I just need the comforts of town. It's fine being up here by yourself when you're younger, but you know it always snows up here even when there's nothing in the lowlands and, well…you just can't be too careful when you live by yourself."

"Have you decided where you're going to relocate?" Jake asked.

"Oh yes!" said the sinewy little man. "Based on the glowing things Sam has reported to me, I've purchased a small home in Arrow Bay. Even has a little greenhouse in the back so I can continue puttering away until they're ready to plant me!"

"Well, we look forward to having you as a neighbor," said Jake. "We'll have to have you over when Sam gets back."

They bade Professor Mills good-bye then climbed into the Jaguar. Alex started the luxury car and raced down the mountainside, the engine rumbling pleasantly as they sped through Glacier Meadows and barreled down to Concrete, kicking up gold maple leaves from the speedily drying pavement.

Just after they'd zoomed past Concrete, Jake asked Alex to stop and turn down a nearly overgrown logging road that disappeared into the thicket of crimson vine maple and sodden bows of cedar.

"You want me to turn down there?" Alex asked skeptically.

"If you don't mind. I've been meaning to show you this for a while," Jake said.

Guiding the Jaguar carefully down the rutted road, Alex announced they would be walking when the fallen trunk of an alder blocked their path. Jake and Alex stepped out of the car and into the oppressive copse, the sound of rushing water several yards in front of them. The road narrowed to little more than a path, and then abruptly the trees broke into a clearing on the riverbank.

Rising out of the river were the decaying remains of a long-forgotten ferryboat. The vessel's one-hundred-fifty-five-foot length lay buried in the mud up to the car deck. The superstructure, once painted white, now was bare and weathered gray. A rusty lifeboat davit stretched out over the port side, holding only air. The windows were mostly broken, moss streaked along the few intact panes along the passenger cabin. Ferns sprung out of the promenade deck, and the forward part of the cabin had caved in.

Two odd things stuck out: the smokestack was painted in a fresh coat of crimson, and the name had also recently been touched up along her crew cabin planking: R O S A R I O. Under that, in the same red as the smokestack were the words KEEP OUT!

"My God!" Alex breathed. "How did she end up here?" he asked as Jake stepped over a half-wrecked wooden gate onto a rickety gangplank.

"The state sold her a few months after they took over from privately owned Black Ball in 1951."

"Just like that?"

"Well, she was a small, single-ended, all-wood ferry that could only hold thirty-three cars even back then," Jake said, walking along the promenade deck. Ferns and lichen covered the surface, and he could hear the steady drip of water. "She was used as a cannery for years, then when they were done with her, she got towed up here to be used as a fishing camp. When that didn't work out, she just got left here." He paused, looking at the slightly open door leading down into the cabin. "Arden?" he shouted.

"Who's Arden?" Alex asked.

"The old hermit who lives on her," Jake said. "Sam and I found him out here the first time we came across the old girl. He was going to chase us off until I told him I worked for the ferries and was interested in her history." Jake looked up over the top of the cabin at the smokestack and frowned. "There's no smoke. I wonder if he's here?"

"Are you sure it's safe?" Alex asked. "Well, more to the point, that this Arden fellow is safe?"

"He's in his sixties if he's a day, Alex," Jake said. "Though it's odd he's not here. He's been here the better part of ten years as far as I know. He stumbled across the boat while fishing and he just…moved in. He'd taken the section of the boat that was the most undamaged—amidships on the starboard side," Jake said, pointing, "and set up a home there. He cut into the smokestack casing and made a firebox to heat the place and made some repairs and improvements to the boat, including keeping the smokestack freshly painted."

"Why'd he do that?" Alex asked.

Jake shrugged. "I've no idea. I mean, he knew it was hopeless. For some reason, he always wanted that stack bright red."

"Do many people know about this place?" Alex asked.

"The locals do. Beyond that, I doubt it. This place is pretty forgotten, and Arden chases all the kids away."

Arden told Jake and Sam he was considering leaving the place last winter. Last time they had seen him, Arden had gifted most of the last of the *Rosario*'s historic treasures to Jake and Sam: her name boards, her compass and telegraph, and her starboard navigation light. He'd given Jake all her brass signage and her mast lights to Sam.

"Something isn't right," Jake said, stepping into the small foyer at the head of the stairs. He started down, Alex right behind him. "Fourteen, four, and two," he said.

"Fourteen, four, and two," Alex repeated. "And that is?"

"The steps to avoid so as not to fall through them."

"Handy to know," Alex said. "Counting up from the bottom?"

"Er, yeah," Jake said. As he started down them, he noticed that stair number two had been smashed through, a gaping hole that had taken out most of the third stair with it. "Careful here, there's some damage," he said.

"What a gift for understatement you have," said Alex dryly from behind him. "You remind me of Marilyn Quayle when she toured San Francisco after the earthquake. That, Jacob, is a *crater*."

"Well, it is a pretty good-sized hole," Jake admitted, treading carefully down the rest of the stairs.

Inside the musty cabin, dust motes danced in the shadowy light filtering through the cedar boughs. The slate gray tile was peeling up from the floor, which groaned uneasily as Jake put his weight on it. Moving forward, he peered through a gently arched doorway where a startled crow burst into furious flight through a collapsed section of the dining room ceiling. Jake knew that section had not been open to the sky the last time he'd visited. Stepping carefully around to the starboard side of the passenger cabin, Jake inched his way to the partitioned section amidships where Arden had made his home. The doorway, knocked together from part of the mahogany paneling that had peeled away from the dining room bulkheads, leaned ominously outward. Poking his nose in, Jake noticed the absence of the neatly stacked cases of Mountain Dew and Stagg chili. The coffeepot was gone, and the bunk was empty of all blankets.

"He's gone," Jake said, a bit wistfully.

"Someone has been here, though," Alex observed, pointing to a collection of cigarette butts on the floor.

Jake looked around the little room, eyes lighting on the section in the wall that had been cut out for the firebox. A few ashes lingered in the makeshift hearth, with a half-charred piece of wood next to them. Bordering the firebox was an old apple crate with a few pieces of notebook paper and a gutted candle. "Not Arden. He didn't smoke." Jake glanced around again, detecting some strange, sweet smell in the air. He glanced at the floor, where heavy boot tread could be seen. Crouching down, he inspected the tread closer, frowning. He tapped one with his finger. "These aren't Arden's."

"How can you tell?"

"Arden's a little guy. Tiny feet. These are a size ten or eleven, I'd estimate." He looked over to the wall next to the broken cot where the old hermit had once slept. A calendar had not been flipped over from September to October. "He left sometime in the last two months would be my guess," said Jake.

"Would he just...leave like that?" asked Alex.

Jake shrugged, rising. He pointed toward the forward part of the vessel, which was largely caved in. "That wasn't there last time I was here, just at the start of June. I can't say for sure when it collapsed, but probably last month, maybe late August. Arden probably got scared he was going to go right through the deck," said Jake, listening to the sound of water running below them.

"Can't say I blame him," Alex admitted.

"Someone *has* been here. You're right about that." said Jake, looking aft. He walked carefully over to the port side of the vessel. "Look here, Alex."

Alex furrowed his brow as he joined Jake. Near the aft end of the vessel, one of the large passenger windows that had been intact had been smashed out, a crude gangplank made up from boards likely pulled from the side of the ferry laid flat on the sill.

"Stern is closest to land here," Jake said. "Not more than four feet," he continued, walking toward the plank across the room as the floor gave an uncomfortable groan.

"Jake, be careful!" Alex shouted.

"No worries, Size Eleven made it across," he said, noting the tracks cut a path across the dust. This made him uncomfortable: the rains had only started within the last week after a record dry October. Whoever had size eleven shoes had been here recently. The absence of beer bottles or any drug paraphernalia led Jake to deduce it wasn't kids looking for a quiet place to get drunk or stoned and have sex. The tracks were in a straight line to where the ferry had once been used as a habitat. Whoever had come in was checking for people.

"I didn't even see this when we got on the boat," Alex said, moving cautiously up behind him.

"No," Jake agreed. "It's been placed in a spot you can't see from the clearing," he said, frowning.

"What is it?"

Jake pointed to the boards and said, "Those aren't from the side of the boat. That's brand-new pressure-treated lumber jammed into the riverbank. That doesn't look temporary to me."

"Where are you going?" Alex asked as Jake moved away from the window.

"I'm going to look around for a second. Stay here."

"Oh, I think not," Alex said. "I've seen that movie. That line is usually followed with the poor sucker left behind getting hacked to death by the maniac with the machete."

Jake crossed back over the groaning floor to where Arden had once slept. He moved forward again, creeping toward the doorway, the creak of the timbers punctuated by a few loud pops.

"Easy, Jake," Alex said.

"It's okay, I know my way around." He crept forward a bit more until he cleared the archway. Alex stayed behind.

The forward part of what had once been an elegant dining room had caved in on the corner of both the starboard and port sides. Jake looked up at the fallen ceiling and could see some of the casing for the wheelhouse shifting through. The gracefully curved windows had all been smashed. The framing had peeled away from the ceiling, yawning out into the daylight.

A few more crows cawed at Jake as he entered the room, taking flight up into the trees. He took another step, the last he dared as the gaping hole in the floor was merely inches away. Suddenly, the sound of crunching glass came from under his foot. He looked down. Red glass was scattered all over the floor. He turned to his right, and back at the archway. The brass frame of the port running light had been smashed against the mahogany paneling.

He was about to turn back when he noticed a sheet from the Seattle *Outlander* on the floor. Jake picked it up, examining for a moment. It was from Section B, the local news, and was detailing some local business that had gone the extra mile and was now doing business internationally. The date on the paper was a week old.

Jake dropped the paper and made his way back to the archway, then stepped into what had been Arden's home. The floor under the windows was indeed giving way, showing traces of the silt-filled car deck below. Alex was poking around Arden's cot when he made an odd noise and jerked upright, something in his hand. He held it up for Jake to see. It was a black-and-white snapshot of a young boy.

"Jimmy, 1959," Alex read off the back. "I wonder who he was?"

Jake looked at the photo more closely. The boy in the photo appeared to be about twelve. He was dressed in a button-up shirt and had horn-rimmed glasses on. Jake closed his eyes briefly and summoned up the mental image of Arden from memory. He looked back at the boy in the photo, noting the same jawline, the same deep-set eyes.

"Offhand I'd say it was Arden's son."

Alex looked at him. "That's odd. I wonder why he left it here?"

"Overlooked?" Jake said, not believing it as he said it. Arden may have been a transient, but he'd kept a photo from 1959 with him. Why leave it now? He looked at the photo as Alex handed it to him. "In all the times we were up here, he never mentioned a son. We used to come up quite a bit once we started talking to him. We'd sell him some food and talk for hours."

"*Sell?*" Alex said, taken aback.

"Not like *that*. Arden wouldn't just take food. He refused to be a charity case, living mostly off the land by fishing and hunting. We started to bring him things we thought he might have needed—coffee and the like—but he got very angry and said he wouldn't take anything. So he offered to buy the things we brought him for the price of his life stories. The guy had lived in Seattle forever and knew it inside and out. Knew all the good seedy stories, who slept with who, where all the bodies were buried, so to speak. I have no idea how much of it was true, but it was fascinating nonetheless," said Jake, looking at the photo again, frowning. "But he never mentioned a son." He thought for a moment. "Come to think of it, he never really said anything about his personal life."

Alex looked at Jake quizzically for a moment. "I wonder if he knew my family?" he asked, looking around at the dilapidated vessel. "How'd he end up here?"

Jake shrugged. "He didn't go into details," Jake said. "He said he'd gotten tired of living in the city and of people in general and came up here to be left alone. Never said what he had done in his past life." Jake sighed, slipping the photo in the pocket of his jacket. "I suspected he was in law enforcement. He knew things about the city and how it worked like someone who had personal experience dealing with the inner workings a great deal."

"So, if he's been gone a month or more, who's been in here since?" Alex asked, curious. He looked around again. "No beer cans or cigarettes, no stub ends of joints…"

"I was thinking the same thing," Jake admitted. "Not teenagers." He looked down at the size eleven shoeprints again, and at the prints added by his size nines and Alex's size twelves. The vessel had been cased, he could feel it. It had been checked out completely to make sure no one was around. The fresh boards thrown into the passenger cabin meant that Size Eleven would be back. And the amount of brush surrounding the area meant he wouldn't be seen.

Visions of drug deals, guns and meth addicts began spinning through his head. The room suddenly seemed darker and more desolate. He looked at Alex. "Look, let's get out of here."

Alex nodded and without another word, they left the corpse of the vessel, the sigh of the river at their heels. A crow squawked loudly as it flew overhead, making Jake jump. The wind whistled slightly as it shook the boughs of the cedar trees.

"I'm not a superstitious person by nature," Alex admitted as they approached the Jaguar, "but something wasn't right there."

"Well, I *am* a superstitious person," said Jake. "I think you're right."

A thought bounced through Jake's head as they neared the car. He eyed the large alder across the roadway. Jake hopped over it and asked Alex to get into the Jaguar and start her up. He followed the tree down to its base in the brush.

The alder stump rested in a bed of fresh sawdust. The cut wasn't more than a few days old.

He turned to leave when a scattering of Mountain Dew cans caught his eye. Curious, he moved forward, sensing something amiss. Jake had moved five feet beyond the stump when he heard the snapping of branches along the river bank, moving toward him. He spun around, looking around wildly.

Nothing. But he could no longer see the blue Jaguar.

Jake walked rapidly back to the car, heart racing in his chest. A sense of menace bore down on him like a torrent of rushing water. When he got to the car, he hopped into the passenger side and snapped the lock shut. Without a word, Alex backed the car up quickly. He turned around in the nearest clearing and drove the car down the rutted road as fast as he dared.

They didn't speak and Jake didn't complain when Alex, upon reaching the paved highway, accelerated and left the carcass of the ferry behind them as rapidly as he could.

CHAPTER THREE

Back at 100 High Street, Jake wrestled the Japanese maple out of the backseat of the Jaguar and plopped it next to the boxwood, one whiff of which made him think that the smelly bush might get the ax after all. Alex helped him unload the plants from the trunk and accepted an offer of a glass of iced tea. Jake brought out two glasses from the kitchen so they could enjoy the late autumn sun on the front porch.

"You've made some changes to the yard," he observed while sipping his tea. "I am sensing a Japanese influence."

"Very much so," said Jake, pleased that Alex had noticed.

"It looks good, continue with it. A lot of harmony here," said Alex. "Except for that fence."

"That's Mrs. Weinberg's fence. She put it in when she found out we had a dog," said Jake.

"Ah. It's a shame. Everything else is in balance here." A pained expression suddenly crossed his face. "Those aren't *lawn dwarfs*?" said Alex, aghast, looking over at Leona Weinberg's yard.

"Unfortunately, yes," said Jake.

"Unbelievable. I knew the old bat had terrible taste, but not quite *that* bad." He shrugged. "Then again, she is a friend of my father's, so I don't know what I expected," he said, shaking his head.

"I didn't know that," Jake said.

"Oh yes," said Alex. "He and Leona go way back. I once suspected they had an affair actually, back in the days before Leona started looking like Phyllis Schlafly."

"There *is* an uncanny resemblance," Jake admitted.

"Attend a town council meeting and see just how much," said Alex with a wry grin. He faced the Jaguar and said with a sigh, "Well, is it enough to ooh and ahh over?"

Jake noticed that Alex's voice was etched with an undertone of consternation. Jake turned his attention back to the sparkling blue Jaguar, realizing he was now expected to pass judgment on the car.

"It's gorgeous, Alex."

"It is ostentatious, gas-guzzling, and impractical," Alex said, frowning a bit. "And materialistic and totally goes against the tenets of most of my beliefs," he said. Then he smiled. "But then sometimes you have to say eh, what the hell. I don't do much driving anyway."

"No, that's true," Jake said. "Most of the time I see you around on your bicycle."

"The Internet makes it possible for me to do most of my work from home," Alex said. "Given my dislike of Seattle traffic, that is truly a wonderful thing."

"Part of me is going to miss the Black Beast," said Jake.

"I know," Alex agreed with a heavy sigh. "It was Gran's car. That's why I held on to it as long as I did, even though it was well past senile. I can't say I wasn't upset when I was notified of the accident." He shook his head. "Then I realized that it was just a *thing*. It may have been Gran's, but it wasn't *her*. I still have the memories."

Jake looked at Alex, surprised. Alex was normally quite circumspect. Even now, Jake wasn't sure what lurked in Alex's past, but he respected Alex's privacy. Sudden admissions like this one left Jake feeling slightly uncomfortable, as he was never sure how to react to them.

"I really should get going," Alex said suddenly. "I've goofed off all day and will have to play catch up all afternoon."

"Yes, and I have some plants I need to get planted."

"Thank you for a pleasantly distracting morning," Alex said. "I needed it."

"Yes, distracted from *what* exactly?" Jake asked.

"I am...ha ha," Alex said, grinning again. "Almost got me there, kiddo. All in good time."

"I'm growing tired of hearing that, Mr. Blackburn," Jake said, giving Alex a disapproving look.

"Would you prefer 'if I tell you I'd have to kill you'?"

Jake winced. "Oh please. *Never* a cliché. Anything but that."

"Well then, you'll just have to wait," said Alex.

"Very well, then," Jake said with a sigh. "If I had known I was befriending a spy, I'd have had second thoughts."

Alex laughed. "Oh, if *only* it were that glamorous. The tedium sometimes…" He shook his head as he slipped behind the wheel of his car.

"Very well, then," repeated Jake. "Back to the coal mine with you."

Alex chuckled. "As a way of placating your curiosity somewhat, can I take you to breakfast Sunday? Free food, all you can eat. Catered buffet…I know you can't resist a buffet."

"Damn it. There you go again, appealing to my stomach," Jake said. "Okay, sure. As long as we're back by early afternoon. Sam should be arriving Sunday evening."

"You're not going down to SeaTac?"

"No, right here in town. He's hired a puddle jumper to take him to the Arrow Bay airport. The silly man actually *likes* to fly."

"Not anxious to see you, is he?" Alex asked.

"Not much," Jake said, smiling broadly.

"See you Sunday, then," Alex said, backing out of the drive. He put the Jag into first and tore down High Street, eliciting a laugh from Jake.

As he stepped back onto the porch, he saw the curtains behind the front window at number 98 twitch. Leona Weinberg had once again been peering out the window at him. Jake shook his head and said, "Withered old clam."

An hour later, he had finished with the flowerboxes on the porch. The dead annuals, used for Halloween props, had been disposed of, and the fresh plants added a much needed splash of color.

He cleaned up his trowel and tools before heading upstairs to shower and get ready for work. He was in the process of gathering up food for his lunch when the phone rang. "Hello," he said.

"Your brother has gone off the deep end."

Jake cringed. He cursed himself for not checking the caller ID first to see that it was his mother.

Jake loved his mother. Of that he was completely sure. He didn't particularly *like* the woman much. Ingrid Finnigan was known for her preferential treatment of her only daughter and her critical attitude toward her sons. She was disapproving beyond comprehension and *nothing* her two sons did had ever met her approval. Neither Jake nor Jason blamed Amy for this, but it became tiring to talk to their mother for any length. The rare occasions she wasn't heaping praise on Amy or her granola and wheat germ lifestyle, she was usually delivering news of some disaster.

Ingrid's only notable deviation from her normal behavior was the news of Jake coming out; over that she hadn't issued a single statement, other than complete support. She hadn't always approved of Jake's "companions," as she called them, but she adored Sam.

"Hello, Mother, how are you?" Jake asked, bracing himself.

"I suppose you haven't heard what I've said."

"I heard. It's the usual custom to say hello and inquire about the individual you are speaking to before issuing edicts about others," he said with a sigh. "So Jason's gone off the deep end. What else is new?" Jake said, feeling an unhappy pang at the thought of his older brother.

While Jason and Jake had been polar opposites most of their life, they were still extremely close. Only eighteen months apart, they had grown up more as friends, with their deviation in interests forming an odd bond. Jason was the athlete. He'd played baseball and football in high school, lettering in both sports. He loved fishing and hunting, often spending weeks alone each year in the woods, though sometimes their father Allen went along.

Jake had always been a bookworm. Jason did share a love of reading, though, just as Jake enjoyed the outdoors. He would often accompany Jason on his forays into the wilderness, but to enjoy being in the forest, not to fish or hunt. Jason would bring the fishing poles, Jake his notebook and camera.

Oddly, Jake's interest in photography led to Jason's career path. Jason discovered he had a knack for photography on those outings, taking brilliant photos of the natural world. Jason had graduated with a degree in photojournalism from Western Washington University and gotten jobs at a few small papers in Washington before he landed a position in San Francisco. Positive notices for his work flowed in, followed by several awards.

His behavior over the last year had become erratic, something Jake had attributed to Jason's recent choice of girlfriend. She had been the cause of their falling out. Jason had refused to believe that in his absence, Jennifer had said violently homophobic things to both Jake and Sam, at one point telling Jake that she felt that both he and Sam should be put to death for their "unnatural ways." Jake had calmly told her that homosexuality was perfectly natural in nearly every animal species on the planet, and that if she didn't get out of his kitchen *right then* he would personally kick her ass physically out the door. Jennifer had fled, taking Jason with her, and the two hadn't spoken since. It still hurt Jake that Jason not only had not believed Jake, but that he had taken her side.

Ingrid Finnigan sighed. "He's left the *Chronicle*. He's staying at some sort of flophouse in Seattle. He won't talk to me or your father or your sister, and he hasn't got a job."

Jake considered this for a moment. Jason not talking to his mother or sister was no big surprise, but not talking to their father was. He took a deep breath and said, "Okay, that's a bit of deep end. He won't say anything?"

"You know he never talks to anyone but you, Jake."

"Not lately, Mom. Not since he was such a jackass."

"You boys," said Ingrid Finnigan, clucking her tongue, and then to someone in the room, "Put them up there with the geology books, and we'll sort them out later."

"New help?" Jake asked, irritated she was being so dismissive. He pictured his mother's bookstore instead to calm himself. It was a large store lined row after row with thousands of new and used books. Jake had spent many a happy hour there roaming the shelves.

"Kelly Graham. You know, Anthony's little sister. Did you get his book I sent you?"

"What?" Jake asked, his thoughts having turned into a muddy boil over the mention of his ex, Tony Graham. His mother had been talking to him for some time.

"I said he's done quite well for himself," said Ingrid.

"He's made a name for himself," said Jake, thinking *the attention-seeking git.* "Was there something you wanted, Mom?"

She sighed heavily. "Well, I was wondering if I left you Jason's phone number if you'd call him."

"Not until he apologizes," said Jake steadfastly.

"Yes, I was rather sure that would be your answer, too," she said. "Too?"

"Well, I did try to call Amy. She's such the peacemaker, and I thought maybe she could talk some sense into you *boys*," Ingrid said.

Jake couldn't help but notice the way she spat the word *boys* but let it pass.

"You didn't get that stubborn streak from me, you know," Ingrid continued. "That's all from your father."

Jake was about to object, but upon reflection he knew it was true.

"If Amy is such the peacemaker, why'd she refuse to talk to him?" Jake asked sweetly.

"Well," Ingrid said her voice tight, "it seems that Jennifer person said something to Amy as well."

"Yeah, I heard about that one. Something about getting the space shuttle to land for more than five minutes. On that score I think her comment was fairly apt," Jake said, shaking his head. "Is Amy still seeing that goofball?"

"If you mean *Professor* Sugg, yes," Ingrid said, starch in her voice.

"Hector Sugg. What were his parents thinking?"

"I nearly named *you* Dashiell."

Jake said a silent prayer thanking his father, who must have intervened. He thought of his sister trying to talk to Jason about realigning his chakras or that all he needed was a big glass of wheat germ or some such nonsense. He sighed. "Give me his number."

After finishing the phone call with his mother, he sat down for lunch, over which he completed the *New York Times* crossword puzzle, keeping one eye on the clock. At three, he had cleaned up his dishes and packed his large lunch sack. He debated about calling his brother, but knew he wouldn't have time. He'd leave it until the next afternoon and see if he could talk to him without shouting into the phone what a thickheaded cretin he'd been.

He made sure Barnaby had food and water and that the dog flap was open for him before climbing the stairs, cursing the fact that another day had passed and he hadn't had a chance to write anything. He let it go quickly, though, knowing there was no sense in winding himself up about it. He'd enjoyed the trip up into the mountains and was happy to have the plants on the front porch to give Sam a cheerful welcome back.

The writing wasn't going particularly well, anyway. For nearly a decade he'd been laboring over a fictionalized account of the death of his best friend, but some days, he couldn't face going back to that moment. He'd tried to write about other things, but nothing seemed to flow or spark the way his story about Chris Aponte did. Every time he looked around himself for inspiration, the well had come up dry.

Maybe Sam coming back will help, he thought.

He winced as the razor cut into his skin, drawing blood. A small rivulet ran down his cheek. Jake splashed water on his face, ignoring the sting, then blotted the cut dry until it stopped bleeding. He washed the drops of blood swirling down the sink, sighing. After drying his hands he stepped into his uniform and played with Barnaby in the backyard for a bit before driving down to the Arrow Bay ferry terminal. The *Elwha* stood at the ready.

Jake clambered up the steps from the car deck and cut through the cabin, heading directly for his room. He stowed his overnight bag in his bunk before going into the crew day room where he crammed his lunch sack into an already burgeoning fridge. He made his way back through the cabin, saying hello to the crew before heading up to the wheelhouse. Neither the captain nor the mate had arrived, leaving Jake to stare out at Ferryboat Channel, lines of prose running through his head.

The next morning had not started off well. Jake awoke late when, for some reason, his alarm didn't go off. He got into his uniform as quickly as possible then ran up into the wheelhouse.

"Was just about to send someone down for you," said Captain Trelawney.

"I'm sorry. My stupid alarm didn't go off. Bloody clock. It's only a year old!"

"No worries," said Rhoda Trelawney, waving her hand dismissively. "You're not actually late."

Jake *hated* being late nevertheless, even if he had made it to the wheelhouse on time. The rest of the day seemed as if everything was off balance.

The *Elwha* seemed to be under the same effect as Jake. The first two cars on the boat smacked into one another and the two passengers nearly came to blows. First Mate Fred was grumpy about all the paperwork, and he bawled out Chris Ditmeyer, one of the able-bodied seamen on the car deck, for not paying attention. One of the passengers admitted it was *his* fault for not watching the car in front of him, but things remained frosty between Fred and Ditmeyer the rest of the day.

As they sailed eastbound to Arrow Bay into a blazing red sunrise to pick up the traffic for Sidney, Jake couldn't help thinking of the old adage about "red sky in the morning." On the heels of that thought, deckhand Sally Conway slipped and fell in the galley just before docking. They picked up another crewmember to relieve Sally since the Coast Guard–issued Certificate of Inspection prohibited them from sailing through international waters without a full crew.

On the way back from Sidney, matters had only gotten worse.

The stool in the pilothouse broke, and no one could find a replacement. The coffeepot flooded because someone didn't line up the carafe, spilling hot coffee all over the chart table. The halyard for the flag had broken, leaving the Canadian flag in the up position. Chris Ditmeyer had yanked the flag down manually with a pike pole, only to have a gust of wind snatch the flag from his hands and send it over the rail into the waters of Haro Strait. While getting a soda in the galley to go with his lunch, Jake had to yell at a small child for writing on the bulkhead wall with a Magic Marker. On his way back to get his lunch, he found someone had jammed gum in all the locks on the doors to the car deck head.

Just when he felt the day couldn't get any worse, Jake pulled his lunch sack out of the fridge to find that someone had pilfered some of it. His Hostess Cupcakes were missing again.

The bastard will pay, he thought.

He looked over at Chris Ditmeyer, who was reading *The Clock Struck Murder* that Jake had loaned him and chewing on a carrot stick. "You know, Chris, it's a damn good thing it's our Friday."

Chris arched an eyebrow. "What now?"

"Some son of a bitch stole my cupcakes."

Chris shook his head, smiling. "Beats me how you can eat those things anyway." He caught a look at Jake's crushed expression. "But still, someone shouldn't have been in your lunch. It's not like we don't know which one is yours, with the treasure trove of snack cakes, chips, and sub sandwiches."

Jake knew Fred Phillips had plundered his lunch but not how to prove it, and accusing an officer wouldn't sit well with the captain unless he had proof. He ate the rest of his meal in a foul mood, though he and Ditmeyer talked a bit about how Spievens's writing was slipping. Jake had just finished his lunch as the *Elwha* reached Friday Harbor. He was due back on the wheel for their final departure from the Harbor to head eastbound back to Arrow Bay. He wished he could have spent it resting, but the thought of Sam being back Sunday afternoon fluttered through his mind and cheered him up. By the time he'd reached the number one pilothouse, he was whistling under his breath.

"Knock that off, Finnigan!" scolded Captain Trelawney.

"Huh?" Jake asked, confused. Then he caught himself. *Whistling up trouble*, he thought. "Sorry, Captain."

"That's okay," she said, knocking on a piece of wood trim. She peered down through her glasses at the cars being loaded onto the *Elwha*. "Going to be a full load on the way back."

"Friday," Jake responded, watching the last of the big trucks drive down the main tunnel.

"That everybody, Mike?" The bosun's voice crackled over the radio to the Friday Harbor dock agent.

"Two more real quick," said Mike. "This Toyota will do it."

Jake watched the Toyota drive on to the boat. The purser stepped back on board, having completed his work with Customs for the international travelers who had left the boat at Friday Harbor. Jake went out the pilothouse door heading for the end number two wheelhouse, nearly slipping on the wet deck. He popped back into the wheelhouse just as Fred appeared. Jake took his place at the tiller, waiting for the all clear from the bosun and the order from Fred before pulling out of the Harbor to head back to Arrow Bay.

"All clear on deck," came the bosun's voice over the radio.

"Offshore manned and ready," Jake replied.

"Transferred steering and propulsion." Captain Trelawney said over the radio from the wheelhouse at the Friday Harbor end of the ferry.

"Slow ahead, Jake," ordered Fred.

Jake sounded the departure whistle and eased the big ferry ahead slowly.

Thankfully, the rest of the trip back was uneventful. As the *Elwha* passed Upright Head on Lopez Island, Ben Roberts, the bosun, came up to the wheelhouse to relieve him.

"Sally's back on board. Just a good sprain. Few days off it at home and she'll be fine, but she might miss the first tour after days off."

"I'm glad she wasn't hurt too badly," said Jake, standing aside for Ben to take the tiller.

"No. Bertha in the galley feels awful about it. The kid had *just* spilled the soda when Sally came around the corner."

"Nothing Bertha could have done that quickly," Fred said.

Jake was glad Fred seemed to be in a better mood—no doubt because he was full of Jake's cupcakes—but he was also glad to be leaving the wheelhouse. He had just clomped down the stairs to the shelter deck and stepped out of the security enclosed staircase when he nearly ran into a passenger standing just outside the gate.

"Mierda!"

"Whoa, slow down there, guy!" said Jake to the individual who had just crashed into him and kept on going. Jake caught sight of a stocky man in jeans and a green nylon flyer jacket entering the cabin at a rapid pace, disappearing into the Wolverines football team from Friday Harbor High School.

Jake avoided the group of rowdy teens, crossing the cabin and jogging up the aft stairs to collect his gym bag. On his way down, he stopped in the day room to grab his lunch bag. He opened it up, sighing over his pilfered cupcakes, pitching the rest of his lunch into the bin. The half-eaten apple clunked loudly on the side of the can. He left the room and stepped down into the passenger cabin, gazing out at the rain. He wished he'd taken some time off for Sam's homecoming.

Jake sat down at the forward end of the passenger cabin with his bag as the *Elwha* lined up with the dock to pull in. Mike Davis stood by the door, waiting until the last minute to step out into the rain and onto the pickle fork to open the gate for the overhead walkway.

"Arrow Bay, this is the *Elwha.* Slip One?" Jake heard Fred's voice snap over Mike's radio.

"Slip one, *Elwha*," replied the dock.

"Well, at least it's over," Jake said, watching Mike bound onto the pickle fork as the boat glided into the slip. The ferry came to rest with a gentle bump. A few minutes later, the overhead ramp came down, and Mike pulled back the net, letting the walk-ons exit and head down through U.S. Customs.

Jake stood up, stretching. The cabin was empty of passengers, and Jake headed downstairs to exit off the car deck. On his way down, he heard someone's radio pop in with Mike's voice, reporting the cabin clear.

Stepping down onto the car deck, Jake watched the last vehicle pull off the boat. Ben Roberts and Chris Ditmeyer were about to secure the *Elwha* with the tie-up lines when Jake heard Chris yell out, "Aw shit! We've got an abandoned vehicle in the tunnel."

"Oh hell," Jake said, setting his bag down. Ditmeyer radioed up to the wheelhouse as he and Ben Roberts walked the length of the car deck, Jake close behind them.

"Yeah, Arrow Bay, could you check with the walk-on passengers to see if any of them forgot they drove their car on?" said Ben Roberts into his radio as they reached the white Toyota.

Jake, Ditmeyer, and Roberts peered into the car. Jake noticed it was a rental with Avis tags in the window. He also saw the keys dangling from the ignition. Instantly, a feeling of discomfort started to creep up his spine.

"All walk-on passengers have cleared Customs, Ben," the dock agent said. "No one forgot a car."

Fred had now appeared, having dropped his overnight bag at the front of the boat before walking back to the abandoned car. "Guys! Back up!" he shouted. "Roberts, radio Customs to come down here with the dog."

"Fred's right, guys," Captain Trelawney agreed. "Let the bomb dog get down here first."

The three men backed away from the car to wait for Daisy, the bomb-sniffing dog, to arrive from downtown. Jake wasn't too terribly concerned with a bomb. Passengers accustomed to walking on sometimes brought their cars with them, and then forgot they had driven. But this car was a rental, which made Jake uneasy. It indicated the person wasn't likely a commuter used to walking on the vessel and wouldn't have been apt to accidentally leave the car. The keys in the ignition also made him apprehensive.

"Did that car load at Friday Harbor?" Jake asked Ben.

Roberts nodded. "Yeah, one of the last ones on."

"You remember who was driving it?"

"Who pays attention to the driver? I'm always watching the car to make sure it doesn't run my ass over."

Daisy arrived with two U.S. Customs agents, Trudy Mundy and Jeff Hibbert.

"Back up, guys," barked Trudy, a stout woman with a kind face but very businesslike demeanor. She took the dog to the car and let Daisy sniff all around the vehicle. After a minute or two, Daisy gave no indication of any kind of explosives.

"It's clean," Jeff announced.

"Who the hell…" Ben muttered.

"Rhoda!" Fred shouted, taking a few steps back from the Toyota. He was visibly shaking, the color draining from his face. His countenance had stopped all of them in their tracks. He said nothing, grimacing bleakly as he pointed to the deck under the trunk of the Toyota. A small drip of blood had seeped out from under the aluminum frame of the car and had started pooling on the damp car deck.

"Why didn't the dog catch that?" Ben asked.

"They're trained for bombs, not blood," Jake replied.

"Oh, hell," spat Captain Rhoda, cursing uncharacteristically. "Hibbert, come over here!"

Jeff Hibbert thumped over to the car where the crew was gathered. Hibbert had always reminded Jake of a redwood tree that had taken on human form.

"What is it, Captain Trelawney? The car's clear, call a tow—" Jeff looked down at the pool of blood. "Oh shit!" He looked into the car and at the keys in the ignition. "Anyone touch the car?"

As one, they shook their heads.

Hibbert, his hands already gloved, gingerly tried the driver's side door. It popped open. He found the remote trunk release and raised the lever. The trunk lid banged open. A rush of sweet-smelling air hit Jake's nose, mixed in with the thick scent of copper.

"Oh God," said Captain Trelawney, turning her head away.

Jake felt his stomach lurch, a sudden sense of déjà vu overtaking him. It took all his concerted effort not to say the name *Chris*, but the body in the trunk wasn't his long-dead best friend.

It was a woman.

Neatly wrapped in plastic, just as Chris Aponte had been, her face was left out of the folds of clear wrapping. Her eyes, pale blue, stared sightlessly into space. A jagged cut raced across her throat, blood soaking her blouse. In what had to be the worst case of overkill imaginable, in the center of her forehead was a bullet hole, burned black into her skull.

CHAPTER FOUR

The next two hours passed in a blur for Jake. The Arrow Bay police arrived and immediately secured the boat, but they were too late. Nearly all the domestic traffic had been through Customs and only a handful of the international traffic remained. Initially, the entire dock was shut down but was allowed to reopen and move traffic to the second ferry slip so the other vessels could continue servicing the islands. The crime scene, after all, was confined to the *Elwha*. As police began taking statements from the crew, forensic technicians snapped photos of the car at the stern end of the boat, and the *Elwha* was locked down. The *Elwha*'s remaining sailings for the day were canceled.

Jake sat at the foot of the number two end stairs leading up to the passenger cabin, his arms clamped tightly around himself. The rain had stopped, and it wasn't particularly cold, but Jake could not stop shaking. Every time he closed his eyes, he saw Chris Aponte instead of the dead woman. Jake found the parallel between her and his murdered best friend deeply disturbing.

A group of men and women from the Arrow Bay PD were huddled by the ramp. Jake watched them carefully for a moment, then looked up the ramp to the legion of squad cars clustered near the terminal building. A white van with the seal of Kulshan County pulled onto the boat. Jake wondered if it was the crime processing team, as Arrow Bay was far too small to have its own crime lab.

A lanky man with dark brown hair and a neatly trimmed goatee looked Jake's way. Jake returned his gaze, only looking away when he jumped at the sound of the van's door slamming shut. The man said something to his colleagues who nodded as he stepped away.

He strode over to Jake, the heels of his shoes clacking softly on the car deck. Jake knew at once he was a detective. He was dressed in a spotless suit and a black raincoat. Other than the goatee and the fact that he appeared to be Jake's age if not younger, he fit the current standard for "detective" as seen on every incarnation of *Law & Order*.

"You all right?" the man asked.

Jake nodded but said nothing. The man had expressive chocolate brown eyes, not unlike Sam's. The sudden thought of Sam had a calming effect on Jake, and he quit shivering.

"Were you one of the ones that discovered the body?" the man asked.

Jake nodded again, his tongue too thick to talk. He noted the detective's comforting, soft baritone.

"My name is Adam Haggerty. I'm a detective with the Arrow Bay Police Department," he said, showing Jake his badge.

"I know," Jake said.

"You know?" Haggerty asked, surprised.

"You dress like every detective I've seen on television," Jake said with a shrug.

Haggerty smiled. "We all shop at the same store," he replied. "Brooks Brothers has a discount for detectives."

Jake appreciated the attempt to lighten the situation. "Jake Finnigan," he said, shaking the man's hand and rising. Jake found himself staring at Haggerty's tie tack. Looking up he said, "How tall *are* you?"

"Six foot five," Haggerty said, smiling again. He suddenly became somber. "I have to ask you some questions, Mr. Finnigan. I realize it will be difficult, given the circumstances. And you'll forgive me if I say you look a bit more shaken than the other crew."

A wry look crossed Jake's face before he could stop it. Haggerty had already scored points with him for being observant. Jake nodded and said, "Not all of us got a good look at…" He nodded toward the car. "I did. And I have an eidetic memory, so can't help *not* seeing it again and again."

"Well, that may be very useful to us in the future, you see—"

A siren cut Haggerty off in mid-sentence, blaring until the green Kulshan County sheriff's cruiser got to the point of the ramp. It lurched to an abrupt stop. The doors flew open, and several uniformed county officers popped out, followed by a large blond-haired man in a blue suit. He thundered down to the ferry and shouted, "That's enough! You lot from Arrow Bay, clear off!"

Haggerty looked bewildered, as did the other men and women from the Arrow Bay police. No one said anything for a moment. The lighting flashes from the cameras abruptly ceased, the silence filled by the mournful cry of a gull. Everyone glanced at one another, not sure what to say until at last an attractive woman in a tailored gray suit and curly, shoulder-length black hair said, "Excuse me?"

"I said you lot can clear out," the man in the blue suit said again. The jacket over his belly was stretched tight, the buttons quivering against the fabric. Jake suspected anyone standing close to the man when one of the brass buttons finally decided to let go stood a good chance of losing an eye.

"*Go?*" the woman asked.

"You heard me. I want everyone who isn't a Kulshan County deputy off this boat. *I've* got jurisdiction here. This dock is on *county* property, not *city* property, and I'll be damned if I'll have you screwing up *my* investigation!"

Jake saw the woman was about to say something to protest until Detective Haggerty said "Sharon" quite calmly, with a nearly imperceptible shake of the head.

The woman named Sharon threw up her hands and said, "Right. Fine."

Haggerty looked at Jake, gave an apologetic shrug, and stalked off, shouting down the tunnel of the car deck, "Let's go, Arrow Bay PD! This is *county* business."

Jake had no idea what had just taken place. He'd read in countless mysteries that law enforcement agencies didn't often work well together. The clash between local and federal law enforcement was a well-publicized *fact*. He'd never heard of any difficulty between county and city law enforcement before, but he didn't *know* anyone in either jurisdiction.

Jake watched as the Arrow Bay Police grudgingly filtered back to their cars. Jake caught one last look at Detective Haggerty, who seemed to be on the verge of saying something to him. He then shook his head and slid behind the wheel of his car. Within a few minutes, the cars had all backed up and filed up the hill from the terminal in a single line.

Jake had no idea who the fat man in the ill-fitting blue suit was, but the way he blustered around the boat, he suspected it had to be the sheriff of Kulshan County. Jake hoped he wouldn't have to answer questions from him.

"Hey, can I get all the crew of the boat over here please!" he shouted a few minutes later.

Jake stayed where he was, in close enough proximity to the man barking orders. The rest of the deck crew approached and gathered around Jake. The man came up to them and said, "Look, you're all obviously traumatized by this event. We've got all your names, and we'll get your statements from the Arrow Bay Police. If we need anything more, we'll be sure to call you. Meantime, just go home and try to relax."

In the back of Jake's head, an alarm bell rang. *Go home and try to relax?* Was he kidding? Even though Jake's experience on crime scene investigation was limited to television and books, summarily dismissing all the witnesses seemed to run contrary to common sense. Looking into the puffed, red face of the county sheriff, Jake was not about to question him. Instead, he shrugged his uneasy feeling aside, all too happy to get away from the *Elwha* and what lay in the abandoned Toyota a few yards away from him. He got up and walked back to the stairwell to pick up his bag, marching rapidly off the boat.

❖

Jake, while not wanting to admit it to anyone, was hungry. Most of the crew of the *Elwha* had headed straight for home, but a few made mention of a drink. Jake, Chris Ditmeyer, and Ben Roberts had agreed to meet at the Bitter End.

The Bitter End, named after the nautical term for the end of a rope or chain on a vessel, was housed in the lower floor of a solidly built, turn-of-the-century gray brick building that had at one time been Arrow Bay Savings and Loan. The dark stained Douglas fir floors had worn to a soft, scuffed glow from years of use. The ceiling of pressed tin squares in a Celtic pattern was painted off-white, with crown molding originally painted maroon that had faded to a soft purple. Sconces that looked like ships' running lights lined the walls, casting a muted glow over the entire dining area. Against the northern facing wall was an antique bar ringed by a dozen green upholstered stools. Behind the bar, a huge mirror held in an ornate gold frame ran the length of the wall; it was losing its silver and reflected everything with a dark, haunted look. Row upon row of spirits lined the shelf in front of the mirror in glittering, multicolored bottles. The Bitter End knew every range of customer, and stocked rotgut to bottles of brandy and Scotch that ran over a hundred dollars for a shot.

"I thought you might be in tonight," the bartender, Caleb Rivers, said, setting a double Jameson and Pepsi in front of Jake.

"How'd you know?"

Caleb jerked his head toward the flat screen television mounted above the hallway to the kitchen and bathrooms. The KABW six o'clock news was just starting, and the top story was what had transpired on the ferry earlier that day. The station was broadcasting live from the dock in their typically amateurish manner, with peroxided local celebrity and newscaster Roxie Eggans doing the live reporting. Despite the grim nature of the story, Roxie's usual collagen smile was plastered on her face, her teeth looking acres wide and whiter than an Alaskan blizzard. Jake groaned as they ran the story shot earlier in the day, which showed him and other crewmembers of the *Elwha* gathered around the front of the boat.

Jake took a seat at the bar stool closest to the end of the counter under the green running light, looking at the marble chessboard, its white and black onyx chessmen bathed in the unearthly glow. It had been there at least seven years, ever since Sam and Caleb had discovered their mutual love for the game. No one touched the board except for Caleb or Sam. At the moment it sat frozen, waiting for Sam to come back and make his next move.

Jake took a sip of his drink while the others from the boat sat down at the table nearest him. Caleb, who knew almost every crew from the ferry system that came into the bar, began taking orders.

"Ben?"

"McNaughton's and Coke," replied Ben.

"Mr. Ditmeyer?"

"A Guinness, please," requested Chris.

Jake joined the group at the table, looking for a moment at the chessboard. He eyed his glass then said, "Guys, I won't be able to drive home if I have this on an empty stomach. Would it offend anyone if I ate?"

As it turned out, the others were waiting for someone to make the first move, and Jake figured he was likely the one they were waiting for. He ordered fish and chips as did Ben, while Ditmeyer opted for a grilled turkey sandwich and fries.

They all avoided the ketchup.

Jake ordered a second drink, this time a single, unable to shake the visage of the woman from his eyes. He looked at the group and said, "*How?* I mean, how the hell does something like this happen?"

"I've been thinking the same thing," said Ditmeyer.

"I saw that damn car come on," Ben almost moaned. "I pointed to the driver to pull forward. And I can't remember a damn thing about the driver! I'm thinking, and I'm wracking my brain, and I can't even think of a single detail."

"Who pays attention to the drivers?" asked Ditmeyer. "I'm always looking to make sure they're pulling up enough, staying off the hatch, or not running me over."

"I know. After a while, you kind of forget the people are there, unless they're loud about it," agreed Ben. "Did you see anyone, Jake?"

Jake shook his head. "Rhoda and I watched the boat load. I saw the car come on, but the windshield was reflecting the sky, and I only looked for a minute. I was more interested to see if any more cars were rushing down the hill. I glanced at it for a second but didn't think twice about it. It was a Camry, one of God only knows how many others on the road. They're *the* nondescript car of the last two decades."

"Who...?" Ben started.

"We'll find out soon enough," said Ditmeyer, misinterpreting Ben's train of thought. "It'll be in the papers by morning."

Jake looked at Ben, knowing what he had really intended: *who would do such a thing?* He'd been mulling over every detail, no matter how seemingly insignificant, since he'd left the *Elwha*. He couldn't think of a single thing out of the ordinary. What could there have been to notice anyway? The car drove on, he watched it, he left for the other pilothouse to take the boat out of the Harbor.

On the whole, he felt very...*irritated.* A lifelong fan of mysteries, he wondered how *anyone* could be so stupid as to leave a body on the international ferry, knowing full well that everyone was subject to U.S. Customs inspection upon reaching Arrow Bay. Why risk the exposure? Why not take one of the other ferries from Friday Harbor? One not subject to any kind of inspection whatsoever, save for the odd bomb-sniffing dog?

He closed his eyes, thinking about the car. He could see it coming down the ramp. It had been raining, but the sky was not dark. The reflection of the gray sky had been nearly impenetrable. He could only remember the briefest hint of having seen a glimpse of hands in black leather driving gloves, and not long enough to even determine if they were male or female, a fact that aggravated him.

By the end of the meal, he still hadn't come to any concrete conclusions. The car hadn't driven itself on, that was for sure. A murderer had been on the *Elwha* today and had walked off scot-free, at least for the moment. He hoped the Kulshan County Sheriff's Office would be quick in solving the crime.

"What the hell happened there at the end?" Ditmeyer asked.

"A pissing match," Jake said.

"Jurisdictional conflict," said Ben, being more diplomatic. "Arrow Bay Police don't have jurisdiction on county property, and the terminal is still leased from Kulshan County."

"I thought they extended the city limits years ago?" Ben asked.

"They did, but that bit of land hasn't been annexed off," Jake replied. "It's a big bone of contention because the county has been getting the money from the lease, and the city doesn't get squat."

Ditmeyer snorted. "Other than millions in tourism dollars coming from people on their way to Sidney and the islands."

"That's basically the county's view as well," Jake said, swallowing another sip of his drink.

"What about Customs?" Ditmeyer asked.

"Not their job," Ben replied.

"Arrow Bay PD sure was *not* happy when they found out just about everyone had already made it through Customs before they thought to shut it down."

"We had…what? Fifteen cars from Sidney on the trip back today?" Jake asked. "It was all domestic from Harbor. Doesn't take long to clear out domestic traffic, and they had all the lanes open up there today."

"What are they going to do with the *Elwha*?" Chris asked.

"She goes back into service as far as I know," said Ben. "They had canceled the evening runs and were going to have the *Kaleetan* make an extra sailing. The crime guys—"

"Forensic technicians," said Ditmeyer and Jake in unison. They read the same books and were used to the vocabulary.

"Yeah. They were going to go over the car with a fine-tooth comb, dust it for fingerprints, that kind of thing. They said it would take several hours, then they'd have the car towed off, and the *Elwha* will go back into service," said Ditmeyer.

"I don't like it," said Ben softly. "It's a bad omen for the boat."

"As if it needed any more," said Ditmeyer. "The damn boat is infamous for being a troublemaker. Ever since it hit the rock back in the eighties. Can you think of any other ferry in the fleet that has a rock, a song, and a drink all named after it? I'll be glad when the damn thing goes out for maintenance soon."

Jake shook his head. "Don't let it get to you. It isn't the boat's fault. You might just as well say the same thing about Toyotas," he chided, but, deep down he knew better. Sailors were superstitious, and he couldn't imagine anything worse than finding a body on board. The *Elwha*'s lingering shadow was going to deepen, at least as far as the crews in the islands would be concerned. Over the years, she had slowly lost the aura of being a "hoodoo" boat as the years went by without any unlucky incident. Now, with the horrific discovery they'd made, the hoodoo talk would undoubtedly come back.

"I am profoundly happy that we are on days off," said Ditmeyer, staring at his empty glass.

"Me too," agreed Jake, remembering again that Sam would be home in two days. The thought flushed him with warmth and he felt a little better. It also filled him with an urge to go home. Not only would the cats and Barnaby be very cross at him for being late with their dinner, he wanted to soak in a hot bath and let the day ebb out of him.

The group broke up after finishing dinner. Ditmeyer left first, after Jake exacted a promise from him that he'd call if he needed anything. Jake found himself not liking the haggard look on Ditmeyer's face and figured that this had impacted him more than he was letting on.

"You going to be okay?" Jake asked Ben.

"I'll be okay. I'm just gonna try and not think about it," he said on his way out the door.

Jake paused by the bar long enough to thank Caleb and give him a slightly larger than usual tip. Caleb nodded and said, "Come back if you need anything. I'm always here."

"Thanks, Caleb. When Sam gets back, we'll have you over for that long talked about dinner."

"You're on," he said, sliding a beer to a customer.

Jake walked out of the Bitter End and to his rain-soaked car. Sliding behind the wheel of the Cruiser, he fired it up and killed the radio, not wanting to hear the yammering of DJs or the strains of any music. He was quite content to listen to the sound of the rain and the steady beat of the windshield wipers.

He took the long way home, winding past Wilde Park. The lights of the houses—snug little ramblers built in the fifties for the refinery workers—all bundled tight against the night, bright squares of curtained windows casting diffused light into the darkness. Pausing at the turn onto Dawson Road, he marveled at the intensity of the rain, looking like quicksilver in the unnaturally bright light of the streetlamp. He speeded up the wipers and made the turn, happy to see the weathered sign for High Street appear a short time later.

Shivering again, he pulled into the driveway, curious as to why the porch lights were on. He was sure he hadn't left them on the afternoon before, and they weren't on timers. It had to have been Evelyn, Sam's mother, stopping by and leaving him something for dinner. Since Sam had been gone, she'd snuck up to the house five or six times to surprise him. He'd call in the morning and thank her.

He dashed from the car to the porch and unlocked the front door. By the time he snapped on the foyer light, he was wondering why Barnaby hadn't come running to the door. Frowning, he took off his coat and slung it over the newel post, whistling for the dog.

"Barnaby! Here boy!"

Someone came up behind Jake and wrapped their arms around him tightly, nearly crushing his ribs.

"Surprise!"

The murder of the woman fresh on his mind, Jake slammed his elbow into the solar plexus of his attacker. He heard a grunt followed by a loud thud to the floor. Jake whirled around, ready to deliver a kick to the head with his steel-toed boot, when he looked down into the pain-laced face of his partner, Sam.

"Oh, bloody hell, Sam! Oh, gods, I'm sorry!" he said, helping Sam to his feet.

"Ugh," Sam managed, as Jake led him into the living room and set him down on the couch.

"I'm so sorry!" Jake said, shaking.

"I didn't mean to startle you," said Sam, rubbing his midriff. "I just thought I'd surprise you by coming home a few days early."

"Oh, you did!" said Jake, hugging Sam tightly to him. "I'm so happy to see you!"

"You have an unusual way of showing your affection," said Sam, grinning.

Jake hugged him again. Sam still looked the same, only deeply tanned. His dark hair was in need of a trim and had lightened a bit in the sun. As always, his beard was neatly clipped and his glasses ever so slightly down the bridge of his nose so he could peer over the top of them. His feet were clad in Chuck Taylor All Stars as normal, but *uncharacteristically* he was dressed in cargo shorts and a long maroon short-sleeved T-shirt with KOALA FERRIES written on it in white, a high-speed catamaran under the script lettering. He'd lost some weight, but still looked like Silent Bob. Jake kissed him passionately until Sam broke it off.

"What's wrong?" Jake asked.

"You. You're not in the habit of elbowing someone in the solar plexus because they've startled you." He paused, smacking his lips. "And you taste of Jameson. That means you've had a rough day. What gives?"

"Later, okay? I promise? Right now I want nothing more than to be with you."

Sam grinned. "Okay. But afterward, you tell me everything, okay?"

Jake nodded, and they all but ran up the stairs.

❖

The sound of the rain on the roof was thunderous. Dorothy and Sophia slept in their baskets while Barnaby had curled up in a ball at the foot of the king-sized bed that took up most of the room. Jake, freshly showered, pleasantly tired and still flushed, was telling Sam about the events of that afternoon and evening.

"Hieth shhet, errr ooo kerridng muhh?" Sam asked through the buzz of his Sonicare toothbrush.

Jake smiled, loving the new pajamas Sam had picked up—blue flannel with Bugs Bunny on them with Count Bloodcount. The words "abra-ca-pocus" and "pocus-cadabra" and "Newport News" and "Walla Walla Washington" floated around in a ghastly shade of green, along with the various transformations Bloodcount turned into when Bugs uttered the magic words. He said, "Finish brushing your teeth, you goof. I can't understand a word you're saying."

Sam spat his mouthful of toothpaste out and then rinsed with mouthwash. He shut the bathroom light off and crossed over to the bedroom, sliding into bed with Jake, shivering.

"Are you cold?"

"A little. And don't be offended if I drop off suddenly. I took an Ambien to help me reset my clock. It's a little after two p.m. tomorrow in Sydney, don't forget."

"Pretty cool, you getting a day of your life back," said Jake, snuggling next to him. He closed his eyes and breathed in Sam's smell:

toothpaste, Kirkland laundry soap, Irish Spring, and the ever so slight smell of cloves. "I missed you so much."

Sam hugged Jake. "I missed you, too. I'm never leaving you that long again. Not ever. If it weren't for the money—"

"We had that talk before you left. Financial security for many years to come was a welcome trade-off," said Jake. "Besides, it made me appreciate you all the more."

"Me too," Sam agreed. "Murdered and left on the ferry, huh?"

Jake opened his eyes again, the face of the woman leaping in front of him. "Throat cut. Not a nice wound, either. Jagged. Bullet hole to the head, close enough to have left powder burns."

"How—oh. Well, Spievens, I suppose."

"Not to mention the dozens of others I've read, *CSI*, *Bones*… and every show on Discovery and Court TV. You pick stuff up after a while."

"Especially with your memory," said Sam.

"Exactly. I couldn't see her hands, but the way her arms were bent back, I suspected they were tied behind her. Come to think of it, I think she may have been hogtied." Jake thought on this for a moment, recalling what he'd seen. Her arms *had* been behind her back, and while he couldn't see under the plastic, he would have bet money that she was indeed hogtied. Given the size and depth of the trunk, she had to have been slight in build and not particularly tall. And not dead for very long, either.

"What makes you say that?" asked Sam.

Jake hadn't realized he'd articulated any of his thoughts aloud. "I can't be positive, but it didn't look like rigor mortis had set in."

"I thought rigor left the body after a few hours?"

Jake shook his head. "Takes anywhere from three to six hours to set in, then up to thirty-six to leave the body."

"*The Crawfish Murder*?" Sam asked.

"*Homicide on the Homeric*," Jake replied dutifully. "One of the Captain Cedric Rostron mysteries. The one where the captain finds the body of Arthur Densmore stuffed into the cowl vent on the fantail and can't figure out how the murderer got him in there with the rigor mortis since Densmore had been seen at the dinner table the night before."

"Right," said Sam, the basic plot bouncing into his head. "Wasn't it the cousin who'd bumped him off?"

"Right. He was going to assume his identity once they'd landed in America."

"Crime never pays," observed Sam.

"Not in the books of Kent C. Spievens," Jake agreed. "I'm not so sure about the woman on the ferry."

"I'm sure they'll know more once the woman is identified," said Sam.

"I hope so," said Jake, closing his eyes again. His memory brought up the face of the woman, her pale, blue eyes staring sightlessly out from the folds of clear plastic sheeting.

"You thought of Chris, didn't you," Sam said. It was not a question.

Jake nodded. "I think I would have in any circumstance. But…"

"The plastic sheeting," Sam said.

Jake nodded. "Hard not to note the similarity."

Sam sighed. "You don't think they're related, do you?"

"The two murders?" Jake asked. "I don't see how they could be. I mean, I suppose it's possible. No one ever found Chris's killer. However, it just…" He looked into Sam's soulful eyes. "It doesn't feel the same. This was just so…*illogical*," said Jake, thinking of the circumstances again.

"What, Mr. Spock?" said Sam, running his hand randomly up and down Jake's washboard stomach.

"Taking the bloody international ferry in from Friday Harbor."

"Ah, I see your point," said Sam, leaning back against the pillows. "Why run the risk of having to go through Customs?" He yawned.

"Exactly," agreed Jake.

"Well, it's been my long and painful experience, Jacob, that people aren't all that observant. Perhaps this joker got into the ferry line and didn't realize the vessel was in-bound from Sidney."

"They hand out a flyer that says you'll have to go through Customs upon arrival in Arrow Bay," Jake pointed out.

"Right, but where would it be easier to ditch the car? Not in the parking lot in Friday Harbor. Too easy to be observed, right?"

Jake thought this over for a second, nodding. While it was possible to leave the car with the pretext of getting a bite to eat or something else, legions of people remained seated in their cars, particularly the closer it came to the vessel arriving. It would be impossible not to be observed leaving a vehicle. On the other hand, if you drove onto the boat, waited until the car deck was clear of passengers heading up to the cabin, and *then* left the vehicle, it would be easy to mix in with the walk-on passengers and disembark the vessel in Arrow Bay without calling attention to yourself. This fact troubled Jake even further. It meant that whoever had driven on with the body had gotten through Customs without arousing suspicion. Customs officers since 9/11 had become more observant than usual. Anyone acting suspicious, nervous, or otherwise untoward would likely be detained for further questioning. This person, or persons, Jake amended mentally, had slipped by without Customs batting an eyelash.

Whoever had driven the car on the ferry might not have known. what was in the trunk. Perhaps the killer instructed the driver to leave the car on the vessel, and someone already on board would pick up the car and drive it off. Jake found that highly unlikely, but conceded, however remotely, that it was possible.

He wondered how long it had taken the blood to slip through the layers of plastic to pool in the trunk and saturate the carpeting enough to drip through onto the car deck. How long had that body been in there? How long had it been wrapped in plastic? Where had she been murdered? What had been that funny sweet smell?

"Smell," said Jake.

"I just showered, thank you," retorted Sam sleepily.

"Not you, goofus. The trunk. When it was opened, there was a… smell…" He mentally added "under the coppery smell of blood," not wanting to upset Sam, before saying, "Something sweet. Floral maybe."

"Maybe she had perfume on," said Sam, the effects of the Ambien taking over. His eyes were beginning to close slowly.

"Could be," said Jake, but somehow he doubted it. The woman hadn't a scrap of makeup on, and her suit was very staid and didn't suggest frivolity like perfume. Jake shook his head, wanting to rid himself of the images of corpses.

"I love you, Samuel Patrick O'Conner," he said softly.

"Love you, too," said Sam. He snorted a short snore.

"Lie down, Sam," said Jake, gently easing Sam under the covers.

"Hassawakino," replied Sam.

Jake smiled, shutting off the light and curling up next to Sam, who was snoring lightly. He stayed like that for some time, listening to the deep breathing and the pounding rain on the roof. An uneasy wind stirred in from the Southwest, making the chimney cap moan in an unearthly voice. The minutes ticked by, and he was unable to sleep.

Finally, as the clock ticked past midnight he was able to drift off. In the deafening rain he did not hear the car on High Street start up and pull away, and as dreams of the day's events played through his head he was not aware that he'd been under surveillance for hours.

CHAPTER FIVE

Jake awoke Saturday morning wondering for a few seconds if the events of the previous day had been nothing more than a bad dream. He reached over for Sam, but the bed was empty save for Sophia, who was fast asleep next to him in a gray ball. He was just starting to question his sanity when the aroma of coffee hit his nostrils, and he could just hear the strains of Vince Guaraldi drifting up from downstairs. Sam was awake already.

He jumped out of bed and crossed over to the bathroom where he took a quick hot shower. After drying off, Jake returned to the bedroom, pulling on a pair of faded jeans, old Doc Martens boots and a snug-fitting black T-shirt. He'd had to confront Sam about buying him shirts a size too small to accentuate his muscles. Sam had shrugged and said, "I've got a trophy husband. I'm going to show him off."

Jake would have been slightly irked at being paraded like a prize cow at the county fair, but he found it refreshing that after nearly a decade together nothing had diminished in Sam's attraction to him.

As he laced his boot, he counted himself lucky and, in a brief superstitious moment, tapped the wood of the dresser in front of him. Many of their gay friends who had been in serious, committed relationships had split up after five years together. Jake knew that the "divorce" rate didn't really vary between gays and straights, at least as far as he could tell. Half made it work, half didn't.

He laced up the other boot and tromped down the stairs, about to ask Sam what his plans were for the day, but was interrupted by the phone ringing. He was about to pick it up when Sam burst in from the kitchen, yelling, "I'm not here! I'm not here!"

"What? You mean you don't want to talk to anyone? It's probably Evelyn."

"*Especially* if it's Mom! I told *no one* I was coming home early!"

"Are you out of your mind?" Jake said, aghast. "She's going to go nuts if she finds out. She's been saying all week how much she's looking forward to seeing you."

"So don't let her find out," said Sam.

"I hate lying to people," Jake hissed. "Moreover, you know I can't do it. Maybe I just won't pick up the phone."

"No! If you don't answer she'll come over here."

"You've put me in a very awkward position, Sam. I don't like it."

"Silly me, I wanted to spend some time with you after not seeing you for six months. Well-meaning as Ma is, she'll take over everything, and I won't get to even see you."

"What do you want me to do?"

"Make up some clever little story. There's a bat in the attic or something."

"We don't *have* an attic!" moaned Jake.

"Basement?" suggested Sam.

"What kind of a bat hangs out in a *basement*?"

"Pick it up! Pick it up! The machine is going to answer it!"

"I'll pretend like I just woke up," said Jake, picking the receiver up off the cradle. He mustered up a very tired-sounding "Huuhhhlooww?" through a half yawn.

"Jake darling? I'm sorry, did I wake you?" Evelyn asked.

"Um. Yeah," he said, forcing another yawn.

"I was going to see if you wanted breakfast. Would you like a rain check?" she asked.

She sounded somewhat preoccupied to Jake. In the background, he heard someone saying, "Evelyn, where do you keep the soap?" which she attempted to block out by coughing suddenly.

"I'm sorry, I didn't quite catch that," said Jake.

"Rain check? Tomorrow maybe?" she asked hurriedly.

"Actually, I'm having brunch with Alex tomorrow," said Jake, just recalling he'd made plans. "How about dinner Monday when Sam is back home?"

"That's a good idea. Meanwhile, get back to sleep and get some rest. Monday it is. Have to go, dear!" she said loudly when Jake distinctly heard "Hey, Evvie, are you going to come in here and wash my back for me?"

He laughed as he put the receiver down.

"What's funny?"

"Your mother had a man in her shower."

"Oh, yeah. She's been seeing Baldo Ludich for quite a while now. She said they'd gotten chummy."

"I gathered. He was in the shower wanting to know if she could wash his back."

"Please," said Sam, holding out his hand and wincing. "I'm happy Mom has a boyfriend, really, but I do *not* need details like that. Ugh. Now I'm going to be picturing that big Scot in Mom's shower holding a loofah and a bar of Irish Spring."

Jake chuckled and said, "A Scot use Irish Spring? Surely your mother uses Camay, or some natural thing."

"She's surprisingly set in her ways when it comes to soap. She's an Irish Spring gal all the way."

"I hate lying to people, Sam," Jake said, gazing deeply into Sam's chocolate brown eyes.

"I'm sorry. But you won't really be lying. I mean, you can always go back up to bed after breakfast."

"That's a nice thought, but I won't be sleepy," said Jake.

"I can help you nod off, I think," said Sam, grinning lecherously.

"Mr. O'Conner," said Jake. "I do love the way your mind works."

After breakfast, they had indeed gone back up to bed, and Jake ended up falling back asleep. When he awoke, he found himself on the darkened car deck of the *Elwha*, the white Camry in a spotlight at the end of the tunnel. He knew what waited in the car and didn't want to get near it, but he drew nearer and nearer, as if he were on a moving sidewalk dragging him closer to the abandoned car. He was soon at the trunk, which popped open like a jack-in-the-box. Wisps of lavender smoke issued from the trunk in separate tendrils, rising toward the roof of the tunnel.

The woman was inside, staring sightlessly out at Jake. Jake went to turn his head away, but couldn't, his mind etching in every minute detail...

"Jake!"

Jake sat straight up in bed, his body covered in sweat. He soon realized where he was and buried his face in his hands, his breath in rapid stitches.

Sam gently put his arm around him. "Jake, are you okay? You were moaning in your sleep."

"Nightmare," replied Jake.

Sam pressed Jake closer to him. "It's okay, it was just a dream, just a dream," he said reassuringly.

After Jake had calmed down, he leaned back against the headboard and sighed. "I suppose it's not too surprising, given the events of yesterday."

"No, I guess not," said Sam. "Are you sure you're okay?"

"I'm okay," Jake persisted.

"Tell you what? Let's get out of here. Why don't we go on out to Friday Harbor or Orcas and spend the day there?"

"You want me to get on a *ferry* on my day off?"

"Er, okay. How about Seattle? Get some good Chinese food? Hit the museums, take in a movie at the Cinerama?"

Jake smiled gratefully. "I'd like that," he said.

"We could even stay the night if you wanted."

"Can't do that. Got brunch with Alex tomorrow."

"Right," said Sam, unable to hide the disappointment in his voice.

"You're coming, you know. I wouldn't think of leaving you here."

"I know," he said.

"You don't sound all that happy."

"Well, you know Alex and I don't exactly get on," said Sam.

"That's not entirely true," said Jake. "Alex likes *you* a great deal. You don't trust Alex."

"I admit a certain amount of prejudice goes along with the Blackburn name. He was at the UW the same time I was, remember. I can still see him strutting around campus…"

"Very well, Professor Snape," jabbed Jake. "After all, Lord knows measuring someone by their family is something you're completely known for…"

It was a remark aimed squarely south of the belt line, and Jake knew it. Upon seeing the hurt in Sam's eyes, he regretted it at once. He took Sam's hand into his and said, "Hey, I'm sorry."

"No, I deserved that," Sam said. "You're absolutely right. I shouldn't tar Alex with the same Blackburn brush as the rest of his family. Especially if the measure is his father. Given the way my father was, I've no right to do that."

"Well, no, you don't," Jake said.

Sam blinked and sighed heavily. "Ah, that refreshing Finnigan honesty. I missed it. I think."

"Sorry, handsome," Jake said.

"It's all right. I had it coming, like I say. I shall endeavor to do my best to give po' Mr. Blackburn a second chance."

Jake rolled his eyes. "I hate it when you talk like Burl Ives in *Cat on a Hot Tin Roof.* It always gives me the sudden desire for pecan pie."

"Auh don't see *anything* wrong with that," Sam said, tickling Jake's ribs.

"Ack! Stop it! Foul! Foul!"

In the early afternoon, the couple headed south in Jake's PT Cruiser, Sam doing the driving in the rain. As they approached Seattle, the clouds broke up and the sun filtered through, making the roadway a slick band of silver snaking down into the city. They debated on going to a movie or a museum and ended up at Volunteer Park on Capitol Hill. They wandered around the grounds and toured the Victorian conservatory. Jake studied each orchid carefully, noting the delicate curves and colors, and the way the petals seemed to form stars or faces. He and Sam enjoyed the warmth of the conservatory and just the simple presence of one another after six long months apart.

As the sun had slipped down behind the Olympic Mountains, they discussed what to do for dinner. Sam wanted to treat Jake to an expensive meal, but Jake, still not entirely adjusted to their suddenly padded bank account, begged off the idea of going to Canlis and instead settled for the Red Robin on the waterfront. Jake stared out the window as the lighted hull of the ferry *Wenatchee* pulled away from Colman Dock, bound for Winslow, Bainbridge Island across the Sound.

"And after that, I'll start playing the tuba naked on top of the Olympic Hotel," Sam said.

Jake shook his head. "What did you say?"

"You're a million miles away, Jake," Sam chided.

"Sorry," he said. "I'm just happy you're here." He sighed.

"So am I," he said, gazing at Jake. "I really missed you."

"I missed you, too."

"I'll never miss another birthday, Jake. I promise."

"I missed yours, too, don't forget," he pointed out.

"I know, I know, but I was the one who instigated this trip. I wanted that fat paycheck so I could slow down a little and you could quit your job."

"About that…" Jake started, and seeing Sam's expression, trailed off.

"No, Jake. C'mon, we talked about this. You didn't bust your ass for nearly half a decade getting me established so you can continue working for the ferry system. That is *not* the plan, remember? It's your turn now."

"You knew it wasn't going to be easy for me," said Jake, picking at a French fry. "Finnigans—"

"Always pull their own weight, yeah, I remember," said Sam, sitting back and folding his arms across his chest. "You pulled yours *and* mine for years, Tiger. Not an insubstantial amount," he said, poking his belly through his waistcoat and making Jake laugh.

"Okay," said Jake. "Just give me a little time. Through the first of the year, okay? Maybe a little longer. I get my ten years in, I get a decent pension."

"Acceptable," said Sam, sitting back.

"Oh, and one more thing."

"Yes?" Sam asked.

"You get that piano you've been putting off buying for, oh, what? Seven years?"

Sam stopped in mid-chew. "You don't like my practicing on that vintage Casio?"

"It sounds like we're being invaded by a very bad eighties sci-fi horror flick," replied Jake. "So, no."

"I'll start looking into it," said Sam amiably.

The *Hyak*, incoming from Bremerton, sounded its landing whistle, making Jake jump. He looked out at the sister ferry to the *Elwha*, shivering.

"You okay, Jake?" Sam asked.

"I'm having a hard time shaking what happened yesterday," he said as the waiter returned with another basket of steak fries.

"I'm not surprised," Sam said. "I won't tell you not to dwell on it. That would be pretty insensitive. I just would try to get you to not focus so much on it."

"I'm trying not to," he said.

"Let's talk about something else, then," said Sam. "How is the writing going?"

"It's strange. Good, but strange. And a bit slow." He shrugged. "I do live in fear that once I get this one out, I'll just dry up and that'll be the end of it."

Sam ate a few steak fries before answering. "I think it's just the opposite. I think this story you've been working on for so long, because it's about Chris's murder...I think it's holding you back. Once it's done, you'll be surprised at how many ideas come your way."

"I wish I had your confidence," Jake said.

Sam smiled wryly. "I do love a neurotic, don't I?"

"Thank you awfully."

"Glad to help," Sam said, grinning back. He bit into another fry. "There's something else I wanted to tell you," he said slowly.

"Oh?"

"Well, before I left for Australia, there was another big contract out that I thought I'd try for..."

"Uh-oh," said Jake, apprehensive. "It's not out of the country again, is it?"

"No, no, nothing like that. And frankly it was a long shot. I honestly didn't think I'd get it. I know I've worked on and designed some fairly big projects..."

"Fifteen catamarans, two two-hundred-fifty-foot dinner boats, one Mississippi paddle wheeler, one Alaska paddle wheeler, four Alaska tour boats, three fire boats, seven passenger-only fast ferries, and the complete overhaul for the *Santa Rosa*," said Jake, counting them off on his fingers. "To name a few."

Sam couldn't help but smile. "I'm impressed. You really do follow my work."

"I'm proud of my man, the preeminent maritime designer on the West Coast," said Jake with a smile. "And don't forget, my name is on the business, too."

"True," Sam agreed. "And I don't know about preeminent, but I'm not bad."

"Go on," Jake insisted.

"Well, I actually didn't think I'd get this one."

"What is it?"

"The next three ferries to be built for the state."

Jake blinked a few times. "You're kidding me."

"No. I just found out."

"The replacements for the Evergreen State Class?"

"Yes. I haven't found out what they're going to call them yet, but

I've heard they're going to name them after some of the major rivers in the state, so I was thinking River Class."

"Have they awarded a builder yet?"

"Not yet. Three are in the running, including Sutherland in Arrow Bay. I told them I'd accept, conditionally, based on who got the yard contract. I don't want to be running down to Seattle all the time…"

"I know how those contracts work, Sam. You can't *conditionally* accept anything."

"Well, no," Sam said, looking down into his basket.

"I'm very proud of you."

"Thank you," Sam said.

"Now, are you going to let them know they've been suckered, and that you've had plans for this replacement class of ferries drawn up for years as something of a—let me see if I can recall the exact words—'fun thing to do on weekends'?" said Jake, eyeing the dessert menu.

Sam gave Jake a withering look. "Ha ha. There will be all sorts of changes to get them up to the state specifications. That's a lot of work."

"But not *nearly* as much as drawing them up from scratch," Jake said, smiling innocently at Sam.

"Well, no."

"How much did you get?"

"Well, I *was* the low bidder. They didn't want to do this with an in-house design again."

"Let me guess," said Jake, covering his eyes. "I really don't want to know how much, do I?"

"Er," said Sam, embarrassed. "Not really. The entire project is three hundred eighty three million. My cut of that is pretty small."

Jake knew even one percent of that was a huge amount of money. "Well then," said Jake. "You're buying dinner."

Sam smiled. "I can do that."

Jake and Sam ordered another round of drinks and toasted to the success of another O'Conner-Finnigan Maritime Designs project.

As they were leaving, Jake spotted a *Times* newspaper box. He peered inside, gazing at a gloomy photo of the *Elwha* next to the headline reading BODY FOUND ON STATE FERRY. Out of quarters, the pair scanned the article quickly through the Plexiglas.

"I wonder why Arrow Bay is 'assisting.' Seems to me the State Patrol would have jurisdiction over the county anyway. The ferry dock and boats are state property, aren't they?"

"County," said Jake. "There was some kind of conflict just before we all left the boat. County sheriff arrived, and some balding guy in a poorly fitting suit ordered all the Arrow Bay police off the boat."

"Blond hair? Looks like he had a perpetual three-gin blush?"

"Now that you mention it, yes."

"Danvers," said Sam knowingly.

"You said that like clichéd scientists say *aha!* when they've had the breakthrough that usually leads to some many-tentacled thing popping up out of a test tube."

"Oh, let's just say I'm not surprised to hear something like that happening if it was Sheriff Danvers. I've heard some stories about him."

"From who?" Jake asked.

"Whom, Mr. English Major," Sam shot back as they walked out of the restaurant.

"Don't try to distract me with grammar."

"Mr. Sutherland, for one. Don't forget he's lived in Kulshan County all his life. I think he went to school with Dwight Danvers. Said he was a bully back then, and that continues right up to the present."

Jake grunted. "Given what I saw down at the dock, I'd have to agree."

"If I were Chief Sanderson, I'd be watching myself. I think he might find he just stepped into something warm, brown, and unpleasant."

"The coffee at the bowling alley?"

Sam shot him a contemptuous look. "That'll do, as there isn't much difference between bowling alley coffee and what I was thinking of, O obtuse one."

"You aren't kidding there," Jake agreed.

"I'm sorry you saw that newspaper," Sam said softly. "I'd hoped to take your mind off of things for a while." He sighed. "I'd be willing to bet you were the 'big fella white as a sheet.'"

"That'd be me," said Jake. "I couldn't stop shivering." He looked at Sam and said, "You did take my mind off things. Finding out you've added millions of dollars to our bank account always leaves me distracted."

Sam laughed. "Well, don't count your millions before they're hatched."

"I've had a wonderful day," Jake said seriously. "Let's head home, though. I'd just like to be on the couch with you and Barnaby and the cats and maybe a good movie. Maybe a fire."

"Fire is easily done, turn on the switch," said Sam with a grin.

"Well then, is it a date?"

"Still dating after all these years. And they say romance is dead after the first two."

Jake pulled a face at Sam. "Har har. Let's not forget who the romantic one is in this relationship."

"That would be the dog at this point, I think. Although Dorothy did bring me her toy mouse when I got home."

"Let it never be said you're not appreciated," Jake pointed out as they got into his Cruiser.

"Yes, I know. I'm worth the value of a catnip mouse," said Sam vaguely.

"I'll have you know that's the highest praise from a cat," said Jake. He considered for a moment. "Well, a *real* mouse would have been, I suppose, but I'd rather not have dead rodents dragged into the house."

"Ick, me either. Too *Whatever Happened to Baby Jane*?"

"And thus completes the gayest thing you've said today," said Jake, grinning.

"What, that beats the 'what a fabulous window treatment' you uttered when we passed Nordstrom?" Sam asked.

"I did *not* say that," protested Jake. "I merely said the curtains in the display were nice."

"You said *drapery* and the word *fabulous* was in there. I'm sure of it."

"Rubbish," said Jake. "Besides, you referenced a film with both Bette Davis *and* Joan Crawford, the two oldest divas of the gay world."

"You're giving me hives," said Sam.

"You said it, not me," Jake said, unable to contain his giggle.

"God I missed you," Sam said again, heading up Aurora to get onto I-5.

"I missed you, too, Sam. Welcome home."

"Love you," Sam said.

"I love you back," said Jake.

CHAPTER SIX

Jake stood at the front of the ferry *Quinault* as it cut through the waters of Admiralty Inlet. Dead ahead of the old ferry was the city of Port Jefferson, the pointed and gabled roofs of its Victorian downtown core coming into sharper focus. A prominent house loomed on the bluff overlooking the town, its square cupola looking out over the water. Jake stared at it and shivered, drawing his arms around himself.

"You really hate coming back here, don't you?" Sam asked.

Jake nodded his head. "I do. It's been a lot of years but still…" His eyes were drawn back to the mansion on the bluff. Scaffolding surrounded it, and Jake could tell even from out on the water that restoration work had been going on for quite some time.

"Looks like they're doing work on the Aponte house," Sam noted.

"The *Nethercutt*-Aponte house. The Aponte family never lets Jim forget he was adopted," Jake pointed out. "But that's the house Chris grew up in, yes."

"It's quite a place."

"It's been a wreck for years. I think I told you how the Apontes pawned it off on Chris's father, Jim, as a token inheritance from old man Aponte. They thought they were leaving him with an albatross," said Jake.

"But it turns out their part of the property included a right of way for the airport," Sam said. "Jim Aponte sold that and a few other choice bits of real estate attached to the house and made a bundle. The best revenge is indeed living well."

"That and having lots of real estate," Jake agreed, turning away from the house. The *Quinault* made a course correction, leaning heavily for a moment and causing Jake to stumble into Sam.

"Well, hello there," Sam said.

"Come here often, do you?" Jake said, smiling.

"Only when shanghaied by a certain attractive man I live with."

"The cad," said Jake, returning to the rail. "I'm going to miss this old boat."

"She's had a good run. Nearly eighty years, in fact. Not that I approve of her replacement," Sam said somewhat disdainfully.

"That's because you didn't design it."

"It's because I don't think the sixty-four-car boat they replaced her with has much use in the ferry system," Sam replied truthfully.

"Well, no arguments on that," Jake said. "Where'd Alex go?"

"Headed back to that German deathtrap," Sam replied.

"English deathtrap," Jake replied. "And he's been driving it pretty calmly from what I've witnessed in the past."

"Easy for you to say. You're in the front seat."

"I *did* say you could take the front, Captain Martyr."

Sam stuck his tongue out at Jake. "Let's go. We're nearly to the dock."

❖

Back in the Jaguar with his legs crunched up nearly to his chest, Sam made a vow to take the front seat on the way back. Alex drove the new Jaguar off the ferry and into Port Jefferson.

Sam wasn't happy at the surprise announcement they'd be traveling to Jake's hometown. He knew too many demons wandered the streets for Jake. In all the years they'd been together, they'd been to Port Jefferson maybe two dozen times.

To make matters worse, Alex disclosed that the brunch was actually a Blackburn Enterprises company meeting held in the Marmot Hotel, the town's pretentious, century-old Victorian castle that sat hunched on the hill above the city like an expectant vulture.

"I always think of Hill House when it comes to that place," said Jake as they approached the looming, gray stone structure.

"Not at those prices," said Sam under his breath.

"I'm really, really sorry, you guys. This totally slipped my mind. I've had so much on my plate lately, I can't recall if I'm coming or going," Alex said with a frown. "At least the food will be top notch. If anyone asks who you are, just say you're personal consultants of mine."

"Consultants for what?" asked Sam.

"Well, let's see. Jake, how about personal fitness?"

"That's easy enough to buy, I suppose," said Jake, scratching his goatee absently.

"And Sam...um. Let me see. Travel consultant? You just got back from Australia. Meanwhile enjoy the food, and I'll try to wrap everything up as quickly as possible. And by way of apology, I'll take you both to the Cliff House some other time soon."

Sam jabbed his knee in the back of Jake's seat, making him stop what was undoubtedly going to be a protest of some sort. Sam would find it gratifying to soak Alex Blackburn for an expensive meal at the Cliff House as penance for not only insisting they take the Jaguar, but for torpedoing his entire unfettered second day alone with Jake.

They entered the lobby of the hotel, which *did* look like an old English castle. The ceilings were cavernous, with massive box beams stretching across the length of the lobby. Two dusty suits of armor guarded the front door. Alex crossed the lobby to the front desk where a stout man with thinning red hair eyed him warily.

"Blackburn Enterprises meeting?" Alex inquired.

"Windsor Room, first door to your right down the hall," the man at the desk replied, eyeing Jake suspiciously. "Hey, aren't you—"

"Thank you," Alex said, flashing his thousand-dollar smile and leading Jake and Sam down a dark, wood paneled hallway.

"Friend of yours?" Sam asked.

"Allen McIntyer. He was a pain in the ass in high school. Couldn't manage to write a single thing for the paper that somehow didn't involve him," Jake grumbled.

"The humble type," Sam replied.

"God's gift to everything," said Jake. "It's somewhat satisfying to see him as a bellhop."

"I think he prefers *concierge*," said Alex.

"He can prefer concierge all he wants," said Jake. "I'm going to keep thinking of him as McIntyer, the bellhop."

Alex took a deep breath and said, "Are you comfortable with your assumed roles?"

"Why the subterfuge, Alex?" Jake complained. "I hate lying to people."

"Not to mention you're lousy at it," Sam confirmed. "Your right eyebrow begins to twitch, and you look down at the floor so fast, I think I can hear a small sonic boom emanating from your neck."

"He's right, you know," Jake said.

Alex sighed. "Well, again, I apologize. I let this slip my mind and was planning on going to the buffet at the Illahee Inn. Trying to explain who you two are might cause complications."

"Because we're gay?" Sam asked. "We promise we won't make out in the corner or exclaim too loudly about the bold use of color in the dining room."

Jake rolled his eyes. "Like you've ever said anything like that in your life."

Alex was trying very hard not to laugh. He quickly regained his composure and said, "Nothing like that. These people are all rather cutthroat business types, and they might infer something incorrectly if they find out Sam's one of the most wanted marine architects in the country."

"Told you so," said Jake under his breath.

"They may get the wrong impression."

"And what impression might they get about me?" Jake asked, eyebrows raised.

"Gigolo. Boy toy. Possible high-class hooker."

"*Hustler*, you altar boy. At least get the terminology correct," Jake groaned.

"You really should go on the road," Alex said.

"It's six months of being apart," quipped Jake. "We've got a lot of catching up to do."

"I see that," said Alex. "Anyway, that's the reason for the low profile."

"Very well," said Jake. "But you owe us one."

"Like I said, dinner at the Cliff House," Alex replied.

"No, that's just the *meal* you owe us," replied Sam with a slightly nefarious grin. "We'll think of something else for the cloak and dagger act. After you, Joe Buck," Sam said, pushing Jake into the room.

The Windsor Room was as vast as the lobby, finished in Jake's second most despised style, Tudor. The white ceiling had black walnut box beams and Jake did appreciate the darkly stained oak wainscoting, but the fireplace was overwrought and looked as if it might collapse under its own weight. Even the blaze inside it did nothing to make it more cheery. The walls had been painted a dusty rose color and were lined with large framed prints of the hotel's construction.

"Help yourselves to the buffet," Alex said. "I have to talk to some people."

Before either of them could reply, Alex had melted into the crowd. Jake looked at Sam and shrugged, heading toward the long, narrow table under a bank of floor-to-ceiling windows where an astounding amount of food was spread, attended by a staff of waiters and waitresses dressed in spotless crisp white linen.

"You feel underdressed?" Sam asked, looking at the room filled with immaculately clothed men in tailored suits and women in formal business attire.

Jake looked down at his black leather pea coat, sweatshirt, and jeans and shrugged. "Me, maybe. You look good as always."

Sam, as usual, was in his cargo pants, blue flannel shirt and mildly clattering waistcoat. He shrugged in response and said, "I'm changing my story. I'm an eccentric Internet millionaire."

Several heads swiveled to stare blankly at them as they made their way to the buffet. Sam theatrically pulled out his pocket watch and consulted it for a moment.

"What are you looking at?" Jake prodded under his breath.

"Just making a note of what time it was when we entered hell," Sam answered.

"I think you mean purgatory, my handsome friend. Hell wouldn't have a string quartet or this good a spread," said Jake, eyeing the buffet table.

"Never underestimate the power of good marketing," retorted Sam. "And the cellist keeps hitting flat notes," he said with a wince.

"I'm hot," Jake said, slipping out of his jacket and sweatshirt.

Sam couldn't repress his laugh as heads swiveled around to get a closer look at Jake. He had worn a black T-shirt under his sweatshirt, which showed off his biceps and pectorals. Sam made a mental note to buy more of them the next time he was at the Jockey outlet store.

"Hello," said a woman with iron gray hair and svelte figure.

She held out a hand to Jake, who wasn't sure if he was supposed to kiss it or shake it. He chose the latter. "Jacob Finnigan."

"Felicia Graysmith," she said. "Are you part of the Blackburn team?"

"Oh no," said Jake. "Personal trainer to Mr. Blackburn," he replied, rubbing his right eyebrow.

"Subtle as a tsunami," murmured Sam, shaking his head.

"This is Mr. Thwacklehurst," Jake said icily, pointing to Sam. "He runs an Internet company. Selling…what was it again, Mr. Thwacklehurst?"

"The machines that put casings around sausages and hot dogs," Sam replied breezily, enjoying the look of astonishment on Jake's face.

"Is there much of a call for that?" the man at Felicia Graysmith's side asked.

"Oh, more than you might think, Mr....?"

"Harrison. Stanley Harrison. Marketing."

"Mr. Harrison. Oh yes, you'd be surprised at the resurgence in home sausage making. It seems people have begun to question the failings of the FDA, particularly under the current regime."

"Regime?" Felicia Graysmith asked.

"Oh, certainly. I mean, you get the Supreme Court to halt the counting of votes, sounds like a dictatorship to me."

Alex had reappeared, clearing his throat loudly. "Fascinating, the difference of opinion we can all have, isn't it, Felicia?" he asked, not able to bite back the smile on his face.

"Oh bother, all that political crap," replied Stanley Harrison from marketing. "I want to hear more about Mr. Thwacklehurst's home sausage casing machine."

Jake couldn't help but burst out laughing, which he attempted to cover in a fit of coughing. He excused himself to get a drink at the buffet table, watching with admiration as Sam, making some wild hand gestures, began to go into the ins and outs of making sausage.

❖

"I think you should be the writer," said Jake, watching Sam fill up his plate at the buffet. "Where on earth did you get a machine for home sausage making?"

"It was going to be a home condom maker, but I changed my mind at the last second."

"How come?" Jake asked, loading up his plate with eggs Benedict.

"I couldn't get my head around how you could vulcanize the rubber without burning the house down," Sam admitted.

"Nearly ten years, and you never cease to amaze me. Though I thought you nice Catholic boys never told lies," Jake admonished.

"When it comes to saving your own neck, you're allowed to fudge a little bit. I'll say some Hail Marys when we get home," said Sam, looking around. "These people are *sharks*, in case you haven't noticed. And I think one of them may have recognized me, anyway. There was some murmuring about 'Alex's pet project' that I didn't like the sound of being connected to my name."

"Thwacklehurst?" Jake asked, sitting down at a table not too far from the buffet.

"No, nitwit, the real one. *Thwacklehurst*. Where in God's name did you pick that one up?"

"A linguistics textbook," Jake admitted, biting into his eggs. "You look like you could be a Thwacklehurst."

"Don't talk with your mouth full," said Sam, beaming. "I swear, there are more people undressing you mentally under one roof than I've ever seen in my life."

Jake rolled his eyes. "Oof outta eee kdddikfh muh."

"I'm not kidding you, and I know you're doing that just to bug me," said Sam.

Jake swallowed mightily. "Mr. Thwacklehurst is perturbed."

"Despite everything, I'm actually enjoying myself. A tiny fraction of me is anyway. I'm still annoyed."

"Truthfully, I am too," Jake said. "Enjoying myself, that is. Except old Ice Bucket over there."

"Who?" Sam asked.

"Whom, grammar Nazi," replied Jake. "Over there, talking to Alex."

Sam turned slowly around, spotting Alex standing off to the side in a shadowy corner of the room. A large moose head on the wall looked balefully out at the group of business people, shadowing Alex and the woman. Alex looked preoccupied, but the woman he was with was not, staring at Sam and Jake with cerulean eyes colder than a glacier.

"What the hell is she staring at?" said Sam under his breath to Jake.

"Beats me. I'm staring right back."

"Never one to be intimidated, are you Jacob?" Sam asked.

She was tall and painfully thin, and her black hair was perfectly coiffed, not a hair daring to be out of place. She wore a jade green and black pinstriped Chanel suit, something Sam had gleaned because one of the other guests had enviously commented on it. Her black patent leather pumps had six-inch heels that made Sam's spine hurt just looking at them.

The conversations at the gathering were deadly boring. Before Sam had taken his seat with Jake at the table with the uncomfortable

Tudor chairs upholstered in purple silk, he had listened in to a steady litany of "profit margin" and "quarterly reports."

"What's he playing at?" Jake asked.

"I've no idea. Maybe we're about to find out," Sam noted as Alex walked abruptly away from the Ice Bucket and headed their direction.

He had just gotten up to them, a pained expression on his face, when the Ice Bucket came up directly behind him and said loudly in a silky, but distinctly acidic voice, "I see the old saying is true."

Alex went slightly pale and cleared his throat. "Excuse me," he said to Sam and Jake before turning on one heel, grabbing the Ice Bucket not too gently by the elbow and leading her out of the room.

"Should we follow them?" Jake asked Sam.

"Absolutely not," said Sam, already on his feet.

They trailed behind Alex long enough to see him and the Ice Bucket disappear across the hall into a parlor and slide the doors shut behind them. Sam could hear the raised voice of the Ice Bucket alternating with Alex's calm monotone. The heavy oak doors muted most of their conversation, and the monotonous murmur from the main dining room behind them made it difficult to hear until they got closer to the door.

"...gall, Alex," Sam heard Ice Bucket say. "And guess who came sniffing around last week? Said she was an 'old friend of the family' that owed you one. Exactly *what* did that bitch owe you, Alex?"

Whoever the *she* was had evidently hit home. Alex's voice suddenly rose.

"Nothing! I haven't seen her in *years*. What the hell was she talking about!"

"Don't lie to me, Alex! Don't be so naïve as to think I don't know what has and what *is* going on!"

Sam looked over at Jake, his eyebrows raised.

"...for over eight years. Nothing. I *swear*," said Alex, seeming to have regained control.

"You think that matters where *she's* concerned?" demanded the Ice Bucket. "How long do you intend to keep this a secret?"

"Zandra, don't worry about it," said Alex. "It's all going exactly as planned. Once this is over, it'll all be fine. Have I *ever* lied to you?"

Sam mentally cursed the Ice Queen for taking this particular moment to mumble. Sam heard a small scuffle behind the door. He grabbed Jake's arm, taking off in a cartoon-like fashion with one foot raised when he heard a hand fall on the knob directly on the other side of the door. Hoofing it rapidly into the nearest empty room, Sam slammed the doors shut behind them and found themselves in the library. "What the *heck* was that all about?" he demanded.

"I've no idea. It didn't sound like your typical business arrangements to me, though."

"You can say that again," said Sam. "See, I told you. *Secrets.* I don't trust that man. I don't trust him any farther than I could throw him. And I bet the sod weighs about two-twenty!" he barked in a harsh whisper.

"Shh!" said Jake, picking up an abandoned Sunday *New York Times.* He flipped to the crossword puzzle and began looking for a pen. "Do you want him to hear you?"

"Oh, who cares?" said Sam in his normal voice, crossing his arms.

They returned to the buffet where, much to Sam's disappointment, the food had been cleared away, and the meeting, such as it was, was wrapping up. Guests put on their coats and issued choruses of "we must get together soon." Sam stuck out his tongue and blew them a raspberry. Several heads turned in Sam's direction, but he had stopped. Jake had to turn away and face the windows to make sure no one caught him laughing.

As the room cleared out, they found themselves back at the same table in the same horrific chairs. Sam blew another raspberry, and they both burst into gales of laughter so hard tears ran from their eyes and their faces were red. Alex found them a short time later, after all the Blackburn Enterprises people had cleared out. He gave them a questioning look but said nothing, making them erupt in fresh peals of laughter.

They caught the next ferry back to Whidbey Island.

"Can I get you some coffee?" asked Alex once they'd stepped onto the car deck.

"If I have any more coffee, I'm going to jitter out of the car," remarked Jake.

"I think I'd like a hot dog," said Sam.

"You didn't get enough to eat?" Alex asked, surprised.

"Not exactly," said Jake quickly. "We went to look around the hotel, and by the time we got back, the buffet had been cleared up."

"Just got a few bites, really," said Sam as they headed up the stairs from the car deck.

"Your grandfather worked this route, didn't he, Jake?" Alex asked.

"Captain Jacob Jason Finnigan, master of the M/V *Defiance* and later the *San Diego* before the state took over from Olympic Ferries. He worked for WSF for a few years before his retirement."

Sam and Jake left to claim his hot dog but seeing the line, Jake set off to find Alex. He found him standing in front of the newspaper box, a frozen look on his face. Jake watched him carefully for a few moments, until a kid with red hair and an Elmo backpack bumped into Alex's leg, breaking his concentration. Alex then dug in his pocket, put two quarters in the box, and pulled out the *Seattle Times*. Jake watched Alex as he read the front of the paper, flinging it open for a moment to reveal the headline: BODY ON FERRY IDENTIFIED, INVESTIGATION CONTINUES.

Jake observed Alex reading the article for nearly a solid minute. Alex's face was scrunched up in…what? Jake couldn't exactly decide if it was concern, fear, or something else. He stepped away before Alex could notice him, stopping by one of the newspaper recycling bins to pull a discarded paper out of the bin. He sat at a table in the galley, waiting for Sam to return with his hot dog, which he did a moment later.

"How was your snack?"

"Atrocious. Just like I remembered them," said Sam wistfully.

"Take a look at the article," said Jake, tapping the paper on the table. He looked around for Alex, giving Sam a moment to finish the article.

"Oh," said Sam. "Her."

"Her? You know her?"

"*Of* her," Sam corrected. "You do too, if you think about it. Says in the article, Susan Crane, daughter of Richard Gordon, that crooked state senator who got a kick back from the developer who built all those houses that later fell into the Snohomish River."

"Yeah, I remember that, but did you know she was the one who ratted out her father and sent him up the river for twenty years?"

"You've been watching too many old gangster movies again," Sam chided.

"Not the point," said Jake, knowing Sam was right. "Can you imagine sending your own parent to prison?"

Sam arched an eyebrow at him and said, "Really? With my abusive father and you having Ingrid Finnigan as your mother?"

"Okay, bad example," Jake said.

"Jake, I know you well enough to know that if either your mother or father had been responsible for destroying the life investment of… what was it?" Sam asked, looking back at the article. "Thirty-seven people, not to mention polluting the ecosystem *and* making a pot load of illegal cash to boot? You'd happily see them in prison."

"Prison, maybe, but her father killed himself."

"Is it cynical of me to say only because he got caught?" Sam asked, taking the final bite of his hot dog.

"Tremendously, but probably true," Jake agreed.

"Sad mess all the way around," Sam noted. "I didn't know that bit about the builder going out of business and putting all those people out of work."

"I don't remember any of that last bit, or that he had killed himself," Jake said, looking out the galley window, still unable to see Alex.

"Well, that would have been the time you were up in Bellingham two counties away and getting your degree and everything," Sam pointed out.

Jake and Sam stepped out of the galley and onto the promenade deck, spotting Alex sitting on a bench. The day was cold, but clear. Mount Baker rose to the northeast, a snowy sentinel on the horizon. A few cirrus clouds streaked across the blue sky like gigantic goose feathers. The sun flickered on the dark, cobalt waters of Admiralty Inlet like sparks, broken by the occasional small whitecap whipped up by the steady fifteen-knot breeze. The *Quinault* plodded slowly but steadily toward the narrow harbor at Keystone, rising and falling ever so slightly, ever so gently.

Alex appeared lost in thought, his eyes fixed north on the flank of Mount Baker. He didn't move until Jake sat next to him and poked him in the shoulder.

"Something wrong?"

"It's just so damn beautiful around here," Alex said. "I don't think I ever appreciated it as a kid, you know? Running around all over Europe…"

"I don't think you'll ever find any place so beautiful as here," he said, somewhat defensively.

"No, I agree with you, Sam," Alex said softly.

"I'd have liked to have seen it a century ago," Sam said. "Century and a half. I keep forgetting that saying a hundred years any more now drops you at the early part of the twentieth century."

Alex chortled. "You're showing your age, my friend."

"Oh bah," said Sam, making Jake chuckle. "Well, a little," he conceded. "But still, by 1905, there had been a lot of logging. The horizon would have been altered. I'd like to have been on that first canoe trip up the Sound with Doc Maynard. Back when those centuries old three-hundred-foot-tall Douglas firs grew right up to the waterline. When the forest grew so thick, the rain couldn't reach the floor below."

"You're a romantic, Sam."

"Not really," countered Sam "I'd have then throttled Maynard for introducing dandelions to the Pacific Northwest."

Jake and Alex both laughed.

"I think Sam and I were born about a hundred years too late," Jake said.

"Hundred and fifty," Alex reminded him.

"Well, no. On that, I'd give a hundred. I'd like to have been around when the Mosquito Fleet was sailing. To have been captain on one of those fast little boats," said Jake.

"You aspire to be captain someday?"

"I don't know anymore," Jake said. He looked at Alex closely, a thought occurring to him. "Did you know her?"

Alex looked back at Mount Baker. "Whom?"

"See," Jake pointed out to Sam. "He says *whom*."

"And you call *me* a grammar Nazi. Back off, kiddo, or you'll end up *hanged* out to dry," said Sam with a grin.

Jake refused to rise to the bait. He turned his attention back to Alex. "Did you see the paper? They identified the woman found on my boat. Susan Crane. Did you know her?"

"I knew *of* her," Alex said slowly. "She had a reputation for being a ballbuster."

"In what regard?" asked Sam.

Alex raised an eyebrow quizzically. "In every regard. She'd hound people mercilessly to get a story. She'd bleed people dry to get details. I've heard she threatened, blackmailed, or intimidated people into giving incriminating evidence in an effort to make public officials look foolish."

"Ha," said Sam. "It's been my experience they need little help with that."

Alex snorted. "I tend to agree. Susan Crane, however, had a particular brand of venom. She above all liked to drag out embarrassing personal details about people. She succeeded on a regular basis. You have to remember the scandal over Senator Brad Jefferson?"

"The sexual harassment thing?" asked Sam.

"Right. Crane was the one who broke that story. Then there was the unhappy incident with the lead detective of the Seattle PD..."

"That one I don't know about," Jake admitted.

"I'm surprised. Your old friend took up the mantle on *that* one. Susan Crane got some very incriminating emails, showing the guy to all but be a member of the KKK. One had a whole vitriolic rant about Capitol Hill and the gay residents living there."

"Oh," said Jake, remembering Tony Graham's guest column in the *Seattle Times* after the incident. "I *do* remember that."

"What happened to him, anyway?" Sam asked. "The detective."

"Run out of town on a rail. I heard he went to Arkansas? Alabama? Somewhere in the south. I *do* know the Seattle PD and the state attorney general were plenty pissed off. The flood of negative press cost old Randolph Buchanan, the AG, his job. The chief of police nearly resigned over it. I'm glad he didn't. He's a hell of a nice guy and a decent man."

Jake shook his head. "She sounds like a lovely woman. The kind that should have been running an orphanage in the Dickensian era."

"Huh?"

"You can take the English major out of the classroom..." said Sam thoughtfully.

"Nothing," said Jake. "She seems to have had a laundry list of adversaries."

"You could say that. Though you generally don't have to look too far for a killer. It tends to be someone the victim knew fairly closely," Alex said, eyes clouding over in thought again.

Jake observed Alex closely, studying the secluded countenance and the haunted look in Alex's eye. He knew something was off there, and wondered if Sam had caught it. Glancing out toward the east, the dock at Keystone was just ahead of them. Silently they made their way down the narrow stairs to the car deck, climbing into the Jag.

The rest of the way home, Alex still seemed remote and preoccupied. Jake wondered why, and could tell by Sam's expression he was probably wondering the same thing. Was it the argument he'd had with the Ice Bucket? Something else entirely? The only thing Jake was certain of was that given Alex's behavior, he couldn't argue that Sam's distrust of Alex Blackburn was unfounded. Alex's behavior today certainly hadn't given Sam any reason to feel differently.

Halfway across Whidbey Island, Alex said out of the blue, "I'm sorry."

"What for?" Jake asked with a yawn.

"Breakfast. I really did intend to take you to the Illahee Inn like I said. I'd forgotten about this stupid meeting and only just remembered this morning. I hope you weren't uncomfortable."

"Actually, I quite enjoyed myself," Sam admitted.

"Everyone was too self-involved to make me feel uncomfortable," Jake said honestly, not wanting to go into the details of precisely *why* Sam had enjoyed himself, figuring Alex would be finding out soon enough.

"Except the Ice Bucket," Sam amended.

"Ice Bucket?" Alex asked perplexed.

"Chanel suit and the hair piled up like a pineapple," Jake clarified, giving Sam a backward glance.

"Zandra Morgan. She's an old family friend."

"I didn't think you kept in touch with friends of the family," Jake asked bluntly.

"I don't keep in touch with friends of my *father.* Some friends of the family, yes. The Morgans were great friends of my grandmother. Zandra and I went to school together."

"I see," Jake said, but didn't. Mentioning Alex's little tête-à-tête in the empty parlor wasn't worth bringing up because he shouldn't know anything about it. He glanced back at Sam, who raised his eyebrows, but also said nothing.

"I was more uncomfortable at being back at Port Jefferson than at your meeting. It's always uncomfortable going there," Jake said.

"You don't too often, do you?" Alex asked.

"No. I don't like bumping into people I know from over there."

"Like the concierge," Alex said, his voice regretful.

"Yes. People aren't used to seeing me how I look now. They look at me and want to know what the hell happened. I did the reverse, you know. You're supposed to go bald and fat after high school."

"That's true," Alex agreed.

"People there…it's like they're in a time warp. The ones I went to school with. The people that stayed, anyway. They can't seem to get their head around the fact I'm not the fat little brother of Jason Finnigan. And, of course, there's the whole rhinoceros in the study thing," he said, shaking his head.

"The what?"

"My articulate partner is avoiding a cliché rather un-artfully," Sam said. "He means 'the elephant in the room.' "

"Oh," Alex said, catching on. "The…" Alex hesitated.

"Unsolved murder of my best friend," Jake finished. "People go so much out of their way *not* to mention it, it becomes more painful than if they just brought it up straight."

"Sometimes people trying to be kind can inflict more pain, however inadvertent," Alex observed.

"True," Sam said from the backseat.

Jake lapsed into silence, thinking back on his childhood in Port Jefferson. It hadn't been idyllic, with a distant, indifferent mother and a father who worked all the time. Even with those difficulties, his life had been ordinary, he supposed. If Chris hadn't died, Port Jefferson would be less of a pall over him, but he still wouldn't like going back to it anymore.

"…later?"

"Huh?" Jake said, shaken out of his thoughts. Alex was now coming up to the Deception Pass Bridge.

"I said I'll take you out to the Cliff House later this week. But at least you both got to ride in the car."

"This is true," Jake said, feeling Sam's knees in his back. He couldn't remember ever being in another car with leather upholstery. It felt like sitting in the palm of someone's hand. He supposed Sam would have said more like a clenched fist, but to his credit he hadn't complained once—at least not to Alex.

"I'll call you guys later in the week. What day do you both go back to work?"

"Wednesday for me. I think they're going send up the *Chelan* while the *Elwha* is going out for maintenance." Jake also found himself superstitiously hoping it was going in for some sort of cleansing. Not being religious, he wasn't sure what you did in such situations. Call in a priest, he supposed, but that didn't seem appropriate. At least one member of the crew was Jewish, one a Buddhist, and at least one a stark atheist who'd chew your ear off on the subject given half the chance. Perhaps he'd just give the *Elwha* a kick and tell it not to get any ideas about collecting more hoodoo because of this incident.

"Will you get the *Elwha* back?"

"We'll probably get it back for a while. The *Chelan* still has to sit in at Mukilteo for one of the other boats' maintenance cycle."

The miles back to Arrow Bay and 100 High Street slipped away, and before they knew it they were back at their front porch. Alex promised again he'd take them out for a "make up" meal at a later date and bid them good-bye, the bright blue Jaguar disappearing around the corner.

"Well, *that* was interesting," said Sam.

"What's that?" Jake asked.

"Tiger, I know you like to see the best in people, which can sometimes give you blinders the size of airplane wings, but you *had* to notice how rapidly Alex shifted the conversation away from Susan Crane *and* Zandra Morgan."

Jake sighed and said, "It could have been out of consideration, possibly. Alex knew how upset I was about the entire incident."

Sam appeared to consider this for a moment and said, "You're right. It is possible he was taking your feelings into account. I apologize for being an overly suspicious old goat."

"Bear, not goat," Jake corrected.

"I note you left the *old* bit uncorrected."

"Well," Jake started as they walked up the porch steps. He stopped at the top step, thinking.

"What?" asked Sam.

"Really, that only explains *one*, not the other, doesn't it? I mean, I can see him steering things away from Susan Crane out of respect for me, but Zandra Morgan doesn't figure into it."

Sam sighed and said, "I can't help it, Jake. I can't shake the feeling that there is something Alex wasn't saying about Old Ice Queen Zandra *or* Susan Crane."

"Really, Zandra Morgan is none of our business, when you get right down to it. And I still think he was just trying to be nice about the Susan Crane thing," said Jake, opening the door and picking up Barnaby after he came running up to them.

"I just don't buy that," said Sam, but he said it so low Jake couldn't hear him.

CHAPTER SEVEN

Monday morning, Jake woke again to the sounds of Vince Guaraldi and the aroma of coffee and bacon drifting up from the kitchen. Jake looked over at Sam's side of the bed and into the face of Barnaby. He thumped his tail on the mattress at seeing Jake awake.

"You are not supposed to be on the sheets, sir, and you know it."

Thump thump thump.

Jake patted him on the head and sat up, looking over at the alarm clock. Sam was not an early riser by nature, and Jake figured his internal clock was still out of whack. Sam wouldn't be awake and cooking breakfast at 6:37 in the morning otherwise.

Knowing he had to work out, Jake slipped out of bed and into his usual workout outfit and padded down the stairs, Barnaby at his heels. Entering the kitchen, he slipped up behind Sam and gave him a kiss on the back of the neck and a bear hug.

"Did I wake you?"

"The intoxicating aroma of bacon did it," said Jake, nabbing a piece off the plate sitting on the drain board.

"You want some eggs?"

Jake shook his head. "After I work out."

"I already took Barnaby out for his walk around the pond," Sam said, setting some more bacon aside from the frying pan.

"What time did you wake up?"

"Around three. I made myself go back to sleep and finally gave up at five."

"Wasn't it a little dark to be walking around Stark's Pond?"

"We managed," Sam replied. "What are your plans for today?"

"You've just gotten home, remember? We're having a welcome home dinner for you with Evelyn," Jake said.

"Oh, right. Can't we get out of that?" Sam asked, looking over the top of his glasses with a grin.

"Get out of dinner with your mother? To painfully overwork an old saying, I think the camel will get through the eye of the needle before we get out of dinner with Evelyn."

Sam sighed. "I know it. It's not that I don't want to see Mom, it's just I expect she'll have an update on my sister—"

The phone rang, cutting him off. Jake looked at Sam thinking, *who the hell could that be?* Jake shrugged and picked up the receiver. "Hello?"

"My God! Are you okay? Why didn't you *call* me?"

"Sadie McKee!" Jake said, calling his best girlfriend Rachel as he had since their days in elementary school. "As I live and breathe! Just when I was about to send an email to the DA to see if you were still alive."

"Very funny, Gobo," she replied. "Seriously, are you okay? Mom emailed me the articles about the body they found on the ferry. I wasn't sure if it was your boat, as I can never keep track of which damn one you are on, but one of the articles said it was the international ferry. I was pretty certain you said you were on that route this fall."

"I did and it was. And thank you for calling."

"I feel like a heel for not calling sooner. Especially with Sam away."

"Erm," said Jake, while Sam starting singing "Cast Your Fate to the Wind."

"He's there, isn't he?" Rachel asked.

"Got in a few days early. The night of the incident on the boat, as a matter of fact."

"Well, I feel marginally less guilty," she said. "At least someone was there for you. Tell me what happened."

Jake related the incident to Rachel, being careful not to miss a detail. After answering a few questions, he lapsed into silence and waited for her to say something.

"There's a reason they came up with the word *overkill*. I think you were looking at a prime example. Why cut the throat *and* shoot in the head?"

"I'm actually not sure which came first," Jake said.

"Well, if she were already dead beforehand, the wound wouldn't have bled. No heart to pump the blood, ergo—"

"Rachel, I haven't even had *breakfast* yet, do you mind?" Jake said, feeling queasy.

"Sorry," she said. "Oh, yeah, I guess it isn't nine thirty there, is it? Oh jeez, Gobo, I'm sorry. I read the articles and picked up the phone without even looking."

"That's okay. I've missed you."

"Work, you know, has been highly unpleasant lately. Everyone knows I'm going on vacation through the holidays and is determined to pile up as much on me as they possibly can."

"Sorry to hear that," Jake said, meaning it. "I wasn't sure if you were...you know, busy or wrapped up with some mook again," Jake said as Sam winced and shook his head.

"Ah, that refreshing Finnigan directness," she said without irony. "If anyone else but you said that to me, Gobo, they'd be crumpled to the floor clutching their testicles."

"I *am* quoting you," Jake pointed out.

"I know," she said. "Sometimes I think that memory of yours is not such an asset."

"Believe me," Jake said, the face of Susan Crane flashing in front of his eyes. "I know what you mean."

"Have they I.D.'d the victim yet?"

"Yesterday. Susan Crane. Some reporter for—"

"The *Outsider*," Rachel finished. "I know who she is. She covered a couple of my trials before I left for D.C."

"Alex indicated she was kind of a troll," Jake said.

"I'm surprised Alex limited his description to something so flat," Rachel said. "She was a conniving, vicious little two-faced bitch."

"*The Parent Trap*," Jake said. "The original one. Minus the bitch part."

"Two points," Rachel retorted. "But it applies. Susan Crane had a way of eviscerating someone without them being aware of it. They'd spill their guts to her, and she'd come right back and smack them with it in the press."

"You aren't speaking from personal experience, I hope?" Jake asked.

"No, no. I was small potatoes for Susie at that time. She tried to nail me down for a quote on a case, and I threw the standard 'no comment' back at her. In her next story, I was referred to as a 'somewhat glamorous, but vapid young prosecutor with more style than substance' whose career was on the short track to nowhere."

"Ouch," Jake replied, motioning to Sam to hand him another piece of bacon.

"And since she didn't use names, I couldn't even sue the cow for libel," Rachel grumbled. "I don't envy the police on this one."

"Why's that?" Jake asked.

"Well, if you threw a rock in Seattle, you just *might* be able to hit someone who didn't want to do her in. I wouldn't put any bets on it though."

"Aha. So Kulshan County has its work cut out for it."

"Kulshan County?" Rachel asked. "Isn't the ferry dock considered state property?"

"It's leased from the county," Jake replied.

"Is Danvers still sheriff up there?" Rachel asked.

Jake didn't like the note of apprehension in her voice. "Yes. Why?"

Rachel whistled through her teeth. "No reason."

"Rachel Louise Parker!" Jake scolded.

"Oh, you used the L-word. I am *so* not saying anything now."

"Fine, fine," said Jake. "What can you tell me about Danvers?"

"Nothing on the phone. This may be D.C. but…never mind. I'm coming out there. Are you up for some company?"

"Rachel's coming out," said Jake.

"Really? When did that happen?" Sam asked.

"Not like that, you goof. She's headed out here. Can you stand some company?"

"If, and only if," Sam said, loud enough for her to hear, "there is the patented Parker mac and cheese in the offing."

"I didn't quite get that," Rachel said. "I suspect there was something about mac and cheese said, however."

"You get the two points this time," Jake replied.

"Tell her we'd be delighted to have her stay with us through the holidays," Sam said. "Though she'll have to share space with Gavin and Jeff."

"She knows the drill," said Jake.

"It'll be nice to see her, especially since she ditched us *last* holiday season. I don't care if it *was* Fiji and the man's butt was 'round and supple as a ripe apricot,' I believe, was the phrase?" Sam said, leaving the kitchen to Jake and his peals of laughter. "I'm going to get in the shower."

"Sometimes I don't know why I am still friends with you two. You're like Heckle and Jeckle. A girl doesn't have a chance."

"The day you can't hold your own, Sadie, is the day they wheel the both of us into the Raisin Ranch."

"And Sam's memory isn't as good as yours. It was a ripe *peach*. I hate apricots."

Jake laughed again. "Seriously, Rachel, it would be good to have you out here. *Especially* on the holidays. And I know Gavin and Jeff will be happy to see you," he said.

"I've missed my second favorite couple," Rachel said with a sigh. "I miss the West Coast, actually."

"Well, we've been trying to get you back here for years," he said. "I miss you like hell, Sadie McKee, and I don't mind admitting..." He took a deep breath. "What happened on the *Elwha*..." He trailed off.

"It brought up memories of Chris," said Rachel knowingly. "I'm not surprised."

"She was wrapped in plastic," Jake said, his voice cracking.

"Oh, God, Jake. You don't think..." She hesitated, not wanting to say it. "You don't think there's a connection, do you?"

"No," Jake said truthfully. "It doesn't *feel* like it, which is about as scientifically supportable as proving leprechauns exist. I can't explain it any better than that."

"Knowing how hard-headed you are, that's enough for me," she confessed.

"I'll ignore that," said Jake. "Are you in the mood for more bad news?"

"Oh, why not?" she asked. "I've a strong heart."

"Jason's gone off the deep end, according to my mother."

"My, you are a bastion of good news today, Gobo," she sighed. "Dear, sweet Ingrid," said Rachel, and Jake could see her rolling her eyes as she said it. "She does have a way with words. What's up with your brother?"

Jake explained the situation to Rachel, stretching out to try and snag another piece of cooling bacon off the drain board. Sam reappeared from his shower and picked up the plate.

"You are evil," Jake said to him. "Evil to the core!"

"Well, if *that's* your attitude, I won't offer you my opinion," Rachel said. "Wait—what is Sam doing?"

"Holding the bacon plate just out of my grasp."

"You're bigger than he is. Knock him down and take it. He who rules the bacon rules the house."

"I am *not* bigger than he is," Jake said, as Sam moved the plate an inch closer to him, then jerked the plate away, laughing so hard tears leaked from his eyes. "Which just goes to show how long you've been away from here, lady."

"Point taken, point taken. Pick me up at SeaTac on…oh, how's the sixteenth sound?"

"Like a day I have to work," he replied. "Sam, could you get Rachel on the sixteenth at SeaTac?"

"What day is that?" Sam asked, leaning in to look at the calendar behind Jake's head.

Jake snagged the plate from Sam's hand. He grabbed a piece of bacon and began eating it. "Wednesday," he replied, smiling triumphantly up at Sam.

"If you get a gut ache before working out, it isn't my fault," Sam replied. "And tell her yes."

"It's a go," said Jake.

"I'll email with times," she said. "Meanwhile, watch yourself, okay?"

"Ha," said Jake. "Which part? Jason, or…?"

"The murder, you nitwit," Rachel said. "If Danvers is involved, I half expect things to turn ugly is all. Just be careful, okay?"

"You're starting to alarm me just a little," Jake said honestly.

"Good," replied Rachel. "You're listening, then."

They rang off, leaving Jake to face Sam's quizzical expression. He related the gist of the conversation along with Rachel's warning about Sheriff Danvers.

"Rachel obviously knows something about Danvers," he said.

"You did say you'd heard some stories."

Sam nodded. "I'll ask Mr. Sutherland when I see him tomorrow. Meanwhile, I think we'd be wise to do what Rachel says. She's never steered you wrong in the past, has she?"

"Rachel?" Jake asked, thinking of their many years of friendship. "No. Never."

❖

Evelyn called just after Jake had finished working out in the basement. She was confirming plans for dinner, and checking when Sam was due in from Australia. Jake recited the time Sam *would* have been in, glad he wasn't looking at her face-to-face.

"Why don't you ask Baldo along?" said Jake, not too subtly.

"Baldo?" said Evelyn innocently. "Whatever do you mean?"

"Oh, come now, Evelyn. He was calling for a back scrub in the shower."

"Along with your memory, you're also blessed with good hearing," said Evelyn O'Conner sourly. "As it happens, Baldo is busy this evening."

Jake erupted in giggles. "Why the subterfuge, Evelyn?"

"Oh, because it's casual, Jacob," said Evelyn. "It's very nice and uncomplicated, and I don't like to make a big deal of it because my son is still so very Catholic."

"I think you underestimate him at times," said Jake.

"Possibly," she allowed. "What time?"

"Oh, seven. Sam should be done tinkering around the house by then. He's been at it all morning."

"What was that?" asked Evelyn suspiciously.

"Nothing!" said Jake in a panic, realizing his slip. "Gotta go, Evelyn, there's a—a—ah—bat in the basement!" Jake said, hanging up.

❖

The doorbell rang at half past seven. Jake yelled that the door was open just as he pulled the hulking pan of bubbling lasagna out of the oven. Another wave of aromatic smells drifted from the dish as Evelyn swept into the kitchen.

"Oh, my!" said Evelyn happily, having had Jake's specialty before. She hugged Jake before marching over to her son and wrapping him in her arms tightly.

"God, Ma, what are you trying to do, squeeze my guts out of my ears?" he asked, hugging her heavily back.

"I've missed you," she said. "You are my only son, you know. Is there something wrong with that?"

"'Course not," he said. "I've missed you, too, but Jake was here to keep you company."

"Oh," she said, waving an arm of her black silk kimono-style blouse. "We had some lovely dinners and conversations, to be sure. You know I love you as if you were my own, Jake, but that work schedule of yours is supremely irritating and nearly impossible to work around."

"Don't I know it," Jake agreed.

"Don't you think it's about time you quit that job and worked on your *real* career?" asked Evelyn, ignoring Sam's warning glance.

"Ma," he said. "Leave it alone."

"Have I said something?" Evelyn asked, perplexed.

"About ten minutes and we can eat," Jake said, sliding the garlic bread in the oven. "And no, you haven't. We're just still discussing it."

"I thought we'd decided," Sam said sourly.

"I brought you some lemon chiffon cheesecake," said Evelyn. She went back to the counter and put the cheesecake in the fridge. She gave Jake a critical look, as if about to say something, then winked at him and said, "I understand, dear. It's hard to let go. You need to. Don't worry so much."

"Ma," said Sam, pinching the bridge of his nose.

Jake gazed directly back at her and smiled. He reached out and squeezed her hand. "Thanks, Evelyn. You know it won't be easy."

"In your own time, Jacob, but don't linger too long. That passion you have for writing will burn you up if you stay too long," she warned. Abruptly clapping her hands together, she said, "Now, how about a drink?"

For the next hour and a half, they discussed Australia and Sam's work for Koala Ferries over dinner, moving on to various projects they wanted to accomplish by the onset of truly bad weather in winter. Evelyn gave her own list of projects she had for some galleries and clients back east, and then inquired about the holidays.

"Are the boys coming up from San Francisco?"

"Christmas, not Thanksgiving," said Jake. "Gavin said the Ashworth clan is meeting in Santa Fe for the holiday."

"Lovely town," said Evelyn. "I've got some pots there. Or had. I can't remember. I sold some to someone there. Who knows if they stayed?"

"Boys, Mom, really? Gavin and Jeff are in their thirties," Sam pointed out.

"When you get to my age, anyone under forty-five is a boy," Evelyn said.

"Like you're so old," said Jake. "You've not even hit sixty yet."

"Perilously close, dear, perilously close," she pointed out. "The days of being able to claim I'm Sam's older sister are long behind me."

Sam dropped his fork. "When did you do that?"

"I was a young mother with two kids," said Evelyn. "Do you realize how hard it was to attract an eligible bachelor in the late 1970s with that kind of baggage?"

"Baggage?" Sam said, folding his arms across his chest.

"As do I with you two," she said. "I'm so very glad you're home, Sam."

"Me too," Sam agreed.

"Don't be so stubborn, Jake," she said as they walked through the dining room to the foyer where she put on her coat and picked up her purse. "It's your time now. Take advantage of it. You've both worked so hard."

"Thanks, Evelyn," said Jake.

"You don't need to walk me out, Sam. This is a quiet little town, recent events notwithstanding. I'm quite sure no one will jump out of the boxwood and attack me," she said, stepping out the front door. She paused for a minute, looked back at Jake and said, "Still, please be careful, will you, Jake? There's just something not right here. I can't put my finger on it. And knowing who the victim was, there's bound to be trouble."

Jake looked at Sam. He shrugged, watching his mother until she was in her car and driving down High Street.

"What'd she mean?" asked Jake, shutting the door and flipping the deadbolt.

"Well, you know Ma. She's got a spooky sixth sense about these things sometimes."

"You think I should heed her warning."

"Can't hurt," Sam acknowledged.

"Okay then," said Jake. "Now, let's clean up the mess."

Back in the kitchen, Jake put the plates into the dishwasher as Sam rinsed and handed them off to him.

"What'd you two talk about?"

"Mom and I? Just catching up on the family," Sam said quietly.

"Ah," Jake said knowingly.

"You can ask, you know."

"Okay, what about?"

Sam shook his head and sighed tiredly. "My sister Nora wants to drag the past up and shake it until something falls out. She's in therapy now and bugging Mom incessantly. Mom, understandably, doesn't want to talk about it."

"It has something to do with your father?"

"It does. What else?"

"I can't blame Evelyn for not wanting to talk about it," said Jake. "Who wants to bring up your abusive ex-husband?"

"Nora does, for whatever reason," said Sam. "I mean, I can

understand working through it so you don't repeat the same mistakes," he said, his voice trembling.

"Hey," said Jake, setting the dishes aside and putting an arm around Sam. "All that's in the past, Sam. Yeah, you got wrapped up with a bad guy who…"

"Beat me just like Dad did," Sam finished. "It's not that I can't handle that fact, it's just that I was so dumb I didn't see it coming—"

"Stop it," Jake said. "You know better. Intelligence had nothing to do with it. Tom White was a sociopath and fooled *everyone*, not just you. Even Evelyn thought he was a hell of a nice guy at first."

"Sorry, sorry," Sam said, taking a deep, shuddering breath. "Every darn time I think I'm over it—"

"Sam, you can say *damn*. Even the Hays Office allowed that for *Gone with the Wind*."

Sam laughed and said, "If it makes you feel better, every damn time I think I'm over it, something brings it up—"

"Nora brings it up."

"—and I end up reliving part of it," he said.

"We both have wooden beams across our shoulders to bear at times," said Jake. "This business has brought up a lot about Chris's death I thought I'd worked through."

"At least yours was by accident. You didn't have an annoying sister bring it up," Sam pointed out.

"True," Jake agreed. "But I honestly think if you weren't jetlagged and exhausted you'd probably be better equipped to deal with it."

"Probably," Sam agreed.

"Why'd Evelyn even bring it up?" Jake asked. "She had to have known you were tired."

"She did, but she thought she'd better warn me," Sam said. "Nora knows I'm back and will probably start trying to badger me by phone."

"Ah, got it," said Jake. "So we are adequately forewarned now."

"Exactly."

Jake gazed into Sam's eyes and asked, "You sure you're okay?"

"I'm okay, Jake," Sam said.

"Okay then. Now quit stalling and help me finish cleaning up the kitchen."

"Ha," said Sam. "I'm jetlagged from my horribly long flight, remember?" He yawned. "I couldn't *possibly* do anything."

Jake threw the dish towel at him. "Fine then, I'll just leave it here for you in the morning."

"After that sumptuous breakfast I cooked you?"

"That was *hours* ago," said Jake, waving a hand dismissively. "What have you done for me lately?"

Sam wrapped his arms around Jake again, kissing him passionately. "How's that?"

"Needs work. Best try again."

Sam repeated the kiss.

"Oh, I like that second effort," said Jake with a smile.

"I want nothing more than the next forty-eight hours with you. Alone. I don't care if we just stare at each other across the room, or read on the couch, or watch documentaries on ants. I just want to be alone with you and only you."

"You old softy, you," said Jake with a grin.

"I can't help it. It's the deep Irish soul in me."

"Well, deep Irish soul, I'm tired and going to bed."

They slipped into bed, accompanied by Dorothy and Sophia, while Barnaby took up residence in his basket across the room next to the furnace vent. Sam started reading *Steamboat Bill* and fell asleep within three minutes. Jake leaned over his partner to shut off the bedside light, then, after a moment's thought, shut off the light on his side of the bed as well and snuggled up next to Sam. Within minutes he too was asleep.

Above them in the blackened sky, huge billowing clouds began to blot out the stars. Inky blackness enfolded Arrow Bay with a brisk wind as the temperature dropped.

The storm was just beginning.

CHAPTER EIGHT

Jake picked up the green receiver off his desk. "Hello?"

"Have you seen the papers today?"

It was Rachel. He could tell by her voice she was upset.

"No…what's wrong?"

"Do you have your computer on?"

"No. I'm upstairs."

"Go pull up the *Seattle Times* web page," she said.

In the background, Jake could hear the sounds of her heels clacking on the floor as she paced.

"All right," he said irritably. "Hang on, I'll pick up in my office," said Jake, setting the phone down and heading downstairs.

"What's up?" Sam asked, entering the kitchen.

"Rachel said something about the *Seattle Times*. Pick up the receiver, and I'll go back down and hang up."

"Okay," he said. "What am I looking for?"

"Ask Rachel," said Jake, running back downstairs.

"What's up, Rachel?" Sam asked, picking up the phone.

"Go to the local section," said Rachel. "I was checking up on the Susan Crane thing. She'd been out here once or twice in the last month doing some sniffing around, and I was curious to see how the investigation was going. I wasn't prepared for this."

"Hang on," said Sam, placing the receiver back on the cradle and heading down into the basement to join Jake at the computer. Jake had just brought the story up.

"Notorious reporter's death ruled as a suicide," Jake read aloud. "*Suicide*," he said again, unable to believe what he'd read. "I don't know what to say," he said. "I'm just too—I just can't…"

"Something's rotten in the state of Sweden," said Rachel.

"Denmark, Sadie," Jake automatically corrected.

"I don't get it."

"Hamlet, you know. Shakespeare," said Jake patiently.

"I know the quote, Jake. If what you said was accurate, something is seriously, seriously wrong."

"Is the Kulshan County sheriff that dumb or has he got something to hide? I don't like this, Rachel. I mean, we saw her! The entire crew did, just about. She was shot in the head with her hands tied behind her back!"

"How many of you *actually* saw the body, Jake?" Rachel asked.

"I did. Ben and Captain Trelawney did for sure. Chris Ditmeyer, I think." Jake felt as if he'd been fighting ten foot swells in Haro Strait. He was thankful he was sitting down; he was pretty sure he would have stumbled and fallen if he hadn't. He realized his hand was shaking as he moved the mouse over to print the article.

"Jake, I want you to listen to me," Rachel said. "Don't do anything stupid."

"What do you mean don't do anything stupid? What would I do?"

"You have a history of antagonizing local law enforcement," Rachel pointed out.

"That," said Jake, through gritted teeth, "was in high school. And it was my best friend! Yours too, remember?"

"I'm not going to call you an asshole for that because I realize you're upset," Rachel replied, voice replete with frost. "I am going to caution you that Dwight Danvers is not someone you want to cross. Nor are you an eighteen-year-old kid any longer. Keep out of it, at least until I get there."

"Do you have any idea what is going on? I mean, this just reeks of a..."

"Cover-up?" Rachel suggested.

"I was avoiding that word," Jake admitted. "It sounds too melodramatic."

"It could be a ruse," said Sam thoughtfully. "Designed to flush the killer out into the open."

Jake put his hand over the mouthpiece. "That only works in books," he said.

"Just an idea, handsome," said Sam.

"Wouldn't sell."

"I don't know," Rachel said. "You get the right actress, some decent lighting and it'd make a fairly believable film for the Lifetime Movie Network."

Jake couldn't help but laugh. "Okay, Sadie McKee," he said, looking out the window at the side yard. He hated when November didn't get cold enough to stop the grass from growing. By Thanksgiving, it'd look like a mossy green sponge.

"Look, I have to go. I'm already half packed and will try to get out of here earlier if I can."

"Well, that would be great," Jake said. "I don't like this one bit."

"I know," Rachel replied. "We'll talk more about this situation later. Meanwhile, try to do something else and get your mind off it."

She rang off and left Jake staring at the photo of Susan Crane looking slightly smug in her jade suit, her eyes sharp, her short blond hair neatly coiffed. He kept going back to her eyes again and again. Blue, perceptive eyes, full of…full of what exactly? Certainly not hatred or complacency. Determination, perhaps. Susan Crane looked like she took no prisoners.

He toyed with the idea of Googling her name and decided against it. Rachel had the best advice. Keep occupied by something and not think about it.

Suicide.

Impossible.

"You look like you do when someone steals one of the cupcakes out of your lunch," said Sam cautiously.

"I just can't believe it Sam. I saw her. There is no way in hell that it could be suicide."

"Jake," said Sam, resting his hands on his partner's shoulders. "Don't get mad at me. However…"

Jake glowered at him. "What is it you have to say, Mr. O'Conner?"

"Just a little advice," he said. "I have no doubt of what any of you saw. And because of that, I am going to caution you to please stay away from this."

"Sam—"

"Hear me out, Jake," Sam said, placing his hand on Jake's shoulder to prevent him from getting up. "This case was a homicide from the start, like you said. The fact that the sheriff has come out publicly with a ruling of suicide indicates that there is something very, very wrong here. Poking your cute little nose into things could be very, very dangerous." Sam took a deep breath and walked to the east window. "It could be very dangerous already."

"What do you mean?" Jake asked.

"I mean you saw Susan Crane's body. Supposing someone doesn't like that? Supposing someone might want to make sure that doesn't get out?"

Jake shivered, feeling as if the temperature had just plummeted. "I hadn't thought of that."

"Just keep a low profile, okay? Don't go and do anything half-cocked."

"All right, Sam," said Jake. "You and Rachel have me convinced."

"She told you to stay out of it too?" Sam asked.

"Yes," said Jake, leaving out the "until I get there" part.

"Sensible woman, Rachel. I have always liked her." Sam walked back to his partner, giving him a long, forceful hug. "I don't know what I'd do without you, you know."

"Me either, Sam," said Jake. "Me either."

By the time dinner rolled around, neither one of them felt like cooking. They opted for the fish and chips at the Bitter End, which were the best in Arrow Bay. Sam ordered the two-piece and Jake the three-piece, followed by two slices of pie. Over the meal they pointedly talked about nothing involved with the ferry *Elwha*. Instead, Caleb and Sam continued with their chess game while Jake distracted himself with the crossword in the *Seattle PI*. After killing a few hours at the bar, they went back home where again they made a point of not discussing the day's events while Jake continued to silently stew about it, still feeling a great sense of injustice.

He was about to say something to Sam when the phone rang. He let Sam pick it up and was surprised when Sam called down from upstairs that his brother was on the phone.

"Jason?" Jake asked.

"That is your brother, isn't it?" Sam shouted down.

"Yes, I'm just, well, surprised is all," Jake said, reaching for the phone. "Hello?"

"I'm sorry."

"What? Jason?"

"I was wrong. Very, very, wrong."

"Apology accepted," said Jake simply, feeling light-headed from shock. "Now, what the hell is going on?"

"I…" Jason sighed. "I can't explain everything to you right now. There's too much going on. I just need some time to get my head straight on some things. Something Mother is incapable of understanding," said Jason sharply.

"Oh, she's capable, just unwilling," Jake said, trying not to smile. "I have to confess, she was in fine form the last time she called. Typical kamikaze phone call. Not so much as a hello before she launched into 'your brother's gone off the deep end.'"

"Classic Ingrid," Jason agreed. "I've got one for you. Amy and that Hector Sugg person are engaged."

"Oh gods! No!"

"You think I'd lie about a thing like that?"

"No. You're not that cruel," Jake agreed. "Please tell me there are no little Suggs on the way."

"Not yet. Amy wants to finish her degree first."

"Well, there's a relief. She'd have to decide on something to major in, something she's not managed in a decade."

"No kidding. Not unless they allow you to major in being a dilettante," said Jason with a chuckle.

"It's good to hear from you, J.D.," said Jake.

"Well, I know Thanksgiving is coming up, and I've been thinking about you a lot and what you said…"

"Hey, we don't have to go into that," said Jake.

"I was wrong, Jake. You weren't butting into my life. And as far as Jennifer O'Hara goes…well, I know you and I have not been as close as we used to be. I'm to blame for that. Things in California went very wrong and I—I had to get out of there."

"I understand, Jason," said Jake, knowing he really meant it. His brother didn't apologize easily.

"Mom said Sam is back?"

"Snuck in on Friday. Right after—" He stopped, having suddenly brought Susan Crane's face back to the front of his mind. He'd been so surprised by his brother's phone call, he'd not been thinking of her or the suicide ruling in several minutes.

"After what? Was that your boat they were talking about on the news?"

"Yeah," said Jake. "We found her."

"Damn Mom," Jason spat. "She told me it couldn't possibly have been your boat, otherwise you would have called her."

"Oh, as if I'd call her about it! I would have had to listen to her claim how I found a dead body on the boat to spite her somehow. No thank you."

"It doesn't take much for Mother to make it all about her," said Jason ominously. "You'd have loved the stuff about unemployment and starting new careers in your thirties, finding someone to marry after thirty and how embarrassing all that was to *her*."

"Are you having any problems on that front?" asked Jake. "Financially, I mean. It'd be no problem to send you some cash."

Jake waited through a long pause before Jason answered. "No, I'm okay for a while. I've been doing a little freelance work while waiting for things to pan out."

"All right. But if you need anything, don't hesitate to ask, okay?"

"Okay, I appreciate that," said Jason. "Now, what happened on the ferry?"

Jake related to Jason what had happened, up to and including the unbelievable ruling by the Kulshan County Sheriff's Office. He waited for Jason to say something, hoping his brother would pick up on his disgust.

"Hmm. Odd. Very, very odd. That woman's name is ringing a bell too."

"She had a laundry list of nasty stories, it seems. Alex said she was a bit of a barracuda."

"I wonder..." said Jason distantly.

"Yes?" Jake asked anxiously.

"I know some people at the *Outsider* still. Maybe I could give them a call and see if there isn't something more to this Susan Crane. And the Kulshan County sheriff," added Jason.

Jake said a silent "thank you" to whatever higher power was around. "Well, if you're sure it would be no trouble."

"None at all. I'm pretty sure one reporter I used to work with would be very keen on the idea of poking around, in fact."

They rang off, leaving Jake to think about Sam's request. He hadn't *technically* violated it. He was not getting involved. Nor was Jason, really. Jason's friend was a journalist who had every right to look into the story.

He realized someone would likely find out one of the people on the dock had seen something that didn't jive with the sheriff's ruling.

He supposed he could be held accountable for that, but so could Captain Trelawney or Ben Roberts.

He looked out the window glumly. If Sam did find out, he would be getting a lecture. He supposed he should just come out and tell Sam, and he would—after the reporter got back to Jason.

After all, there was no sense in counting chickens before they'd booted off the last bit of shell. There might be nothing to find out at all.

Alex Blackburn watched the setting sun color the glaciers on Mount Baker an unblemished shade of magenta as the light fell from the western horizon. He swirled his glass of Johnnie Walker Blue Label absently, looking again at the story on Susan Crane on the local section of the *Seattle Times*. Her picture was now washed with pink light, making her appear as if she were a victim of carbon monoxide poisoning.

He leaned back in his green leather easy chair, sighing heavily. He felt the same guilty pang going through his stomach again. He'd lied to Jake for the first time ever.

He knew Susan Crane.

He knew her well enough to both respect and despise her, knew her to be not only a ballbuster, but a meddlesome, obsessively driven woman who grabbed onto a scheme and squeezed it until it was bleeding.

Her father had been a case in point. Alex knew him well enough; he had been an associate of *his* father's for decades. Alex had always been surprised Alexander Blackburn Junior hadn't been dragged down in the political debacle of Richard Gordon. He suspected his grandmother might have stepped in and done something to prevent it. He was never sure one way or the other, and he had never dared ask her about it.

Susan hadn't been around much when he'd been growing up. She was older by five years, and Alex was in school. He'd only met her after her divorce from Edmund Crane and after she'd already begun the process of tearing her father down. She'd tried to enlist Alex to help with the latter.

He closed his eyes, swirling another swig of Scotch around his tongue before swallowing. He remembered the scene vividly. He'd been thirty, and about to embark for Ireland for the first time. Susan had sent him a message, peculiarly via courier, calling him to her home office in

Seattle. Alex had only gone because he was amused by the novelty of the method of communication, he being something of a Luddite.

He'd thought her office overdone. Persian rugs with peacocks in the weave, ponderous mahogany furniture lurking in the corners, a table, a chair, and a brass lamp. Behind a massive desk was a floor-to-ceiling window, which gave a sweeping panorama of Elliott Bay. All of it was chosen to convey authority, to intimidate, to disparage. Alex found it laughable.

Oddly, Susan Crane was not devoured by her decorating efforts, or her huge antique desk. On the contrary, it seemed to cower from her. She sat ramrod straight behind it, her iron gray suit looking like a prison matron's outfit, her blond hair arranged so casually it had to have taken hours. Her hands were folded on the desk, nails unpolished and trimmed short.

"I asked you here so you might possibly help me," she said. Her voice was deep and slightly mannish. Alex had figured she worked at it.

"To what end?"

"I beg your pardon?"

"What's in it for me?" Alex remembered saying, realizing now he'd been a cocky idiot.

A strange look crossed her face. "In it? For you? How about not going down in flames like your dirtbag of a father? Does that interest you?"

He'd laughed at her. Thinking back, it had been a pretty foolish thing to do, considering all the things his father was involved in. He hadn't known the half of it then. A few years later, he realized she'd had a pretty solid threat against him, but she would have had to take on his grandmother. Few people had ever come out of a scuffle with Ruby Blackburn undamaged.

"You're pretty confident in yourself. I like that."

"Thank you. So are you."

She smiled crookedly. "Let's cut the bullshit here. Your father has copies of some documents I need. I understand you have access to your father's files. Can you get them for me?"

"Without getting caught? Just how stupid do you think my father is?"

"Stupid enough not to know his son is screwing his business partner's wife." She looked at him carefully.

He supposed he'd blanched at that. He wouldn't have been able to help it, not back then, when he was still trying to keep that a secret.

Alex sighed, getting up long enough to get another glass of Johnnie Walker Blue and some ice from the kitchen. Susan Crane had been the start of Alex's undoing. He'd walked out of her office that day, and he never purposefully contacted her again.

She'd followed through on her threat, revealing the affair to his father. Oh, he knew he couldn't prove she'd had her hand in it, but when John Parish, junior executive assistant, suddenly arrived at the office one day in a new car, he knew where the money had come from. Alex had gotten even with Parish, turning stool pigeon on him. He let it slip to Parish's father that his son was frequenting the gay leather bar in Seattle. Parish then tracked Alex down and whacked him over the head with a beer bottle. Parish wasn't ready to be outed. Oddly, they had become good friends in the ensuing years. Parish had gone on to breeding basset hounds and living with a nice fellow named Andre from Belgium.

The lesson was clear. Alex had learned not to cross Susan Crane. In retrospect he had to admit the truth coming out was actually the best thing that could have happened. He no longer had to pretend to be something he wasn't around his father. If he couldn't deal with it, that was his damn problem.

Somehow, she'd gotten copies of those documents from the Blackburn Industries files. Alex never knew for sure, but he had his suspicions. The rumor in the family had been that his father had hand-delivered the copies to Susan Crane himself, with a promise she'd make it known to the grand jury he'd had no hand in Gordon's business dealings. Knowing his father as he did, Alex figured that was probably what had happened. It wouldn't be beyond his father to sell out his own friend. He had wondered from time to time how his old man felt about his best friend killing himself as a result of his actions.

After destroying her own father, Susan Crane went on to wipe out two state legislators, at least three lawyers, and two well-regarded detectives in the Seattle Police Department. SPD was so infuriated by that stunt that when she had a break-in at her apartment and was assaulted by the intruder, she claimed SPD took over an hour to show up. No one could seem to back her up on that accusation, and the matter was dropped.

Seeing her name in the paper had shaken him. He'd lied to Jake because he didn't want Jake to know how foul some of the demons from his past were. Alex had done much to atone for the mistakes in his youth, and suddenly there was Susan Crane's face in the paper to bring it all back and expose it. Even from beyond the grave, her filthy hands still had the power to incriminate.

He drank the last mouthful of Scotch from his glass, and rather than hinder himself from getting properly drunk, grabbed the bottle and took a deep pull from it, letting the warm taste of the Johnnie Blue surge over his tongue before it slid like liquid silk down his throat.

Alex let out a bitter laugh. Even dead she was dangerous. He had no doubt she had been murdered. Alex could count six people off the top of his head that would have happily murdered her, though he suspected none of them had the guts to do it. He also knew most of them lacked the intelligence and would have left all but a trail of bloody footprints leading up to their front door.

No, whoever had gotten Susan Crane had connections. The murderer wielded enough power to get that ridiculous suicide ruling. Alex had no doubt about what Jake had seen. Jake's eyes were too keen and his nearly photographic memory wasn't to be questioned.

And that worried him, too. Jake wouldn't let it rest as a suicide ruling. It would bring up all the unresolved feelings around the unsolved murder of his best friend. Alex knew Sam would probably try and prevent him from getting involved, but Jake and his highly developed sense of right and wrong wouldn't *allow* him to let it go.

Thinking of Jake and Sam, Alex reached out to the phone and picked the receiver off the cradle. From memory he punched up the number.

Three rings went past before a husky "Hello?" greeted him.

"Alex here. I've got a job for you."

CHAPTER NINE

Wednesday morning, Jake slipped down to his office in the basement. After working out and making sure Sam was busy, he got online and Googled "Susan Crane." He justified his actions by saying to himself he wasn't *really* getting involved; he just wanted to understand more about the woman who'd ended up dead on his boat.

He frowned at the screen, both because he knew he really *was* meddling to some degree, and also because of the surprising lack of results. Adding the words "Seattle" and "reporter" turned up the website for the *Outsider* where, curiously, almost everything about her seemed to have vanished. The only stories listed were covering the ones Alex had mentioned.

Tapping a pencil on his lip, he switched the search over to "news" and instantly was rewarded with a list of hits, but most of them were about the recent discovery of her body. Jake combed back through the first four pages to get rid of those and began turning up more informative documents from sources other than the *Outsider*.

He was perplexed by the first results outside of the murder. For someone who had been described as a tenacious reporter, the stories attached to her name were fairly pedestrian. She wasn't even the main player, her name only appearing in passing as being co-reporter for a number of stories that the now-defunct weekly *Seattle Star* had been covering. The most *potentially* incendiary story involved the civil rights violation of a Somali man accused of terrorism. In that instance she wasn't even listed as co-reporter—merely "additional materials contributed by."

Frustrated, he went back to the *Seattle Times* archives directly and put in her name. Again, the same oddly blank period between roughly 2000 and the present. It was as if for the past several years, she'd been relegated to the shadows. Prior to 2000, however, Jake found her name popping up with regularity, each item getting nastier. She'd sued someone at the *Seattle Star* for sexual harassment and settled out of court. State Representative Inez Cookson had accused Crane of "character assassination" after Crane had somehow unearthed some bills of sale showing how Cookson had profited from an illegal timber sale that had wiped out some wetlands.

The earliest results dated back to 1997. Crane's investigation had resulted in most of the senior staff at the Quilceda County Sheriff's Office getting thrown out of a job due to widespread corruption. The sheriff, Reginald McManus, who had been highly respected up to that point, had died of a heart attack on the witness stand when made to recount the number of bribes he'd been taking over the years.

Also in 1997, Crane had personally sued a neighbor for illegally cutting down trees on public property. Crane's evidence included photos of the man cutting down the trees, but in a bizarre turn of events, several photos of the man engaged in sexual relations with another man in the backyard of his home were mixed in with the slides. Arnold Witcher had been married, and the public outing had destroyed his marriage and reputation.

Crane had apologized for accidentally displaying the photos at the trial, but the damage to the man's personal life had been done. The press ran with the story, and subsequently Witcher had been forced out of his father-in-law's law firm, and his wife had divorced him. Jake found himself disliking Susan Crane more and more. She seemed to seek out stories that triggered a lot of personal pain for the people involved. More disturbing were the intimations from other sources that she had *delighted* in that fact. The *Times* had described her as "gleeful" on the witness stand.

Just what kind of a warped individual had this woman been?

The next flood of search results detailed Crane's father having committed suicide, and all the troubles the Gordon scandal had caused. Crane had shown no remorse in testifying on the witness stand against her father, stating that when the evidence had come to light it was her "moral and legal obligation to report on and come forward with the information," and that "not even family ties were above the law."

What she hadn't said was *where* the evidence had come from, a pattern becoming all too apparent to Jake. The defense claimed the documents had been obtained illegally, and true to form, Susan Crane refused to name her source. The prosecution cited attorney-client privilege, and because the defense had no proof the documents had been obtained illegally, the evidence had ultimately been admitted. The sound of prison doors must have gone off in her father's mind. He hanged himself a short while later.

Jake's eyes were growing weary from having read all the entries. He was about to give up when they abruptly came to an end. The earliest entry appeared at the bottom of the screen, dated in 1996. Susan Crane, a new reporter for a paper Jake hadn't heard of, was defending Alfonso Lopez, who had been arrested by the Seattle PD for arson at the University of Washington. The police had labeled him an "eco-terrorist." The case against him had been strong and conviction almost assured when Crane suddenly appeared with evidence that Lopez had not been Mirandized at the time of his confession. An investigation revealed that Crane had been correct in her assertion and the case against Lopez was thrown out. The prosecutor openly questioned where and how Crane had gotten the evidence. Setting what would become the established trait for Crane, she refused to answer.

The Lopez story seemed to be the only one in which she'd not actively destroyed someone's life, Jake noted. The two Seattle officers had been suspended without pay for six weeks, but apparently went back to work on the force. Jake found himself wondering if the story Alex had related about the SPD not showing up in a timely fashion at her call had some validity after all. Clearly Susan Crane had not been one of the more popular residents of the city of Seattle.

Sighing, Jake printed the articles and stuffed them in a file labeled "pending." He then tromped upstairs and took a shower. After getting dressed, he popped into Sam's office to say good-bye before heading down to the library to pick up a book that had been on hold. Sam, who had his head buried in a file cabinet, reminded him to meet for lunch after Jake was done at the library.

"You are distracted," Sam said to Jake, who was staring out the window of the Bitter End watching traffic zipping past on Center Street.

"What?"

"My point exactly," said Sam, giving him the hairy eyeball. "What gives?"

"Oh, it's this whole Susan Crane thing," said Jake. "I can't believe they're trying to pass it off as a suicide."

"I'm finding that difficult to believe as well," said Sam slowly.

"And our county police doing nothing," said Jake, even more annoyed. "*Someone* there has to realize that something isn't right."

"I thought you weren't getting involved?" said Sam patiently.

"I'm not," Jake said, irritated. "I just happened to, uh, look some things up on her," he said, swirling a French fry into his ketchup.

"Just magically appeared on your computer, did they?" asked Sam.

"Look, Sam, I'm not getting actively involved in the investigation. I'm not pounding on doors or tracking down suspects or anything."

Sam sighed heavily. "No, I suppose not," he said. "And it's not as if you could do any harm by looking stuff up on the computer," he said, slicing a piece of chicken and popping it into his mouth. "They've really outdone themselves this time. This Hawaiian chicken is incredible."

"'The Bitter End never disappoints,'" said Jake, quoting their slogan.

"You got that right," said Sam, swallowing with a smile. "So what did you find out?"

"I thought you weren't interested?"

"I didn't say that," said Sam, jabbing a fork in Jake's direction. "I said stay out of it. I didn't say I wasn't interested. Far from it. Woman turns up dead in the trunk of a Toyota, I'm as interested as the next person. Which is your fault, too."

"Me?" said Jake, wounded. "Why me?"

"All those bloody mysteries you've turned me on to. It's hard to not wonder what's going on."

"This sounds like getting *involved* to me," said Jake. "I thought you said we weren't getting involved?"

"We're not," Sam reiterated. "And this is *not* a mystery novel. You get my point?"

"Yes, yes. Loud and clear," said Jake, stabbing his salad sullenly. "Well?"

"Well what?"

"What did you find out?"

"Samuel Patrick O'Conner, you are the most infuriating man. You tell me not to get involved, scold me for looking stuff up on Susan Crane, and then you grill me for details!"

"I stated clearly that reading up on her was *not* getting involved," said Sam, swigging down a gulp of Pepsi. "So you may as well give it up."

Jake recounted the first several stories he'd read about Susan Crane while Sam nodded vigorously. "Will you quit doing that?" Jake said.

"Doing what?"

"Nodding like you'd already heard all this before!"

"Well, most of it I have. Not *quite* that detailed, though. The *Examiner* had an interesting little bio, however. Up to the McManus thing. They skipped over the gay tree abuser and Lopez, the greenhouse arsonist."

"The *Examiner*?" Jake asked, incredulous.

Sam pointed to the latest copy of the *Arrow Bay Examiner* sitting on the bar next to Caleb. "You ever *read* our local paper?"

"You know I don't. Reed Longhoffer, the anti-union Republican editor, is constantly harping on the ferries. Their crossword is pedestrian at best as well," Jake said, pushing his half-eaten meal aside. For once in his life he wasn't interested in his food.

"I agree with you on Longhoffer, but you really should give it a read, if only to keep up on the local stuff," Sam said. "And I don't even mean anything about Gladys Nyberg assaulting another tourist with her umbrella. They've got a new writer who seems to be very keen on upgrading the image of the paper."

Jake grinned at the mention of Gladys Nyberg, the town eccentric. A lady in her late fifties, she routinely dressed in combat boots with woolen socks, a tweed green plaid skirt, and a heavy maroon sweater. She wore a bucket hat the same color as the sweater, squashed over a thick head of gray hair. She regularly accosted people asking if they'd seen and/or sent a "Paige Farelley" after her. If they didn't answer appropriately she'd occasionally smack them with her umbrella, something she carried with her night and day. She'd never done anyone lasting harm, though she *had* regularly knocked pedestrians off the path in Wilde Park while riding her ancient green Schwinn. Locals had learned to listen for the familiar squeak emanating from the iron basket attached to the handlebars while walking the trails at Wilde Park, particularly after twilight.

"I always felt that the *Examiner* was good for announcing the latest bake sale or lining the bottom of a parakeet's cage and not much more," Jake said, grabbing up the paper and reading over the story.

"I think they're trying a new tactic. Even our paragon of fair and balanced—"

"And dull," Caleb chimed in.

"—reporter since 1964, Marian Burd, is showing new life because of this Derek Brauer fellow," Sam added, ignoring Caleb's jab.

"That's not a bad thing," Jake conceded, thinking. "That's a familiar name."

"It is?" Sam asked.

"I'm associating it with Gavin," said Jake, the mental file cabinets opening in his memory. "Not Gavin, exactly, but San Francisco."

Sam looked up and said, "You're right. Gavin did mention him. A friend of Jason's, wasn't it?"

Jake scoffed. "Can't be the same guy. Gotta be a coincidence. Can you see a reporter from the *San Francisco Chronicle* coming up here to the middle of nowhere to be a reporter for the *Arrow Bay Examiner?*" Jake asked.

"No, I can't."

Jake ate, letting the din of the bar settle over them. His eyes drifted back to the *Examiner* article on Susan Crane, particularly the last sentence: *I honestly think something is terribly wrong with the ruling on her death from the Kulshan County Sheriff's Office. I'm starting to wonder if this case shouldn't be handed over to someone else.*

"You read the story. Did you spot the last line?" asked Jake.

"Yes."

"I'm not the only one that thinks something is wrong here."

"No, you're not," Sam replied. "And I wonder if Derek Brauer values his safety as much as I value yours."

Jake scowled. "Phooey. He's a reporter. He's *expected* to dig up things. I hope he does so."

"So do I," Sam said, taking a bite out of a French fry.

"You do?"

"Yes. It'll keep you from poking your nose in. It's none of your business, Jake."

"You're wrong there, Sam. Someone *made* it my business when they dumped her body on my boat. Mariners are a superstitious lot, you know that more than anyone because you design ships. I already know one or two people who aren't going to take watches on the *Elwha* anymore."

"That's stretching the point," Sam said. "You need to stay out of this."

"I can't. Her *eyes*, Sam. Her *eyes*." He shook his head. "No one deserves that. To be *discarded* like that. She was thrown away on my boat, Sam. And now the police are doing the same thing. No one deserves that," he repeated softly, eyes glazing over.

"Jake…" Sam started. "We both know what's going on here."

"We do?" Jake asked, turning away.

"You are projecting," said Sam. "And I don't mean that unkindly. I know that this has to bring up a lot of unresolved things about Chris's death."

Jake nodded but remained mute. As usual, Sam was tuned in on *exactly* what was happening with him. He couldn't stop seeing the parallels between the two cases. The plastic wrapping, the cruel way in which both victims had been so utterly discarded, as though they were nothing. He *knew* the cases weren't related, but it didn't stop the feelings from losing Chris coming to the surface again, as raw and painful as ever.

Sam took Jake's hand and gave it a squeeze and said, "I've always got your back, Tiger."

"I'm sensing a *but* about to hit me here," said Jake.

"Like a mountain goat, buddy," Sam confirmed. "I've heard that level of conviction in your voice before, every time you get obsessive about a project of some sort."

"Obsessive?!" Jake barked.

Sam help up a hand, cutting him off, and said, "Does pneumonia and a hospital stay sound remotely familiar to you? Even though I told you to quit working in the basement when you had a cold."

"Okay, okay. Uncle."

Sam smiled and said, "Gonna be a long winter, isn't it?"

Wednesday was a crisp autumn day, one of the last good ones with November marching relentlessly toward December. A breeze blew out of the southeast, stiff enough to cream the tops of the waves in Ferryboat Channel but not enough to cause the *Chelan* to rock. Jake was on the car deck watching Ben Roberts load the ferry, still thinking about the last line in the *Examiner*.

Jake left Ben to finish up the loading, heading up the stairs through the passenger cabin. He crossed over through the galley and out the number two end doors, opening the locked gate to the stairwell leading up to the hurricane deck. Entering the wheelhouse, he spotted Fred standing at the helm watching the *Yakima* come in, while Captain Trelawney was making some notes in the log.

"I'd forgotten what a pain that car deck can be," Jake said.

"Yes," Captain Trelawney said, looking out the window toward the north. "That has been a problem with her since they added the second car deck," she observed, glancing at her watch. "Got a bit of a wind up."

"Nothing bad," Fred said. "Gusts up to twenty."

"Full load?"

"Nearly."

At 5:05, Captain Trelawney took the boat out herself. Jake figured she wanted to get reacquainted with how the *Chelan* handled before turning the boat over to Fred. Jake wouldn't take the wheel until after they left Friday Harbor, and with Sue Rafferty acting as quartermaster, he was free to leave the wheelhouse.

Jake went down to the passenger cabin to say hello to his coworkers and see how they were, given the events that had taken place before their days off. Everyone appeared to be fine, but Jake noted that everyone was making a concerted effort *not* to talk about it, save for the comment by Chris Ditmeyer that he was happy to be back on the *Chelan*.

Making his way back to the wheelhouse, he cut through the cabin where he saw a woman with short blond hair talking into a cell phone, sniffling. She didn't appear to be too outwardly distraught, but something about her made Jake take a look back, at which point he walked right into another passenger.

"Watch where you're going, idiot!" snapped an elderly woman.

"Terribly sorry, ma'am," Jake said, stepping out onto the shelter deck where a brooding man with a pockmarked face smoked a nauseatingly sweet-smelling cigar, the smoke billowing about him as he puffed away. His tailored suit was a hideous shade of avocado green. He eyed Jake from head to toe, seeming to size him up. Jake stared right back.

Washington State had banned smoking onboard the ferries the previous year. Signs in big block letters that read SMOKING IS NOT ALLOWED ON WASHINGTON STATE FERRIES were all over the shelter deck. People had adjusted quickly, and they rarely had to admonish any one or threaten them with the hundred-dollar fine.

Whoever this was, he was either legally blind or purposefully ignoring the signs.

Stepping outside, Jake called out, "Excuse me, sir?"

Jake felt himself inwardly squirm when the man blew out a long gust of pale blue smoke from his lungs, his beady black eyes lingering on him for an uncomfortable period of time. He looked him up, then down, his eyes boring into Jake's skull.

"Sí, señor, qué usted desea?"

Jake was losing his patience at this point. "You have to put your cigar out. Smoking is not allowed on the vessels."

"Oh...*No hablo ingles.*"

My ass you don't speak English, thought Jake. *"No se permite,"* he said with irritation as he jabbed a finger at the man's cigar.

"Sí, señor," said the man, tossing the cigar over the side of the *Chelan.*

Something in the man's eyes gave Jake a nasty twinge. It kicked his flight response into overdrive. He felt the urge to get the hell out of there, and fast. Instead, he returned the man's stare and said, *"Gracias."*

"Sure, mister, anything you say," said the pockmarked man. He continued to stare out into the fading light as Jake swiped his badge over the keypad and entered the staircase up to the hurricane deck. He made sure the gate locked behind him before walking up, resisting the urge to turn back and stare at the man, as he was positive the creep was leering at him.

Something else was bothering him, though. He kept trying to place what it was but couldn't. He shrugged it off and stopped in the day room, ignoring the disgruntled look he got from Fred Phillips as he went through the wheelhouse.

The *Chelan* made the trip in just over an hour, good time for any ferry. Jake stood at the helm, looking down as the cars offloaded. Through the moon roof of a black BMW, he saw the head of the woman he had seen dabbing tears away in the passenger cabin. He was struck with another uncomfortable twinge again, this time not at all related to the pockmarked man.

It was because he clearly knew now what it was that caught his attention in the passenger cabin. This same teary-eyed woman was the one talking on the cell phone.

The woman was Susan Crane.

❖

Jake went to the Front Street Ale House after the *Chelan* had finished her runs and tied up for the night. Jake was still feeling shaken and ordered a lemon drop, wishing he were home to spend time with Sam. The more time went on, the less Sam liked Jake's overnight stays in Friday Harbor every other evening. If he were home right now, he knew they'd be snuggled up in bed, reading, Barnaby and the cats at the foot of the bed. His heart ached a little bit. Sam had only been home for four days and already they were apart again.

"It sucks," he said aloud, then blushed. He hadn't intended to say anything, but he was feeling pretty relaxed after the stout lemon drop. He dug out his cell phone and dialed Rachel's number.

"Gobo," she said tiredly, having picked up on the second ring. "Do you have any idea what time it is?"

"Slightly later than six thirty in the morning when *you* called last," Jake said, checking his watch. It was just after 12:30 in D.C., and he knew Rachel hadn't been anywhere close to sleep.

"Well, what's up?" Rachel asked.

"Nothing," he said. "Well, something. I think I saw Susan Crane."

"In a Haley Joel Osment 'I see dead people' kind of way, or are we talking *Night of the Living Dead* in the flesh kind of way?"

"I've been thinking about that. Ghosts in my experience do not use cell phones."

"How do you know I haven't been hit by a presidential limo, and you're talking to a ghost right now?" Rachel asked.

"It would have made the news for one thing, and despite your stature as a prosecuting attorney for the feds, I don't think you're much of a threat to the current powers that be to warrant running over with the presidential limo," Jake replied.

"Damn," Rachel said. "There's always a catch."

"And if everything about zombies in the movies is true—" said Jake.

"Hollywood lead us astray? You're joking!" replied Rachel.

"—I can't see them having the mental or physical dexterity to operate a cell phone. Besides, who would they call?"

"Hmm," said Rachel. "Unless there's a twenty-four-hour brain emporium open, I can't imagine who. The conversations would be fairly dull, I'll give you that. And frankly I can't see your average zombie vacationing in the San Juans at this time of year."

"Lack of tourists to feed upon?"

"More like hungry bald eagles," Rachel replied. "What else?"

"What makes you think there's a 'what else'?" Jake asked.

"You called me after midnight on a Wednesday to report the potential sighting of a ghost-and-or-zombie of the nefarious reporter recently offed on your boat. If that isn't an open end for a 'what else' I don't know what is."

"How about a sinister man with a pockmarked face like six miles of bad moonscape?" Jake asked.

"That makes the picture a bit more complete," Rachel said.

"He was annoyed when I asked him to quit smoking that foul sweet-smelling cigar," Jake said, something pinging in the back of his head. He couldn't figure out what it was and dismissed it.

"Well, the ferries are non-smoking now, right?" Rachel asked. "He probably didn't know and was miffed."

"No, there was more to it than that. He was…sizing me up somehow."

"Were your work pants terribly tight?"

"What?" Jake asked, confused. He sighed. "You and Sam really should put together an act."

"A dirty mind is a terrible thing to waste," Rachel replied.

"That is *exactly* what Sam said."

"Great minds run the same way," Rachel quipped. "Seriously though, what else is bothering you?"

"It was more than being pissed off about the smoking. This guy looked like he was in a controlled rage. He looked like he could cut the heart out of someone and not even flinch."

"A real charmer," she said. "Sounds like half the men who want to date me."

"So where does this leave me? I spot a psychotic and someone who looks a lot like our recent murder victim."

"Suicide victim, remember?" Rachel said. "I thought you led a dull life out there in Arrow Bay?"

"Right, suicide," said Jake. "Because it's so easy to tie your hands behind your back, climb into the back of a car, and then shoot yourself point blank in the forehead. Oh, and cut your throat. I nearly forgot."

"It's always the little details that escape you," Rachel joked.

A gust of wind rattled the windows, and the patrons of the restaurant looked up. Through the glass, Jake spotted the *Evergreen State* tying up next to the *Chelan.*

"I have to admit, Gobo, the more you tell me, the less I like it," she continued.

"I'm not wild about it either," Jake agreed.

"Well, keep your shirt on. I'll be leaving the day after tomorrow. I dumped a load of work on an underling. I'm not at all popular right now, but dammit, I don't like you being alone on this." she said.

"Well, I'm not actually acting alone on this, I mean Sam..." he started.

"Did Sam suddenly get replaced by a pod person and become ecstatically happy about you poking around a highly suspicious death?"

"I wish people would quit using that phrase," Jake sighed. "I have *not* poked around."

"But I bet Sam asked you not to."

"Well yes," Jake conceded.

"That sounds more like the Samuel P. O'Conner I know and love," said Rachel. "Ever practical. And he's right, you know."

"You're a fine one to talk."

"He didn't ask *me* not to," she pointed out. "As I know you don't take your promises to Sam lightly."

"No, that's true, I don't," Jake said.

"And if I make some inquires, you don't even have to get out of the car."

Jake pinched the bridge of his nose. "That is somewhat duplicitous, Rachel."

"I work in Washington D.C. What do you expect?" she replied. "Besides, that way you won't be going against anything Sam said and won't be staring at the floor when you try to talk to him."

"You've thought about this a little too much. I can see we need to get you back home as soon as possible. That place has been a terrible influence on you."

"I can't argue with you there," said Rachel. "And I'll promise you I won't directly involve you in anything. I'll be subtle as a church mouse."

"*Subtle?* Rachel, your entire wardrobe is based off classic Joan Crawford films from the thirties. You spent a year looking for the Patriot Red lipstick she used to wear."

"Don't exaggerate, Jacob. Yes, my *favorite* outfits are all vintage and Crawfordesque, but not *all.* I couldn't very well show up to court in Sadie McKee shoulder pads, could I? I can look downright dowdy if I have to."

Jake could picture Rachel, who was slightly taller than he was with long, shapely legs, a full bust, and chestnut colored, shoulder-length hair. With her dazzling Egyptian blue eyes, high cheekbones, and dimples Jake knew making her look dowdy would take some work.

"What do you want to do?" Jake asked cautiously.

"Just do a little poking around. Nothing serious."

Jake scratched his goatee. "I don't know, Rachel."

"I have a lot of contacts," she insisted. "I may not have to do that much poking around myself."

"There is something *rotten* about this," said Jake. "It's affecting everyone on the crew."

"You don't want this hanging over your heads forever, Jake," said Rachel. "It's bad enough we still have to deal with knowing that whoever killed Chris is still out there."

Jake knew she was right. Chris's murder never left him. Leaving the death of Susan Crane to remain a suicide would add more salt to the wound.

"Okay," said Jake. "But I won't do anything to hurt Sam."

"Wouldn't dream of it, Gobo. Discretion is the name of the game. You'll see. I bet we won't even have to do anything. I bet someone else is already looking into it."

Chapter Ten

In the fog, the *Elwha* skulked. Even with the glow of the lights in the passenger cabin and with the running lights shining through the mist, Jake couldn't help but think the ferry looked hunkered down and menacing. He shook his head. *It's just a damn boat*, he thought. He glanced at Ben Roberts and could tell by the look on the bosun's face he wasn't alone in feeling apprehensive about stepping on the car deck of the ferry again. He looked over at the *Chelan* in the tie-up slip, a relief crew readying her to sail southward to the Clinton-Mukilteo run. Jake found himself sorely missing the smaller ferry.

Shrugging, he slung his bag over his shoulder and walked down the transfer span onto the car deck of the *Elwha*. He knew First Mate Phillips and Captain Trelawney were already in the wheelhouse. After saying hello to Chris Ditmeyer, he was about to go up the stairs when the piquant smell of sage drifted over his nostrils.

He turned, went back down the steps, and walked the length of the car deck toward the number one end of the ferry. Ben was there, waving around a bushel of burning white sage.

"What exactly are you doing, Ben?"

"I...uh...well. I have this new-agey type friend who said burning sage kind of purifies a place."

"Ben?"

"Yes, Jake?"

"You're Catholic."

"I could post pictures of the Pope and sprinkle holy water around, but you think our resident atheist would take lightly to that?" asked Ben, referring to Phillips.

"Er. Carry on," Jake said.

He left the car deck and went up to the crew quarters, dropping off his bag on his bed. Ben poked his nose in a few minutes later, stowing his stuff in his locker.

"Feel better?" Jake asked, and not sarcastically.

Ben shrugged. "Well, you know. I figured it couldn't hurt."

"No, I guess not," Jake agreed. "You know, we really ought to change our way of thinking. It isn't the ferry's fault."

"No, I know," Ben agreed, turning to leave.

"The sage wasn't a bad thought, Ben," Jake said. Ben turned back at Jake, smiled and shrugged, and then turned and left to go back down to the car deck.

Jake got up and headed toward the forward wheelhouse, where Captain Trelawney stared intensely at a raft of paperwork and Fred stood sipping a cup of tea, listening to his radio to get the all clear for departure.

Twenty minutes later, Jake pulled the ferry out of the dock, making the course corrections Fred called out to take the *Elwha* to San Juan Island. He could feel the difference in the handling between the *Elwha* and the *Chelan* right away. The *Elwha* didn't respond as well, or so he thought as darkness began to fall over the San Juans.

Burning sage is not a bad idea, he thought again absently, knowing it was used in purification rituals by Native Americans. *Superstition or not, everything around Crane seems less than pure. It can't hurt.* Jake was disappointed to be back at work and was again raging with mutinous feelings about how it interfered with what he really wanted to be doing, like writing or picking up Rachel at the airport. Sam was right. It was time to hand in his notice.

Jake was even more anxious than usual to talk to Rachel. She had sent him a large envelope overnight delivery from Washington D.C. Rachel had done some prodigious prodding into Susan Crane's background. So far everything she had turned up painted Susan Crane in a more negative light. Rachel had accessed court records and public documents, leaving Jake to wonder what the personal stories were like. Nothing in the public record was tremendously insightful other than the obvious, that Crane had been brutal to the subjects of her stories.

Martin Gore, a prosecutor for King County, had locked horns with Crane early in her career. He had sued her for libel over a story she'd written about him having a relationship with a witness on a case he was prosecuting. Crane had responded by writing an entire series of stories about him alleging that Gore had frequented a "massage parlor"

that was known for prostitution. Abruptly the libel suit was dropped—
and a retraction printed by the *Star* on the prostitution allegation only.
There was no retraction on the allegation that Gore should have recused
himself from the earlier case.

Rachel had included a note with the article: *No further mention
of this case anywhere. No internal investigation done. What the hell?*

Rachel had also turned up the missing stories on the *Outsider*'s
web page, the series of articles Susan Crane had most recently been
attached to. It was the case of Bowman vs. the State of Washington.
Rachel hadn't gotten access to the case files, as it had yet to go to a
jury. The *Outsider* had made mention of it and had said the case was
postponed. The lawyer for Jack Bowman, a bullish-looking man with
gray hair and close-centered piggish eyes, had requested and been
granted an extension.

Jake knew he could soon divest himself of the guilt he had in
digging around Susan Crane's background, though he reminded himself
again it was *Rachel* who was doing the actual digging. Even with the
background information on Crane consistently painting her character
blacker and blacker, they had reached a dead end.

One last story had appeared, one that made Jake feel less guilty
about what they were doing—one not sent in the packet of papers from
Rachel, but in Arrow Bay's own little *Examiner*.

It hadn't even gone to the mainline Seattle papers, which seemed
to have tired of the antics of Susan Crane, character assassin for the
Outsider. Jake wondered if that wasn't symptomatic of the city itself.
Seattle seemed to have lanced a large boil in the form of Susan Crane.
Her destructive career that had shattered so many lives on what seemed
to be a little more than a whim had ended abruptly. It seemed as far as
the Seattle papers were concerned, so had the story.

No, Seattle had *ignored* the story. *This* story had been courtesy
of Derek Brauer, the new reporter at the *Examiner*. In big, bold letters
the Brauer story had exclaimed: Danvers Says Witnesses Unreliable;
Crane Case Closed.

It was in a special edition of the weekly paper—something Jake
wasn't sure had ever happened in the *Arrow Bay Examiner*'s history.
Jake had taken up the paper with interest after having been admonished
by Sam for not paying attention to the local rag. Sam had looked across
the table at the sound of Jake's grinding teeth when Jake had reached the
part where Brauer had quoted Danvers saying, "Anyone who says this
was anything but a suicide is just plain wrong. I don't care what they

say they saw or thought they saw. Anyone will tell you eyewitnesses supply the worst evidence. Those that discovered the body weren't trained in forensics or had any kind of knowledge to make any kind of determination as to what kind of wounds or anything Ms. Crane may have suffered."

After arriving at Friday Harbor on the first trip that evening, Jake stopped by the day room to see if anyone else had caught the story. He was not surprised to see the *Examiner* lying open on the table in the break room.

Mike Davis looked at Jake as he sat down at the table.

"Did you get a look at this crap?" he spat.

"Oh yes," said Jake.

"I'm a vet from the Gulf War," he said, barely able to control his fury. "The *first* one, that is. I spent a year in Iraq. I sure as *hell* know what a bullet wound looks like! And since when did anyone committing suicide ever do anything but shoot themselves in the temple?"

Ben and Captain Trelawney entered the room a moment later.

"We're doing drills," she said.

"We are?"

"Yes, as far as the dock is concerned, we're doing drills," she replied. "Which is why we're not loading yet."

"Got it," replied Jake.

"We were talking about that," Rhoda Trelawney said, pointing at the *Examiner* on the table.

"And thought we should check in with you. It seems you beat us to it," said Ben.

"I can't agree with you more, Mike. We all know what we saw," said Captain Trelawney.

"There is no way someone—she cut her own throat, and *then* shot herself in the head?" Ben exclaimed.

"Or the other way around for that matter," said Captain Trelawney. She sighed heavily. "I know I can't officially order you not to talk about this to anyone," she said, her voice etched with concern. "But I have a bad feeling about this. Something is amiss here. The sheriff has ruled the case closed, and I think so far as we should be concerned, that's good enough, regardless of what any of us may or may not have seen," she said quickly when Jake opened his mouth to protest. "I think it would just be wise to say that we support the findings of the sheriff and leave it at that. Like I say, I can't order you to abide by that, but it might be in our best interests to do just that—at least for now."

Ben, Mike, Jake, and Rhoda all looked at one another, letting her words sink in. Mike was the first to nod in agreement.

"I've heard some stories about Danvers..." he started.

"So have I," Captain Trelawney said. "None of them good."

Rachel and Sam's words rang in Jake's ears on the same subject. He looked at his fellow crew and nodded. "So have I."

"It's all kind of..." Captain Trelawney started.

"Shakespearian?" Jake offered.

She nodded with a wry smile. "Very."

"Who the hell *was* this chick?" Mike Davis asked.

Jake looked him in the eye and said, "That's the million dollar question, isn't it?" and then winced at his use of the cliché.

❖

That had been the last of it. They hadn't even talked about it among themselves, though Jake had smelled sage twice more that night curling up from the car deck.

Friday Harbor, Orcas, Lopez, Arrow Bay, back to Friday Harbor. They tied the *Elwha* up that night, the evening run having gone flawlessly. Jake breathed a sigh of relief. Perhaps the boat had shaken any hoodoo that might have been attached at the violent death of Susan Crane. Or perhaps Ben's burned sage had purged the boat of anything negative after all.

After securing the boat for the evening, Jake changed out of his uniform into a tight-fitting sweatshirt and tight blue jeans. He reminded himself to have that talk with Sam about his clothes again as he clomped down the stairs of the *Elwha* to the car deck. Jake stopped for a moment to stare at the spot the white Toyota had occupied, visualizing again what he had seen that day. In his mind he saw the car pull slowly onto the boat, the windshield awash in a glittering reflection of the sun that had chosen that particular moment to break through the clouds. The memory was as impenetrable as the windshield had been that day.

The car deck yielded no hint of anything awry. He saw no mysterious reappearing pool of blood, no phantom handprint. The air felt cold, but that was normal for November. He was staring at the blank gray skid paint when a hand fell on his shoulder.

He whirled around, his fist at the ready, only to be greeted by Ben, who'd backed away with his fist clenched as well. They both laughed. Jake dropped his fist, shaking his head. "God, Ben, don't do that again."

Ben relaxed, dropping his fist. "Sorry. I didn't mean to startle you," he said, pulling his coat tighter to himself. "I was just going to, uh…"

"Use the last of the sage?" Jake suggested.

"Well, yeah," said Ben, looking around, embarrassed.

"Carry on then," Jake said, patting Ben on the shoulder as he walked passed.

"Where're you off to?" Ben asked.

"Late dinner," Jake replied half truthfully.

He walked up the ramp and out the security gate on the dock. Even though the dock was well lighted, inky pools of blackness seemed to cling around every corner and odd angle. He was happy to leave the dock and step onto Front Street, which was illuminated by the faux antique streetlamps Friday Harbor had installed. Jake made his way to the Front Street Ale House, taking a seat by the window. Below him, the cabin lights to the *Elwha* burned brightly, casting flickering confetti of luminosity across the waters of Friday Harbor. The temperature had dropped in the weeks since Jake's birthday on Halloween. With Thanksgiving only a little over a week away, Jake wondered if the threat of snow that had been forecast was actually going to materialize.

He ordered an appetizer of onion rings and a large Sprite, not wanting to be caffeinated and unable to sleep. He pulled out his cell phone and dialed his home number.

"O'Conner's pack mule service," Sam answered on the fourth ring.

"How many pieces of luggage *did* she bring?" Jake asked, knowing Rachel's inability to travel lightly.

"Seven. That's two down from the last visit. I'm impressed," Sam replied.

"That *is* an improvement, though I think it is down three from the last time," Jake said, burning his finger on a hot ring. "Ow. Dammit."

"What are you doing?" Sam asked suspiciously.

"Having some onion rings at the Front Street Ale House," Jake declared. "I packed kind of a light lunch."

"Light for you or a water buffalo?" Sam asked. "And you were right, it *is* down three from last time," he added, laughing. "You wish to talk to her?"

"Yes please," Jake said.

"Okay, here she is. Love you."

"Love you back," said Jake, hearing the fumble of the phone as Sam handed the receiver over to Rachel Parker.

"Sam, I think I left my makeup bag in the Subaru."

"What? Where did you stow it? Under the seat?"

"Would you be a dear and go look?"

Jake heard Sam mutter something indistinctly, followed by the sound of the front door opening and closing.

"Hiya, Gobo."

"Hello, my Sadie McKee. How are you?"

"Tired," she confessed. "And I owe you an apology."

"For what?" Jake asked.

"Well, for…not doing everything I said I would. In regard to you-know-who," she said, lowering her voice.

"Voldemort?"

"Be serious," she said. "Crane."

"Well, you said 'you-know-who,' and in my world lately that means *Voldemort*. Maybe we should come up with a code name." He thought for a moment. "Why the hell are we whispering?"

"I am because I don't want Sam to hear me," she said. "I can't answer for you, goofball."

"Ah, right," Jake replied, thinking. "Maybe you-know-who isn't such a bad idea. I half expected to see the grim shade of Ms. Crane go floating across the car deck this afternoon."

"Not her style, from everything I've read," replied Rachel.

"I expect not. Still, the bosun burned a whole bundle of sage on the car deck just in case."

"Not a bad idea," Rachel replied. "Although I'd have gone in for a full exorcism myself. Priests, rabbis, shaman, holy water, the whole ball of wax."

Jake pressed back to the issue at hand. "Why are you apologizing?"

"Well, I know it was my job to track down some of the people she knew so we could maybe talk to them, but I haven't had much of a chance. I had a bunch of last-minute things to take care of at the office."

"You don't need to apologize. I mean, you are—were—clear

across the country, after all. Getting copies of her recent stories was plenty. Oh, and speaking of which, did you see the story one of our own Arrow Bay reporters did about Ms. Goody Two Shoes today?"

"Oh yeah," she said. "Sam pointed it out."

"Pointed what out?" said Sam's voice drifting over the line.

"The new…" Rachel started.

"Uh-huh," Jake heard Sam say. "I'll leave you and Nancy Drew to talk about whatever it was I was not supposed to hear about Susan Crane," Sam called out to Jake. "Makeup bag indeed."

"Okay, we get an F for subtlety," Rachel said, slumping into the chair by the phone.

"Well, it beats the whole you-know-who shtick," Jake replied.

"Agreed," Rachel said. "Aww, you're a sweetie."

"I am?"

"Not you, Sam. He just brought me a Manhattan."

"He never brings *me* a Manhattan," Jake said.

"If he's telling you I never bring him Manhattans, remind him he doesn't like them," said Sam in the background.

"He says—"

"I heard," Jake said. "And I haven't been a complete slacker. I did find some things out."

"What'd you find?"

"Well—" he started, as the waiter came by to fill his water glass, "It's weird. Prior to the stories on the Lopez case, she was a nobody. Then all of sudden, she's listed in glowing terms at the *Seattle Star* and getting some stories senior reporters should have gotten."

"There is nothing about her personal life out there," said Rachel. "Not surprising though. I was checking mostly public records stuff."

"No, I guess not," he said, taking a bite of another onion ring. "Then for reasons I can't figure out, this no-name Crane ends up with exonerating evidence for the Lopez case."

"That's the eco-terrorist?"

"Right. It's the case that establishes a pattern for her. After Lopez, she barbecued Inez Cookson."

"There was someone in between, wasn't there?" Rachel asked.

"Right, the sexual harassment case while working at the *Star.* This was the company that dropped the *GreenBelt* stories in her lap. She wasn't even an environmental reporter."

"Who was that?" Rachel asked. "The one she sued."

Jake never had to take notes. His memory came through with

alarming clarity, back to early childhood. "Jeremy Young," he said, taking a bite of his salad. "And the paper, of course."

"Go on."

"I cross-referenced this guy. *He* was an environmental reporter. Major stories that were published in the *Star* and for *GreenBelt*."

"What's their magazine called?" Rachel asked. "I know it has gotten some awards."

"*GreenBelt*," Jake replied. "Not very imaginative."

"So wait, the guy she sues for sexual harassment just happens to be the noted reporter for said group?"

"Yeah," said Jake. "Thus paving her way to get the job."

"Because true or not, once the allegation of such a thing is out there..."

"Exactly. And settling out of court creates even more doubt, at least in the minds of some," Jake pointed out.

"And a short time later, the *Star* closes its doors."

"After she breaks the Cookson story," Jake said.

"Having once again supplied the incriminating evidence herself."

"Right," said Jake.

"Well then, perhaps she resorted to the second oldest profession," Rachel mused.

"Baking?"

"Blackmail, you idiot," said Rachel. "How else would these incriminating documents always seem to turn up rather conveniently?"

Jake shook his head, exasperated. "We'll never figure anything out using news reports and public records. Talking to the people who knew her is the only way we're going to figure this out. Her editor at the *Outsider*. Waterman. He's one of the few that didn't describe her as some sort of demon spawn."

"I *did* try to call him," said Rachel. "He's out of the office until after the Thanksgiving holiday, according to his office voice mail. I couldn't find his home number."

"No worries. Thanksgiving's a little over a week away."

"Who else knew her?" Rachel asked.

"Waterman, for sure. Lopez. Her grandmother. Her sister." Something occurred to Jake. "I wonder what *she* looks like?"

"The sister? Probably like Crane did—wait, hello. Who gets the award for being the most clueless this week?"

"Dual prize?" Jake asked. "That has to be who I saw going to the Harbor. Lila Gordon-Beyers," said Jake. His steak and shrimp had arrived. Having assaulted his salad and onion rings, he balanced the phone between his shoulder and ear and cut up the steak into bite-sized pieces, digging into it with zest.

"Which brings up a whole host of questions," Rachel said.

Chewing his first bite thoughtfully, he said, "I wonder what she was doing up here?"

"And the charming fellow you suspect as her companion," Rachel replied. "It seems odd to me that Gordon-Beyers would be up here on the same ferry her sister clocked out on."

"Don't be giving the *Elwha* unnecessary bad karma," Jake chided. "Remember, someone punched Crane's time card long before she got on the ferry. Not to mention that we're the final departure out of Arrow Bay to the Harbor. That she would end up on the *Elwha* is hardly a coincidence. As it was, it was the *Chelan* the woman got on."

"True, true," said Rachel. "Lord knows I don't want to embroider."

"That being said," Jake said sheepishly, "the *Elwha* is heading into the yard for some extended maintenance."

"Aha," said Rachel. "Relieved?"

"Yes," Jake acknowledged.

"I can't blame you," she conceded. "Let her have a crew that has no associations. I'm sure she'll be an okay boat, just…"

Jake smiled. "I carry too much baggage around as it is."

"You know, Gobo, we've been awfully thick," Rachel said.

"What?" Jake asked, cutting up the last two bites of his steak.

"What was Crane's father's name?"

"Gordon," Jake said automatically. "Oh hell."

"Where did Crane come from?" Rachel said.

"Well, she either changed her name herself, which is entirely possible, given how she seems to have felt about her family," Jake pondered.

"Or she was married," said Rachel.

"They didn't list a spouse as a survivor," Jake remembered.

"They wouldn't if he was an *ex*-spouse," Rachel pointed out.

"I wonder if he's from around here," Jake said.

"Public records search would turn up any marriage certificate," said Rachel.

"If they were married in this state," Jake said. "I'll check with Alex, he might know." He took a sip of water, thinking. "Come to that, I haven't heard from Alex in a while," he said quietly.

"Gobo, are you *eating* something?" Rachel asked.

"Um. I *was*," he said, looking at his decimated plate.

"Well, as charming as it is to hear you smack and slurp, I think we'll finish this conversation tomorrow, agreed?"

"Okay," he said. "Put Sam on again, will you?"

"You got it," she said, calling out for Sam.

"How goes it, Trouble?" Sam asked picking up the phone.

"You know, don't you?"

"Let me see, my heart is beating, I can get one eye open…yes, yes, I have figured out that as usual you've ignored my well-tendered advice."

"I'm glad you're not bitter or cynical about it."

"What am I going to do with you two?" Sam asked.

"Love us and shower us with gifts!" said Rachel in the distance.

"Loving you both is the easy part," Sam said. "Keeping you two out of trouble…"

"No trouble," Jake said.

"Promise?"

"Er," Jake faltered.

"Thought so. Good night, love of my life. Sleep well."

"Good night, Sam," Jake said, feeling somewhat guilty. "I love you."

Jake finished his soda, lost in a myriad of thoughts and emotions. His eyes were drawn to the flickering light radiating from the *Elwha*. Abruptly they vanished as one of the crew on board extinguished the lights in the cabin. The ferry lay hunkering in the dark as the first heavy splats of rain began to tumble down from the sky above.

He paid the bill and left the restaurant, walking slowly down the hill to the harbor's shore. Traffic was nonexistent. Three months earlier, the sky would still have been streaked with light and the streets of Friday Harbor bustling with tourists. In the dark of the approaching winter, the streets seemed to brood.

Jake stopped suddenly. He turned around, looking back up Front Street. Rain swirled like silver sparks in the sodium vapor light of the streetlamps. The large elms in Memorial Park shifted uneasily in the wind, the rain hissing slightly through the branches.

What is it? Jake thought.

He wasn't sure. He stared back down the street into the park. The light flickered and moved from the shadows of the branches and the movement of the rain. "Nothing," he said aloud.

Jake continued back to the ferry, making sure the security gate was locked behind him. He made his way back onto the car deck and up the stairs, unable to shake the feeling he'd had back on Front Street.

He was being watched, he was sure of it. He couldn't dismiss the feeling in the pit of his stomach, and it lingered well past his shutting the light off in his quarters. He stared into the darkness, unable to sleep, listening to the uneasy sound of the *Elwha* as she shifted against the tide and the wind. Around midnight Jake finally drifted off to sleep, his mind still on edge.

A short time later, a green Chrysler strategically parked at Memorial Park in order to observe both the street and the *Elwha* started up abruptly. Moving slowly down Front Street without headlights, it paused briefly near the dock. The driver's side window dropped a fraction of an inch, a plume of blue, sweet-smelling smoke pouring out into the night. A moment later, the headlights snapped on and the car lurched forward. It turned up Spring Street and disappeared into the darkness.

❖

Arriving back at Arrow Bay the next afternoon, Jake had just gotten to the Cruiser when Barnaby ran up and began sniffing his feet. The beagle looked up at him and woofed once expectantly.

"Hey, Barnaby! What are you doing here?" Jake asked the dog, bending down to pick the beagle up.

"He was hoping that he could convince you to come down to Seattle overnight," said Sam, coming down the trail from the public lot into the employee parking area.

"What's in Seattle?" Jake asked.

"A boring meeting in the morning that you can sleep through."

"I have to be back here by four."

"No worries," Sam said, smiling. "So can I kidnap you?"

Jake smiled back. "Sure. Let me get out of these clothes, and we'll head out." He stopped. "What about Rachel?"

"She is headed over to Port Jefferson for an overnight stay at her parents' house. She was disappointed not to see you, but, as she put it, 'at least it gets the family visit the hell out of the way.'"

Jake smiled. "That's my Sadie."

Two hours later, they were in the thick of evening traffic heading for downtown Seattle. Luckily the main thrust of the commute was headed out of the city rather than in, making their journey less difficult. They checked into a suite at the Westin overlooking Seattle Center and the Space Needle. Jake had balked at the price, but Sam insisted. It had soured his mood briefly, but after lounging in the mammoth bed and allowing Sam to give him a long back and shoulder rub, he felt refreshed and decided to ignore the money issue. They ordered room service and watched *Mythbusters* while finishing cherry cheesecake and sipping strawberry daiquiris made with Baileys instead of rum.

"What time is your meeting tomorrow?" asked Jake, sipping the last of his drink.

"Early, seven."

"Wake me up when you go, okay?"

"What for?"

"Oh, there are some things I can get done while I'm here," Jake replied vaguely.

Sam raised an eyebrow. "Like what, exactly, pray tell?"

"Take advantage of some early Christmas shopping," he said matter-of-factly. "You know how much I *love* coming down here, but since we're here I may as well take advantage of it," said Jake sincerely.

"Well, that's true enough. Getting you out of Arrow Bay is like practicing dentistry with seventeenth-century tools."

"Farm tools," Jake agreed.

"I'm going to take a shower. I've gotten all sticky."

Jake raised an eyebrow.

"From the drink I just spilled down my chest," said Sam.

"I offered to help you with that," said Jake agreeably.

"I thought joining me in the shower might be more fun," Sam said, grinning, as he got up and walked into the bathroom.

"Be there in a minute," Jake called once Sam turned on the water. Almost at once, he heard Sam singing "Night and Day" in his rich baritone. He was about to get up and peel off his clothes when a thought occurred to him. He sat back down and after a moment's hesitation dialed Alex's phone number.

"Blackburn," snapped a gruff reply after the second ring.

"What, no hello?" Jake said, somewhat taken aback.

"Oh. Jake. Hello. How are you?" Alex replied.

"I'm okay. You don't sound your normal self. Is something wrong, Alex?"

"Hmm? Oh, no, no. What's on your mind?"

"You're definitely distracted."

"Well, I was expecting someone else, to be perfectly honest," Alex said. "Where are you? The number came up with a Seattle area code."

"The Westin. Sam has some meeting with the bigwigs and asked me to tag along."

"Ah. Things are okay then?" Alex asked.

"Fine," Jake said, relieved that Alex was sounding a little more like his usual self. "Making up for the six months Sam was gone, I guess."

"Ah, that would explain why you haven't been around lately," Alex said.

"*Me?* I seem to recall you said you'd get hold of me after your little luncheon from hell."

"Oh, that," Alex said, sounding shamefaced. "Yeah, I'm sorry about that. I still owe you two a proper meal, don't I?"

"You do," Jake agreed. He smiled as Sam started singing "Fly Me to The Moon" in the shower.

"How about the day after tomorrow?"

"Friday? Make it dinner. I'm not off until three thirty."

"Dinner then. The Cliff House?"

"Sure," Jake said, knowing Sam would be pleased that Alex was sticking to his promise of the only four-star restaurant in Kulshan County.

"Absolutely. We can make a night of it. Hit the casino afterward, maybe."

"Not sure about that. We've got company here."

"Oh. Well, bring them along!"

"Are you sure?" Jake asked.

"Yes. The more the merrier, as the saying goes."

"As the cliché goes," said Jake, shaking his head.

"I'll see you Friday. Say five thirty?" Alex asked, appearing not to have heard.

"Okay. See you then," Jake said.

"Okay. Bye, Jake," Alex said.

"By—Oh! Wait! I forgot I was going to ask you something!"

"Hmm? What do you need?"

"Susan Crane. Do you happen to know who she was married to?"

Silence from the other end of the phone. For a moment, Jake thought he'd lost the connection. "Hello?"

"I'm still here," Alex said quietly.

"Do you know? I thought you might, or at least might have access to the public records or—"

"Dennis Crane," Alex said again, his voice oddly strained.

"Dennis Crane," repeated Jake. "Any middle name or initial?"

"I've no idea," Alex replied. Jake heard a click on the phone. "Jake, I've got another call waiting, probably the one I've been expecting."

"Okay. See you Friday."

"All right. Take care of yourself, Jake," Alex said, ringing off.

Jake put the phone receiver on the cradle, frowning. Something about Alex's tone had made his last sentence sound like a warning.

"Are you coming in here, or do I have to go through another verse?"

"On my way," Jake said, hopping into the shower with Sam. He quickly forgot all about the odd tone in Alex's voice.

CHAPTER ELEVEN

November dawn on a rare clear day over the Puget Sound Basin comes in stages. In the lower Puget Sound region, light begins to creep into the sky, shifting it from black to a cobalt blue. Mount Rainier emerges from a star-devoid cone-shaped section on the horizon to a silhouette as the eastern sky begins to flicker with color. As the sun marches into the sky, hues seep into the glaciers swathing the volcano. The sky will deepen to shades of rose and periwinkle long before the sun ever appears, bathing the crest of the Cascades in pastels of pink and pale blue. Rainier's glaciers begin to glow pink; the Olympics on the western side of the Sound shimmer in gold. The sun will break over the Cascades, intensifying the blue; the Olympics shine a blinding white with the first fresh snowfall of the year.

Western Washington cherishes clear days in November, a time when the skies normally glower with gray, and heavy rains propelled by steady twenty-knot winds hug the land.

On this day, the nearly faultless blue sky was only decorated lightly with high cirrus clouds feathered over the arch of sky from the Cascades to the Olympics. Temperatures were abnormally cold for so early into the season, hovering just above freezing. The inversion of cold air and warmer water caused the clear dawn to be suddenly overtaken by fog as the mist rose thickly from the water.

Sam rose early as he regularly did, letting Jake sleep a while longer while he showered and dressed. Before he left at six thirty, he gently roused Jake into wakefulness. Jake agreed to meet him back no later than eleven so they could be back home well before Jake's start time at quarter after four.

Jake slipped on his swimming trunks and enjoyed the Westin's heated indoor pool for thirty minutes before taking advantage of the twenty four-hour gym. After showering and dressing, he enjoyed a continental breakfast despite his stern appearance. He spent the entire meal glaring at a list he was drawing up:

Jack Bowman
Martin Gore
Jeremy Young
Inez Cookson
Kelly & Nunamaker
Reginald McManus
Arnold Witcher

He had left off the name of Brad Jefferson, the senator, as he was dead. The racist Seattle detective had been named Seth Black, and he was dead also, killed in a car accident not long after leaving the Seattle PD.

He underlined the name Jack Bowman several times, wondering what the case was to be about and what angle Susan Crane had on him. Nothing had turned up in the paper, which meant it was either another pedestrian story she'd been assigned to, or the press hadn't done much digging. How much Crane had turned up was anyone's guess at this juncture, and who knew where she had kept her evidence? His own research on the web had produced a John Bowman and Sons Construction Company, but little beyond that, and certainly nothing that would indicate any kind of lawsuit.

Martin Gore, the onetime county prosecutor, had since retired. Crane had certainly vexed him, but enough to come after her and cut her throat and shoot her in the head eight years after they'd last confronted one another in court? Jake impatiently crossed the name off his list.

Jeremy Young's career had been undoubtedly trashed as a result of Crane's sexual harassment suit and the publicity it had generated, yet Young had not been fired from the *Star*. Jake wondered where the reporters of the *Star* had scattered and what had happened to Jeremy Young. He marked a few checkmarks by the name, and mentally made a note to look further into the whereabouts of Mr. Young.

Inez Cookson…well, that was easy enough. She had died the past summer from natural causes. Her political career had been ruined, but it hadn't stopped her from running a successful temp agency in the Bellingham area right up until her death. Since Susan Crane hadn't been responsible for Cookson's death and certainly wasn't causing any problems for Cookson otherwise, Jake crossed her off the list as well.

He drew a few lazy circles around Kelly and Nunamaker. He wondered what had happened to them since they'd bungled the Alfonso Lopez case. Could they still possibly hold enmity? It seemed to Jake a rather long time to harbor feelings of antipathy. Still, he wondered if he might be able to get hold of them. He placed a star next to their names and continued down the list.

He crossed out Reginald McManus since he knew the Gray Gentleman of Seattle had passed away a number of years back. Next to it, he scribbled a series of question marks, adding, *relatives? friends?* before crossing out that lot as well. It too was nearly ten years in the past—a long time to harbor a grudge.

That left Arnold Witcher, the gay tree-cutter whom Crane had publicly humiliated by outing him and destroying his marriage. That had been in 1997, also an awfully long time to foster malice.

He sighed and put the pen down. Folding up the paper carefully, he berated himself for having read too many Kent C. Spievens novels. Dr. Claypool made a list of suspects in nearly every novel, and it always seemed to help *him*. All this was pointing out to Jake was that the likely suspects had all been a decade away from having collided with Susan Crane. While it was possible any one of them *could* have murdered her, it didn't seem likely.

So much for your lists, Spievens, Jake thought.

Nothing worked the way it did in books. Perhaps that was the problem. He was approaching Susan Crane's murder as if it were one of the Harvey Wallace Claypoole Mysteries, or one of the Sir Cedric Rostron thrillers. Real life, it seemed, was not that neat. There *were* no tidy endings. Sometimes people were murdered and no one ever found out who the killer was—something Jake knew all too well.

Susan Crane was something different, though. Chris Aponte's murder had been marked by a stunning lack of evidence. There had been nothing to go on, little physical evidence, no suspects, and no obvious motive. With Susan Crane there seemed to be any number of suspects and plenty of motives, and he knew there *had* to have been tremendous amounts of evidence in that trunk. It was all being brushed under the braided rug. Why?

He picked up the piece of paper and decided it was time he stuck to his word. He left the Westin and walked through Seattle with shopping on his mind. He'd put on a blue cotton dress shirt and jeans he knew probably fit him too snugly, but under his heavy black leather jacket it didn't matter much. A thick, impenetrable fog had settled in after the clear dawn, obscuring the sky. The sun, however, was winning the battle, and the miasma was already starting to break apart. He could hear the ferries out in the bay blasting their horns as they sailed slowly toward Colman Dock. By the time he reached Pine Street and Westlake Center, patches of blue were starting to show through the fog.

Jake avoided Macy's, still annoyed they'd done away with the Bon Marche name. Instead he went to Nordstrom, the last Seattle department store still holding on. The flagship store was located in the old Frederick and Nelson building, yet another Seattle icon long lost. The store was not yet decorated for Christmas. Nordstrom proudly displayed signs saying they preferred to celebrate one holiday at a time, and the Christmas decorations would be up *after* Thanksgiving. He quickly found a pair of hand-crafted art deco silver earrings for Rachel. He knew they would look attractive on her, and she cherished anything that harkened back to the era of Hollywood glamour and the 1930s.

Walking through the clothing department, he stopped at the counter selling cologne and perfume, figuring he'd get his mother her yearly bottle of Chanel No. 5 and perhaps find something for Sam. Sam had worn Obsession for years and Jake usually purchased a new bottle for him at Christmas. It wasn't a surprise, but it was always appreciated. Lately, Jake found himself thinking the scent was a bit too old for Sam, and he thought he might find something more appropriate.

He was about to ask the advice of the saleswoman at the counter when he saw an Obsession bottle in dark blue next to the familiar amber-colored original. It said Obsession Night. He wondered how different it could be.

"Can I help you?" the woman said.

"Actually, yes," said Jake, smiling. The attractive brunette dressed immaculately in a blue blazer and skirt was giving him the eye, which made him blush. Her name badge said *Alyssa*. "I was just wondering how different this one is from the original."

"Well, I'll let you judge for yourself," she said, spraying the cologne on a tester strip.

Jake inhaled deeply, instantly liking the warm smells. "Vanilla… sandalwood…something else in there…"

"You've got a good nose. It does have both those in there, along with anapear, woods, and leather."

"Leather?" Jake arched an eyebrow, not entirely sure that was what he was smelling. "I'll take it. The big bottle. And can you gift wrap it, please?"

"Certainly, sir," answered Alyssa, flashing Jake a smile with very white, even teeth.

Jake figured having it wrapped was worth the extra money since Sam was an overgrown kid around Christmas, often "accidentally" stumbling over gifts Jake purchased in advance.

Jake paid for the gift and was about to leave when something occurred to him. He closed his eyes for a brief second trying to recall the strange smell that had wafted out from the trunk when it had been opened. He tried to focus his mind off the immediate stronger smells— the coppery scent of blood and the burned smell of cordite. Something else...

"Was there something else, sir?" the clerk asked perplexed.

"Patchouli, woods, something musky in the base. And a little citrus as well."

"Men's or women's?"

"This was on a woman," he said, regretting the awkward sound of the statement. "I mean I think it was a women's perfume."

"Hmm," said Alyssa, thinking. "Patchouli...and something musky?"

"An earthy smell, I guess."

"Kind of sensual?" she asked, smiling as Jake blushed again.

"Yeah, I guess."

"That sounds like Diana," she said, wandering down the counter a bit to the women's section of the perfume counter. She retrieved a diamond-shaped bottle and sprayed it on a card, handing it over to Jake.

Jake took a deep breath of it and winced, the scene of the open trunk flooding back into view as if it stood before him. For a moment, he actually saw Susan Crane's dead eyes superimposed over the sales woman, making him jump back.

"Are you all right?"

"Fine," said Jake catching his breath. "Fine." He looked at the bottle. "Diana. Roman goddess of the moon and hunting, the protectress of women. Ironic, that."

"I'm sorry?"

Jake shook his head. "Nothing." He smiled at her. "Have you got anything the polar opposite of this? Something soft and floral...kind of..."

"Sensual?"

"Yes," Jake said, not liking her repeated use of the word. "But also feminine…in a very determined kind of way," said Jake, thinking of Rachel. "I don't suppose they make Jungle Gardenia anymore, do they?" he asked.

"No," she said. "I don't think so. But if you're thinking of gardenia, there's a new one by Kenneth Cole…it's called Black."

"I have the men's version," Jake said, which he knew was citrus in nature.

"Try it," she said, spraying another card and handing it to him. One sniff and he knew Rachel would love it. "I'll take that," he told her.

❖

Twenty minutes later, he emerged feeling as if he'd bought out half the perfume counter. He hoped Rachel would like the Black as much as he had, and not only because it had driven away the musky, heavy scent of the perfume clinging to the corpse of Susan Crane.

For the next hour and a half, he wandered around the shopping areas near Pine Street, startled to find it was only ten o'clock. He looked up from his watch to see a phone booth. An unwelcome idea clanged into his head, niggling at him as he paced back and forth in front of the phone booth. Finally, he got inside and picked up the courtesy phone book. He flipped rapidly through the directory under newspaper, finding the *Outsider* listed on a page that had been torn in half.

The address given was surprising: Columbia Tower, Seattle's highest building. He walked down Fifth Avenue until he reached the imposing structure at 701. These were pretty posh digs for the way he'd always thought reporters worked—newsrooms with cubicles and desks brimming with stacks of paper stained with coffee, and everywhere the sound of phones ringing and the clack of computer keyboards.

He was about to enter the building when he caught sight of a husky, gray-haired man in a pea coat, his hair squashed under a black baseball cap. The man was conspicuously tying his shoe, a smoldering cigarette tucked in the corner of his mouth, his eyes shielded by a pair of black Aviators. Jake gave him a beady glance as he walked by. He had seen the same man earlier at Nordstorm tying his shoe. He wanted to ask him if he required some assistance in securing his shoelace, since it seemed to be a recurring problem. He decided against it, pushing his way through the revolving door and entering into the cavernous lobby of the Columbia Tower. He found the directory on a flat panel near the elevators, which listed the *Outsider* in Suite 6300 on the 63rd floor.

Jake paused at the elevator, feeling guilty for not adhering to his promise to stay out of trouble. Sam's soulful brown eyes loomed up in his mind, and he hesitated in punching the button to summon the elevator. *Okay, you're really not doing anything wrong. Just getting a look at where she worked...that kind of thing. That can't possibly be trouble*, he thought, pressing the button.

Jake stepped out into a quiet, shadowy reception room, lushly carpeted with an intricate Asian pattern in hues of purple and maroon, the walls painted pale blue. Original watercolors depicting Seattle scenes lined the walls.

Jake approached the large reception desk cautiously. This was clearly not a newsroom. He wasn't sure if he was in the right place until he saw the EMPIRE PUBLISHING placard behind the huge reception desk. It listed, among its many publications, the *Outsider*. Jake noted the pair of faux Tiffany lamps on either end of the desk, both dark. He peered around the desk at the left-centered computer terminal, which was also switched off. A bundle of ballpoint pens jammed into a crudely made ceramic cup were to the left of the computer terminal. Jake looked down at the calendar ledger, which was annoyingly blank. A small brass frame containing a photo of a woman and young boy was to the right side of the desk.

Jake stepped back, irritated the left-handed receptionist had been so tidy. He didn't even see a directory. If this was the headquarters for the publishing company, it seemed unlikely Crane would have had an office here.

Jake studied the list of publications again. The *Outsider*, *Health Today*, *Outdoorsman*, *Ladies Weekly*, *Cascade Journal*, *Nor'wester*, *Tempo*, *Infusion*, *Cigar Month*, *Spirits Classique*...all respectable publications, and presented in large print. Below in much *smaller* print was a list of magazines Jake's mother had always referred to as pulp rags: *Main Street Detective*, *True Crimes of Passion*, *Melodrama Weekly*, *Red Herring*, *Shock! and More Shock!*, *Highly Confidential*, *Hollywood Gossip*, *Passion*, *Men's Playthings*, *Sappho's Closet*, *Raging Stallion*, *Torn Curtain*, and, in the smallest print of all, *Leather Weekly*. Jake suddenly understood how Empire Publishing could afford such luxurious digs. They may have printed some award-winning stories in the *Outsider*, *Ladies Weekly*, and *Health Today*, but they were pulling in the money on all the trash in small print.

"Can I help you?" barked a voice from behind him, making him jump.

Jake looked up into the weary face of a security guard. Jake generally always looked up, being just over five and a half feet tall, but this time he looked up *and* up. The security guard towered over him by well over a foot.

"Um," said Jake, thinking *articulate bugger, aren't you, Finnigan?*

"You one of the movers Waterman called?" the guard asked, eyeing Jake's arms.

"Sure," said Jake, quickly followed by, "am!" He was aware he was now looking at the carpet.

"Go on back," said the guard.

Jake blinked, incredulous, and said, "Thanks."

As he made his way down the corridor, it became evident why the guard hadn't bothered asking for an ID badge of any kind: the entire floor was nearly cleared out. Only one office had any furniture in it, and the name written on masking tape on the door explained why: Crane.

Jake glanced at the door for Susan Crane's name placard, but he could only see a faint outline under the tape of where the brass plate had been. He peeked through the open door, looking at nothing more startling than a swatch of olive-hued carpet. He pushed the door open with his shopping bag. A mammoth mahogany desk stood in front of a massive floor-to-ceiling window with sunlight streaming through it. Two floors below lay the fog, which eclipsed nearly all of downtown and all of Elliott Bay.

Susan Crane's monstrously huge desk was obscenely ornate and overwrought, with scenes carved into the wood that seemed somewhat familiar. "Purgatory," he said to himself softly. "Dante's view of Purgatory," he said, remembering the text from his medieval literature class. He even recognized the winding mountain strewn with unfortunates working their way up the edifice.

"Can I help you?" a voice directly behind him said, making him jump. He mentally cursed his coffee consumption and pulled himself together.

"I'm sorry. I was just admiring the view," Jake said. It sounded lame even to his ears.

"Yes, it is quite something," said the owner of the reedy voice, a man about forty-five with salt-and-pepper hair and a neatly trimmed beard. He was about Jake's height and very slender, dressed in suit pants and a lavender shirt with the sleeves hiked up to the elbows and no tie. "Were you looking for someone?"

Jake felt like he was under a laser. The man looked him up one side and down the other. Jake was glad he'd dressed a little better than he normally did, but he still felt awkward. Seeing no reason to lie, he said simply, "I was looking for Susan Crane's office."

"I see. Did you know Susan?"

"Not exactly," Jake said slowly.

"How exactly *did* you know her, Mister…?"

"Finnigan. Jacob Finnigan," he said, wincing. *You just introduced yourself like James Bond, idiot.* "And I didn't actually know her. I was one of the crew on board the *Elwha* that found her body."

A look of astonishment crossed the man's face. "Well, this is something of a coincidence. My name is Tomas Waterman, Mr. Finnigan. I've been trying to get hold of someone from your crew for days. I've been stonewalled at every turn. And now here you are."

I'm going to have to give up on my theory of no such thing as coincidences, Jake thought. "Was this her office?" he asked.

Waterman pushed the door open completely, walking past him into the room. Jake could now see the boxes stacked on the floor and on one corner of the desk. A pile of framed photos leaned against one of the mahogany bookcases. Jake couldn't keep his eyes off the desk, and he took four steps into the room when he felt something stab his leg. He stepped back suddenly, hearing his pants rip. Looking down, he saw he'd been gashed with a bronze arrow held by an elaborate three-foot high-statue of the goddess Diana. He reached down to his thigh and brought up bloody fingers.

Diana. Well, isn't that a bit of irony for you? he thought.

"I'm sorry, I should have told you to watch for that," Waterman said, grabbing a tissue from the haphazard stack of boxes on the lumbering desk. "Are you cut badly?"

"My cats have done more damage," Jake said, though the puncture stung like hell.

"Have you had a tetanus shot recently?"

"My last physical. Dr. Masuoka thought it was a good idea with me working on the boats."

"You should be fine then," Waterman said. "Just another thing to add to the list of woes around Susan," he said somewhat cryptically.

Jake wadded up the tissue, throwing it in a nearby bin. "Why were you trying to get hold of me, Mr. Waterman?"

"Call me Tomas, please," he said, sitting on the edge of the desk. "And I wasn't. Not you specifically. *Anyone* who might be able to give me an answer."

"To what?"

"Susan. Her wounds." His face tightened suddenly. Jake thought he was having an attack of some kind, but instead he said in a guttural whisper, "Was her wound self-inflicted?"

Jake was taken aback but recovered rapidly. He glanced at a high-backed maroon leather chair, looking to Waterman, who nodded. Jake set his Nordstrom bag down and then sat in the chair. He quickly discovered it was the single most uncomfortable chair he'd ever sat in. Almost at once, his back started to give him discomfort.

Waterman chuckled. "Uncomfortable?"

"Extremely," Jake said, sitting up straighter.

"She looked for the most disagreeable chair she could find. I believe it took her three weeks. Susan liked to keep her interviewees distressed. She could maintain an edge over them better that way, she felt."

"Forgive me, Mr. Waterman, but this office seems rather sumptuous for a reporter. Especially since this clearly is a publishing headquarters and not a newsroom."

"Yes, it does, doesn't it?" Waterman said without irony. "We all wondered why the old man put her up here. My office is in Fremont, with the rest of the *Outsider* staff. I was specifically asked by Mr. Buckman to clean out her office."

"How long had she been here?" Jake asked.

"Not long. A year maybe. We were all a bit surprised when she said she was making the move. We *assumed* it meant she had taken a job somewhere within the publishing company and was leaving the *Outsider*. Her stories kept coming in via email, however. More and more infrequently, though."

"And her excuse for moving here was?"

"Her work needed extra privacy she couldn't get at the *Outsider* offices." Waterman gave Jake an appraising look. "You know much about her work, Mr. Finnigan?"

"I do," Jake said, having become very familiar with her writing style.

"Then you'll agree that in fact she probably *did* require more privacy than the rest of us," Waterman said.

Jake shifted in the chair again, finding it impossible to get comfortable. "I assume that was the purpose of the desk as well," said Jake, looking at the figures with their eyes sewn shut. "I know that would put me off."

"She hunted all over Europe until she found this…*thing*. It wasn't originally a desk, you see. The panels were taken from an Italian villa somewhere outside of Florence. She alleged that Alastair Crowley had the thing built into a desk around the turn of the century, but I think she was making that up." Waterman looked at the desk disapprovingly.

"What will you do with it?"

"She left it to the Smithsonian in her will. Oh, don't look so surprised. It wasn't so much generosity on her part as it was a preventative measure from any of us taking a fire ax to it." Waterman smiled wryly. He turned back to Jake. "Can you tell me what you saw?"

Jake moved toward the edge of the chair, where he gained a modicum of comfort. "Well, I can tell you, Mr. Waterman—"

"Tomas."

"Tomas. Even if you had contacted the crewmembers, only a few of us could have helped you." He thought a moment. "Not many caught a clear look at the body."

Waterman leaned forward. "What did you see?"

Jake closed his eyes, remembering in vivid detail. "I remember seeing a blond woman with pale blue eyes. She was wearing what appeared to be a gray or light blue suit. She had on pearl earrings and a matching pearl necklace. Her hair was pulled back…" He hesitated, not wanting to recall the corpse in vivid detail but unable to prevent it. "She was shot in the forehead," he continued. "Directly in the center. There were dark marks around the wound which I think were powder burns. Her eyes were open, and she was…"

He hesitated, the mental image of Chris Aponte swimming up in his eyes. He'd never seen Chris's body, but he knew all too well he'd been wrapped in clear plastic, just as Laura Palmer had been. The parallels between the infamous murder on the cult series *Twin Peaks* had been enough to cause serious concern in the Port Jefferson Police Department, fearing a copycat killer might have been loose. The similarities had ended at the plastic, however.

"Mr. Finnigan?"

"I'm sorry," Jake said, regaining his composure. His throat felt dry, and his voice cracked as he continued. "Wrapped in clear plastic. There was a jagged wound to her throat that *looked* fatal. Her arms were tied behind her back...actually I *believe* her arms were tied behind her back," Jake opened his eyes. "I didn't see her hands, just that her arms were pulled behind her. That's what I recall." *Other than the scent of what I know now is Diana perfume*, he thought, looking at the statuette that had wounded him.

"Was the gun in the trunk?"

Jake closed his eyes again, thinking. "It wasn't a large trunk. The body and the plastic were taking up most of it. No, I didn't see a gun, but that doesn't mean one wasn't there. The trunk was carpeted—gray, I remember that. There was a tag on the lid with the rental agency logo on it, and that was it." He opened his eyes again. "That's it."

"You have a remarkable memory for detail."

"It's pretty good," Jake acknowledged. "I've always been able to remember things very vividly. Family trait."

"Your family trait may be a danger to you, Mr. Finnigan. I would be *very* careful of whom you spoke to about this."

"I've heard this before, Mr. Waterman. As I take it you're not threatening me personally, you *do* seem to be implying there is a threat of some sort," Jake said.

"I feel there is, yes. You've seen what the official ruling from the Kulshan County Sheriff's Office has been."

"Yes, I have," said Jake slowly.

"Given what you've seen, would you agree it is physically possible to cut your own throat and shoot yourself in the head?"

"I suppose in theory it *is* possible," Jake said, "but not with your arms tied behind your back, and it would certainly hamper your ability to wrap yourself in plastic and lock yourself in the back of a trunk."

"Yes, that *would* be difficult," Waterman agreed.

"However, I am apparently an unreliable eyewitness according to Sheriff Danvers."

"You don't strike me as unreliable," said Waterman.

"No. Neither are the rest of my crew. We don't have to have the dead rodent swung under our noses to smell it. We've been advised—unofficially, mind you—by our captain to stick with what the sheriff says."

"Your captain is a wise man," said Waterman. "There is indeed something very wrong in Kulshan County. I've got some leads on what has been going on and hopefully can apply some pressure. Meanwhile, I'd do exactly what your captain advised you to do."

"And aren't you in some way possibly in danger yourself?" asked Jake. "You were quoted in the paper as saying she was not 'despondent or depressed or upset in any way' and that 'Susan was not, I repeat emphatically, *not* suicidal.' That's my stress on the second *not*," said Jake.

"Right on the money. I stand by it, too," he said. "As for feeling threatened, believe me, I am taking precautions. Being a highly visible editor of a well-respected newspaper helps. My sudden disappearance would be noticed," Waterman said.

"Aside from my having confirmed the physical evidence, what else made you so certain Susan Crane hadn't killed herself?" Jake asked.

Waterman gave him an unpleasant smile. "Susan Crane was one of the meanest, most spiteful, backstabbing bitches on the face of the earth."

Jake wasn't entirely surprised to hear the late Susan Crane described this way. But he *was* taken slightly aback by the vitriolic way Waterman spat out the words.

"You don't agree with my assessment?" he asked Jake.

"It's not that. It's just it seemed at first that, well…" Jake trailed off.

"Oh, I respected her. In the same way you respect a poisonous snake when it's lurking somewhere in your bedroom."

"Ah," Jake said, understanding.

"She took *pleasure* out of crushing people under her heels. No, if Susan Crane was found dead it was because someone made it happen," he said, shaking his head. "And frankly I'm not sure how I feel about it."

"Meaning?" Jake asked.

"Meaning there's a big part of me that feels like letting the suicide ruling stand and forgetting the whole thing. I feel personally the world without Susan Crane is a hell of a better place."

❖

Sam's meeting with state officials had been mind-numbing. Three cups of coffee hadn't been able to keep him awake while members of the DOT rattled on about ridership statistics, funding issues, and the next legislative session. Sam had been there only to unveil his initial design for the new ferries, which he had done to general fanfare and nods of approval. He took a few questions and then, mercifully, his part of the meeting was over early. He walked back to the hotel room, packing their things, and got them ready for check-out. He figured they could start the trek back north early and take a more leisurely pace.

It took very little time to get their things in order, and knowing Jake wouldn't be back until eleven, Sam dialed room service and ordered more coffee. He was feeling a bit hungry. The continental breakfast provided at the meeting was skimpy, but he figured he'd wait until Jake got back and they could have an early lunch. Waiting for the coffee, he picked up the *Seattle Times* and started glancing through it, noting that Jake had already killed off the crossword puzzle.

The phone rang abruptly, making him jump. He picked up the receiver and said, "O'Conner."

"Oh," wheezed an asthmatic voice on the other end. "I'm sorry. I think I must have the wrong number."

"That all depends. Who were you looking for?"

"Um, I was...nothing. Thank you." *Click.*

Sam looked at the receiver for a moment before setting it down. He hadn't recognized the voice on the end, an unpleasant croaky, elderly-sounding voice. He had been able to discern a phlegmy rasp that reminded him of chest congestion or the death rattle of emphysema. It gave him a shiver.

He went back to reading the paper, his eye on the clock next to the bed. It clicked past ten fifteen as room service knocked at the door. Sam tipped the valet and poured himself a cup of coffee from the carafe. He resumed reading the paper, not looking up until eleven thirty. It was unlike Jake to be late. Sam wasn't worried just yet, knowing how Jake was when he started Christmas shopping.

The phone rang again. Sam picked it up and said, "O'Conner."

Silence.

"Hello?"

Click.

Eleven forty-five. He was now officially worried, and he was about to get up and check the department stores where Jake might be lingering when the door opened and Jake burst in.

"Where the hell have you been?" said Sam, harsher than he'd meant to.

"Sorry, Sam. I got caught up."

"In the department store?"

"No. I've got a lot to tell you," he said. "And, well…"

"What?"

"I can't believe I'm saying this. It sounds so melodramatic."

"Oh?" said Sam, cocking an eyebrow. "What's that?"

Jake sighed, slumping his shoulders. "I think someone is following me."

❖

Sam drove through the winding back roads of Capitol Hill, cutting through Volunteer Park, and then down to the University Bridge. He looped through Fremont and into Ballard before heading back to I-5 and starting northward back to Arrow Bay. The entire time he maneuvered the Outback around Seattle, Jake looked furtively into the rearview mirror on his side of the car. Satisfied no one was following them, he'd finally relaxed and started talking.

"First of all, don't get mad."

Sam glanced over at him, scowling. "I hate it when you start a sentence like that."

"Well, I just—well…"

"See, it automatically sets me up to *get* mad," said Sam, as they whizzed past Shoreline. "And it automatically makes me assume you're guilty of something."

"Guilty?"

"Yes. You never say that unless you've already done something you know I'll get angry about."

Jake sighed. "Very well. I guess I should get it over with," he said. "I went to Susan Crane's office."

"See, now, here is where you're wrong," said Sam through gritted teeth. "I'm not angry."

"No?"

"Disappointed is a better word."

"I see," muttered Jake.

Sam chuckled and said, "Not in the way you think, Tiger. You should know by now you can trust me," he sighed. "I don't know why I have to be married to Curious George. Telling you to stay out of trouble just reminds me of that panel of George with the ether bottle."

"I *did* go shopping," Jake said. "Heading over to her office was just a spur-of-the moment idea. I didn't think anyone would be there, I just thought if I could see her office it might...I don't know, help explain something." He paused. "I'm sorry. I promised you I wouldn't get involved, and here I am poking my nose right into it."

Sam sighed again. "I realize asking you to promise that was tremendously unfair. You've got a colossal sense of what is right and what is just, and I know this situation flies in the face of that. Asking you to keep out of it was like telling a leopard to suddenly jump out of its spots."

"We'll come back to that analogy in a moment," said Jake, not entirely sure he liked where Sam had gone, but relieved he wasn't angry. "It's—it's just..."

"It's wrapped up in Chris's death," Sam said, taking Jake's hand and giving it a squeeze. "And it's only natural that when presented with a similar homicide, you'd want to figure out what the hell."

"I still shouldn't have gone to her office," Jake said.

"Well, I would have preferred you waited for me. Or at least called and let me know where you were going. You probably shouldn't be doing things like that alone."

"Breaking Rule One of Spievens's Rules for Investigation," said Jake.

"Rule Two," Sam pointed out. "Rule One is 'never go willingly into the killer's lair.'"

"Right right," Jake agreed. "Like the dreaded basement or creepy room with aluminum foil on all the windows."

"Exactly. Rule Two is 'never go anywhere alone, it shortens the life expectancy.'"

"To about twenty pages," Jake agreed. "You're right, I should have called you."

"Forget it," said Sam squeezing Jake's hand again. "I'm glad you told me, though."

"I couldn't *not* tell you."

"I know. I'm just worried, is all. Something peculiar happened while you were out," Sam admitted.

"What?"

"I'll tell you later, after you tell me."

"Okay. Well, I talked to Tomas Waterman. He was there cleaning out her office." He shook his head. "God, you wouldn't believe the hideous desk and furniture she had!"

"Waterman. That name sounds familiar."

"He was the fellow that was quoted in the *Times* as saying Crane's death couldn't possibly be a suicide. Now I figured—as probably did anyone who was reading it—that it was the usual skeptical It-Can't-Happen-to-My-Friend kind of deal," said Jake, catching his breath. "That's how I took it, anyway."

"So did I," Sam conceded.

"I was wrong, though. Waterman said the *only* way Susan Crane would have ended up dead is if someone punched her ticket for her. She had too many irons in the fire. Did I just use that old cliché?"

"You did. Bad English major. No Dickinson omnibus for you."

Jake scowled at Sam, then continued. "Waterman didn't know what she was up to, but he did say she had to have been on to something."

"Wait a minute, aren't the *Outsider*'s offices out in Fremont?"

"Yes."

"How the hell did you get to Fremont and back so soon?"

"That's the other thing. Crane was holed up in the publisher's *corporate* offices in Columbia Tower. Plush office, hell of a view."

"For a *reporter*?" Sam asked.

"Yeah, that was my reaction. Waterman said Crane told him she needed special privacy because of the types of interviews she did."

"Right, the ones where she was likely blackmailing the teeth out of people."

"Yeah, those," Jake agreed, grinning. "Waterman wouldn't say anything specific, but I got the feeling he thought she had something on the owner."

"That would make sense. Go on."

"I got a little information on her modus operandi," said Jake.

"You're sexy when you speak Latin."

"Pay attention, Samuel," Jake said, unable to stop himself from smiling. "Waterman said Crane spent a *month* in county court, just watching the prosecutor. She made copious notes on how he acted, how he presented the case, everything."

"I could see that if she were a lawyer. It'd be tactical. You'd know what you'd be facing," said Sam.

"Right, but Crane was no lawyer. Waterman said there was some other element to it. When she was in court with Martin Gore, the head King County prosecutor, she said something in court while being questioned that struck everyone as odd. She wasn't even looking at her lawyer; she was staring right at Gore."

"What was it?"

"He was paraphrasing, but it was something like, 'Documents about your personal life can turn up *anywhere*. Sometimes they just fall into the wrong hands.'"

"That's paraphrasing?"

"He didn't have a transcript with him, but that's what was implied."

"What else?"

"Just that it was a pattern, something Rachel and I already figured out. Susan Crane only got on to a story when she could personally gain from it. Waterman seemed to think her real joy was destroying people, like Senator Cookson in Whatcom County."

"Why? I mean, did she have anything specific against these people?"

"He didn't know. Other than her father. He knew very well why she ruined him."

"You going to tell me, or are you going to make me guess?"

"Getting there, getting there. Patience, my handsome friend, patience," Jake said, thinking a moment. "You know, no matter how bad my relationship with my mother has been I don't think I could ever do anything like that to her. I mean, it would have to be something awful that she'd done to me. Even then I'd probably let the law take its natural course, but—"

"Jacob!"

"Huh? Sorry. It seems that she'd been holding a grudge ever since her father divorced her mother when she was sixteen or thereabouts. Her mother ended up in Western."

"You're talking the state hospital, not the school," Sam said.

"Er, yeah, the local basket weaving academy, yes. Complete breakdown. She's still there. She never recovered, apparently. Waterman said Susan visited her once a week without fail."

"But she never forgave the father," Sam said.

"No. And I guess she was pretty successful in engineering the breakup of his second marriage. And that *still* wasn't enough. Waterman didn't know where or how she got it, but she managed to dig up the dirt on her father—and ruin him politically. She didn't anticipate his suicide. Or at least Waterman didn't *think* she anticipated his suicide."

"Did she say anything about that?" Sam asked, squirming a bit in his seat. His bladder had become uncomfortably full from the three cups of coffee he'd consumed while waiting for Jake to reappear.

"Not to him, although he did say she never seemed upset over the whole thing," Jake said, glancing in the rear view again. He was keeping his eye on an elderly Oldsmobile two cars back, but it exited onto the Everett Mall Parkway.

"So we know why she went after her father. You said something about a sexual harassment suit at one point."

"At the *Star*. Waterman told me I'd have to talk to Jeremy Young myself to find out the specifics, but he doubts if Crane was harassed. He said she was so prickly no one would have bothered."

Sam chortled. "Well, where's this Jeremy Young located?"

"Bellingham. Mr. Waterman gave me his card. Also he said that Crane's ex-husband lives up there, or did as of two years ago."

"Aha," said Sam, squirming again. "So Rachel was right." He paused. "Isn't a rest stop ahead?"

"Just outside of Marysville."

"Okay, good."

Abruptly a flash of illumination rippled through his brain. "Wait— 'Rachel was right'?"

"Oh. Well. Um," said Sam, blushing.

"You've known all along what we've been up to, haven't you?" Jake said, grinning crookedly.

"Let's face it, Jake, you and Rachel have not been subtle. I don't make a habit of listening in on people's conversations, but I did get the gist of what was going on the other night. And that effort to get me out of the house was pretty ham-handed."

"Yes, that was a bit—er—awkward," said Jake, making a mental note to harangue Rachel as soon as they got back.

"And just so you know, I read her the riot act as well. I *still* don't think any of us should be poking around, especially with Sheriff Danvers publicly stating you've all got faulty memories and that Susan Crane killed herself."

"You sound like Captain Trelawney," said Jake. "I wouldn't worry, nothing we've done is really traceable."

"Mm, yes, right. That's why you thought you were being followed," replied Sam acerbically.

"Oh *damn it!*" Jake said suddenly. "I forgot."

"Mr. Photographic Memory forgot something?"

"It does happen," Jake said, grumbling. "Particularly if I'm thinking about something else or distracted. Like by all things bright and shiny," he said, shaking his head.

"Your *corvidae* tendencies are your undoing sometimes," Sam agreed.

"How do you feel about dinner at the Cliff House on Friday?" asked Jake, somberness overcoming him again.

"You know, sometimes I do struggle to keep up with the way that wonderful brain of yours works," Sam stated. "I'm not sure how you got from being followed to dinner at the Cliff House."

"Followed made me think of car, which made me think of how Rachel is getting home from the ferry terminal—"

"She picked up a rental in Mount Burlington," Sam replied. "She *said* it was to run errands. It was at that point I accused of her playing Nancy Drew."

"Which led me to think of car rentals, believe it or not, and then to new cars, which led me to Alex—"

"Stop," said Sam, holding out a hand. "If I ever ask you to explain your thought process again, please just tell me you happened to think of it."

"I happened to think of it," Jake said.

"Much better," Sam said. "So is Alex finally living up to his end of the agreement?" asked Sam. "When did you talk to him?"

"Last night while you were in the shower. Before I joined you. I called to see if he knew what Susan Crane's husband's name was, if she had one."

"Okay, sure. I'm getting the Copper River salmon though," he said, grinning evilly.

"That's what, fifty, sixty clams?"

"Something like that," he agreed.

Jake smiled back. "I'm sure Alex won't care. Money doesn't mean a whole lot to him."

"I've noticed."

"I wish you two got on better," said Jake. "I've never understood what it is about him that grates on you so."

"I've told you. I think he's a big phony. And I always feel like I'm being sized up somehow."

"I—" Jake started to say something in defense of Alex but abruptly cut himself off. He valued Alex as a friend as he always offered consideration and sound advice to any problem. He was always willing to give help when needed and could, for the most part, be counted on in an emergency, but Alex *was* Byzantine by nature. He held his inner thoughts and feelings to himself. Despite Alex's sage advice and generally obliging nature, Jake still did not feel tremendously close to him, even after all the years they'd known each other. Alex kept people at arm's length, something Jake had also found maddening, and yet Jake knew he was probably the closest person in Alex's life since his grandmother had passed away.

"Yes?" asked Sam.

He sighed, still thinking as Sam pulled into the rest stop. "You're not jealous of him, are you?"

Sam chuckled again. "Ouch. There goes that Finnigan honesty again."

He shrugged. "I believe in being direct. Life is too damn short to be playing silly buggers in the bushes."

"I—" Sam stopped, pulling into a parking spot next to the public bathroom. "Playing *what*?"

"Figure of speech," Jake said, with a dismissive wave of the hand.

"Not one I've heard."

"We don't read all the same books, you know," said Jake, grinning.

"Tell me, how does one play 'silly buggers in the blueberry bushes'? I'd very much like to know."

"If you're very good, I may show you some warm spring day," Jake said.

"Uh-huh. I'm going to go relieve my bladder. And just remember, blueberries are ripe in the fall, my green-eyed friend."

"Who said anything about blueberries? *I* merely mentioned the *bushes*."

Sam opened the door, laughing. "I'll be right back."

"And you didn't answer the question!" Jake shot back at him as Sam got out of the car.

Jake sat back in the comfortable seat of the Outback, watching a few of the larger chrome-laden sixteen-wheelers pull in. On his left, a family piled out of a red minivan, the disheveled mother yelling at two red-haired children to wait until she got there before they went charging into the bathroom. Jake watched her go as another car pulled in behind, then went past the Outback slowly, parking five spots down.

Jake didn't move a muscle or pretend he'd even noticed. He then slowly turned toward the right. The man in the car had his back to him, but he could see a familiar black baseball cap and gray hair poking out from under it.

"Son of a bitch!" he whispered harshly.

He watched for several minutes until he was able to discern the glint of Aviator sunglasses perched on the man's face. More annoyed than afraid, he told Sam to get in the car quickly when he returned from the bathroom.

"What?" said Sam, slipping into the driver's seat.

Jake had been so intent observing the man in the car he hadn't heard Sam open the door. He cursed his inattentiveness. "That car down there. Guy with the black baseball cap?"

"It's a Pontiac, I think," said Sam, starting the Subaru.

"Lose it."

Sam cocked an eyebrow. "I thought you didn't like to sound melodramatic, eh?" he asked.

"Just get out of here as fast as you can! I'm serious, Sam!" said Jake. "That is the guy following me, I'm sure of it! He was on foot outside the Columbia Tower, and I'm positive he followed me back to the Westin."

Sam pulled out of the rest stop at normal speed. He waited to see if the car was following, and when he determined it *had* left the rest stop at the same time, he slammed the accelerator to the floor. The Subaru took off up I-5.

"What are we going to do? It won't take long for him to catch up with us at this rate."

"I'm not sure," Sam said. "Wait a minute! I've got an idea," he said, shooting down the off ramp. He took the first available right into the parking lot of a Subaru dealership that faced the highway. Sam pulled his blue two-year-old Outback into a row of nearly identical 2006 Outback wagons.

"Remind me to kiss you when we get home," Jake said. "That was bloody brilliant."

"It was good timing," Sam quipped. "Did you get the license plate?"

"No. Damn, I didn't even think about it, I was too worried about ditching the guy."

"No worries."

"I sound paranoid, don't I?"

"Maybe not," said Sam. "There!" he exclaimed.

The bruise-hued Pontiac Sunfire raced up the interstate at a faster pace than any of the cars around it. Jake saw Sam watching it with his eyebrows raised. Sam took out his cell phone, dialed the number for the state patrol, and reported the approximate location of a Pontiac driving recklessly.

"You're good, you know that?" Jake said.

"Did you get a look at the guy?"

"Not close. Gray hair, which might not be his, black baseball cap, black Aviators. He kept ducking behind things. Pretty inexpertly, too. He kept tying his shoe whenever I looked at him."

"Hmm," Sam said, pondering. "Makes you wonder," he said, telling Jake about the phone calls he'd gotten at the hotel. "Could be a total coincidence, though."

"Sam, you know I don't—" Jake said.

He laughed, knowing what Jake's mantra on coincidences was. "Believe in coincidences, I know. Things *do* work out that way sometimes, though."

Jake sighed resignedly. "I suppose, maybe. If it *is* the same fellow, then no coincidence."

"That remains to be seen. Meanwhile, we'll take the back way up to Arrow Bay. Just in case."

"You don't want to see if the guy got nailed?"

"Well, yes, I do, but on the other hand, routine traffic stops take very little time. He could catch up to us before we ditch him again."

"True," Jake conceded.

"On to home, then. Lucky you get to work today."

"Ugh, don't remind me. I had such a nice time at the hotel."

"Me too."

Sam was just about to start up the Outback when someone knocked heavily on the glass of the driver's side door, making them both leap in their seats. Sam, annoyed, rolled down the window and testily said, "Yes?"

A man in a beige suit and lightly windswept blond hair looked in at them and said through a toothy grin, "Hey gents, you in the mood for an upgrade?"

Sam looked at Jake, smiling affectionately. "Nah, that's okay. I think I'll keep him."

"Harrumph," said Jake. "Like you could afford to replace me."

Sam pulled out of the Subaru dealership, leaving a perplexed salesman behind. Instead of turning back onto I-5, Sam turned toward Arlington, driving to the interchange for Highway 9 northward.

As he did, he was completely unaware of the green Chrysler that had pulled into a Denny's two blocks from the car lot just after they had exited the highway. The car had also been at the rest stop, but a discreet distance away. The tinted driver's side window dropped down a few inches, releasing a cloud of cigar smoke. A moment later, the car started up and left the parking lot. In no time, it was back on I-5, heading toward Arrow Bay.

CHAPTER TWELVE

The main dining room of the Cliff House had been modeled loosely on the same room aboard the *Queen Mary*, though Sam could only see a bare resemblance. The walls had a similar highly polished mahogany veneer, and some authentic-looking art deco wall sconces looked the part, but very little else. The tables were completely modern, covered in crisp white linen, and the silverware was of a contemporary pattern. The ceiling was totally wrong, with four crystal chandeliers spaced out over the length of the room between a mural of the view outside the window, had it been light enough to see.

Light jazz piano drifted from the far corner of the room, a dozen couples dancing on the oak dance floor adjacent to the black grand Steinway. They all seemed to be enjoying the mellow tunes. The intoxicating aroma of spiced oranges, prime rib, and vanilla mixed in with expensive perfume and cologne, creating a wonderful aromatic pastiche. The low murmur of conversation mixed in with the notes of the piano.

Sam found himself thinking cynically for the third time that evening, *what are you up to, Alex Blackburn?*

Alex was engaged in very active conversation with Rachel, seeming to have been instantly taken with her elegant but approachable beauty. Sam had nearly laughed out loud when she had inadvertently spilled Alex's smoked oysters into his lap.

Rachel was not letting Alex get away with anything, Sam was delighted to see. She shot his flirtations down at every turn, but in a polite way. Sam wondered what Rachel was like cross-examining someone.

The conversation had flowed pleasantly, from various areas of the maritime industry to the latest plans for the new class of ferries that Sam was currently working on, subjects so benign Sam started tracking what Alex *wasn't* saying to see if he could place what was bothering him. And then, it dawned on Sam. Alex wasn't the least bit nervous or upset in any way, taking all of Rachel's deflections with good humor. Alex seemed keenly focused and not distracted at all. He was conducting the dinner like a business meeting, working very hard to control the tone and subject matter of the conversation. Jake seemed oblivious to what Alex was doing, because he kept saying things to derail the current thread. Sam was having an easier time of it once the food came, as Jake took a deep and abiding interest in his prime rib instead of the conversation.

"Huh?" Jake said, looking up from his plate.

"I said you're leaving the ferry system," Sam said.

"Oh," Jake said. "Well, yes. Takes up too much of my time, and I haven't been too zealous with the place given everything that has happened lately, and the stupid way Kulshan County has been handling things."

"Kulshan County government has a lot of issues," Alex said. "Their permitting process is entirely too cumbersome, and their time getting back to you is measured glacially, I think," Alex replied.

That was somewhat artful, Sam thought, looking at Rachel.

"So tell me, Mr. Blackburn—"

"Alex."

"Alex," Rachel nearly purred.

Sam saw Jake wasn't completely involved in his meal; he rolled his eyes over Rachel's remark. Sam was thinking about how cute Jake looked in his black suit and nearly missed out when Alex started describing his duties at Blackburn Industries.

"The board is comprised of two factions," he said, his voice laconic. "The younger set in the family—"

"Such as yourself," Rachel said, leaning closer to Alex.

"Correct," Alex replied. "And the older generation that is increasingly out of touch."

"Bunch of buck-toothed old mummies?" Rachel inquired, making Sam choke on his cider and Jake burst out laughing.

"*Simpsons*," said Jake. "Homer's letter to Mr. Burns after Bart gives him several pints of his blood to save his life."

"Full points," said Rachel.

"And after said letter, Mr. Burns feels some remorse and decided that the Simpson family needs a far grander reward," said Sam.

"Resulting in the purchase and gifting of Xt'Tapalatakettle," said Jake. "That's the—"

"Ancient Olmec head that resides in the Simpsons basement," Alex replied with a smile.

"Very good," Rachel said. "I'm impressed."

"This prime rib is excellent," said Jake.

"I could hardly tell," said Sam under his breath. "You've barely come up for air since it arrived."

"What? Oh," Jake said, setting his knife and fork down. "I'm sorry. I hadn't eaten all day."

"That's okay," said Sam, resting his chin on his hands and gazing lovingly at Jake. "I like a man with an appetite."

The conversation resumed, Sam smiling at Rachel's ability to pin Alex down on certain subjects. Rachel was straightforward and blunt to the point of bruising, just like Jake. Sam could tell that Rachel was also very aware that Alex was navigating around certain issues and decided to drop them. She finally asked him to dance, and they joined the other couples on the floor.

"That was interesting," Sam said to Jake as the waiter took their plates away.

"Which part? The part where Alex suddenly started talking about Blackburn Industries or the part earlier where he let it slip that he was a major stockholder due to his inheritance?"

"You *were* paying attention!" Sam said, genuinely impressed.

"Of course I was," Jake said. "And I have a theory of what he's up to."

"Do tell," Sam said, watching as Rachel and Alex drifted ably across the dance floor. "They're both excellent dancers."

"Rachel's better," Jake said, looking over at them.

"How do you figure?" Sam asked.

"She's going backwards and is in three-inch heels," Jake replied.

"Got me on that one."

"I may appreciate the fine flavors of a truly succulent prime rib, but that does not mean I eat through my ear holes, Sam. I've been listening to every word he's spoken tonight. And *not* spoken."

"He doesn't seem to want to talk about—"

"Shh! Here they come!" whispered Jake.

"Sorry, we seem to have interrupted something," Alex said.

"I was asking Sam if he'd read that article," Jake said, staring down at the white linen tablecloth.

"Which article was that?" Sam asked, unable to hide his delight at Jake's awkwardness.

"The old *Sechelt Queen*. I saw something about it being sold," Jake said, regaining his composure.

"Ah, yes, I saw that too. I was trying to find out who bought her. She's an interesting vessel. Gibbs designed her, you know. For Black Ball back in the late '40s for the Seattle to Victoria run," said Alex.

"Gibbs?" inquired Rachel.

"William Francis," Jake said. "The guy who designed and built the S.S. *United States*."

"Oh, I've seen that ship," Rachel said. "She's over in Philadelphia. I had no idea that the same man had designed a vessel for use out here."

"She was the *Chinook* back then," Jake said. "There was a really big tourist industry going to Victoria."

"I'd love to redesign that boat," Sam said wistfully. "Beautiful lines. She originally had staterooms. She was Black Ball's night ferry to Canada, and ran up to Victoria from Seattle. Then Peabody turned her into a regular ferry up at Horseshoe Bay. Cut off her bow. Made her look like she'd stubbed her toe or something."

"Sechelt…it means *the people*, if I remember right," Alex said.

"I think you're right," said Jake. "I read that somewhere. B.C. Ferries isn't into their Native American names as much as WSF. They have a fair few that have native names, though."

"True," Alex said, sipping his Johnnie Walker Blue Label Scotch thoughtfully. "Place names are interesting. Washington has a whole host of interesting place names derived from Chinook Jargon. I think my favorite is *Wollochet*, which means *squirting clams*."

Jake chuckled. "They considered that for a ferry name once. Personally I'm glad that they dropped it. That and *Sequim*."

"If you boys are going to talk boats, I'm going right out to the car and going home," said Rachel. "I love you dearly, but as you've just seen, Alex, they can go on about their ships."

"I do apologize, I was heading in that direction as well," he said gallantly. "I, too, am a fan of all things nautical."

"Do you own a boat, Alex?" asked Rachel, focusing all her attention on him again.

Jake snorted, and Sam thumped Jake's shin under the table with his foot. He didn't want Rachel's spell to be broken.

"Ow! Watch it, Sasquatch!"

"Terribly sorry," Sam said, giving Jake a look.

"What else are you a fan of, Alex?" Rachel asked, taking a sip of her drink.

"History. Local history in particular."

"Ah, then you can answer a question for me my pair of favorite mooks have not been able to," she said.

Sam looked at Jake. "Are we mooks?"

"From one mook to the next," replied Jake, "pass me the salt, would you?"

Alex looked at Jake and Sam with amusement and asked Rachel, "And that would be?"

"How'd Arrow Bay get its name?" Rachel asked.

Alex pushed aside his quiche and smiled. "It started as Alexia, a pretty-sounding name that means *an aphasia marked by the loss of the ability to read.* They renamed it Arrow Bay as *alexia* didn't have quite the ring they thought it did."

"How'd the Arrow Bay come about then?" she asked.

"The shape of the bay itself is on the pointy side," said Jake.

"Somewhere near the present site of the town, a couple of tribes had some sort of skirmish. As the town was being platted, workers kept coming upon *kaleetans* in the soil they were digging up."

"Aha," said Jake knowingly.

"I'm at a disadvantage here," said Rachel.

"*Kaleetan* means *arrow*," Alex said. "And I guess they found *kaleetan* tips more than anything else. For a time they were going to call it Kaleetan Bay but in a fit of anti-Indian sentiment, they chose the English translation."

"Typical," Jake said, shaking his head. "I don't know why they can't leave well enough alone when it comes to things like that. Mount Baker is a boring name. *Koma Kulshan* has some style."

"I agree," said Rachel.

"There are some neat old journals about the whole history of the town," Alex said. "I'd love to look them over, but can't. The current holder is over in Europe," he said, sighing. "I wish David Longhoffer would come back not only for that, but also to fire that brother of his that's ruining the *Arrow Bay Examiner.* I get so tired of reading his right-wing editorials, I could scream some times."

"Now now," teased Jake. "That doesn't sound like a good Buddhist to me."

"I never claimed to be a good one. I'm still a novice and trying to learn more every day," said Alex with a tired grin.

"How long have you lived in Arrow Bay, Alex?" asked Rachel, taking a bite of her cheesecake.

"Full time? Six years. My folks lived mainly in Seattle but had a summerhouse on Orcas for decades. My grandmother retired to the Bay and I spent a lot of time with her…" he trailed off. "I took care of her during her illness and just settled here." He looked at Rachel and smiled. "How do you like D.C.?"

"I loathe it," she replied. "Except for the museums and monuments. I guess the old adage about taking a girl out of the small town is true."

"You ever think of coming back here?"

"Constantly."

"Then you should," said Alex with a simple nod. "I think I know of at least two fellas who would love to see you back."

"Hear hear," said Jake and Sam in unison as they dug into their cheesecake.

"And maybe three?" she asked so low only he could hear her.

"Oh, I'd say three is a good number."

❖

"He's full of shit," Rachel said after dessert. "But I don't think there's anything malicious to him."

"Is it polite to talk about someone who's gone to the bathroom?" Jake asked.

"You can't very well while he's at the table," said Sam.

"Tends to shorten the meal," Rachel agreed. "And he's paying, don't forget."

"Shh! He's coming back," Jake said as Alex crossed the room, heading toward their table.

"I was looking at your website the other day, Sam," Alex said, sitting back at the table. "I didn't realize you'd tackled so much work."

Now what do you mean by that? thought Sam. From the look on Rachel's face, she was apparently thinking the same thing. He shrugged and said, "I've done very well for myself. In the last eight years I've worked continuously. The time in Sydney was spent modernizing their fleet. I've been approached by a few private companies to design dinner boats. When I found out the state was going to be building some new boats I threw my hat in for that. I didn't really think I'd get it," he admitted.

"Well, the fleet here is in desperate need of modernizing," Alex said. "I understand your design is easily converted to liquefied natural gas engines in the future?"

"You hadn't told me that," Jake said.

"I hadn't told *anyone* that," said Sam suspiciously. "How'd you know?"

"Oops," said Alex, smiling. "Don't be mad with Mr. Sutherland. Blackburn may have a project with him, and we were just shooting the breeze. I guess he let it slip. He speaks very highly of you," Alex said.

Sam smiled wryly. "Well, Sutherland's a good man."

"The fleet *is* getting old," said Jake.

"The Steel Electrics, Evergreen State class, and the Supers all need replacing," Sam pointed out. "Ships have a life span, just like people. It's frankly amazing the state has kept as many of the old vessels it has in such good shape."

Alex ordered another round of drinks and a second piece of cheesecake for dessert for Jake. Sam excused himself to go to the bathroom. Jake was about to dig into his second piece of cheesecake when Rachel said to him, "Shouldn't you go with him?"

"Sam's perfectly capable of—ow!" he said, Rachel's foot connecting with his right shin. Scowling at her, he said, "Well, I *did* want to see the bathrooms before we left." Looking sadly at his cheesecake, he left the table. "Perhaps they'll have some ice for my shins, as I have a pair of matching bruises now," he muttered as they walked away.

"He's a good guy, isn't he?" Alex said, apropos of nothing.

"Jake? One of the best."

"Yes."

"I'm a little worried about how obsessive he's getting over this whole Susan Crane thing," Rachel said, noticing how Alex stiffened when she mentioned the name.

"Obsessed?"

"He's determined to find out all he can about her."

"Maybe you could deter him."

Rachel arched her eyebrows. "And why should I do that?"

"I knew Susan Crane. She was *not* a nice person. Jake could be getting in over his head."

Rachel sat back in her chair, crossing her legs. "What exactly do you know about her?"

"Enough. She was dangerous. I'm sure you've found that out, or has Jake not filled you in?" he asked pointedly.

Okay, asshole, thought Rachel. *That does it.* "Oh no," said Rachel, batting her long lashes at Alex. "Jake, unlike some people I know, is very forthcoming."

Alex looked at Rachel. He paused for a moment before taking a breath and speaking. "You don't like me much, do you?"

Rachel thought a moment. "That's not true."

"It isn't?"

"No. I don't like you at all."

Alex laughed. "I like your honesty, Ms. Parker."

Rachel shrugged. "I don't know how to be anything else."

"I'm curious, Rachel," said Alex, downing the last of his Scotch and motioning to the waiter for another one. "Why don't you like me?"

"Not for the reason you think," she said carefully.

"Oh? And what might that be?"

"You calculate on being disliked for being wealthy, good-looking, and arrogant. And a Blackburn. More than anything else, you *count* on being disliked for that."

Alex cleared his throat and asked, "So why don't you like me?"

"I don't like you because of that phony air you put on. You're shrewd and thoughtful, and I suspect you care deeply about a great many things, but from what I've been able to glean, you cover that all up by surrounding yourself with sycophants or people who can be of benefit to you in some way. You use them to carry out whatever it is you're doing behind the scenes at Blackburn Industries. You get them to do things to irritate your father or someone on the board you don't like," said Rachel smoothly. "I don't know why you didn't like Susan Crane, Alex. It sounds like in that regard you had an awful lot in common."

He swallowed thickly. "If that is true, then why do I—"

"Why do you keep Jake and Sam around?" Rachel shook her head. "I can only guess. I do know Jake genuinely cares about you."

"And what about Sam?"

"Sam doesn't trust you, but he can't figure out why."

"I see," Alex said, his voice hoarse.

"Count yourself lucky, Mr. Blackburn," said Rachel, her voice going flinty. "It's the fact that Jake is in your corner that makes my opinion one of general distaste for you and not outright hatred."

"And why is that?"

"There's one thing about Jake," Rachel continued. "And Sam,

for that matter. They accept people for who they are. They love them unconditionally. Jake manages to find the good in everyone and bring it out. I think he could have done that with Hitler."

"I would agree with you," Alex said.

"Sam's a bit more cynical. He's had to be. He's had horrors in his life no one should have to see," she said. She smiled at Alex, her eyes frozen on his. "You know what I think, Alexander Joseph Blackburn the Third? I think you're a fraud. Everything about you, from denying your wealth to wrapping yourself in environmental causes. It's a ruse." She considered this for a moment and shook her head. "No, not a ruse, a persona. One that affords you a level of comfort and safety. You may believe in some of your causes. I hope you do for your sake. But I've seen bravado like this before." She smiled wickedly. "I have *crucified* people like you on the witness stand. They *all* break down. You know why?"

"I suspect you're going to tell me whether I want to hear it or not."

"Because under it all, you're a scared little boy who wants to be loved and accepted just like everyone else." She sat back. "And you can't find it anyplace. You're a dilettante always searching for the cure for that cold, empty ache inside of you that you can't kill off with booze or Buddhism or denying yourself of the things you really want."

"Are you quite finished?" Alex whispered.

"No." She leaned closer to Alex. "You know what I really think, Alex? I think you're a decent guy. Just can the crap and be yourself. If you allow yourself to be who you are instead of who you *think* you are, or what you think other people think you should be, you might be surprised to find you actually like yourself."

"What if…" Alex started. He sat back, throwing Rachel a haunted look.

"There's nothing good inside to allow you to be yourself?" asked Rachel, as if reading Alex's thoughts. "You're not the bad person you think you are, Alex. And I know a *lot* more than Jake does, believe me. I didn't get where I am at in my job for nothing."

"You checked me out, didn't you?"

"Of course I did. Jake's mentioned you for years, but it's only been recently that you've gotten closer to him and Sam, and I wondered why."

"And you think you know?" he asked, smiling for the first time.

"Oh, I do," she said, sitting back and taking a sip from her drink.

"Care to share your penetrating insight?"

"No," she said with a grin. "This game is one you lose, Mr. Blackburn."

"Jake is right," Alex said, his voice thoughtful. He downed his Scotch as soon as it arrived. "You are a remarkable woman."

"And you, sir, are a remarkable man. If you weren't, Jake wouldn't have anything to do with you." She smiled. "You may not be forthcoming with your past, Alex, but Jake has an unerring sense when it comes to character. His trust in you reveals more about you than you think."

"So it would seem," he said.

"Trust is big with Jake and Sam," Rachel said. "I know what you're trying to do. Given your family history, I applaud your efforts." She smiled. "*Trust them.* I think you'll find it is worth it."

"Anything else?" Alex asked.

"Yes," Rachel replied. "You're an excellent dancer."

Alex laughed heartily at this remark, just as Jake and Sam arrived at the table, debating some small point in *The Clock Struck Murder.*

"Worst book ever," said Sam.

"No, trust me, it is not. That had to be—"

"Boys, it's getting late," Rachel said. "Shall we?"

"Boys, she says," said Jake.

Rachel rolled her eyes. "Big, burly, strong manly men, it's getting late. Is that better?"

"Yes," Jake said. "You agree, O strong and manly one?"

"Assuredly I do, big and burly," said Sam. "And besides, the lady is right."

"Good night, Alex. It's been a fascinating evening," Rachel said.

"Indeed it has, Ms. Rachel Parker," he said. Looking at Sam and Jake, he said, "Good night, manly men of Arrow Bay."

"Unngh!" grunted Sam, tossing a wave to Alex and walking away, his neck scrunched into his suit, lumbering like a caveman.

"God, I love that man," said Jake. "Take it easy, Alex," he said, then following suit, scrunched his neck down and followed after Sam.

"It's like living with Heckle and Jeckle," said Rachel, shaking her head. "Good night again, Alex. Think about what I said."

"More like Mac and Tosh," said Alex. "And I will."

❖

"What did you say to Alex?" asked Jake as they waited for the valet to bring Sam's blue Subaru to the front door. It was a chilly night, so Jake zipped his coat up.

"The duck was excellent, as was the cheesecake," said Rachel, refusing to be cornered.

Jake would have none of it. "Don't play games with me, Rachel. It's beneath you. Alex looked like you'd punched him in the gut," he said, stepping around the back of the car to get in on the passenger side.

She slipped into the backseat. "I'm sure I don't know what you're talking about."

"Methinks the lady doth protest too much," said Sam, tipping the valet.

"Gracias," said the valet.

Jake's heart did an unpleasant flip. He tried to catch a look out the window as Sam pulled out onto Chuckanut Drive, heading south.

"What's wrong?" Sam asked him.

"Nothing," said Jake, sitting back. "You're being evasive, Rachel."

"Okay," said Rachel as Sam rounded a corner on the winding road. "I may have said something to him. But he provoked it."

"Rachel," Jake groaned. "You weren't rude, were you?"

"Not exactly," said Rachel. "I just called him on a few things is all."

"Damn," Sam moaned. "Of all the times to have to go to the bathroom."

"He was more forthcoming tonight than I've ever seen him," Jake said. "You had an interesting influence on him."

"It must have been my charm and allure."

"More like the way you cross-examine," said Sam.

"You're supposed to be on *my* side, Sam," Rachel pointed out.

"I take no sides in issues relating to Alexander Blackburn."

"His business is his life, and he won't let anyone in on that. I get the feeling something big is brewing there, but he won't tell me what it…" Jake trailed off, a voice pinging in the back of his head. In his mind he saw a closed oak door, set into a wall with floral Victorian wallpaper, and behind a voice saying, *Once this is over, it'll all be fine. I swear.*

The Ice Queen and Alex, at the hotel. And the Ice Queen shrieking back, *and how much longer, Alex?* And his reply. *Six months at the most. I swear.*

"You're thinking," said Sam.

"Recalling a conversation, actually," replied Jake.

"Port Jefferson?" asked Sam.

"Exactly," said Jake. "Six months, he said. Remember?"

"Hello," Rachel said. "Someone not privy to that conversation would like a little filling in."

Jake related the events at the hotel, watching Rachel quietly listening.

"Interesting," she said after he'd finished.

"Interesting what?" Jake asked.

"Nothing," she said. "You've never been a bad judge of people, Jake. I think your basic assessment of Alex is a good one. I think at heart he's a decent guy. I suspect he's trying to make up for a rather wild and misspent youth."

"Typical rich guy," Sam said, shaking his head.

"And you, Mr. O'Conner, surprise me. I've never known you not to cut someone some slack, certainly when it comes to having a less than stellar family. It might do you good to get to know Alex Blackburn a little better," she said, choosing her next words very carefully. "I *suspect* you might find you have some things in common."

Jake turned around and looked at Rachel, eyes narrowed. "You checked him out, didn't you?"

"Whatever do you mean, Gobo?"

"Rachel Louise Parker! You checked him out!"

"Wish I had thought of that," said Sam under his breath, earning him a withering look from Jake.

"I merely wanted to see if there was any reason to be concerned," she said. "His father *is* a very bad man," she said. "I sound like I'm four years old. He's a very *corrupt* man. Father and son are nothing alike, I'm happy to report." She put her hand on Sam's shoulder. "You can appreciate that, I'm sure, Sam."

He nodded and gave Rachel's hand a little squeeze. "Yeah, I can."

Behind them, the bright lights of another car filled the rearview mirror. Sam sped up as much as he dared. Chuckanut Drive was a winding piece of two-lane highway that ran up the side of Chuckanut Mountain on its way from rural Kulshan County up to Bellingham. Prone to rockslides, it was not a road to drive incautiously. The Subaru's wheels screamed as they rounded the next bend.

"Sam," said Jake, tensing up. "What's the big hurry? Slow down."

The Subaru's tires squealed again as Sam rounded the next corner. "Um," Sam said. "Promise you won't get upset?"

"What? This road scares the hell out of me, and you know it. Slow down."

"That car behind us. I think we're being followed."

"Let him follow," said Jake. "I don't like the idea of being—"

BANG!

The car behind them smashed into the back end of the Subaru, and Sam nearly lost control of the car. He righted the wheel and slammed down the accelerator, squealing around the next corner.

"Jesus, Mary, and Joseph!" Rachel screamed. "That maniac son of a bitch hit us!"

"Oh, come on!" Jake yelled.

"What?" Sam asked, slamming his foot on the accelerator.

"This is so stereotyped!" shouted Jake as they tore through another corner, narrowly missing an oncoming car. "Trying to run someone off the road is as old a chestnut as you can get!"

"Old chestnut or not, he's doing it!" shouted Rachel.

"Don't worry. I used to drive Chuckanut all the time when I was running up to the Bellingham yard. I know it like the back of my hand."

"I don't care whose hand you know, slow down for that next one or we're going over!" she replied.

"Okay, okay, hang on!"

"He's going to hit us again!" she yelled, bracing herself for the crash.

BANG!

Sam slowed down to make the corner, but the car behind him didn't. It ricocheted off the Outback and skidded as they rounded the next hairpin, giving Sam time to leap forward. The trees dropped off to the side of the road on the right, revealing the moonlit water some two hundred feet below. Sam jerked the wheel to the right as they screamed around another hairpin corner.

The car behind them was gaining again. Jake whirled around to try to catch any detail of the vehicle, but all he saw was a blazing wash of white headlights. The circles of light grew steadily closer, and he braced himself for another impact.

BANG!

The Subaru jerked to the right, heading toward the cliff. The front bumper smashed into the guardrail as Sam let out a grunt and jerked the wheel to the left. Sparks flew up, and the front fender let out a scream of agony as it bounced off the rail. The car screeched back onto the roadway, narrowly missing an oncoming car. Sam jerked the wheel to the right, hitting the rail again and shattering the headlight before regaining control of the car and punching the accelerator.

"You sure you know what you're doing?!" Jake shouted.

"Would you like to come over here and drive for a bit?" asked Sam, hearing Rachel muttering prayers from the backseat. She suddenly burst out laughing.

"I'm glad you find something humorous about this!" Jake snapped.

"Who am I praying to? I'm an atheist!" she said, laughing uncontrollably.

The car was gaining again. Sam gunned the engine, which was erupting steam from under the hood.

"That's not exactly comforting, you know," Jake yelled, his eyes glued to the speedometer, which had just leapt past eighty.

"Just a little further," said Sam through gritted teeth.

Jake looked in the rearview mirror, where a pinpoint of light was gaining on them again. He looked out the window where the cliff had fallen away, revealing the open stretch of salt marsh not far off. If they could just get to that…

He braked the car for control, then aimed directly toward the wide corner of an oncoming turnout.

"What the hell are you doing, Sam?" Jake shouted in terror.

"Hang on, we're gonna make it!" Sam bellowed back.

The car smashed into the back of the Subaru, shattering the rear window. Rachel screamed as a fine spray of safety glass covered them. They roared forward toward the shoulder, headed for the cliff and the guardrail when Sam suddenly jerked the wheel to the left as hard as it could go. All four tires bit into the pavement as the anti-lock brakes grabbed the all-wheel-drive car and threw it sideways across the road, slamming it into the deep ditch on the other side. The Subaru's engine cut out as the airbags deployed. Jake felt the air gush out of his lungs as the car smashed to a halt on the cliff wall. He heard Sam grunt and the sound of glass shattering.

And then all was very, very quiet.

CHAPTER THIRTEEN

Is everyone okay?" Sam asked.

Jake opened his eyes. Over the airbag, he could see a spider-webbed windshield and the headlights of the Outback pointing up the mountainside. The dome light popped on, and Jake was flooded with relief to see Sam was okay other than a small cut on his forehead.

"Next time I really must decline the invitation to dinner," Rachel said from the backseat.

Jake heard her seat belt pop open. He looked back to see her opening the door, reaching for her purse. "I think we should get out, don't you?"

It wasn't a particularly deep ditch on the mountain side of the road, a few feet down. The Subaru had landed upright, leaned over on its left side. Once Jake clambered out of the car, Sam crawled over the passenger side to get out.

"You okay?" Jake asked.

"My neck is a bit stiff, but the airbags did their job," Sam said, massaging his neck.

"Sadie?"

"I think so," she said, pulling her cell phone out and dialing 911. "We should get checked out, anyway."

"Who are you calling?" Jake asked.

"The police. Someone just tried to kill us, in case you hadn't noticed!"

"Speaking of which," Sam said, running across the road. Jake and Rachel quickly joined him.

They had been coming off the mountain at the last curve. The light from the city of Mount Burlington bounced off the low clouds, illuminating the large field of potatoes below them. Jake suspected the land once had been marsh: the green Explorer that had run them off the road lay on its side, half buried in the muck, its unbroken headlight cutting through the night with a jaundiced beam. The driver's side door hung open, but no one was to be seen.

"Sadly, that looks survivable," Rachel said, looking down at the wrecked car.

"It does," Sam agreed.

"Do you think whoever it was can get back up here?" Rachel asked, looking down the steep hill.

"Not unless they're part mountain goat," said Jake. "My guess is they're hoofing it off in that direction, toward Mount Burlington." He couldn't see anything moving in the shadows.

"Or calling for backup," said Sam.

They moved away from the pullout, not wanting to be seen. Rachel completed the call to the Washington State Patrol. They went back to the battered Subaru, waiting. "They should be here in a few minutes. They're sending the aid car as well."

"We're fine," said Jake.

"My poor car," said Sam, his voice filled with sorrow.

"It's insured," said Jake.

"Of course it's insured! That's not the point! You just can't replace something like that, you know! What are you thinking!"

"Why are you yelling at me?"

"Because someone tried to kill us, and I'm scared, you nitwit!" Sam shouted back, taking Jake into his arms and squeezing him. "God, if anything had happened to you—"

"Nothing did," said Jake. "Sam—Rachel."

Sam let go of Jake and walked over to Rachel, picking her up and setting her next to Jake. He then grabbed them both in his huge bear hug, squeezing them.

"Uh, Sam," said Rachel.

"Go with it," Jake advised.

A few minutes later, a stream of cars poured down off the mountain. One or two pulled over to render assistance, but the rest continued on their way down Chuckanut Drive. Jake scowled at the lot of them as they continued driving.

"Where the hell were *they* fifteen minutes ago? If all that traffic had been around, this wouldn't have happened!"

The state patrol and the aid car arrived. The EMT checked Rachel over to make sure she was okay. Jake noted she was lightly flirting with the burly blond paramedic and knew she couldn't be feeling *that* bad. Sam was giving his statement to the officer when the man requested a breathalyzer.

"You've got to be kidding me," said Jake, losing his patience rapidly. "You can see the back of our car is bashed in! Another car down the hill there, and you're giving Sam a breathalyzer!"

"Jake, it's standard procedure," Sam said. He turned to the officer. "Don't mind him, he's just a little stressed out."

"Sam hasn't had anything to drink but sparkling apple cider tonight," said Jake, approaching the officer. "In fact—"

And that was when he slipped on a wet rock and went skidding headfirst into the ditch.

Evelyn O'Conner closed the hospital room door behind her as the nurse left. "What happened?" she asked calmly.

The trio had been silent about the entire incident since she'd arrived at the hospital. "Someone ran us off the road," said Sam slowly.

"So you said to the police."

"I think they must have been drunk," Rachel volunteered. Sam and Jake looked over at her, gratitude flooding their faces. "We had just left the restaurant," she started.

"He just missed that last corner and went sailing right out there," said Jake.

"Yes," Rachel agreed. "Sailing right out there."

"Was it Jimmy Durante with the money from the tuna cannery?" Evelyn asked acerbically.

"What?" Jake and Rachel said in unison.

"Two points, Mom," Sam said, covering his eyes with his hand and shaking his head. "You two were quoting Milton Berle in *It's a Mad, Mad, Mad, Mad World* when Smiler Grogan drives off the cliff."

"Oh," said Jake.

"Um," said Rachel.

"Yes, well. You children spend far too much time watching television," said Evelyn, her face sketched with obvious skepticism. "What I would like to know is what happened to your drunk driver."

"What do you mean?" Jake asked.

"According to the nice state patrol officer out there—who doesn't believe your story either, for the record—no one knows where the driver went. The car was empty when they got there," said Evelyn.

"Apparently they were well enough to walk away from it," Sam said.

"Probably didn't want to get hit with another DUI," said Rachel. "I don't suppose they serve Cosmopolitans here?"

"You're in line behind me, Ms. Parker," Evelyn quipped.

"How far could he have gone? I mean, how long was it between when the Explorer went over and the ambulance arrived?" Jake asked no one in particular.

"That, I don't know. Probably not too far. They sure as hell didn't come *up*. State patrol arrived in five to seven minutes. No one else came down the mountain." Sam looked down at Jake, squeezing his hand. "How's the pain?"

"Oh, not so bad. They gave me some Percocet. The doctor said it's a grade three sprain, and I should be good to go after Christmas."

"You left out torn ligaments," Rachel said.

"Torn ligaments?" said Sam.

"That's what makes it a grade three," Jake added.

Sam squeezed Jake to his chest. "My poor loveable klutz."

"I called dispatch at the ferry system for you," Evelyn said. "A very nice man told me to have you call back when you knew the extent of your injury."

"Good thing I have sick leave saved up," said Jake.

"Mom, will you excuse us a moment?" Sam asked.

"Sam, if you give me one more line of bull—"

"Easy does it," Sam said, winking at her. "See if you can find Jake's doctor so he can let us know when they're springing us from this joint."

"Sam, you are the most exasperating person," Evelyn said.

"Ha!" said Jake.

Sam stuck his tongue out at Jake.

"Very well. I'll see what's up," she said, kissing Sam on the cheek and leaving the room.

Once she had gone, Rachel said, "Not much gets by your mother, does it?"

"Let me put it this way," said Sam. "You're looking at your future self."

"Oh, I hope. Your mother has fantastic taste and is a class act. If a bit too perceptive."

"You'll note the similarity."

"So she's already talked to the state patrol," Rachel said.

"She's right, you know," Sam replied. "They were plenty suspicious. At first they thought I might have been racing the jerk down the side of the mountain, but I guess once they checked my record out and searched the other car, they figured I wasn't racing."

"Sadie McKee and her sexy dress helped," Jake said, feeling mellow with the pain pills. "The cop had trouble meeting her eyes," he said, giggling.

"Er—yeah," said Sam, looking at Jake with his eyebrows arched. "I forgot you have a funny reaction to painkillers."

"Well, he's right," Rachel agreed. "But he must have also figured that no one racing a car would have a passenger in the back wearing an evening dress."

"What pedestrian lives they must lead," mused Jake.

"I agree, Gobo," she said, rising from the chair. She stroked his hair a few times and looked at Sam. "You okay?"

"We're lucky to be alive. My car is totaled. I'm very thankful I only had sparkling cider at the restaurant."

"What *did* you tell them?" she asked. "I was a little worried because we didn't have time to get our stories straight before they showed up." She stopped. "Sam, why the hell didn't we tell them the truth?"

"I don't know. Instinct took over. I mean, it was *basically* the truth. I told them this guy came barreling down the side of the mountain and bashed into our back end a few times. I fudged the truth a little and said he tried to get around us and was likely drunk but that never happened. Then I said I tried to pull over, took the corner too fast, and the guy went over."

Rachel shook her head and said, "You're not much better at telling a lie than Jake is. They saw how bashed in the back of that Subaru was. They *had* to have known it was deliberate."

"I'm sure they did," Sam said. He was suddenly exhausted. "I don't know what else I could have told him. If I had said the guy was *trying* to drive us off the road, he'd have thought I was nuts." He lowered his voice. "And I'm paranoid about it getting back to Kulshan County."

"Danvers?" Rachel asked.

"Yes!" Sam said, glancing over at Jake, who was nodding off. "Have you heard the stories about him?"

"I've heard the allegations. Corruption, fixing evidence, all tenebrous at best and no one has been able to prove anything." Rachel said.

"That's what I've heard," Sam said. "Mr. Sutherland told me Dwight Danvers is not a man you want to cross. You might suddenly find yourself in a whole lot of trouble with Kulshan County."

"You don't think *he* had anything to do with this, do you?" Rachel asked.

"I don't know," Sam said.

"She was a dangerous woman," said Rachel softly.

"What?" asked Sam.

"Oh, nothing. Something Alex said to me," Rachel replied.

"Susan Crane," said Jake, noticing he made them both jump. "Why else? Waterman warned me I might be in trouble," he said, his head spinning. "I think I'd like a trip to Europe," he said, his thoughts becoming muddled by the Percocet.

"I hate it when you tune in on my thoughts like that, Gobo. I was thinking the same thing. Because of what you saw," Rachel said, ignoring Jake's last comment. "You know, and by default *we* know it was no suicide."

"Yeah, but why go at it so ham-handed?" Sam asked. "Trying to run us off the road. Aside from being remarkably unimaginative..."

"Sam," Rachel said. "This *isn't* a Spievens novel. And even if it were, knocking us off Chuckanut Drive would have been pretty effective, *n'est ce pas?*"

"If it is related to Crane, which I have no doubt, we are once again faced with the big question of why they ruled it a suicide."

"A story she was working on?" Rachel asked.

Jake shook his head. "No. Waterman thought not, anyway. She had been turning in humdrum stuff since her move into the big office. He knew she was working on something, but didn't think a story was in the offing. He did a thorough search of all her office files. Or would have if there had been any," Jake said.

"What do you mean about the files?" Sam asked.

"Cleaned out," said Jake, waving his hands theatrically. "Waterman found a bunch of boring meeting notes and general information, but nothing personal. He said he'd been over to her apartment, too, but nothing there, either."

"I bet those files walked away with someone before Waterman got there," Rachel said. "Someone was taking pains to wipe Susan Crane off the face of the earth. Someone really wants everyone to forget she existed."

"After tonight, I'm inclined to do just that." Jake winced as he shifted in bed. "Unfortunately, we can't now," he said, sitting up. "I'm more appalled by this goon's lack of creativity. He gets an F for that. I mean, come on! Running someone off a mountain road in the middle of the night? It's clichéd! Next thing you know he'll try blowing the car up."

"Don't even, Gobo," said Rachel.

"Yes, let's skip that particular cliché," Sam said.

He wandered over to the large picture window to look out into the darkness. Unexpectedly, he spun around and kicked the wastebasket across the room, which ricocheted off the wall with a thunderous crash. "Who the hell *was* this woman? Everything she touched, even tangentially, even after she is *dead* turns poisonous." He slumped down in the uncomfortable green plastic chair again, holding his head in his hands. "Now she's screwed with us, too."

Silence fell heavily on them. The intercom in the hall echoed through the antiseptic-smelling air, the overheard fluorescent lights droning. Jake stared at the corkboard ceiling, unsure of what to say or do next. His ankle throbbed, but the numbing effects of the painkiller kept him from feeling much of it. His thoughts grew fuzzy as the opiate anesthetized him. "From now on," he said slowly, "we can't be alone."

"I agree," said Rachel.

Jake struggled a few minutes to pull himself out of the fuzziness before speaking again. "Whoever murdered Susan Crane doesn't like us knowing it. Since the book has been closed on her," he said, "if we keep quiet about it and *not* make noise with the police, maybe they'll lay off. If they think they've shut us up, maybe they'll leave us alone."

"They're doing a bang-up job," said Sam, shaking a bit.

"We leave it for a while, then. I can't do anything while this stupid ankle heals anyway," Jake said. "After that…"

"Let's just take 'after that' when it comes. Christmas is coming up. Gavin and Jeff will be arriving soon. I don't want to be worried about the boogeyman jumping up from behind the damn Christmas tree every time I come into the house," said Sam.

The nurse came back and said Jake could be discharged as soon as they were done wrapping his ankle in Ace bandages. Jake was not happy to hear it could be up to six weeks for the ankle to heal properly, and that would have to be followed by physical therapy.

Sam and Rachel joined Evelyn in the waiting room. Evelyn spent the next hour talking very generally with Rachel, wanting to hear about her background and work and what Jake had been like as a little boy. The nurse wheeled Jake back in a short time later, advising them to wait for the doctor. Jake opened his mouth to say something to the nurse when the doctor came in, a short, round, handsome Japanese-American man with round glasses perched on the end of his nose.

"I'm Dr. Masuoka," he said. "Mrs. O'Conner said you had some questions, Mr. Finnigan?"

"I'm not sure we want to hear this, Evelyn. Jake doesn't do well with medical advice. Let's go bring your car around."

Twenty minutes later, Sam and Jake emerged from the hospital. Jake scowled as Sam pushed him out into the parking lot. They spotted Evelyn's Cadillac, and Sam guided the wheelchair toward the car. White exhaust curled up in lazy plumes from the Caddy's dual exhaust. Jake neatly hoisted himself into the car's big front seat while Sam loaded the crutches in the trunk. He took the wheelchair back and returned to the car, sliding into the backseat beside Rachel.

"You look like someone stole your lollipop," said Evelyn.

"The doctor threatened me," grumbled Jake.

"He didn't do anything of the kind," said Sam. "He just said stay off that ankle or he'd put a cast on it."

"That sounds like a threat to me," said Jake.

"Oh, quit complaining. You know as well as I do Dr. Masuoka is tired of you not listening to him. You're lucky he didn't just stick you in a cast. I would have. And don't look at me like that. You can still do your upper body workout," said Sam.

"Is *that* what he's upset about?" asked Evelyn, shifting the Cadillac into drive.

"Yes. We all have our little addictions, don't we?" asked Sam with a smirk.

Jake closed his eyes. "I'll politely pretend I didn't hear that. What a surreal damn day," he said, enjoying the spin of the Percocet.

"Nightmarish, more like," Rachel said, sneezing.

"Bless you," said Jake.

"*Gracias,*" said Rachel.

Jake's eyes snapped open. "Sam, what did the valet look like?"

"What?"

"The valet at the Cliff House. What did he look like?"

"Nondescript, dark hair, thirties maybe."

"Did he have pockmarked skin? Acne scars?" asked Jake quietly.

"Yes, I think so."

"I know who tried to run us off the road," said Jake slowly. "I also know where else I've seen him."

"Where?" asked Rachel.

"On the *Elwha*. On the day that we found Susan Crane's body."

Evelyn pulled the Cadillac over on the side of the road and put the car in park. "Well, this sounds fascinating! Now we're all going to have a nice little chat about what's going on here before I go any further, is that understood?"

Rachel and Sam slid down into their seats. Jake, was out like a light, snoring gently.

"Well, Evelyn," said Rachel, "it's like this."

"You incompetent jackass!" Alex shouted into the phone. "How could you have let something like this happen? What the hell am I paying you for?"

"With all due respect, Mr. Blackburn, you did say *you'd* handle things tonight," said the gravelly voice on the other end of the line.

"McEvoy, I told you I wanted you to keep an eye on him regardless of the circumstances. What I said was, I'd be with them tonight, not that I could handle things. Christ, they were nearly *killed*," said Alex, his voice shaking.

"Well, as long as your friend wants to play amateur sleuth, he's going to be a target. Actually, he may be a target even if he doesn't. He's one of the few people that saw Crane was popped in the head."

"Don't think I don't know it. What have you found out so far?"

"Crane had been pissing off a lot of people lately. She was rattling some cages with the relatives of the old lawyer of the Gordon family. Uh, James, his name was."

"Jack James?" Alex said. "He died years ago."

"I know that. You asked me what she'd been up to."

"What else?"

"Two or three things she was working on. One she was playing really close to the cuff, though, not letting anyone in on it. No, the only one who might know is that Lopez jerk, but he ain't talkin'."

"You've tried?" Alex asked impatiently.

"'Course I did. That's what you're paying me to do, isn't it?"

Alex could have argued that he wasn't getting his money's worth, considering the events of the evening. "Keep at it. And get someone better to keep an eye on them. That complete screw-up Drayton got easily ditched the other day. *And* pulled over, I might add," Alex said, giving a silent nod to Sam O'Conner's aptitude.

"I've got nearly all my men covering this as it is."

"Don't bitch to me. You're being more than adequately compensated."

"There are times when you sound *remarkably* like your father, Alex," McEvoy said.

"Just do what I ask you," he said, annoyed. Then added, "Please. I know you're doing your best, but this really scares the hell out of me."

"Well, it should," said McEvoy. "One of the things Crane was poking into was stuff on Junior."

Alex dropped his glass. It shattered on the impact, shards of crystal scattering over the floor.

"What?"

"You heard me. Crane was looking into your father's business dealings."

"Why?"

"I don't know yet," McEvoy acknowledged. "We're working on it. This case ain't no picnic for us. This whole assignment gives me the creeps. What the hell was she into, anyway?"

"I don't know," Alex said. *But I have some guesses.*

"Well, it wasn't picking daisies in the park. How the hell did this get ruled a suicide anyway?" McEvoy asked.

"Ask Danvers, the Kulshan County sheriff."

"We'll check that out, boss. *Thoroughly.*"

Alex sighed. "Sorry I snapped."

McEvoy chuckled. "I'm sorry I made the crack about your father. You really aren't anything alike, other than you both have a temper. But I'll be goddamned if Junior ever got upset over the welfare of another human being." McEvoy chuckled again.

"We both got the temper from Gram," Alex said, smiling.

"God rest her. All right, we'll keep on it. Check in with you twice a day?"

"Yes. Until this is over."

"You got it."

Alex rang off with McEvoy. He grabbed another glass out of the kitchen and poured himself another Johnnie Walker Blue on the rocks, slumping into his chair, rubbing his eyes. He blamed himself for what happened. He knew he should have been honest with Jake from the beginning. He'd had Jake tailed by Blackburn Industries security because he'd been worried about him ever since he'd told Alex he knew Susan Crane's death hadn't been a suicide. Alex figured it probably wasn't either, knowing Crane's track record, but he hadn't dreamed that someone had the clout to have the investigation ruled a suicide. He had a few suspicions as to why the Kulshan County sheriff did it, but none of them made him any more at ease.

He wanted to call and find out how Jake, Sam, and Rachel were doing, but he technically wasn't supposed to *know* what was going on yet. Having left the Cliff House long after the trio had been taken to Kulshan County General, he hadn't found out about the accident until McEvoy finally reached him on his cell phone, which he'd left in his car.

"Damn," he muttered aloud. He knew he'd have to call in a favor. He hated doing it, even though the people he knew were always more than willing to help him—with the exception of Zandra, of course, but she had her reasons.

Just a few more months, and it'd all be over. Maybe not even that. It could be down to mere weeks now, and then he could finally relax. Things were going very well for him, and very, very badly for his father. With each passing day, his father was losing his grip on the company, falling further into debt. The time was nearly right for Blackburn Industries to collapse. A whole new order would come out of it. The dinosaurs on the board would be gone, and then he'd pull out all the stops. If only he could just hold on a little while longer.

"Damn you, Susan Crane," he said. Even from beyond the grave, she was screwing things up. He hoped McEvoy would come up with some answers soon. He was becoming increasingly worried about Jake and Sam, and now Rachel. He vowed he wouldn't let anything happen to them if he could humanly prevent it.

Outside, the moisture on the grass flashed into ice as winter crept into the night.

CHAPTER FOURTEEN

The days before Christmas slid by at a languid pace. Jake continually scowled at his injured ankle, cursing both his klutziness and the fact that it was healing more slowly than he would have liked. Dr. Masuoka again threatened Jake with a cast and told him to stay off it as much as possible. He continued to work out, however, focusing on his upper body.

Jake heard from his brother Jason more frequently. Jake was still a bit concerned about the tension in Jason's voice, and he knew that something was up even though Jason wasn't saying anything.

"Why'd he leave San Francisco so suddenly?" Rachel asked the day after Thanksgiving.

"I don't know," Jake admitted. "I suspect it had something to do with that bigot he was dating."

"The one that caused the big blowout," Rachel said.

"Yes."

"I never understood why he was with her. Jason's always had a level head on his shoulders. She was not exactly his type."

"She sure had a rope on him for a while," Jake said, staring out the window at the gray day and the steady stream of rain.

"I wonder why?" Rachel mused, staring into the gas fireplace.

"I know that look," Jake said, shifting his ankle onto a pile of pillows on the sofa he was stretched out on.

"What look?" Rachel asked in mock surprise.

"It's the same look you gave me when I brought up Alex's name and you disappeared for several hours. Presumably to do whatever background check you ran on him."

Rachel brushed a lock of hair out of her face and shrugged. "I'm sure I don't know what you're talking about."

"Well," said Jake, "you could always ask Gavin and Jeff when they arrive. I mean, they know San Francisco so well and are bound to have heard something."

"Jacob Allen Finnigan," said Rachel, wearing her scandalized expression. "I wouldn't dream of doing such a thing!"

❖

On the 17th of December, the slate gray sky filled with large, fluffy white flakes that powdered Arrow Bay and the hills around town with three inches of downy snow. With the Festival of Lights taking place nightly downtown, the effect was postcard perfect. Red and green lights were strung across the streets, intertwined with cedar boughs and holly, creating a winter marvel...until it had a chance to pack down and freeze into solid ice, as was the usual pattern in Western Washington.

Sam, Rachel, and Jake viewed the holidays with somewhat cynical eyes, though Jake had never been particularly fond of Christmas. They were all looking forward to the arrival of Jake's former college professor and his partner to liven things up and lessen the oppressive atmosphere. They felt their movements were being watched, and this *was* the case as Alex's security force kept an eye on them. With each renewed report of "everything normal," Alex began to breathe a little easier, waiting until the moment McEvoy produced the results that would, he hoped, shed enough light on Jake, Sam, and Rachel to keep any nefarious plot far from their doorstep.

Something *was* wrong in the wind, though.

"I feel it most acutely heading into work on the *Elwha* each day," Captain Trelawney had said to Jake when he'd gone down to the *Elwha* to get his stuff off the boat. "There are Christmas decorations around the terminal and on the ferry, but I can't shake this feeling of trepidation."

"You think the rest of the crew feels that way?" Jake asked.

"I think the boat will be forever tainted, despite our best efforts to avoid being superstitious."

"Maybe the feeling will be gone once the murderer is caught."

"I hope so," Captain Trelawney confessed. "I don't think the specter of Susan Crane stalks the decks, but there is a *feeling* that her presence dogs the boat."

Jake hadn't let Susan Crane flit too far from his mind. One night just before falling asleep, it occurred to him that despite the results of the crash, if anyone really *wanted* to kill the three of them that night

FINAL DEPARTURE   • 191 •

on Chuckanut Drive, they could easily have done so. They'd been given a stern warning to keep the hell away, something that by outward appearances, they all had been doing.

Tomas Waterman had been aghast to hear of the "accident" when Jake had called him. Jake spent the next hour trying to see if he could wheedle any more information out of Waterman about the list he'd drawn up. Waterman, feeling somewhat responsible for Jake's condition, said he'd check up on the two police officers, Jack Carpenter and Arnold Lloyd, to see what had become of them.

"Have you tried Alfonso Lopez?"

"The fellow Crane got cleared of the eco-terrorism charges?" Jake asked.

"Right. If Susan ever had a friend, he was as close to one as she got."

Jake had taken down the number on his steno pad. The list was now down to Martin Gore, Jeremy Young, the heretofore unknown Jack Bowman, and Arnold Witcher. He would have liked to talk to all of them immediately, but his ankle was still wrapped. He finally gave up and began playing phone tag with Alfonso Lopez. He wouldn't leave a message on Lopez's machine because he didn't want to have his voice recognized. And the name *Lopez* reminded him of a certain pockmarked Hispanic man.

By the third week of house confinement, Jake was going out of his head with boredom. He'd burned through two crossword puzzle books and soundly trounced Sam and Rachel at cribbage eight games in a row last week alone. He knew he was driving Rachel crazy. After one too many games of Five Crowns, she had fled the house in her rental car.

"I have to go Christmas shopping *sometime*," she said that morning.

"Take me with you," Jake pleaded.

"How am I supposed to shop for you if I take you with me?"

Jake called Sam at Sutherland Shipyard where Sam had gone that morning to check in on a few projects. "You have to take me somewhere."

"What's in it for me?"

"Don't be difficult, Sam."

"Well, all right. I was thinking it was about time we replaced the Subaru anyway. Your car sucks in snow."

Car shopping with Sam turned out to not be much of an outing. Sam drove them right to the Arrow Bay Subaru dealership and put down the money on a brand-new, fully loaded Outback wagon in Atlantic blue. Jake was a bit surprised that he got extras like the built-in cooler in the backseat, automatic adjusting mirrors, and a high-priced sound system. The dog gate he could understand and possibly even the bicycle rack. The car wouldn't arrive for another six weeks—there wasn't one with those specifications available in the state and Sam was adamant on Atlantic blue. Jake found himself smiling over Sam's stubborn insistence. Sam had never owned a car that hadn't been painted blue.

They had a good afternoon, making jokes and talking, enjoying the frozen scenery around them. Jake noticed Sam glancing up in the Cruiser's mirror more than he may have normally done in weeks past, but otherwise both of them had been relaxed. Sam asked Jake if he'd like to go into Mount Burlington for a trip to Costco, and Jake agreed, but noticed not long after they'd headed down the highway that Sam was heading toward Chuckanut Drive.

"You have some burning desire to go back to the scene of the crime?" Jake asked, looking out the window. The sky was the color of volcanic ash, fat with moisture. Soon it would start snowing again, and he didn't want to be caught in the Cruiser in a blizzard.

"Kind of," said Sam.

They were soon there, the skid marks left by Sam's demolished Outback clearly visible, along with the scattered bits of chrome and metal from the car that had gone down the hillside.

The insurance company investigating the accident had decided that Sam's story was as close to the truth as they'd want to pursue. The other car had been a rental, with plates switched from an Explorer in Renton the owner hadn't even noticed was missing. The police and insurance company closed the case as Sam being the victim of a drunk driver, the trio having been in the "wrong place at the wrong time." Since they all knew they were neither, they were happy to have the entire matter closed, neatly or not. Sam's insurance company had cut him a check the next week.

Jake carefully got out of the PT Cruiser, using one crutch to get over to the ledge. Looking down on the field still covered with snow, he examined the setting below. The field terminated to the north into marshy ground that would be flooded with the next rain. The cold blue waters of Samish Bay lapped up gently on the shore, the air filled with the heady smell of salt water. To the west, the field stretched out for miles before disappearing into a dense copse of trees, and to the south lay the highway. Behind them rose the forested slopes of Mount Blanchard. On either side of the highway were a number of farmhouses.

"It doesn't make sense. Whoever it was, they sure as hell didn't run up the hill into the woods behind us," Sam said.

"Which leaves a couple of possibilities. Whoever it was either ducked behind one of those farmhouses down there and maybe called someone. Or someone was down there waiting. Maybe checking to see if they'd got the job done," Jake said, surprised at his anger. The fear of what had happened to them had long since evaporated.

"You think there's more than one person?"

"I've thought that from the beginning," Jake said, hopping back into the cruiser and stowing the crutch behind him.

"The car following us on I-5?"

"Possibly," Jake said. "I'm still not sure about that. Given what happened, it makes you want to draw that conclusion. It makes the most sense, but...damn it, why does that feel wrong?"

"I don't know. It does to me too, though," Sam said. He looked into Jake's malachite eyes and smiled. Leaning in, he kissed Jake. "I don't know what I'd have done if anything had happened to you, Jake."

"Me either, Sam," said Jake, shivering against the cold. He looked down the steep slope again, then back up the winding stretch of Chuckanut. "Let's get out of here."

Sam turned up Highway 22 and headed out past Sedro Woolley toward Concrete. "Where are you headed?" asked Jake.

"Well, you said you wanted a drive. I thought I'd buzz past the *Rosario* one last time."

"Er. I'm not sure that's entirely a good idea," said Jake, shifting uncomfortably.

"Was there something else you aren't telling me about the last time you were there? Other than the obvious bit about someone else having been in there and Arden being gone?"

Jake shrugged, unable to articulate what it was he'd felt when he and Alex had last been there. It was a sense of dread, he remembered, a feeling that had broken his arms out in gooseflesh and sent an uncomfortable shiver down his spine. He shivered again thinking of it now. "I had a creepy, something wrong and out of place feeling. I just wanted to get the hell out of there as rapidly as possible."

Sam pondered for a moment. "Did you feel like you were being watched?"

Jake considered for a moment before replying. "Not exactly. More like…I don't know. Like I could sense something off about the place. It was more than just discovering someone else had been tromping through the *Rosario*, though that was disturbing enough."

"I wonder…" said Sam.

"Hmm?"

"Arden. It just seems odd he'd leave so abruptly."

"I found that weird, too."

The snow had begun to fall by the time they started up the road that lead to the hunkering hulk of the *Rosario*. Jake stared out the windshield as the heavy wet flakes made soft splats against the glass. The trees, now denuded of foliage, readily gave up the opening where the ferry was.

"I don't want to linger, Sam. The snow is really starting out heavy."

"Did you want to get anything while we're here?" Sam asked, stopping the Cruiser and stepping out slowly.

"I don't think anything is left. Arden pretty much gave us anything that might have been useful from the boat," Jake said, putting his shoe on and sliding out behind Sam, grabbing his crutches. "Besides, I don't think I should navigate the boat with these babies."

"Probably right," Sam said, looking at the hulk of the *Rosario*. In the absence of any human occupation, moss had started to take over the red funnel. Tree branches from the last windstorm covered the decks and a blanket of wet maple leaves was plastered on every flat surface.

"Down over there," Jake said. "Just on the other side of the tree. I got spooked when I noticed the tree had been recently cut down. I think Alex was uneasy, too, though he never spoke about it afterward," he said, slipping on his coat.

"It's a bit weird without Arden here," Sam agreed, walking around to the front of the Cruiser, staring at the *Rosario*. "Poor old boat."

"No, it was something more than that," Jake said, pointing to the boat. "*She* didn't creep me out. Other than the fact that the decks are in worse shape now than they were before, and there's a good chance I could have been killed." *The footprints bothered me, though*, he thought. *And those new planks*.

"Wheelhouse is halfway into the passenger cabin, did you notice?"

"Uh-huh," Jake said, eyeing the boat. "She won't last through the winter."

"No, she won't." Sam agreed. The flakes danced around him, sticking to his hair, his glasses. "Uh-oh."

"Hmm?"

They approached the area of the tree stump carefully, Jake watching very attentively how Sam made his way through the frozen underbrush. Sam stopped abruptly, wincing. "It was here, wasn't it?"

"Yeah, something there."

"Jake," Sam said patiently. "Can't you *smell* it?"

"Sam, you don't think..." Jake said, crutching his way toward where Sam was heading in the underbrush.

"I do, Jake, I do. Oh *man.*"

They tromped around the stump at the spot where the flash of green had caught Jake's eye two months before. Sam kneeled down and gingerly pushed aside some leaves, revealing unopened cans of Mountain Dew. Just beyond it was a crate of canned goods and coffee. Pushing back further into the brush, the smell assaulted them both. Sam gagged and tried not to vomit. "Oh God, Arden!" he said, looking down.

Leaves and debris had covered the corpse, but the cold temperatures had preserved it somewhat. It wasn't completely skeletonized, but the face was gone. Sam looked down long enough to see the skull looking back up at him. He turned away quickly, closing his eyes.

It had been a quick look, but it was long enough to discern the bullet hole left in Arden's head.

"What have you done to yourself?" Gavin Ashworth asked upon seeing Jake at the front door with crutches.

"A 'hello' would have been nice," said Jake sourly.

"Hello," Gavin said, taking off his trademark ball cap and running his fingers through his black hair. He gave Jake an appraising look, his brow etched with concern. "What's wrong, Jake? And the hell have you done to yourself?"

"You know our Jake," Sam said from behind him. "Tripped over his own feet."

"Aha," said Gavin, stepping into the foyer and setting his bags down to give his friends a proper hug. "I appreciate all the effort of bringing in the snow for us. Jeff is beside himself. He's also annoyed that I didn't let him drive," he said,

Jake knew they were in for it as he watched Gavin's eyes dart back between he and Sam.

"What hell is going on, you guys? You look awful!"

"That's a fine way to greet someone," said Jeff, stepping in behind Gavin and shutting the door behind him. He looked at Jake and Sam and said, "Jesus, you two do look awful!"

"Salt and Pepper have spoken," said Jake.

Jake and Sam jokingly referred to the couple as Salt and Pepper: Jeff, with his sandy blond hair and beard and light blue eyes, was as much the polar opposite of the black-haired, nearly black-eyed and tattooed Gavin as was possible. Gavin, though only a few years older than Jake, held a PhD in English and taught creative writing at Berkeley; Jeff owned his own nursery and landscaping business. The couple had met about a year into Gavin's PhD work. Upon meeting Sam and Jake, they'd all become fast friends and now spent the holidays together, Jake and Sam usually spending Easter and part of spring break in San Francisco or a mutually agreed upon meeting place, and Christmas was nearly always spent at Arrow Bay.

"Joke all you want, Jake, but what's going on?" Gavin insisted.

"How'd the ride up go?" Jake asked, not meeting Gavin's eye and trying to brush off the subject.

"The professor wouldn't let me drive," Jeff said sulkily.

"Well, California boy, tell me exactly how many times *you've* driven in snow?" Gavin asked.

"Well," Jeff confessed sheepishly. "I haven't. It hailed heavily in San Mateo once—"

"Bah," said Gavin, waving a dismissive hand. "Until you've braved Seattle drivers over three inches of packed snow and ice for several weeks, I don't want to hear about it."

"Yeah, yeah," said Jeff. "Nice try to steer the conversation, Jacob, but what the hell happened to your foot?"

"I tripped," said Jake, suddenly staring at his feet. "Dammit."

Gavin cast a knowing glance to Sam and said, "Okay, Sammy, what's going on here?"

"There's been, uh, an incident."

"Would that explain why the Subaru wasn't in the garage?" Gavin asked.

"How'd you know that?" Jake asked.

"Oh," said Sam, lowering his head. "I told them the garage was open and to park in there."

"And you say I can't keep a secret," said Jake, rolling his eyes.

"Hey, remember, Gobo, no secrets. Dangerous things, secrets. Now, what gives?"

"Put your things upstairs," said Jake. "We'll talk when you get settled."

"Perhaps we should wait for Rachel?" Sam suggested.

"Oh, my," said Gavin, a knowing smirk on his face. "Has Rachel gotten in on this, too?"

"Yeah, she has," said Sam. "And it's a little more serious than you think."

❖

Rachel looked up from the counter at Nordstrom, where the salesclerk had just shown her a man's sterling silver ID bracelet she was considering for Jake when she felt the hairs on the back of her neck stand up. She looked in the mirror above the salesclerk and saw a tall blond woman in dark sunglasses behind her.

Rachel thanked the salesclerk for showing her the bracelet, saying she'd think about it. She headed out of the store and into the parking lot where her rental car waited for her. She was nearly to the door when she heard, "Mrs. Finnigan?"

Well, that's a new one, Rachel thought. She turned and faced the blond woman, her heart skipping a beat. She recognized who it was at once. She'd seen her photo in dozens of news clippings. Susan Crane.

Rachel blinked as the woman took her sunglasses off. She had softer eyes and fuller lips. Rachel knew it had to be Lila Gordon-Beyers, Susan Crane's sister.

"Are you Mrs. Finnigan?" asked Lila Beyers.

"Ms. Finnigan," Rachel said. "Can I help you?"

"Yes. My name is Lila Beyers," she said, lighting a cigarette.

"I'm sorry, do I know you?" Rachel trailed off, mildly annoyed as Beyers exhaled a plume of clove scented smoke at her.

"I am Susan Crane's sister," said Beyers, her voice quavering on the edge of tears. "The woman your—?"

"Brother," Rachel supplied.

"Found dead on the ferry," she said.

"I'm very sorry for your loss, Mrs. Beyers," Rachel said carefully.

"Thank you," Lila Beyers said. "I'm sorry to approach you like this. I tried to contact your brother directly but have been unsuccessful. When I saw your car down at the ferry dock the other day with the two of you in it, I just assumed..." She shrugged. "My sister and I hadn't been close for some time. Family issues, you know how that goes, but recently we had made efforts at a reconciliation. Susie was all the family I really have left with our mother being so ill. I just can't fathom what happened to Susie," choked Beyers, breaking down in tears. "I'm sorry," she said, producing a silk handkerchief and dabbing at her eyes. "It's just so hard…so hard…"

Rachel studied the woman. Lila Beyers was obviously very distraught, but Rachel had witnessed similar performances from women on the witness stand, including one who had poisoned six husbands and carefully dismembered them. Tears could be easy to come by if you needed them badly enough.

Very softly she said, "Again, I'm sorry, Mrs. Beyers. Is there anything I can help you with?"

"I don't know! I don't know!" wailed Lila Beyers, making Rachel take a step back. "I just don't know where to turn! After that…that *horrible* little man closed the case—"

"Sheriff Danvers?" Rachel suggested.

"Yes, Danvers, that's it! Insisting it was suicide! I can't—I *won't* believe Susie killed herself, not when we had come to an understanding and were getting so close again! It's just so preposterous! And how she was found, I mean, you can't commit suicide and lock yourself in a trunk, can you?"

"Barney Evers," said Rachel, thinking *here goes nothing*.

"I beg your pardon?" Beyers sniffed.

"Back in school. Barney Evers was the kind of pencil-neck geek no one could stand. He had bad acne, a stutter, and glasses that could have started forest fires they were so thick. My senior year of school, he decided he was going to kill himself. Well, actually, he decided *twice*. The first time, he jumped off the Greenbrooke Bridge, but that wasn't high enough. The second time he tried it, he succeeded. He jumped into the back of the trunk. Used a piece of rope tied to the lock to pull it shut. Shot himself with a .22."

"Well," snuffled Lila Beyers, "I suppose it is *theoretically* possible…" She trailed off, wiping more tears away. "What I came up here to ask…What I wanted to know is if anyone *saw anything* that might lead you to believe it was something other than suicide?"

"Mrs. Beyers," said Rachel, thinking, *Oh Lord, if ever I needed the spirit of Joan Crawford to help me out, now would be it.* "I wish I could be of more help, but the way my dear brother told me, apart from seeing that someone was in the trunk…Well, *none* of the crew saw much of anything, overtaken by the sheer horror of the discovery. Customs shooed everyone away quickly. It was a very traumatic thing for everyone. With all due respect, my brother and the others on the crew are trying not to dwell on it."

Beyers sniffed again, wiping at her eyes. "Yes, thank you, of course...of course. I'm sorry to have bothered you," she said, turning away and walking slowly across the parking lot.

Rachel got into the rental and started it up, watching Lila Beyers until she disappeared among the snow-dusted cars in the parking lot. It might have been her imagination, as Beyers was some distance away, but Rachel could have sworn that she thought she saw the woman suddenly stand more erect, stamp out her cigarette, throw her shoulders back, and march defiantly back into the store.

With Rachel back at home, they spilled the entire story, Gavin and Jeff listening attentively, expressing horror and sympathy at the events that had taken place. Jake and Sam finished the story with the discovery of Arden's body, at which point Rachel excused herself to mix up a pitcher of apple martinis. She handed them out to everyone, Sam and Gavin sitting in front of the fire, Jake and Jeff slumped on the couch.

"Jake, I'm so sorry," Gavin said. He had helped Jake work through the murder of Chris Aponte when they'd both been attending Western Washington University. "Are you doing okay? Have..."

"Have the nightmares come back?" Jeff asked, giving Jake's hand a squeeze.

"Not yet," said Sam softly. "He's had one, but..." He trailed off, looking at Jake.

"Who knows with this last?" said Jake, downing his drink and setting the glass aside. He rubbed his eyes vigorously. "I hate my memory sometimes."

"He was definitely shot?" Rachel asked.

"No mistaking it," said Sam. "You could see the bullet hole."

"Jesus," Gavin muttered. "And you think the two are related?"

"I think they have to be," said Jake. "Poor Arden."

"Well, I'm not surprised Crane ended up dead," said Gavin, folding his tattooed arms over his barrel chest. "I remember the shit she pulled while we were at school."

"I don't," said Jake. "Vaguely, maybe, like something I saw on a newspaper headline or some such, but God, I was so busy with my studies, I didn't keep up with things like that."

"No, I know it," said Gavin, getting up and starting to pace. "What do we do next?"

"We?" Rachel asked.

"You can't expect us to sit idly by after someone kills a friend of yours and tries to kill you lot," Gavin said. "What kind of friends would we be if we did that?" he asked. "And where the hell is your piano?"

"Gavin, love, you're shouting," said Jeff gently.

"Damn right I'm shouting! Someone's tried to kill the people I hold most dear on earth next to you, and it pisses me off!"

"Easy, Prof," said Jake. "Easy."

"We've talked about it at length and have decided we're backing off," Sam said cautiously as Jeff stood up and wrapped his arms around a still-fuming Gavin.

"We were warned, Gavin," Rachel said. "If that guy had wanted to kill us, he could have."

"Forgive me if I take little consolation in that," Jeff replied.

"I agree with that," Gavin said, huffing. "You're just going to sit back and let it go, then?"

Rachel, Sam and Jake all glanced at one another. Rachel opened her mouth to say something when Gavin held out a hand and cut her off.

"No, Sadie McKee, don't even attempt it. I know better," he said slumping into the unoccupied recliner. "And I understand it."

"You do?" asked Jake.

"Don't be dense, Jake. No one but these two know better than I do about what Chris's unsolved homicide has done to you. As much as I'd like to sit on the lot of you to prevent you from doing anything stupid, I know it's not going to work, especially after the death of this Arden fellow."

"No," said Jake. "There isn't much you could say or do."

"I haven't found one yet, Gav, but I swear to God that I'm looking online and hunting antique stores until I find the right one!" Sam blurted.

Gavin looked at him, perplexed and said, "Huh?"

"The piano," said Sam apologetically. "I haven't put it off, really."

Gavin stared at Sam, amazed for a moment, until he let out a chuckle and shook his head. "God, I love you guys."

"For being batshit insane?" asked Jake.

"For reminding me what an utterly quiet, boring life Jeff and I lead," Gavin replied.

They all laughed, breaking the tension that had been building, but unspoken among them was the feeling that things were about to get much worse.

CHAPTER FIFTEEN

So it turns out Arden was a policeman who sort of went out of his head after the death of his family in a drunk driving accident. After that, he became homeless and moved into the abandoned ferry. Unbelievable," Rachel said, putting the paper down and looking at Sam with her eyebrows raised.

"Unbelievable that Arden chucked everything and became a hermit because he was so consumed with grief?" Sam asked.

"No," Rachel replied. "No, that part is incredibly sad. What's unbelievable is the last bit about his body being discovered by two hikers. Two hikers?"

"I had to tell them something," Sam said.

"Yeah, but *hikers*, Sam? Jake's on crutches!" Gavin pointed out.

"Only until Friday, thank God," said Jake. "And now you know why *I'm* the writer in the family. Someone else is better suited to blueprints and figures and all things left-brained."

"Besides which, I don't think the police cared. They knew we had nothing to do with it," Sam assured them.

"How could you have? He'd been dead a long time," Rachel pointed out.

"I'm glad I kept that photo," Jake said.

"Why the hell would he leave that?" Sam said, irritated. "It doesn't make any damn sense."

Jake sat down at the kitchen table across from Sam, thinking a moment. "When Alex and I were there, a layer of dust was on everything. I saw two sets of footprints in there, but neither of them were Arden's. He'd been gone a while before whoever it was started poking around in there."

"What happened?" Jeff asked.

"I'm not sure," Jake acknowledged. "Several possibilities," he said, tapping his finger on the table. "I just had the feeling that place was being used as some sort of meeting house. For what, I don't know."

"What gave you that feeling?" Rachel asked, curious.

"It was more what wasn't there than what was," said Jake. "There weren't the usual indicators that would implicate kids."

"And the lumber," Sam pointed out.

"Lumber?" Rachel asked.

"Yeah, I hadn't thought of that," Jake said. "What kid goes out and buys pressure-treated lumber to make a gangplank?"

"None," Gavin agreed. "You grab what you have handy."

"Exactly. The only reason to have good lumber there is if you want to make damn sure you're going to get from point A to point B without breaking your neck."

"Why *there*, I wonder?" Rachel asked.

"Isolated," Jake said. "While it's known to locals, most avoid it because of Arden. It's far enough off the road that no one would know you're there, while still being fairly protected."

"Unless you take the wrong step," Sam said, holding out his coffee mug for Jeff to fill while he was up. "Thank you."

"It seems so out of the way. Wouldn't a cheap motel be easier?" Jeff asked.

"You still run the risk of someone remembering you," Jake said.

"Well, whatever the reason for it, Arden was shot in the head, there's no mistaking that," Sam said.

"Yeah," said Jake. "Which means we have another murder."

"Why, though?" asked Rachel. "You think it was just to get him out of the way so whoever was meeting there wouldn't have any obstacles?"

"That's the big question, isn't it?" Jake agreed, looking out the window. The snow had stopped, but the bitter cold temperatures remained. The forecast called for more snow, with the possibility of a rare white Christmas for the Northwest. "The cops seemed to think it was drug-related, that they'd been doing something and found Arden there and killed him."

"But you'd already ruled that out," said Gavin.

"Yes," said Jake. "*Nothing* there indicated any drug use. Drug addicts aren't the cleanest of folks, but we didn't see any trash, no beer cans, no discarded needles. They certainly weren't using the *Rosario* to cook up meth."

"Poor Arden." Sam spoke what Jake had in the back of his mind.

"There are too many bodies around here," Jake said, shifting uncomfortably. He'd be glad to get the damn brace off his ankle. It was itching and making him extremely irritable.

"Well, there's only two," Sam pointed out.

"*One* is too many."

"You have a point," Rachel agreed.

"And then there's your *mondo bizarro* encounter with Lila Beyers," said Jake. "Why is she skulking around the ferry dock?"

"It sounds to me like maybe she's not buying Danvers's explanation of events either," said Sam. "She obviously knows something is wrong there, too. Wasn't that your impression, Rachel?"

Rachel sipped her coffee and shook her head. "I don't honestly know. She *seemed* genuinely distraught. It was obvious she'd been crying off and on for a bit, but that doesn't mean a thing. I've seen Oscar-worthy performances on the witness stand before from people who had done some pretty heinous things."

"What does your prosecutor's instinct tell you?" asked Gavin.

"It doesn't, that's what disturbs me," she said. "That isn't normal for me. Granted, it was the only time I'd laid eyes on the woman, but still…" She shook her head. "I just don't know."

"I can't stand this. For the last month, I've been sitting here like a bump on a log," lamented Jake.

Sam arched an eyebrow. "You do remember what happened the last time you went poking about, right?"

"Hang on, Sammy. I seem to recall from your tale last night that you went right along with Jake," Gavin pointed out.

"Ha, he's got you there, Sam," said Jake, suddenly shaking his head. "I can't help but feel Arden is somehow tied into this, though."

"I don't see how," Gavin said, sipping his coffee, and looking out the window distractedly. Barnaby came trotting through the kitchen, with Sophia and Dorothy right behind him.

"Other than the wound, neither do I." Jake shook his head. "There're too many loose ends. From the original list I drew up, there are *still* half a dozen people who could have killed Susan Crane. And we haven't even talked to the Bellingham people yet. Including her ex-husband. Or Lopez."

"Well, you know," Sam said thoughtfully. "I was thinking of taking a day off tomorrow and going up to Bellis Fair to do some Christmas shopping."

"Samuel O'Conner, you big fibber. What would Sister Mary Francis say?" Jake said with mock horror.

"Sister Myrtle Agnes, for your information, and I'd probably get whapped upside the head with that yardstick she kept by the window, miserable old bat."

"You have to be more careful about your fibs," Jake said. "I know you've not shopped for Christmas gifts in a mall since 1997. Other than my forays into Seattle last month, neither have I." He thought a moment. "Weren't there *any* nice nuns at Saint Stephen's?"

"Sister Elizabeth and Sister Gertrude were great. They were younger than the others and had been in a convent barely accepted by the church for being too progressive. It's a wonder I'm not completely warped."

"Being gay and Catholic already puts a strike against you," Rachel teased.

"Spoken like a true heathen," Sam replied. "Speaking of, we don't even have a tree up yet."

"Hard to do with this," Jake said, waving his ankle around dramatically.

"Oh, don't give me that. I've heard you clanking iron down there all week. It won't take but five minutes to drag that moldy old pipe cleaner of a Christmas tree up the stairs."

"Oh, please," Rachel groaned. "You're not *still* having that argument, are you?"

"That tree looks as real as any live tree out in the yard," Jake countered.

"Look, Rachel's right. We're not going to have this discussion again. I will *not* be called a *tree murderer* again."

"If the ankle-strap pump fits—"

"Gobo!" Rachel warned.

Jake leaned over and gave Sam a kiss. "Very well, Sadie. We'll haul up the moldy old pipe cleaner this afternoon."

"Thank you," she said. "I already feel behind as the neighbors have had their lights up since the first."

"Don't let that fool you," Jake said, looking across the street. "They've been up since *last* Christmas."

❖

Alex spent the first half of the day going over his finances, something that gave him a tremendous headache by the time it was halfway over. After his accounting team left him in the quiet of his condo, he opened the blinds and stared out across the bay at the lowering gray sky again threatening snow. Tonight, he vowed mentally, he'd go into town and enjoy the Festival of Lights, which might add some much needed cheer to his otherwise gloomy outlook.

He glanced over at the phone. The light indicated two voice mails had been left during the six-hour conference with the team. He picked up the black receiver and dialed the number.

"Alex," the gruff voice of McEvoy said. "I've been leaning on Lopez a bit down here. I think he's ready to crack. Crane was up to her eyeballs in something. She was going to be booted from the paper. Lopez won't tell me what exactly it was, but as usual if you wave a few dollars, all sorts of doors open. Glad you've got plenty. Oh, your Sheriff Danvers is currently under scrutiny by the FBI. Whether it is over this Crane business or not, I've no idea. My source wouldn't say more than that. I'll keep on it. Meanwhile, the rental car that tried to run your friends off the road was rented by a heavyset guy with bad skin and horrible breath. Name and I.D. given were a fake. Big surprise there. I'll keep on it and give you an update tomorrow. Oh, and thanks for the Christmas bonus. That was damn generous of you. I'm sorry about that crack I made about you being like your father the other day. That tightwad bastard never gave me so much as a thank you in twenty-five years."

That alone had cheered Alex considerably. He was not only happy at the progress McEvoy had made but also very pleased to hear yet again that there was an ocean between the man he'd become and his father.

The second call had been from one of his closest associates, Benjamin Bennett. Alex and Ben had gone to school together and spent a great deal of time together in Europe when Alex had been researching the family's roots. Ben had been a great help to him but refused to come to work directly for Alex as long as his father was still in charge of the family business. He'd become a sort of contract employee, working directly for Alex from time to time. Of late, Ben Bennett had been looking over several pieces of property to acquire for Alex. One had already been purchased and it was this Bennett had been calling about.

"Alex," said Ben into the voice mail. "News is good and bad. Good news is the asbestos problem was cleared out by the previous owner. Bad news is any historic details have been wiped out. Very few original elements remain. I'm still working on getting blueprints. Overall, though, things are in great shape and with a little investment, it should pay off handsomely for you. Also, the piece of property in town you had me look at is available. I am in negotiations to get that settled as quickly and discreetly as possible. The family that owns it needs money and I get the impression the agent wants to wash his hands of it as quickly as possible. I'll update you in forty eight hours, but I give it an eighty-five percent probability of it being in the bag. Incidentally, I think your choice of naval architects is a good one, his work is excellent. I hope you can get him."

This bit of news had elated Alex. All the pieces were now starting to come together, forming an image that would reveal everything with unparalleled clarity for the first time in his life.

Alex stared out his office window in deep contemplation at the snowy cone of Mount Baker, the steam rising from the Essex bio-fuel refinery in great plumes when the phone rang again.

"Blackburn," Alex said.

"Hey boss. McEvoy. Giving you an update."

"Go ahead," said Alex.

"First, I'll start with what I've dug up on your sheriff of Kulshan County," said McEvoy, his voice tinted with stress. "Say, Blackburn, just what have you got me mixed up in?"

"McEvoy, are you all right? You sound…" He trailed off. *Scared* was what came to mind, but he wasn't sure he wanted to say that over the phone. Instead, he said, "Tense."

The man grunted. "A little yes. But I'm okay. Now, let me tell you about the sheriff," he said, clearing his throat. "First of all, I couldn't get the county coroner's report. This struck me as odd, so I started poking around to see what was going on there. Turns out the coroner, a man named Clark, who has no medical training, retired right after the Crane case was closed. He allegedly moved to California where he was supposed to have bought a house in San Francisco. I don't know how much county coroners make these days, but that seemed a little abnormal to me."

"Wait, no medical training?" Alex asked.

"Not a requirement for Kulshan County. You'd be surprised at how common that is across the U.S."

"Go on."

"Well, I went up there in person to request the report. The clerk tells me he can't find it. It's gone missing out of the file cabinet."

"*What?*"

"Yeah, that was my reaction," said McEvoy. "I thought my phony press pass wasn't cutting the ice, but it turns out it is gone. This poor clerk got royally bitched out while I was standing there."

"A line from *Hamlet* comes to mind," said Alex quietly.

"Never one of my favorite plays. Anyway, no one seems to have the forwarding address for Dwayne Clark, the coroner, so I try to contact his assistant who helped him perform the autopsy on Crane. One Gerald McIverson. Well, it seems Mr. McIverson went to his own funeral three weeks after the Crane case was officially closed. I talked to his sister, Myra, who said her brother had been very upset ever since he'd worked on the Crane case. Now, she didn't say that it *was* the Crane case, but it fit the time frame. She said something had scared her brother, and in the last two weeks before his death, he was jumpy and nearly paranoid."

"How'd he die?" Alex asked, his throat dry.

"Suicide. He left a typed, unsigned note on his computer. Then he gave himself a massive shot of his own insulin."

"Jesus," Alex whispered.

"So I tried finding Dwayne Clark again, but this guy has literally dropped off the planet. There's no known residence for him in California. His house in Mount Burlington is still completely furnished, too."

Alex sat straight up. "Come again?"

"Exactly. There appeared to be some evidence of packing going on."

"Okay, what about Sheriff Danvers?"

"On sudden extended medical leave. Currently in Kulshan General with severe peptic ulcers."

Guilt, thought Alex. "For how long?"

"Three days. Deputy Sheriff Langley said he had no idea when Sheriff Danvers was coming back," said McEvoy, sighing. "I trust my gut on things, as you know. I liked the acting sheriff. He seemed completely straight with me. He even told me he thought it was strange

Danvers didn't have him working the Crane case with him, but that isn't too surprising—the guy is new, hired from outside the county."

"Anything else?" He was nearly afraid to ask.

"Nothing officially is being done with the case. The feds claim no interest, but a very reliable source told me they were indeed looking into it. And I need three hundred dollars."

"All right. What for?"

"The coroner, Clark, was renting that house in Mount Burlington. I got the landlady to let me in by paying the three hundred in rent he'd skipped out on."

"Has anyone reported this guy missing?"

"No, which is really strange. This guy falls off the face of the planet, and no one does a thing. The house was damn creepy, Alex. Stuff was half packed, suitcases, a few boxes, but it looked like someone had just run out the door. I didn't see any evidence of foul play or anything, it was just empty. *Hurriedly* empty. It was like being on the *Mary Celeste*. I did, however, find something."

"What?"

"Clark was—" He caught himself. "*Is* methodical. Looking at his desk in his office, everything was lined up to mathematical precision. His closets all had suits on hangers labeled for the day of the week. Very compulsive stuff."

"Another reason to suspect something has happened to him."

"Right. I'm still looking into any relatives he might have gone to. This isn't a guy who'd let anyone needlessly worry about him."

"No," said Alex. "You said you found something?"

"Not just something, the big enchilada. One autopsy report of one Susan Crane."

"Holy shit! Where?"

"The freezer, of course," McEvoy said nonchalantly.

"The…"Alex slapped his head. "Sure. Nice, stable guy, compulsive guy like that. Where did Mom always say to put important documents in case of fire?"

"Exactly. Although I'm not sure putting x-rays in a freezer is a good idea, even if they are in airtight plastic bags."

"No kidding." He took a deep breath. "Official findings?"

"Simply put, murder. Someone whacked this broad, though I think we knew that all along. Clark came to the conclusion that Susan Crane had been shot in the head at point-blank range by a left-handed assailant. She had powder burns on her *eyes*, for Chrissakes. The gun was no more than an inch away, but not pressed to the forehead directly. She had a broken wrist from a defense wound—she'd been in a fight, with contusions to the head and shoulders. Even if you ignore the fact that she had no powder burns on her hands and was locked in her own trunk, for God's sake, she couldn't have tied her hands behind her back or closed the lid of that trunk with a broken wrist!"

Alex could tell now that McEvoy was livid. He got that way when he perceived a miscarriage of justice was taking place. Clearly this was a large one.

"There are notes all throughout the file. Clark disagreed with Sheriff Danvers on every aspect of the case, vehemently refusing to sign off on the report Danvers authorized. Clark intimated the official report was heavily edited, and his name had been forged." McEvoy cleared his throat again. "I saw something on his desk calendar, boss. Two days before he checked out, there was a name written down with 'two p.m.' next to it. Now I know it has been a while since I've had dealings with them, but Sawyer was the name of one of the field agents with the FBI in Seattle a few years ago."

Alex thought for a moment, his eyes following the lazy trail of steam up from the refinery. "One of two possibilities. Either someone found out and made him disappear, or Agent Sawyer figured out what was going on and put our county coroner in a safe house."

"I'm thinking the latter. Which makes me really nervous about having this material, boss. It could have been left there as bait for Danvers."

"But with Danvers in the hospital, no one bothered to pick it up," said Alex. "You've got it with you now?"

"Yes."

"Drop it by. I know where it can do some good."

Alex stared out the window, thinking. He glanced up at the calendar. December 18. Christmas was a week away. He stared at the thick gray miasma that hung over Arrow Bay as the first tentative flakes of snow began to swirl slowly down to the ground. "McEvoy, you're going back to Texas for Christmas, right?"

"I leave Wednesday."

"Okay. Do me a favor. Don't mention this to anyone until you get back."

"All right."

"I appreciate it."

"I trust you, Alex. Your instincts about things are rarely wrong."

"Make sure you have multiple copies of the coroner's report made. Stow them in the usual places."

"Already done."

"Good," Alex said, thinking, *I knew there was a reason I trust you so much.* "We'll break this thing wide open right after Christmas."

"You have a deal." He paused. "There is something I have to tell you."

"Yes?"

"Two nights ago, I was coming home from Lopez's place. I'd just gotten past Gasworks Park on my way home. It was late, two or three in the morning. I noticed a car had been trailing me pretty close for the last couple of blocks. I started to turn toward home then decided not to, heading back over to the Aurora Bridge. This car followed me until I just started to pull into the public safety building. When I was about to turn in the parking lot, whoever it was sped up to me, swerving deliberately at me. A pretty stupid move given where I was, but then this guy doesn't seem to be that good." McEvoy paused. "Or maybe he is. He must have seen me coming out of Lopez's place. Anyway, I need to back off your friends for a while. I'll get Doyle to do it, but I think I better steer clear for a while."

"Did you see what kind of car?"

"It was dark green or black, American made. The lights on the license plate were out."

"I didn't mean to put you in danger, McEvoy."

McEvoy laughed heartily. "This is nothing, kid. You should have seen some of the crap your old man had me do. I just thought I better mention it."

"Thanks, McEvoy. Just keep an eye out, okay? I don't want your last words to be a typed, unsigned suicide note."

"You got a point there, boss."

Alex sighed. "Call me when you get to Texas."

"I will." Another silence fell between them. "I don't like this waiting, Alex."

"I don't either. I wouldn't if it weren't necessary."

"I know it. Like I say, I trust you," McEvoy wheezed.

"I'm glad for it."

"I'll be happy when this one is over, Alex," McEvoy said truthfully. "This bitch was poison. And it has spread."

"You've no idea, McEvoy," said Alex quietly. "You've no idea."

He rang off, walking into the kitchen and pouring himself another shot of Johnnie Walker Blue. His nerves were frazzled, and he wasn't sure how much more he could take. Alex took a heavy swig, setting his glass down and staring at the refrigerator. Something flickered in his mind, and he had a growing suspicion of just who murdered Susan Crane.

CHAPTER SIXTEEN

Christmas was a dreary, rainy day. The temperatures had slowly risen, breaking the cold that had been holding all of Kulshan County in its grip. The wind howled up from the south on Christmas Eve, bringing with it a warm weather front from out of the Hawaiian Pacific and sweeping up with it tons of moisture, raising the freezing level to fifteen hundred feet. The lowlands marinated in heavy showers while the mountains continued to be buried in white.

Jake, his ankle at last unwrapped, was enjoying unencumbered mobility. He worked out early in the morning, leaving Sam to sleep in with all three pets at his feet. He took it easy on his ankle, but was delighted to get back to a normal workout routine. By the time he was finished two hours later, he was sweating freely and feeling like his old self again. He hadn't realized how vulnerable he'd felt with his ankle injured. Having Sam around had been a real blessing, something he intended to demonstrate his appreciation for later; he'd booked a weekend away at the end of January at the Empress Hotel in Victoria.

For the first time in days, he didn't think about the murder or anything at all to do with Susan Crane. He moved from room to room, doing last-minute cleaning, arranging the Christmas decorations, and getting the mammoth twenty-five-pound turkey into the oven. Their dinner plans included Gavin and Jeff, returning from Christmas Eve with Gavin's parents, Jake's brother Jason, and possibly Sam's mother, although Evelyn had celebrated her "Christmas" a few days earlier at the winter solstice.

Jake called Alex the night before, but Alex said he'd be away in Seattle. Jake wasn't sure what Alex did on Christmas, as he knew Alex didn't care for the holiday much since his grandmother, Ruby

Blackburn, had passed away. He respected Alex enough not to badger him about it, but still felt sad for him.

Jake's mood was typically pensive. He knew this was due to the disastrous childhood Christmases that had included unhappy things like Christmas tree fires; fights over the wrong perfume being given; an entire gamut of drunk relatives parading through the house; and a set of delinquent cousins who destroyed his toys before he'd ever gotten a chance to play with them. In adulthood, Jake had endured his mother's continuing wars with her sisters and brothers, tense gift-giving sessions, and disapproval over his or his brother's partners. While Ingrid adored Sam now, that hadn't always been the case.

In addition to his history with Christmas, he also knew Rachel and Gavin and Jeff would soon be returning home. Rachel was already gone for the day, spending the holiday with her brother, sisters, and parents in Port Jefferson. She would be back in Arrow Bay late that evening, hopefully in time for dessert. Jake felt his friends' absence around the house already and tried not to dwell on the thought that Rachel would soon be three thousand miles away, and though San Francisco was closer, Gavin and Jeff would be far away, too. It filled him with a sense of sadness that was hard to overcome.

Sam trudged downstairs and into the kitchen, yawning when the phone rang. He picked it up. Jake went back to the task of stuffing the mammoth turkey when Sam said, "It's for you."

"I'm up to my ass in stuffing," Jake said, wiggling his breading-covered fingers. "Who is it?"

"I don't know. He said you'd called him."

"I'd called him?"

"If you pick up the phone and ask who it is, I'm sure he'd tell you," Sam said. "That's how these things work."

"Listen, laughing boy, if I had wanted sarcasm, I'd have given you a nickel. Now come here and play nice with Mr. Turkey so I can answer the phone," said Jake.

Sam looked as if he'd just stepped into something Barnaby left on the lawn. "I hate stuffing the turkey."

"Yes, but you like *eating* the turkey," said Jake, washing his hands in the sink. "Besides, it's—"

"I don't want to hear it, I know what you're going to say," said Sam, wincing. "Just go take the call, you pervert."

Jake kissed Sam on the cheek. "I was going to say it's nearly done," he said. "Who's the pervert *now*?" He smiled wickedly and headed into the living room to pick up the phone. "Hello?"

"Mr. Finnigan, who are you and why are you bothering me?"

"Merry Christmas to you, too, whoever you are," said Jake irritably. "Just what do you mean I'm bothering you? You called me!"

"My name is Alfonso Lopez. You keep calling me and hanging up," he said angrily.

"That's not true, Mr. Lopez. I keep calling you and not leaving a message when your machine picks up. There's a big difference."

"What do you want?"

"What I want, Mr. Lopez, is some information about Susan Crane."

There was a long pause. Jake could hear Sam singing "It Came Upon a Midnight Clear" in the kitchen, his voice resonant and flawless.

"Why should I tell you anything?"

"Because, Mr. Lopez, I *saw* her. I *found* her body ditched on my ferry. Since that time, Mr. Lopez, I've been assaulted and nearly killed, and I think it is because of what I saw. If you have any answers, I think you at least owe it to me to help protect my family against whoever did this."

Sam came into the room, wiping his hands on the dish towel. Jake motioned for him to come over and sit down. On the receiver, Jake heard a long, drawn-out sigh mixed in with the sound of traffic. He suspected Lopez was calling from either a pay or cell phone.

"What do you want to know?"

"Well, the obvious, of course. Do you know who killed her?"

Lopez laughed. "I wish I did. My life would be so much easier."

"How's that?" Jake asked.

"You must know, Mr. Finnigan. I expect you've done some background research on Susan. You know what she was."

"What was she to *you*, Mr. Lopez?" Jake asked.

Another long silence. "I thought a friend," he finally said. "At first, that is. Now I think I was more a distraction. She played with me like she did all the others."

"Others?" Jake asked.

"You know who I mean."

"My coat pocket," said Jake, motioning to Sam, holding the

receiver away from his mouth. "There's a piece of paper from a steno pad. Get it quick, please!" Returning to Lopez, he said, "What about the cops on your case, Mr. Lopez? What happened to them?"

"Jack Carpenter is now a detective with the Seattle PD. Typically, they rewarded him for his incompetence. Franklin Lloyd was killed while on duty."

Sam hurried back with the piece of paper. Jake quickly opened it, his list of suspects somewhat worn from having spent a long period of time in his coat pocket.

"Ask him about the lawyer in Bellingham," said Sam.

"Shh, I need to know about something else first!" hissed Jake.

"What was that? Is someone listening?" Lopez asked suspiciously.

"No! Not at all. I was just—uh, stuffing the turkey," said Jake, shrugging when Sam clapped his hand over his eyes, shaking his head. "Witcher!" cried Jake, locating the name. "Arnold Witcher. The one she sued for cutting the trees down."

"The faggot lawyer? No, he actually came off for the better. He caters to all the queens on Capitol Hill now, with his disgusting faggot boyfriend," spat Lopez.

Jake had to stop himself from grinding his teeth. "No *animosity*, then?"

"Not hardly. Try again, Mr. Finnigan. You're beginning to bore me."

And I can see why you and Crane were friends, thought Jake. "Martin Gore."

"Gore, now there's a possibility. Susan was going to go after him about something in his past. She wouldn't tell me what. She was going to expose him, she said, and it would ruin his career. He retired instead and moved to Florida. I think he sells fishing lures."

Strike three, thought Jake. *Assuming he's telling the truth.* "Jeremy Young?"

"Look, why don't you ask him yourself? He's still trying to save the planet in Bellingham. And the little creep wouldn't have the balls to face Susan again, much less shoot her. And you're still boring me, Finnigan. Don't try to call me again. I've changed my number. I don't know how you got it in the first place."

"Hang on, hang on!" Jake shouted. "One more question, Lopez. Who was Jack Bowman? I was told she was working on some story against a guy by the name of Jack Bowman. What was it about?"

Lopez laughed. "A property dispute. Pennies, just pennies. She was using that to draw attention away from herself. Bowman's a nobody, a nothing. Now leave me alone, Finnigan."

Click.

"Son of a bitch," said Jake, annoyed.

"I heard most of it," said Sam. "Including the repeated use of the word *faggot*, though I didn't get the context."

"Arnold Witcher, the one Crane pushed out of the closet. Seems he's doing a brisk business on Cap Hill and is quite happy." Jake scowled at the list. "I need to talk to Jeremy Young. And her ex-husband," he said irritably. "I'm running out of suspects, Sam."

"That's not a bad thing, is it?" asked Sam.

"No, that's not what I mean," said Jake wearily. "I mean they're either dead or in the clear. I can't establish a motive for anyone."

"Well, you've actually not proven where anyone was at the time of the murder, have you?"

"Sure I have," said Jake, handing Sam the list. "Inez Cookson, dead. Reginald McManus, dead. Franklin Lloyd, dead. Martin Gore lives in Florida. Jack Carpenter is a detective on the Seattle police force. While it's possible he could have, *why* would he have, ten years later, after he's already been promoted?"

"Okay, but you still haven't established—"

"I know, I know. Harvey Wallace Claypoole would be ashamed of me. I can't call today, but tomorrow I'll damn well find out where Witcher, Carpenter, and Gore were for sure that weekend."

"There's always the possibility of Sheriff Danvers," said Sam.

"Well, it would certainly *fit*," Jake agreed. "The suicide ruling, the attempt to discredit the witnesses, but…?"

"We're back to why. Though if he's as corrupt as Mr. Sutherland claimed, I can see why Danvers would want Susan Crane out of the picture."

Jake ruminated on that idea for a moment but dismissed it, shaking his head. "Why kill her, though? Why so close to home? Why draw all that unnecessary attention right to your doorstep? If you're corrupt and trying to keep a low profile, killing someone in your own backyard is a pretty thick way to go about it."

"I agree," Sam said. "Maybe he killed her in a fit of anger?"

"Possibly, but there's no indication from anyone I've talked to that he was Crane's intended target. Waterman knew she was working on something, but he didn't say what. While it's possible she was after him, Kulshan County isn't exactly a hub of culture and industry. It'd be a minor blip on the radar, and then all would go quiet again," he said, thinking.

"From the look on your face, there's something else."

"The way she was killed. Those wounds were vicious, but calculated. Precise. She was shot dead center in the forehead. The throat…"

"What a cheery Christmas conversation," Sam said, sitting back on the couch. "Perhaps we'd like to break out the albums of dead relatives and dress up like the pair of grim Victorians we're being right now."

"You're right," Jake said. "No more about it today. Nada. From here on out, it's Christmas cheer and sunshine."

"You're going to get drunk on eggnog, aren't you?"

"I don't make it with double rum for nothing," Jake declared as the doorbell rang.

Sam got up and answered the door. Jake sat back on the couch massaging his forehead when a familiar voice floated in from the foyer. He looked up, and standing in the arch was his brother, Jason.

Jake felt a wave of shock. He'd not seen his brother for more than five minutes in several years, after their falling-out. Jake was startled by his appearance. Jason had always been a head taller than Jake and had *always* had an athletic build. His dark brown hair had continuously been cut short, his face clean shaven, and he was dressed in no-nonsense business attire at all times. Jake had never figured out how he'd managed to be a photojournalist while looking like he never broke a crease in his well-ironed pants.

Standing before him now, Jason was still built athletically, but looked like a Hollywood action-adventure hero. He was dressed in baggy cargo pants and a black T-shirt over which he had thrown a flannel camp shirt. A brown bomber jacket was draped over his shoulders and left open, and he was wearing steel-toed Chippewa logger boots. He wore a brown Akubra hat with a silver band, his hair trailing out from under it in long and loose curls. He had grown a thick, full beard and his intense blue eyes sparkled. He had always been a good-looking man, but the clothes and the beard made him look strikingly handsome.

Jake was too stunned to speak. This was *not* the same man he'd had the falling-out with years prior.

"Hey, little brother," Jason said, breaking out into a smile.

"Say something, you goofball!" Sam said softly in Jake's ear.

"Um. Hey, Jason. Merry Christmas."

"You too, Jake," he said quietly. "It's really good to see you," he added.

"You look...different," said Jake, at a loss.

Jason laughed. "Well, yeah. There's been some—"

The doorbell rang. "I'll go get that," Sam said, leaving Jason and Jake to stare at one another.

"Jake," said Jason, his voice shaking, "I'm so, so sorry."

Jake stepped across the room to his brother, embracing him. "I know you are, J.D."

"I've been so damn stupid."

"It's okay, Jason, really."

"It isn't," said Jason solemnly. "I have no right to ask you to forgive me for the things I said."

"I forgive you, Jason," said Jake. "Sometimes we do stupid things when we're in love."

Jason grunted bitterly. "Yeah, love." He gave his brother a bear hug. "Can you forgive me for being such an asshole?"

Jake hugged back. "Sure. And I won't even say I told you so."

"Eh, you should get one or two in. It's only fair."

"I told you so, dimwit."

"Okay, can we space them out a bit?" Jason said with a wink. He pulled his hat off and set it on the newel post.

"Okay. Maybe once every other hour," Jake agreed. "God, I just can't get over how different you look."

"You look good. Both of you look good."

"Thanks," said Jake.

"Hey, remember when you asked me if I knew anything about that woman who got murdered? Well, I did some checking..."

Jake heard Gavin's voice coming in from the foyer. He looked at Jason and shook his head.

"Later, okay?"

Jason nodded. "Gotcha," he said.

Gavin entered the living room, talking at the pace of a machine gun when he caught sight of the two teary-eyed brothers. "Jason? Is that you?" he gasped.

"That's what I've been trying to tell you for the last five minutes," said Sam, shaking his head.

"I'm clearly missing something here," Jeff said to Sam.

"Jake hasn't seen Jason, his brother, in a while. A while back they had a big blowout and haven't spoken since," Sam said quietly. "So this is a big deal."

"Oh, right, I remember," said Jeff. "He was living down our way."

"Photojournalist for the *Chronicle*," Gavin said. "Memory like a sieve, this one," he said, wrapping his arm over Jeff's shoulder.

"Yeah, but when it comes to any plant under the sun, Jeff knows his stuff," said Jake.

"You have a sister, too, right?" Jeff asked. "Is she coming?"

Jason and Jake looked at each other and burst out laughing. "God, no," said Jake.

"Amy's always been somewhat of a flake," said Jason.

"More like a colossal pain in the as—butt," Jake quickly amended, seeing Sam's look of disapproval. "A narcissistic, selfish diva, a—"

"Jake," said Sam, pinching the bridge of his nose. "It's Christmas, after all."

"Oh, very well," Jake agreed.

"Besides, she's got nothing on dear old Mom," Jason said.

"I wouldn't categorize Ingrid as a pain in the butt," Sam said, pondering.

"More like a typhoon," said Jason.

"Tsunami," ventured Gavin.

"Is that fair, Gav?" Jeff asked.

"Trust me, Jeffrey," Gavin said, winking at the brothers. "I've met the woman."

❖

The rest of the morning passed with food preparation and listening to the soundtrack from *A Charlie Brown Christmas* until sitting down to watch the DVD. Jake was still feeling edgy and finally gave up, mixing the eggnog for which he was famous and chugging a large cup down.

"Jake," said Jason slowly. "I need to get my camera equipment out of the car. It's kind of damp out there," he added, noting the rain.

"I'll help you," said Jake, already feeling more relaxed.

He and Jason stepped outside where Jason's aging Toyota 4Runner was parked behind Jake's PT Cruiser. Jake stopped when he saw the car was filled with what he took to be all of Jason's possessions.

"Jason, what's going on?" Jake asked, concerned.

Jason looked at him, dejected. "Jake, I've got no right to ask you this. Can I stay here for a bit? I know I've got a lot of gall to ask. If you say no I understand."

"She cleaned you out, didn't she?" Jake asked, suddenly comprehending.

Jason nodded, swallowing thickly.

"Do you want to talk about it now?" Jake asked.

Jason shook his head. "Not right now, if it's okay. I just need a little time."

"Sure, J.D.," said Jake, hugging him again. "No worries. Let's get your camera equipment in the house. You'll kip on the sofa tonight. Rachel's been with us for nearly a month, and the boys are in the guest room upstairs."

"Rachel's here?" Jason said, his voice taking on a much lighter tone.

"Port Jefferson for the day, but she should be back this evening."

"God, I haven't seen her since she left for D.C. How is she?"

"Tired of D.C.," said Jake, slinging some of his brother's equipment over his shoulders. "She'll be glad to see you."

"She's undoubtedly going to mention the time I dropped the spider on her when I was eight."

"She's still traumatized by it," Jake said with a grin.

Back in the house, Jake took Jason's equipment into the guest room, telling Jason to make himself at home. Jason excused himself to the bathroom while Jake made his way back to the kitchen, where Sam was waiting expectantly.

"What's up?"

"I'm not sure," Jake said. "That Jennifer woman seems to have cleaned him out. He hasn't gone into specifics yet." He looked at Sam. "I said it was okay if he stays here a while."

"As long as he needs," said Sam, smiling. "I like having a house full of friends and family. Er, family we *like*," he quickly amended. "I'm glad you guys are patching things up."

"I never blamed him," said Jake. "Well, only that he didn't believe me when we told him what Jennifer said."

"Love can make us do some dumb things," said Sam. "I'm glad he's back. I know Jason's more like your twin than just a brother."

"He's been a good friend to you, too," Jake said.

"I know. I hated not having him around. I still hate having Gavin and Jeff so far away. And Rachel."

"Well, Rachel's moving back, and we'll just have to work on getting Gavin and Jeff up here," Jake said.

"Turkey smells great," said Jason as he walked into the kitchen.

"Jason!" said Gavin, entering the kitchen and dragging Jeff over to him by the wrist. "I'm sorry, I've lost my manners. This is Jeff, my partner."

Jason shook his hand. "Good to meet you."

"You too."

Another awkward pause fell between them, but Gavin came to the rescue again. "Well, Jason, it looks like we've got you settled. Why don't you get something for Jason to drink, Jake, and we'll meet you in the living room? *Charlie Brown Christmas* for one and all," he said, smiling. "Of course, if Sam had already purchased his piano, he could be playing it for us instead of just listening to it on CD."

"You're as subtle as one of our earthquakes, Gavin," Jeff said, shaking his head.

"You've never heard Sam play," Gavin replied. "I'm tired of hearing excuses, Samuel Patrick O'Conner. Don't make me send one up from the warehouse."

"Hey, there's a thought, though," said Jake.

"What's that?" asked Sam.

"Ashworth Furniture," said Jake.

"But I want an antique," Sam protested.

"The auctions," said Gavin, slapping his forehead. "Of course!" he cried, pulling out his cell phone.

"Clearly, I'm missing something," said Sam.

"Gavin's dad opened a new store," said Jeff. "Antiques and estate items, jewelry and the like. For his retirement, since he's no longer seeing the day-to-day operations of the Ashworth stores."

"He gets in all sorts of cool stuff," said Gavin, listening to the phone ring. "I'm sure he gets pianos. I'll tell him to keep an eye out for—Pop? Yeah, it's me. What do you mean 'me who?' Your son! How many sons do you have?"

Jake, Sam, and Jeff laughed, Jake going over to mix them drinks. "Um. Whatcha want?"

Jason glanced at Jake's glass. "The eggnog looks good, but a shot of Jameson would do me well about now," he said with a crooked grin.

Jake nodded. "I agree wholeheartedly," he said, pouring two doubles. He drank the shot, enjoying the slow burn all the way down. Jason followed suit.

"You know about Mom and Dad in Mexico?"

"Oh yeah. Did they tell you why?" Jason asked.

"Nebulous answers, which means they're hiding something?" Jake said, shaking his head. "Wonder if Evelyn's going to show up?"

"Yikes," Jason said. "I like Sam's mother, but damn, she's worse than a Spanish Inquisitor. I know she'll be asking me about what happened. Another?" he asked, waving his empty glass at Jake.

Jake poured out another shot for each one of them. He looked at Jason and said, "I'll have Sam put in a word to her not to bug you about it. To your good health."

"And yours," he replied. They clicked glasses together and downed the shots.

"Yowza," said Jason.

"Yeah. But I'm starting to feel less anxious about the Finnigan Family Christmas Curse."

"Like the time Uncle Henry came over and broke into the gin?"

"Oh God, I'd forgotten about that," said Jake. "Or blocked it out. No one ever did find out what happened to the turkey, did they?"

"No, but I don't think anyone *did* want to find out. I think some highly unnatural things happened to the turkey that Christmas."

They looked at one another and laughed.

"Jake, I'm really sorry."

"Forget it, J.D."

"I've been stupid and blind. Maybe purposefully blind. It's inexcusable. I'm sorry for the things I said."

"Just don't let it happen again, you big jerk," said Jake.

Jason smiled. "It won't." He looked down at the floor for a minute. "What happened…I was in deeper than I thought. And Jennifer was *not* who I thought she was." He laughed bitterly. "It wasn't even her real name."

"Was she some kind of con artist?" Jake asked.

Jason thought for a moment. "In a way, yes." He looked into his brother's eyes. "Something bad happened. Something really, *really* bad. I'm not even sure how much fallout there has been. I lost everything, but I don't care. I think I'm lucky to even be here, frankly."

"You're starting to scare me a bit, J.D.," Jake said.

"It was worse than that, Jake, it was terrifying, it was—"

Just then the doorbell rang. Jake looked out the kitchen door and through the living room into the foyer. Sam rushed over to open the door. Holding it open and awash in the gray light of the afternoon, Jake caught the astonished look on Sam's face.

"Ah, she did decide to come," Jake said.

"Mom!" Sam said. "Come on in."

In a swirl of jade silk, Evelyn O'Conner swept into the room. She embraced her son, said "Merry Christmas, darling," and placed something small in his hand. She then spied Jake and walked over to him in a rustle of kimono.

"Merry Christmas, son-in-law," she said, kissing his cheek. "Hmm, do I detect a hint of Jameson on your breath there, Jake?" said Evelyn with a wink.

"Er, a little," he said, blushing furiously.

"Be a dear and pour me two fingers, will you?" she asked, adjusting the two chopsticks anchoring her auburn tresses in place. "I've just had the most dreary conversation with my daughter."

"Do I want to know?" asked Jake.

"How's your ankle?" Evelyn replied.

"Aha," said Jake knowingly. "It's fine, Evelyn. Healed up just fine."

"No more car chases down mountainsides?" she asked.

"Ma," said Sam, his voice steely.

"Relax, Samuel, I'll be on my best behavior," she said with another wink, downing the glass once Jake had returned. "Much better," she said with a smile. She spotted Jason and said, "My God, can it be you, Jason?"

"Yes ma'am."

"Well, you look marvelous, Jason. You'll have to sit by me and tell me what you've been up to," she said, taking his arm and giving Jake a third sly wink as she escorted Jason into the living room.

"Any Jameson left?" asked Sam, slinging his arm around Jake.

"Half a liter, give or take," said Jake, patting Sam's backside. "I was going to ask you to ask Evelyn not to interrogate my brother."

"Ha, like *that* would have worked," said Sam.

"I'm glad we have a backup bottle of Jameson. We may need it."

❖

"Everything okay?" asked Gavin as he savaged the boiled potatoes with the masher. "I see Evelyn and Jason are chatting away."

"Well, you know Evelyn," said Jake.

"She's a force to be reckoned with," Gavin agreed. "I quite like her. Always have. And Jeff thinks she's a hoot."

"She likes you guys a lot," said Sam, fretting over the apple pie that was sharing space in the oven with the browning turkey.

"I know it took her a bit to get our friendship," said Gavin.

"Not too many exes spend the holidays together," Sam said. "But I put it to her in terms she understood."

"How'd you manage that?" asked Gavin.

"I told her that if Jake hadn't met you, he and I wouldn't have ever gotten together," said Sam.

"Which is the absolute truth," said Jake.

"Mom's pretty open-minded, and she's into the whole 'path of life' thing," said Sam. "She knows that if Jake and I had met before you, it wouldn't have lasted."

"Because I was a basket case," said Jake.

"You were not," Gavin sighed. "You had a lot to work through, and I'm happy I could help you. Not the least of which because I ended up with two of the best friends I've ever had."

"Who?" asked Sam.

"Us, you goofball," said Jake. "Just how much eggnog have you had?"

"It *is* Christmas, you know," Sam said with a silly grin.

"You're a goof, and I love you," said Jake, kissing Sam long and luxuriously. "Make sure everyone is topped off, will you?"

"Aye aye, Captain," said Sam, shuffling away.

Gavin laughed and said, "It's so odd to see him even slightly buzzed like that."

"Christmas only," said Jake. "You know how he is, what with that bastard of an alcoholic father he had."

"I know," said Gavin. "I can't abide by anyone who beats children. I'm glad the son of a bitch ended up at the bottom of the Harbor Steps."

"I don't think you'll find too many shedding a tear over him," Jake agreed, tossing the green salad. He dropped in a handful of dried cranberries and feta cheese. "Did you see the vase Evelyn gave us?"

"Stunning," pronounced Gavin. "I'm always amazed by her work."

Evelyn had presented Sam and Jake with a superb trumpet-shaped vase glazed in iridescent blue and purple. It shimmered ethereally almost like a hologram.

"Me too," said Jake.

"So what happened to J.D.?"

"She cleaned him out," said Jake. "That's all I know. He's deeply ashamed of what happened, and…" He trailed off.

"What?"

"A little scared, I think."

"*Scared?*" Gavin asked, concern etched in his face. "J.D. hasn't ever struck me as the type of man to get scared. Far from it, in fact."

"No, he doesn't, as a rule," said Jake. "Which is why I'm concerned."

❖

Twenty minutes later, they sat down at the dining room table and began Christmas dinner. They passed the turkey and dressing around the table with the gentle buzz of conversation, everyone thoroughly enjoying the company and the food. Evelyn held their attention, as she tended to do, regaling them all with tales from her childhood, her encounters with well-known artists, and her exploration of palmistry, new age philosophy, homeopathic medicine, crystals, and aura reading.

Jake had the highest respect for his mother-in-law. She was a woman who had survived fifteen years of a physically abusive husband and had made the break from him to thrive on her own. Evelyn had changed the surnames of her children and took back her maiden name to remove the scourge of Phillip Baker from the family forever. She'd gone back to school, earned her degree in art, and opened a studio. Having been successful in Seattle, she made a respectable living as a potter and established her name well enough to start teaching at Considine College in Kulshan County.

Jake also respected Evelyn for thinking outside the box on spirituality. Raised in a rigid Catholic home, she eschewed faith and began looking for greater meaning in her life after breaking free from her abusive husband. She began studying all sorts of religions and beliefs to open her mind to other possibilities. She studied all of them and attended the First Unitarian Church of Arrow Bay, though she confessed she was likely to leave the church soon, as she was moving more and more into Buddhism.

"How's the teaching going?" Gavin asked Evelyn.

"Very well," Evelyn said. "I've got some very talented students this year. You'd love Considine, Gavin."

"Aha!" Gavin cried. "They've gotten to you. Trying the old 'come up and teach at Considine and live closer' ploy."

"The boys are blameless," Evelyn said. "I was merely pointing out that you would find the atmosphere inviting at the college."

"I am sure I would," Gavin said. "There's just one little word that throws the whole thing off."

"Tenure," Jake said.

"You got it," said Gavin.

"Oh, rubbish, Gavin. You've got a PhD, you've published two collections of short stories and four books of poetry. They'd probably bend over backwards to give you tenure if you decided to make the jump," said Evelyn.

"We just can't pack up and leave San Francisco," said Gavin.

"Dunno why not," said Jason. "I did."

"Well, the truth is, I wouldn't mind coming back home at all, but we've got Jeff's family to consider," said Gavin a little too sharply.

"Don't lay this out on me again, Gavin."

"Come off it, Jeff, we both know that's exactly what it is. Your mother hates my guts and has been trying to split us up for nearly a decade," said Gavin. "We should move just to get away from her."

"Gavin, that's not exactly fair—" Jeff started.

"It *is* fair. Your useless brother and sister don't lift a goddamn finger around that place, leaving it all up to you to take care of everything. Every time we talk about moving, suddenly that woman comes down with a new ailment and needs your undivided attention." He looked at Evelyn and said, "I've been trying to get us away from there for the last four years, but every time it looks close, like we're really going to be able to get away from there, out comes another tentacle and we're dragged right back."

"Hey, guys, c'mon," said Sam.

"Gavin, that's not true!" Jeff snapped. "And I'd appreciate if you didn't discuss this anymore!"

"It is true, Jeff, and don't try to deny it. I've given up trying to get you out of there and have concentrated on making our lives as pleasant as possible, even though I have to deal with Eva Braun on Nob Hill trying to wreck our relationship every five months!"

Jeff's mouth snapped open, and he was about to launch into his partner when Rachel suddenly appeared in the doorway, looking resplendent in a red silk dress and black hat with a sprig of holly in the brim.

"Well, I can see as always my timing is impeccable! I've just endured another Parker Family Christmas of half-baked rolls, ham with so much salt in it that it makes the Dead Sea seem positively refreshing, and some sort of runny material that was supposed to be plum pudding," she said, flashing a dazzling smile. "God bless my mother, but she never learned how to cook. Budge up, Sam, I'm *starving*."

They finished their meal without any more tense moments. Afterward, Jake and Sam turned on Vince Guaraldi's music, and they exchanged gifts. Jason sat the exchange out, Barnaby curled up asleep in his lap. Jake watched him carefully for a while, not liking Jason's haunted look as he stared out the window.

As the evening approached and the light began to fade from the sky, Evelyn sat down next to Jake while Jeff, Sam, and Rachel started a spirited game of Trivial Pursuit. Gavin sat next to the fireplace, staring into the flames and saying nothing to anyone.

"You know how happy I am that you and my son have found one another," she said, patting Jake's knee.

"I know you are."

"You're a fine man, Jake. No parent could ask for a better companion for their child. Your brother, however, looks deeply troubled," she said.

"I know it," Jake said. "He's gone through some trouble recently."

"It's wavering around him like a flag in a fifty-knot gale," she said matter-of-factly. "I've made a suggestion to him, Jake, that I hope you don't find forward."

"My goodness, Evelyn, he's a little young, don't you think?"

Evelyn O'Conner picked up a pillow from the couch and swatted him with it. "You are incorrigible, you know that?" she said with a chuckle.

"I'm sorry. Go on."

"Well, Jason seems so lost. I'm glad you offered to let him stay here. He needs an anchor. In the meantime, I offered him the back room of my studio to use as a darkroom. I know they use mostly digital these days, but your brother has always been more of an artist than a photojournalist." She shrugged. "I thought it would be good for him, and he can use some of my gallery space to sell his prints."

"Thanks, Evelyn," said Jake, genuinely touched. "I really appreciate it. I'm sure Jason does as well."

"He thanked me profusely. I'm just happy I have the space down there," she said, turning her gaze back on Jake. "Now what is troubling you?"

"What do you mean?" Jake said, turning away.

"Jacob Allen Finnigan, you are the world's worst liar. You can't ever look anyone in the eye when you attempt to do it." She shook her head. "It's still that dead woman they found on your boat, isn't it?"

"Evelyn, it *is* Christmas after all."

"A holiday *I* do not celebrate, as you well know."

"Some of us do," Jake complained.

"What aren't you telling me?" she asked. "Has anything happened since the night someone ran you three off the road?"

"No," Jake said, cursing when he saw he was now looking at the floor.

"I know you don't want to worry me, which I appreciate…"

"I'm sensing a 'but' or 'however' here," said Jake.

"However, I don't think you've thought all this out."

"What do you mean?" Jake asked.

"You're in more danger than you'll ever know," Evelyn said, again fixing him with a look of steel. "I read that report in the *Examiner*. If the Kulshan County sheriff is covering this up, there's someone out there with a lot of influence and a bankroll to back it up." She sighed. "Have you ever considered *why* she was killed?"

"All the time. It's one of the things I want to find out."

She nodded. "Of course. Did you ever think that maybe it was *meant to be* that it was ruled suicide? That she was even killed in the first place?"

"Well, yeah. Wait, you're not saying this was *justified*, are you? I mean, she was shot in the head and dumped in the trunk of a rental car on *my* boat."

"Put yourself in the mind of the killer, Jake." She paused. "How would you have felt if it had been Adolf Hitler stuffed in that trunk?"

"You can't compare the two," Jake complained.

"Of course I can't. But you know how people's perceptions are warped with time and bitterness. Maybe she caused enough misery and suffering the likes of which few people have known. Maybe she caused wounds so deep they never healed. Left untended, those wounds get deeper and more infected," she said, sitting back.

Jake considered this for a moment. "She was no Little Mary Sunshine, that's for sure."

"Killings like these are extremely personal, Jacob. My feeling is the person who did this felt they were doing the world a favor." She shrugged. "Maybe they were right. From what I gather, Little Mary Sunshine, as you put it, was a nasty bit of work, and the world *is* a better place without her." She sat forward and looked Jake in the eye again. "I do not condone killing. I do not condone violence. I treasure all life. What happened to her was horrendous. Inexcusable. There is no justification for taking another human life." She thought. "Most of the time."

Jake's eyebrow shot up. "Most of the time?"

Evelyn shrugged. "Send me back in time to Vienna when a certain unknown man was not accepted into art school, having been found unacceptable as a painter. Knowing what he'd cause, I'd put a bullet in his head."

Jake watched her carefully, seeing something go cold in Evelyn's eyes, something clouded in memory. He could tell she was light years away from the soft brown sofa, her mind retracing a path.

"Sometimes certain people are better off dead. As sacred as I hold life, there are evil, evil people loose in this world." She blinked and smiled warmly. "But, as you said, it is Christmas. I think I will go back and get another glass of eggnog."

Jake watched her as she retreated into the kitchen in a whirl of green silk. He found himself thinking for the ten thousandth time that he'd probably never fully comprehend Evelyn O'Conner as long as he lived.

He sighed, getting up and striding over to the dining room table, resting his hands on Sam's shoulders, reading the Trivial Pursuit card in his hand. He glanced over at Jason, who was just accepting a glass of eggnog from Evelyn as she sat down beside him, absently patting Barnaby.

❖

Alfonso Lopez had just finished Christmas dinner with his close friend Andrea Bonner and was leaving for home so he could feed Little Pete, the canary he'd inherited from Susan Crane. His apartment, just across from Gasworks Park, would be warm and empty, as it was every night since Susan died. He decided to cut through the park. The evening was fairly warm and the rain had stopped; the alcohol he'd consumed at Andrea's house had left him feeling pleasantly mellow.

That stupid bird, he thought for the umpteenth time. *God* how he hated that bird. And it was only fitting Susan should leave the miserable thing to him. She knew he hated it.

If he hadn't felt somewhat guilty about Susan's death, he'd have let the damn bird out of the cage to fend for itself in Seattle. As it was, he kept coming back again and again to the last conversation he'd had with her the Friday night before she'd gone missing and ended up dead.

He'd been at home, trying to memorize some particularly obscure case reference in preparation for the bar exam when the phone rang. He'd let the machine pick it up, and only when he heard the tone of Susan's voice did he decide to answer.

"Alfonso, it's Susan. Look, I—I have to go away for the weekend. Something has come up that could be a real problem for me and I can't let this one go. Could you have someone check on Little Pete for me if I'm not back by Monday? This may take some time. I—I just have to do this, I—"

He'd snatched up the receiver. "Susan?"

"Alfonso. You're there."

"Where are you going?"

"To a place up north. We used to go there when we were kids. I—I—I—have to go. It's just—just..." she stammered, then seemed to calm herself. "It's business. That's all. I may not be back by Monday, though."

"What's this about? You sound strange."

She'd laughed. "Oh, this could solve a *lot* of problems, Alfonso," she'd said, a note of iciness slipping into her voice. *That* had sounded like the usual Susan. "I think after this weekend, I can put the *Outsider* behind me for good."

"Is that *wise*?" Alfonso had said. "You've got that idiot Bowman breathing down your neck, and the *Outsider* is the only thing that is keeping you safe."

"Shut up!" she'd hissed. "You think this line is secure? What the *hell* are you thinking? Christ, you're so stupid!"

He'd slowly fumed, gritting his teeth until it hurt. "Fine. Have a lovely weekend."

"My bird. Will you check on him?"

"Yes," he'd said angrily. "Although why don't you do us both a favor and not come back?" And he'd slammed down the phone.

Now she was dead. And all that was left of her was a stupid, annoying canary.

Still, the bird was a reminder of the old Susan. The one who'd defended him against the bogus claims the government had charged him with. Back then, Susan had a real love of the truth. She'd seemed to care about him, the case, and making a statement.

Now he wasn't so sure. He could see in retrospect it might have been a carefully constructed façade. Having decided to become a lawyer, he'd taken a great interest in his savior's career. Every rung she advanced on the ladder was always on the back of someone else.

Alfonso had often wondered why she'd kept him around. The words *boy toy* had been bandied about by his colleagues for quite some time. Little did anyone know that part of their relationship had been brief and unfulfilling.

"Bitch," he said aloud, the darkness of the park enfolding him. The lights from the street flickered through the trees, the mammoth steel structures of the old gasworks rising directly in front of him like rows of sharpened teeth.

Lopez scowled at the pavement. He'd also learned too late how the trail of destruction Susan left behind often swept up those around her. First it was the police, and then it was the investigator McEvoy snooping around and haranguing him. He'd seen him twice now, both times McEvoy making it abundantly clear that Lopez knew more than he was telling.

"I think you're lying to me, you little prick," McEvoy had said when confronting him in his office. "You know more than you're saying. I think you know exactly who iced this broad and you're keeping clammed up to protect your ass!"

"What do you think this is, some second-rate Raymond Chandler novel? 'Iced this broad'? Who writes your dialogue, Mr. McEvoy, and what Hollywood B film did they come from?"

"Listen, you little bastard," McEvoy had said. "I happen to know you got off on a technicality on your eco-terrorism charge. But how would you feel if I told you there was some *additional* information that might reopen the case?"

"I'd say you were unfamiliar with the term *double jeopardy*," said Lopez, feeling his stomach do a little flip-flop.

"Who says I'm talking about that?" said McEvoy, tossing a photo down on the table. "You're far from angelic, Lopez. I know all about that little incident in Sodo. They send people up for five to ten for that little trick, don't they?"

Lopez blanched at the photo, which had been taken from a surveillance video. His heart thudded loudly in his chest, sweat breaking out on his brow. He'd looked up at McEvoy and croaked, "Who the hell do you work for?"

"Never you mind that," said McEvoy. "Let's just say this isn't the only copy."

"What do you want?"

"Answers."

"What do you want to know?"

"Crane. What was she up to?"

"I don't know. She wouldn't tell me what. She said it was nothing." He looked up at McEvoy. "That's the *truth*. I swear it."

McEvoy seemed to consider this. "Did you believe her?"

"No," said Lopez. "It was all vague and ridiculous, the way she'd pull the cloak-and-dagger crap. I told her as much, too."

McEvoy grunted. "Who killed her?"

Lopez shook his head. "I don't know. So many people hated her."

"Any ideas?"

"A few. Jack Carpenter was on duty the night she was killed. Martin Gore hasn't left Florida in months. The faggot lawyer was in the hospital with appendicitis. Maybe Jeremy Young finally got his revenge."

"That seem likely to *you*? Could Young get the autopsy report covered up? How did Susan Crane know Sheriff Danvers?"

"I don't know that she did! Look, leave me alone! I've told you all I know!"

McEvoy eyeballed him harshly for several moments. "I doubt that. I'll be back," he had said, getting up to leave. "Oh, one other thing. Someone may call you about this. An interested party. Last name of Finnigan. Brush him off."

"Will you leave me alone if I do?"

McEvoy shrugged. "For now."

After the second encounter, the fat little bastard abruptly began popping up wherever Alfonso happened to be—the university,

Starbucks, the library. Everywhere he turned, McEvoy would be puffing away on a foul-smelling cigar.

He'd all but decided to go to the police about it until he remembered what exactly the name Susan Crane meant to the police department. Dead or alive, she was poison in their eyes; a blue-eyed malicious ice queen who had routinely badmouthed the department in the press and made them look like incompetent, racist fools. He'd have to ditch McEvoy on his own. If *only* he could figure out who the hell he was working for.

Lopez continued trudging through the rain-soaked grass of the park, the heavy, low clouds glowing orange from the lights of the city. Near the parking lot, he spotted a thickly built man dressed in a dark suit. As he drew nearer, he could see the man had heavy acne scars on his face. His black, beady eyes seemed to have no bottom in the street light. He was smoking a cigar, his foot up on the bumper of a black BMW.

McEvoy, Alfonso thought, thinking this had to be another one of his men.

"Amigo," the man called out.

Alfonso ignored him, starting to cross the deserted parking lot for his apartment building just across the street.

"Amigo," said the man again. "Hey, Alfonso, you want to know what happened to your little bitch friend?" he jeered.

Alfonso stopped dead in his tracks, rage filling him. He slowly turned around, walking rapidly back toward the man next to the BMW.

"What did you say?"

"You heard me," he said.

Alfonso nearly gagged at the stench of his breath. "What the hell are you talking about?"

"The dead reporter bitch," said the man, his fetid breath billowing in front of him in a white plume. "You want to know what happened to her? Or maybe you already know. Maybe you've been telling someone about it."

"Piss off," said Alfonso, turning to leave.

The man grabbed his arm, spinning him roughly around. *"Amigo,* don't turn your back on me. You tell me. What have you been saying?"

"Take your hand off me."

"What'd that dead reporter tell you?" the man asked.

"I said—" He trailed off, the glint of a knife in the man's hand flashing in his eyes. *Where the hell did that come from?* he thought. The man had been empty-handed only seconds before.

"You don't want to lie to me, *amigo*," said the man, his breath reeking of decaying molars and tobacco. "You tell me what she said to you."

Keeping his eye on the knife, he said, "Noth—nothing. She said nothing. She said she was leaving town. She wanted me to take care of her bird."

"What else?"

"That's it! I swear!"

"Keep your voice down, friend," cautioned the man. "You sure that's all she said?"

"Yes!"

"You wouldn't lie to me?"

"No!"

The man shook his head. "No, I think you're not telling me all she said. I think I'll stab your lying ass and let you lie here and bleed."

Alfonso swallowed. Any direction he'd try to run to, he'd be stabbed. He could only hope that someone might come by and save him. The way the man was standing, though, would shield the knife from any passerby. To the casual observer, it looked as if two friends were having a chat. It was Christmas night, near midnight, and *no one* was out.

"I'm not lying. She didn't say anything else."

"Maybe you forgot something? Maybe she told you where she was going?"

Alfonso shook his head emphatically. "No, no, no. She only said she was going north."

"She said that? North?"

"Yes," he said, nodding vigorously, hoping that what he said was appeasing the man. Alfonso searched his face, then saw with dread that the mention of the word *north* had hardened something in the man's eyes.

"North, she said? What else? Eh, *amigo*, what else?"

"N-n-n-nothing!" Alfonso stammered. "She said she was going north, that's all, and to feed her bird!" *That goddamn bird*, thought Alfonso. *Stupid goddamn bird!*

"North, that's all she told you," he said, lowering the knife.

"Yes! That's all. To some place she went as a kid."

It was the wrong thing to say, and he knew it once it was out. The man's eyes had widened, then grown icy.

"So she said that. You tell that to anyone?"

"No!"

"Just me?"

"Y-y-yes! J-j-just you!"

The man lowered the knife again. Alfonso watched it, like a cat observing a mouse move across the floor.

"You know what? I think you're telling me the truth."

Alfonso breathed a sigh of relief, eyes still fixed on the knife.

"You know what else, amigo?"

"What?"

"You've been watching the wrong hand."

Alfonso was aware of the flash of metal from the man's left hand as it leveled a .38 at the center of his forehead. Before Alfonso Lopez could utter a word, the man pulled the trigger, sending the bullet into his brain. He was dead before he hit the ground.

The man stepped back from Alfonso, walking around the body, avoiding the pool of blood. Glancing around to make sure no one was watching, he walked around the BMW, walking across the parking lot to where a stolen Buick lay in shadow. Opening the door with his gloved hand, he stepped into the car, started it, and pulled slowly out of the parking lot. A few minutes later he was crossing the University Bridge, where he flung the gun out the car window.

Whistling "Jingle Bells," the man slipped into the heart of the city unseen.

CHAPTER SEVENTEEN

December 26 dawned to a steady drizzle. Sam and Jake snuggled under the sheets for an hour after they awoke, the cats and Barnaby crowded onto the bed. Neither man wanted to break the spell and brave leaving the warmth and comfort under the sheets. Jake was enjoying his last few days of medical leave. Wednesday would bring the start of a new week and his first day back at the job since hurting his ankle.

Jake yawned, sliding the pillows up behind him. Dorothy gave him a disgusted look for disturbing the bed and hopped off. Sophia stretched luxuriously and yawned while Barnaby watched her with one eye open. Deciding no game was afoot, he went back to dozing.

"On the whole, not a bad Christmas," said Sam, kissing Jake on the cheek.

"Not bad at all," Jake agreed, kissing Sam back. "I'm glad Evelyn came."

"I'm glad Rachel showed up when she did," said Sam. "I hate it when Gavin and Jeff argue."

"That's because like us, it happens so infrequently. It's always a shock to see them angry with one another," Jake agreed.

"Do you smell something?" Sam asked.

Jake sat up, sniffing. "Bacon."

"Have we any bacon?"

"You can't have bacon burgers without bacon," Jake said, tickling Sam's ribs.

Sam giggled and pushed him away. "Listen you, stop it!"

Jake inhaled deeply. "You're right. It is bacon. And coffee."

"Sounds like breakfast to me," said Sam, getting out of bed. He was wearing sweats and a T-shirt, but still pulled on his robe.

"Must be Gavin," said Jake.

"Could be Rachel," mused Sam.

"Rachel cooks about once every second moon cycle," Jake said. "She's a fine cook, but she hates doing it, so I doubt it is her."

"Good point," said Sam. "Could be Jason, too."

"Could be. Jason is actually a good cook. He does unbelievable things with salmon and trout."

"You hate salmon and trout."

"My point exactly," said Jake. "He even makes a great mooseburger."

"I sometimes forget your brother is the great outdoorsman," Sam said. "Must have driven him crazy in San Francisco."

"Must have," said Jake, thinking back on his brother's words from the night before. *Something really,* really *bad happened.*

Jake suddenly became aware Sam had been talking to him for some time. He looked up from his woolgathering and said, somewhat chagrined, "I'm sorry. What, Sam?"

"I said I need to go down to the shipyard this week. We're finalizing the plans, and if all goes well, we'll lay the keel plates for the new boat sometime after the first of the year."

"Good," said Jake.

Sam looked at him, exasperated. "You're eight million miles away, Jacob."

"I'm sorry Sam. It's just anxiety."

"About?"

"I'm not sure." He looked into Sam's soulful brown eyes and shrugged. "Okay, Jason."

"I thought as much," said Sam, sitting back on the bed. "You want to talk about it?"

"You mean other than it seems like he's done a one-eighty overnight?"

"Ah, well, it's not overnight, is it?" said Sam, ruffling Jake's hair. "You haven't really spoken to Jason in several years. My advice is to cut him some slack and just let him talk when he's ready."

Jake snorted derisively. "With Jason, that'll be at a glacial pace. Could be a year or more."

"Patience, my fine feathered friend," said Sam, rising and heading out the bedroom door. "For Rome was not built in a day."

"The cliché police are going to come after you," said Jake, hopping up and joining Sam.

They slipped down the stairs quietly and stepped into the kitchen, where Jason was just pulling the bacon out of the frying pan.

Rachel, Gavin, and Jeff sat at the butcher's block table. Gavin and Jeff were dressed, but Rachel sipped coffee in her blue silk robe, her hair pulled up in a ponytail. "I just *love* a man who can cook," she said with a smile as they entered.

"Who doesn't?" asked Jeff.

"Amen to that," said Jake.

"You're a good cook, Rachel," said Gavin, stretching. "Your mac and cheese is legendary."

"Grandma's mac and cheese," she said, waving a dismissive hand. "I just don't like to cook. Which is why I love a man who does."

"Me too," said Sam, pouring himself a cup of coffee. "Jake?"

"You have to ask?"

"Sorry, sorry," Sam said. "Clearly I was out of line."

"Just give me the damn cup," said Jake in mock irritation, making the group laugh.

"I thought the smell of bacon might wake you up," said Jason. "I've never known Jake to pass up a piece of bacon in his life."

"Oh, no," said Jake. "There was the one awful place outside of Forks, remember?"

"Oh, you're right!" Jason said, setting the pan down. "I swear to God that bacon was blue."

"I think it tried to crawl off the plate when I poked it with my fork," said Rachel.

"I can't believe we paid for that meal," Jake said, shaking his head. "I'm glad you made it in time for dinner last night," he said, turning toward Rachel.

"Me too," she said. "Mom's cooking is getting worse, I swear." She looked at Sam. "I had a good talk with your mother. What is wrong with your sister?"

"I wish I knew," Sam said, shaking his head. "Why, what'd Mom tell you?"

"Not much, just that the pace of phone calls had been increasing, and she keeps bringing up your father," she said, looking at Sam. "Sorry."

"You can bring him up, even if he was a bastard," Sam said.

"Anyway, it seems Nora is poking into the family history," said Rachel. "And Evelyn can't figure out why. She seems disturbed by it."

"Anything other than your father dubious, Sammy?" Gavin asked.

"Not to my knowledge," said Sam. "Other than a propensity for a lot of gay uncles, we're all pretty straight."

"If you'll pardon the expression," said Jake and Sam in unison. They sipped their coffee in time as well.

Jason stared at them. "Damn," he said. "That's just eerie."

"It's cute," said Rachel. "In kind of a creepy way."

"You didn't have to do this, Jason," Jake said, ignoring them both.

Jason scooped out eggs and bacon onto their plates. "I know. I just wanted to is all. So I went down to the store and bought the bacon and the newspaper and decided to make breakfast. I was up already, after all."

"Early?" asked Jake.

"Since five," answered Jeff.

"Sorry, guys. Did I wake you?"

"Not this one," said Gavin, jerking a thumb at his partner. "He's always up with the Guernseys. He was up and packed before I'd taken my first pis—urination break for the day."

"God, whatever for?" said Rachel, snapping a piece of bacon in half. "Mmm, cremated. Perfect."

"You, like dear brother over there, always have liked your bacon all but cindered to a crisp," said Jason. "And just up out of habit. Your best light for photographing things is in the morning. Even on gloomy days like this."

"That's true. And this is the *only* way bacon is good," Rachel said. "Any other way brings back the horror of blue bacon and Forks."

"Forks isn't all bad," Jason said. "Good fishing."

"That isn't always a sterling recommendation," said Jake. "Jason, Evelyn told me about her offer to you yesterday. Are you taking her up on it?"

"What offer?" asked Gavin.

"Studio space and room for a darkroom, though I'm doing less and less with film these days," he said. "And I am going to take her up on it. It'll help me get back on my feet, artistically speaking. I haven't touched my equipment in a while."

"Oh, ow," Rachel said.

"Ow?" Jason asked.

"You know how hard it is for me not to say something about that comment?"

"Thank God I wasn't the only one thinking it," said Gavin, getting up to pour himself another cup of coffee.

Jason rolled his eyes. "I'm glad there are things I can always depend on. One of them being this motley crew of friends I've got," he said, a look of sadness creeping into his eyes.

"Damn straight," Rachel replied, taking another bite of bacon.

"You know you can stay here as long as you like, right?" Jake said.

"If you don't mind having me. It would really help me out."

"We'd love to have you, Jason," Sam said.

Barnaby trotted into the kitchen, Sophia and Dorothy trailing behind him. The cats made separate journeys to the litter box and food dish. Barnaby looked up at Sam expectantly.

"This is horrible, horrible stuff, dog."

Barnaby continued his long stare at Sam, He looked at his bowl, then back to Sam.

"Oh very well. *One* piece," he said, tossing a broken bit of bacon to the beagle. Barnaby crunched happily, then trotted out the dog flap.

"You spoil him," Jake chided.

"Oh, as if you don't."

"I didn't say that," said Jake.

"Good eggs, Jason," said Rachel.

"Very," said Jake, taking a large gulp of coffee. He picked up the paper, frowning. "I didn't think the *Examiner* came out before Wednesday."

"It doesn't," said Sam. "That's probably loaded with after-Christmas specials."

Jake opened the front page. His eyes caught the headline, making him swallow his coffee wrong. He coughed violently, choking and gasping for air.

"Jake!" cried Sam. "Are you okay?"

He nodded that he was fine, jabbing the paper with his index finger. "There...there..." he said between spasms.

Sam grabbed the *Arrow Bay Examiner* from Jake. Jason, Rachel, Jeff, and Gavin leaned in to see the headline, sprawled across the front of the paper in block letters was the headline SUSAN CRANE MURDERED.

The story, written by Derek Brauer, went into depth about the disappearance of the county coroner and the allegations against the sheriff of Kulshan County, including how he had given the orders to cover up her homicide. Jake's head reeled at the fact that everything he suspected about the case was suddenly being spelled out in black and white.

"Jake, what is it? You're white as a sheet," said Jason.

"What the hell is going on?"

"Jake," Sam said, handing the paper back. "You realize what this means?"

"It means it goes a whole hell of a lot deeper than we thought," said Jake, holding his head.

"Like hip-wader deep in a very brown and unpleasant stream," Rachel said.

"Damn! With everything that was happening last night, I forgot to tell you!" said Jason, sitting down next to his brother.

"What?" Rachel asked.

"Right after it happened, I mentioned to Jake I probably knew someone who knew something about Susan Crane. The name stuck with me, and I wasn't sure why."

"And?" the group asked him at once.

"My friend at the *Times* heard Susan Crane was going to get canned by the *Outsider*."

"Not exactly surprising," said Rachel. "Given the caliber of her stories had diminished so greatly."

"My friend also said Crane had been put up at the *Outsider*'s publishing headquarters in a really plush office, which struck everyone as strange because as far as anyone knew, she didn't have a job there."

"I've been there," said Jake. "And I talked to her former editor. He said the same thing."

"Did he mention she had suddenly come into scads of money?" Jason asked.

"No," Jake said.

Jason nodded. "New car. New clothes. New jewelry. Talk of purchasing a condo in California. My friend said it could have all been bullshit, at least the part about the condo. The jewelry was real, though."

Jake looked at Sam and Rachel, knowing the same thing was going through their minds at once: *blackmail*.

"This reporter says he's seen the original coroner's report, and it says clearly she was murdered," Sam said, returning to the article. "I wonder where he got it?"

"Knowing Derek, he was able to ferret it out on his own," Jason said.

"You know him?" Jake asked.

Jason nodded. "Yeah. He and I worked together at the *Chronicle*. After…" He dismissed the rest with a shrug. "Derek said he needed a change."

"I *knew* I knew that name!" said Jeff.

"San Francisco to Arrow Bay is one hell of a change," Gavin remarked, incredulous.

"A *major* change," Jason agreed.

"The coroner's gone missing," said Jake.

"I saw that," said Rachel glumly. "Well, Alex said Crane wasn't a nice person. We knew that already."

"She must have been into something *rotten* in order for the Kulshan County Sheriff's Office to want to cover it up," Gavin said. "Can you all please note my concern again?"

"Noted," said Sam.

"The sheriff," Rachel corrected, looking at Gavin. "Not *necessarily* the department, which this Derek Brauer is quick to point out. He also notes the state was already looking into the case after a complaint from the deputy sheriff."

"You're right," said Jake, slumping back into his chair.

"Everyone's heard the rumors," grumbled Sam. "On the take with drug money, covering up or losing records. How does the SOB keep getting elected?"

Gavin grunted and said, "Please, Sam, it's politics."

"You're too cynical for your own good," Jeff said, rubbing Gavin's back. "I love you for it."

"Well, it's a little more simple than pure politics," said Jake.

"How so?" asked Gavin.

"The last two election cycles, Danvers ran unopposed," said Jake with a sigh. "Sounds like the deputy sheriff—" His head shot up. "What did you say?"

"I said, 'How does the SOB keep getting elected.'"

"No, not you. Rachel. Before that. About Alex."

Rachel's blue eyes radiated confusion. "He said she wasn't a nice person. Said he'd known her…somehow, I forget, and she was one to steer clear of."

Jake felt his face go rigid, his jaw clamped tightly.

"Jake, are you okay?" Sam asked.

"I'm going to go down and work out now," he said, rising. "I need to think."

Without saying another word, Jake rose from the table and went down into the basement.

"What was that all about?" Jason asked.

"I don't know," Sam said.

"Whatever it is, he's upset," said Gavin.

"I think I might know," said Rachel, looking at them all with deep concern.

❖

Jake slipped out of the house after his workout, making a pretext of stopping by the library. Jason, Gavin, Jeff, and Rachel watched him with completely doubtful expressions, but Sam ignored it. He knew that if something was up, Jake would tell him in time. Jason offered to go with Jake, but Jake abruptly said no and left without another word.

"What was all that about?" Jason asked, once the electric blue PT Cruiser had backed out of the drive and slipped down High Street.

"I'm not entirely sure," said Sam. "Sadie?"

"Um," she said. "I think you know."

"Alex," said Sam, shaking his head. "Son of a sea cookie," he said angrily.

"You know, Sam, I've never been sure which is more disturbing," Gavin said. "Your self-censorship or what you substitute your curse words with."

Sam looked over at Rachel. "You still think I should trust him?"

Rachel sighed, shaking her head. "My gut feeling is, yes. Hey, don't give me that look," she said to Sam.

"Come on, Rachel. He lied to Jake about knowing Susan Crane!"

"Remember when I said Alex had a lot of regrets about a wild and misspent youth? Things he was deeply ashamed of? If you knew or had anything to do with that viper, would *you* happily admit it?" she asked.

"Well," Sam groused. "No. Probably not."

"And if you were worried about your friend poking his nose into a murder, would you encourage that or discourage that, knowing how potentially dangerous the woman was?"

Sam said nothing, knowing she had a point again.

"I have clearly been away far too long," said Jason, feeling left out.

Sam sighed. He looked over at Jason and said, "You get settled in okay?"

"We'll be out of your way this afternoon, Jason," said Gavin.

"Don't rush off on my account," said Jason. "It's great to see you guys again."

"Unfortunately, we've got some obligations to take care of tomorrow," said Gavin, rolling his eyes. "Otherwise, we'd stay until New Year's like we always do."

"Not happy obligations, I take it?" Jason asked.

Jeff blushed. "I promised my mother I'd help her out with some things around the house."

Gavin took in a deep breath and let it out slowly. "Of course she knew we'd be up here."

"Stop it, you two," Rachel warned. "I will *not* have two of my favorite people fighting. Too much is going on right now, and we need to focus on the events at hand."

"Okay, but I wish we were staying around for that reason," said Gavin. "Jake has a tendency to…"

"Rush into things," Sam finished. He took Gavin's hand and gave it a squeeze. "I could use your influence around here."

"Please, Sam, you're just as bad as Jake," said Gavin. "You want to figure this out as much as he does. It's written all over your face."

"It's gotten Jake so upset, how can I not? I want it to end," Sam growled.

"I can't blame you," Gavin agreed, looking at Jason. "I'm glad you're back, J.D."

"Me too, though I don't want to be any trouble to these guys," he said.

"You won't be," said Sam, frowning as Barnaby made eyes at the cats' food. "No, Barnaby," he said, before returning his attention to Jason. "But while we're on the subject of things being out of kilter, is everything okay with you?"

"Better," he said, vaguely. "Not perfect, but it will be. I'm glad Jake has a big heart."

"He's missed you terribly, you know," said Sam.

Jason nodded. "I know. I've missed him, too. If I hadn't been so self-centered the last…well, decade," he said, then looked at Sam and laughed. "Some of us grow up more quickly than others. Jake…"

"Jake's been about a hundred and seventeen years old since birth," said Sam, knowing what Jason was about to say.

"Light years ahead of me," Jason agreed. "It's not easy for a Finnigan to admit they're wrong."

"Really? I had no idea," said Sam, unable to hide the grin.

"Me either," said Rachel.

"Yeah, you're not very transparent on that issue," said Gavin, rolling his eyes again.

"Ha. You're all too aware of it, I am sure," said Jason.

"As the relative newcomer to this group, even I know that," said Jeff.

"Barnaby, *no.*"

The beagle looked up from Dorothy and Sophia's dish and wagged his tail once, then went back to staring at the mushy mess of cat food.

"What is wrong with you anyway?" Sam asked the dog, walking over to inspect his bowl. The contents of Barnaby's dish had been tipped over. "Oh, I see. Well, that's what you get for harassing the cats." He grabbed a broom from the cupboard and swept up the kibble, tossing it into the neighboring trash can. "Picky little bugger won't eat his food if it has been on the floor."

"Over the last year I've had to do a lot of…well…" Jason hesitated, looking at Gavin.

"Oh, say it, J.D. It's clichéd, but it's been drilled into our heads for the last thirty years—'soul searching,'" he said.

Sam turned his attention to the beagle after refilling his dish. "You do that again and you can just eat off the floor. I'm not about to put up with a haughty dog. I've seen you drink out of the toilet, don't forget."

Barnaby somehow managed to look sheepish for a moment before he buried his head in his food bowl, happily munching kibble.

"Right," said Jason. "I've made some pretty hideous mistakes that I'm trying to atone for, I guess."

"Good Catholic word, that," said Sam. "Go on."

"I just realized sometimes family is all you can count on," said Jason.

"God help us," said Gavin under his breath.

"I heard that," said Jeff.

"Boys," Rachel warned again.

Sam smiled at Jason and said, "Jake hadn't ever given up on you, not really. None of us had."

"You had every right to."

"Jake never does," Rachel said. "Not with the people he loves and cares about."

"Heck, Jason," said Sam. "He still loves Amy, after all."

Jason laughed. "Very true."

"I'm not so sure about Hector Sugg though," said Rachel winking at him.

"I'm right there with him on that one," said Jason. He turned back to Sam and said, "I'm sorry, you guys."

Sam held up a hand. "Jason, I don't want you to worry about it. You've apologized. We've accepted it. What's more important to us—and I think I can speak for your brother as well—is that you be happy."

"Keep working things out and keep *growing*," said Gavin. "Part of changing the things that drag us down into unhappiness is to recognize them and not beat ourselves up over them. Stopping that cycle of negative feelings is a big, positive step."

"I love it when you talk like a Buddhist," said Jeff, kissing Gavin on the cheek.

"I *am* a Buddhist," said Gavin. "But that's one of those life lessons that applies to everyone." He smiled. "I can tell just by looking at you that you've changed."

"You mean I'm not so damned buttoned up and stuffy," said Jason.

"Well, I wouldn't have described it *quite* like that," Sam said.

"I would have," Rachel said. "You weren't nearly so bad in high school. Call it a case of temporary insanity."

"You aren't kidding there," Jason replied.

"I can tell you're a lot more relaxed," said Sam.

Jason loaded up the dishwasher and Sam finished reading the *Examiner*.

"The murder thing, you're not telling me everything," said Jason after he'd put the last dish into the machine.

"Whatever do you mean?" Rachel asked.

"You mean aside from the nose poking remark?" Jason asked, looking at Rachel, who batted her eyelashes at him. "God, if I wasn't sure before, I am *now*," he said. "What else has happened?"

"I don't know what you're talking about," said Sam, hiding his face with the paper.

"Credit me with a little intelligence, you two. I can see it in your faces that there's a lot more going on."

"Not up to me to say," said Gavin. "Though I would like to know what was up with his 'going to the library' story."

"Oh, I've no doubt Jake's going to the library," said Sam.

"How do you know?" asked Jeff.

"Ah," said Gavin, catching on. "He wasn't looking at his shoes when he said it."

"Exactly," said Sam smiling wickedly. "I'd also like to know what he's going to tell me when he gets back from wherever he's gone. It's the day after Christmas—the library is closed."

"Ha," said Rachel. "As if you didn't know."

"This would be the Alex person you were talking about? Isn't he a writer or something? I know Jake has mentioned him before." Jeff asked.

"Alex Blackburn," said Gavin. "Of *the* Blackburns. You see the name painted on all the train cars."

"Oh, *those* Blackburns. I've heard some unpleasant things about them," said Jeff. "I bet Mom knows them."

"I wouldn't be at all surprised," said Gavin under his breath, making Rachel snicker.

"Don't change the subject," said Jason. "Or are you not going to tell me?"

Sam sighed, putting the paper down. "You know your brother. You know how he gets if there's something annoying him. When the sheriff ruled Crane's death a suicide, he—"

"Went ballistic."

Sam winced at the choice of words, Susan Crane's fate on his mind. "Exactly," he agreed. "So, being Jake he—"

"—took it upon himself to find out what really happened. Just like high school all over again."

"Chris Aponte," said Rachel and Gavin in unison.

"Yes. Though he was easier to stonewall at seventeen. I thought he'd let go of that," said Jason.

"He's gotten better about it, but not over it," said Gavin.

"No, you're right," Sam agreed. "I sometimes wonder if that is even possible."

Jason sat down at the table, concern now etched on his face. "Sam, the car accident…that wasn't an accident, was it?"

Rachel cleared her throat and looked the other way.

"Subtle, Miss Crawford," said Gavin, amused.

Sam faced Jason. "It wasn't. I think someone wanted to scare us off. Jake had been poking around a bit into Crane's past, talking to a few people."

"*Jake* had?" Rachel said, giving Sam a skeptical look.

"Well, okay," Sam said. "We all have been a bit."

Gavin shook his head and said, "It's contagious, apparently."

Jason shrugged. "Well, that's Jake. Can you honestly say you'd expect any less, Gavin?"

"No," Gavin confessed. "I don't approve, however. I'm scared shitless. Sorry, Sam."

"No need, I'm right there with you," Sam agreed. "But we're through the looking glass on this one."

"Jake's head would be exploding from all the clichés uttered here in the last hour," Rachel said, a wry smile on her face.

"What you're saying is, even if this Susan Crane was as bad as you say she was," Jeff said, "it doesn't matter."

"No," said Sam. "Because Jake wants the killer caught."

"To make up for not being able to do anything about Chris Aponte," Rachel finished.

"God help us," Gavin sighed.

Jake drove directly to Alex's condo, walking up the stairs to his front door, where he knocked with too much force, rattling the door on its hinges. He wasn't even sure if Alex was home, even though the Jag was in its parking spot.

A few seconds passed, and he heard the pop of the deadbolt sliding and the door opened on a hollow-eyed, disheveled Alexander Blackburn, dressed in a rumpled, stained suit that looked as if he'd slept in it for several days. His hair was completely askew, his face ruddy and his eyes bloodshot. Jake pushed past him without saying a word. He closed the door behind them.

"Well Jake, what brings you here this fine Boxing Day?"

"You lied to me."

Alex looked at the floor.

Jake stared at Alex coldly. "You knew her."

"Knew who?" Alex said, not meeting Jake's eyes.

"Cut the bullshit, Alex. You knew Susan Crane."

"Yes, I did."

"Why did you lie to me?"

"I don't know," he said slumping onto the couch. "No, that's not true. I didn't want you to get hurt."

"Try again, Alex," snapped Jake. "That may be part of the reason, but that isn't all of it," he said, sitting down beside Alex. "God damn it,

Alex! I trusted you! I consider you a friend, and if I can't trust you—"
He studied Alex sharply.

"I had other considerations," Alex said slowly, meeting Jake's
gaze.

"What?"

"I had some concerns about how other people might be affected."

"You considered other people? There's a switch," Jake said. "I
wasn't aware other people crossed your orbit, Alex."

"That's not fair," he said, his voice shaking.

"Oh it's completely fair. I've defended you for years, Alex, and
yet when I really need you, everything everyone tells me about you is
proven correct."

"Everyone?" he asked, brow raised. "You mean Rachel."

"I mean what I said."

"Now who's bullshitting who, Jake? But I'm not surprised. Rachel
could see right through me. A very admirable trait, I might add," he
said, rubbing the excess moisture out of his eyes.

"Dammit, Alex," Jake said, sighing. "Tell me the truth. Why did
you lie to me?"

"Because my past is *ugly*, Jake. I've done a lot of things I'm not
proud of. For a long time I was more like my father than I ever wanted to
admit. I could be ruthless. I could easily step on or over people without
giving a second thought to it. If I had a conscience, I've no idea where
it was," he said sadly. "My heart has never been good, Jake. Even the
stuff I've done for whatever environmental causes—hell, I've always
had less than altruistic motives. They were all about revenge. All about
getting back at my father." He shook his head. "Meeting you and Sam
showed me that there was still some good in the human race. I'd given
up on people. Everyone that crossed my path was out for themselves,
for their own agenda. I know it sounds hackneyed, but it's true."

"Go on," said Jake.

"You two were different. You both gave me hope in people, but
more than that, in *myself*. You were the only people in my life who
showed me true honesty and conviction were not just something
ascribed to a character in a book. They were real and still could be
found! You've no idea how that astonished me. For the longest time I
tried to figure out if it was some sort of act. I realized it wasn't."

"I've only ever been myself, Alex."

"I know," he said. "And you are loyal, honest, and truthful. You've
no idea just how rare those qualities are," he said.

"You've just been hanging out with the wrong people, Alex," said Jake. "I'm surrounded by a lot of people who are exactly like that."

"I've slowly come to realize that and have been maneuvering myself out of the pit of vipers I used to associate with. One by one, I've had to sever the ties to the people in my life who were every bit as false as I was." He looked up at Jake and smiled tiredly. "And I've tried to *mean* everything I've said. Everything I *do*. I shoved all the bitterness and vengeance I felt toward my bastard of a father in one direction, one channel to try and free myself and make things pure. I'm so close, Jake, so close," he said, the exhaustion evident in his voice.

"That's all good and well, Alex, but I still don't understand why you felt you had to *lie* to me. When have I ever given you the slightest indication I've ever given a shit about your past? Haven't I always said I'm more concerned with the man I see today than what happened when you were twenty or whenever?"

"I'm sorry, Jake. You're right of course, I *should* have known better. Susan Crane, though…" He took a shuddery breath. "Susan Crane brought me back to a particularly black period in my life," He shook his head. "God, that evil bitch! Even *dead* her poison spreads. I've allowed her to pollute my relationship with you and Sam, and that hurts me even more."

"Alex," Jake said, taking a deep breath to steady his patience. "For the eleven thousandth time, whatever you've done in your past doesn't bother me in the least. It is who you've become, who you are *now* that matters. Sometimes it takes a long while to find our way and become who we're meant to be. Sometimes the journey there sucks and has a lot of bad in it. It doesn't matter to me, Alex. I love you for who you are *now*, for the man you've become in the eight odd years I've known you."

"You really mean that, don't you?"

"Have I once ever said anything I don't mean?"

Alex chuffed again, looking at his feet. "No, not you. Jake Finnigan is a man of his word, proud and true." He laughed. "You're a damn anomaly in the world today."

"I guess I was just brought up right," he said, and they laughed.

"Someday I'm going to tell you both my whole dark past, Jake."

"We'll be there to listen," Jake said. "It's what friends do."

Alex arched an eyebrow. "You're sure you can handle it?"

"Alex," Jake said. "As my grandmother used to say, 'It's a perilous thing to underestimate a Finnigan.' Do *not* underestimate me. You know better. Don't be afraid to tell us anything. We're your *friends*, we can handle it. I mean what I say." He turned back and looked at Alex. "You are a *good* man. I wouldn't be around you if you weren't."

"I know," said Alex quietly. "Rachel said the same thing. It gives me hope. As for Susan Crane, you've certainly done enough research on your own to find out what happened to people who crossed her."

"Have I ever."

"Ever since the suicide ruling…" He sighed. "A part of me hoped it would stick. It would have buried her. Sometimes the dead are best left buried," he said, rising. He stared out at the rain-swept view of Arrow Bay and the refinery, then looked at Jake and smiled. "I forgot how single-minded you can be at times."

"I'd be insulted by that if it weren't true," said Jake dryly.

"I got scared. I knew you weren't going to let it go." Alex shook his head. "I gave it to the head of security at the company," he said sheepishly. "You know I honestly and truly don't give a damn about my wealth. It *does*, however, have some advantages. Blackburn's security force is second only to the Secret Service, in my opinion."

"Blackburn security! *That's* who's been following me!"

Alex chuckled. "You've given poor McEvoy a run for his money. Remind me to compliment Sam on getting one of his associates pulled over."

"He's lucky that's all that happened," Jake said, a little annoyed.

"Well, you were a little too good at ditching him. Although the three of you getting run off the road and nearly killed the night we had dinner was *my* fault. I should have been watching you guys."

"Alex, you couldn't be with us *every* second."

"No, I realize that. I never, ever thought that anything would happen. Not with me right there. I'll never forgive myself."

"You couldn't have known what was going to happen."

"I *should* have anticipated something was going to happen!" Alex said angrily. "You saw the story in today's paper?"

"Oh yes."

"I gave the reporter the scoop. McEvoy dug up all the information."

"Why give it to the *Examiner*?" asked Jake, curious.

"Kind of as a favor. The paper has been struggling. The reporter has been the only one even interested in the story since the Seattle papers dropped it," said Alex. "You'll be pleased to note that all the major papers have picked up the story since our little fish wrapper published a special edition today."

"Well, that's good. The more light on this, the better."

"That was part of my reason for doing it. This thing is bigger than I ever thought, and now *this*," Alex said, handing the paper to Jake.

"What? I saw all this—"

Alex shook his head. "No, no. This is in the *Times*. Page four. Near the bottom."

Jake scanned the paper. Down at the bottom was a small headline: *Man Found Slain in Gasworks Park*. He read through it quickly. "I'm not sure I understand."

"It doesn't say in the paper who it was, but that was Susan Crane's buddy Lopez. Shot in the head. No witnesses to speak of, but the man who found the body shortly after it happened remembers seeing a heavy-set Hispanic man in the vicinity earlier."

Jake felt his blood run cold. "I just talked to Lopez."

"Did he tell you anything?"

"Other than to bugger off, no. He did tell me I was barking up the wrong tree with Martin Gore and Arnold Witcher. He didn't say anything about the cops, though. Nunamaker and Kelly."

"In that regard, he was correct. Their alibis all check out, according to McEvoy."

"He said the story she was working on was nothing."

"More than that. There *is* a Jack Bowman, but he had nothing to do with Susan Crane. The story she was working on for the *Outsider* was about a man who didn't exist. McEvoy didn't know what she was cooking up, but something wasn't right there."

"How about her ex? Or the guy she sued for harassment. Young."

"After all these years, I can't quite imagine it. You never know, though. Jeremy Young seems harmless."

"So did Lizzie Borden," said Jake.

"She was acquitted, don't forget," Alex pointed out.

"I feel slightly sick," said Jake. Something flickered in the back of his mind. "Read me that part about the description of the man leaving the park."

"'The witness described the person of interest as being a heavy-set man approximately five foot ten with black hair and a dusky complexion.'"

Jake's mind raced back to the day they had found Susan Crane, how he had run into a heavy-set man with black hair who had cursed in Spanish and rushed off. "We've seen him, Alex. Sam and I."

"Where?"

"I saw him on the boat. I saw him on the day we found Susan Crane's body. We saw him at the Cliff House."

Alex was shaking his head. "Coincidence? I don't think so. Whoever this guy is, he's a paid thug, pure and simple. My bet is he's being bankrolled well." He shuddered. "Something did happen that was odd. The Thursday before she was killed," Alex started slowly, "I got a call from her. Out of the blue. I hadn't heard from her in years—by choice, mind you. I was in Seattle, I got the message on my machine when I came back. She sounded weird. Nervous. She said she'd like to talk about something that 'only I would understand' and that she'd call back. I erased it, figuring she was either going to try to blackmail me or ask for something. I put it out of my mind, having no intention of ever speaking to her again. I'm not even sure how the hell she got my phone number. Then on Friday, she turns up dead."

"What did she have on you, Alex?" Jake asked.

Alex stepped away from the window, slumping back on the sofa. "I don't know what she might have *thought* she had on me. She told my father I was having an affair with his partner's wife." He looked up at Jake and shrugged. "I was. It was brief and not particularly memorable. I think Elaine and I were both doing it out of revenge," he said, looking away again. "I told you I wasn't proud of my past."

"Why'd she do it?"

"Huh?" said Alex, breaking out of his reverie. "Oh. She wanted some documents my father had. Pertaining to what, she never did say. She managed to get them, though. That's why I can't figure out why the hell she'd call me. Unless she wanted me snooping in Dad's files again."

Jake glanced at his watch. "I'm sorry, Alex, I should be going."

"I understand," said Alex.

He looked at Alex, his handsome face marred by dark circles under his eyes, his hair unkempt and falling into his eyes. "Look, Alex, I'm sorry about what I said."

"I deserved it." He shrugged. "I've been a fundamentally selfish person the greater part of my life. I'm trying to change that, but it's a hard habit to break. Just don't give up on me yet." He looked into Jake's malachite eyes. "Please."

Jake buttoned up his coat as Alex walked him to the front door. He stopped long enough to give his friend a hug. "I haven't yet, you dope. Be careful."

"You too," he said. "I'm honored to call you both my friends. Maybe Rachel as well in time."

"You've already got a good friend there. She's been defending you ever since she met you at the Cliff House."

"Really?" he asked.

"Rachel has an unerring instinct for people," said Jake, frowning. "Except when it comes to the ones she dates most of the time."

"I don't know what I did to deserve that, but thank her for me."

Jake smiled wryly. "Thank her yourself. But don't be too extravagant. She's not impressed by that kind of thing."

"So noted," Alex said. "Thanks, Jake. I'm sorry."

"Quit being so damn hard on yourself," he said, giving Alex another hug.

"Thanks," he repeated in a hoarse whisper.

Jake smiled and went out the door, leaving Alex to stare at his back until he was gone. Alex then shut the door, seeming to lose all his strength in the act. He slumped against it, feeling as though he'd not have the energy to get to the couch. He stumbled over to it, landing with a sigh of cushions around him, whispering secrets.

After a few minutes passed, he stood up with a start. Alex pulled himself together with a shuddery breath, straightening up to his full height. He walked stalwartly into his office, sat behind his desk, and went about the business of bringing down his father's company.

CHAPTER EIGHTEEN

The year dwindled down, as did Jake's remaining time off. Jake disliked returning to work for the ferry system, his blue funk exacerbated by the departure of Gavin and Jeff. Added to it, the gloomy specter of Susan Crane would be weighing on his mind as he approached the *Elwha* every morning.

The morning he went back to work, he stopped by Rachel's room to find her on the phone with someone in Washington. As soon as he came in, she told the person on the other end of the line to hold.

"You're staying until after New Year's, right?" Jake asked.

"Please. Miss New Year's and Sam's legendary crab cakes? Perish the thought."

"Good," said Jake. "I just think it's…" He shrugged. "Important. Don't ask me why."

"No need to," she replied. "And if it makes you feel any better, I'm talking with someone right now about listing my condo for sale."

That news had cheered him considerably.

Jake tromped downstairs, mulling things over in his mind. He went into the kitchen to get some coffee and found Sam at the butcher's block table, reading through the *Seattle Times*.

"Good morning, handsome," he said. "Did you accidentally knock over Barnaby's food this morning?"

"No. He probably did it tearing after the cats," Jake said, hugging his partner from behind and taking a deep breath. Jake enjoyed the amalgam of scents emanating from his partner: strawberry shampoo, Irish Spring, Obsession Night, and the slightly erotic and arousing musky scent that was simply part of Sam. He breathed this in deeply, taking solace in its familiarity, finding himself thinking how lucky he was.

"Not that I am complaining, but what was that for?"

"Just letting you know I appreciate you."

"That's nice," he said as Jake joined him at the table.

"Rachel's listing her condo."

"Good," Sam replied.

"I know you know how much I've wanted her back here."

"*We've* wanted her back here, Tiger. As you know that I know that you know how much we've both wanted her back here."

"Always the comedian."

"I've got a two-cup advantage on you, which I suppose isn't fair," Sam said.

"No, it isn't," he said. "Jason about?"

"I think he already left. He made mention of the light being good and thought he'd take some photos up at Panama Hat," Sam said.

"It's nice to have him back, too."

Sam nodded. "It is. I've always thought of Jason like a brother. I know he feels bad about what happened."

"Water under the draw span," said Jake, sighing.

"You don't want to go back to work, do you," Sam said. It wasn't a question.

"No," Jake said. "Aside from the prospect of seeing Fred Phillips again, I dislike the idea of going back to that boat."

"Can't blame you," Sam said with a dismissive grunt. "Try not to blame the boat. It wasn't the *Elwha*'s fault, after all."

"I know," he said. "There's also the fact…"

"Short timer's syndrome?"

Jake nodded. "I didn't get any time to write, even with my being laid up with my ankle. I know it's only a few more months, but still…"

"Hang in there, Tiger," said Sam, tousling Jake's hair. "You'll get there."

❖

Dusk was already descending by the time he reached the Washington State Ferry Terminal at Arrow Bay, and the *Elwha* was in Slip 2 at the dock. Sam was right about holding the ferry blameless; it certainly hadn't asked for Susan Crane to come across its decks, nor had it been a party to what had happened to her. Still, he was anxious for the *Chelan* to take her place in the islands and send the *Elwha* southbound. He knew that it was only a week to go before the vessels would be switched,and the winter service schedule would begin.

And maybe, he thought as he parked the Cruiser and grabbed his overnight bag, *maybe this nightmare will be over with.*

It was a blissfully uneventful evening. Traffic to the Islands wasn't too terribly bad, a bonus given the holidays. First mate Fred, evidently feeling some of the Christmas spirit, let Jake land the boat twice and both had gone flawlessly. The tie-up at Friday Harbor was over with quickly and he was in bed before the lights had gone out in the cabin.

Finding sleep was more difficult. He missed Sam's warmth and the animals on the bed. The rocking of the ferry in the slip began to lull him slightly, but his mind would not shut off. He was still focused on this latest murder, the death of Crane's pal Lopez. Whoever had killed him certainly was taking a risk. Gasworks Park, even at night, was well lighted and seldom empty. Jake *thought* the park had a policy of closing at dusk, but it wasn't as if the park was locked up in any way. People could stroll through at all hours of the day or night, and often did.

Why take the chance? he thought, shifting in his sleeping bag on the bunk. An old cliché floated up through his memory: *there is nothing more dangerous than a man with nothing to lose.*

He shifted again, made uncomfortable by the thought. Nothing to lose. *So our pockmarked gun-for-hire has nothing to lose, or he's simply arrogant and thinks he can't get caught.* This would mean he would be bound to make mistakes.

"Screw that," he said aloud. "Who the hell is paying him?" he said to himself, acknowledging that Alex was absolutely right. Whoever he was, he was merely a paid thug. Someone was bankrolling him. That would narrow the field down a bit. He closed his eyes again, drifting off to the thought that he would still need to talk to some of Crane's friends, or, more appropriately, her victims.

❖

"You can't do that," Sam said into the phone, feeling his temperature rise. The man on the other end of the line was the project director for the new ferries, and as far as Sam could tell, knew nothing about the job he was supposed to be performing.

"I don't care what you think," he continued. "You better read the contract again, Albert. I have absolute discretion when it comes to the design of the boat. You don't. And if you want to fire me, you still have to pay me. Yes, I thought you'd see it my way," he said, and rang off. He slumped into his chair feeling a headache beginning to throb as the phone rang again.

"O'Conner-Finnigan Maritime," he said.

"Sam?"

"Rachel?"

"Come back in the house, will you?"

"Where are you calling from?"

"The guest bedroom. Something…can you just come over here, please?"

"Sure…"

"And be careful!" she said, ringing off.

Something was making the hairs on the back of Sam's neck stand up. He glanced over at Barnaby. The dog was asleep in his basket by the easy chair in the corner, completely oblivious to everything around him.

"And you noticed this when?"

"When I was talking on the phone to my assistant," she said. "I just had the creepiest feeling I was being *watched*."

Sam stood in the guest room, looking around. Again, nothing was out of place. Rachel was sitting on the edge of the bed, holding herself with her arms. He crossed over to their bedroom, checking it and the bathroom. The cats were both asleep on the bed.

"When did this start?"

"About an hour ago," she said. "It seems stupid. The house just got so quiet. I heard Jason leave and was just talking away with Marcy when it felt like *someone* was in here." She shrugged. "I looked downstairs and thought you might have come in, but you hadn't."

"Did you check the basement?" Sam asked.

"And violate Spievens's Rule Eight?"

"'Never go alone into the basement,'" Sam recited. "Let's go."

The basement was completely secure and empty. Frowning Sam said, "Go back up to the guest room, but stay away from the window."

Rachel nodded and went back upstairs.

Sam left the basement and, acting casually, retrieved a Diet Pepsi from the fridge and walked back upstairs, making a show of turning on the bedroom light before turning back to the guest room across the hall. He got down on his knees and carefully started crossing the room below the level of the window. Halfway across, Barnaby woke up to see his master crawling on the floor on his hands and knees. He hopped out of his basket and crept up alongside Sam until he was even with Sam's head. He looked at Sam and gave a small bark.

"Beat it, Barnaby, you'll blow my cover," grunted Sam.

"What in God's name are you doing, Sam?" Rachel asked when she came in from the bathroom.

"Shh!" barked Sam. "Get down. Crawl over here."

Rachel did as she was told, sidling up to Sam at the window.

"Stay back here," said Sam, indicating the shadowed corner. He slowly raised his head over the frame of the window, leaving his face in shadow. Anyone looking in wouldn't have been able to see them.

High Street below was nearly deserted, save for the neighbor's car to the right and the lurking form of Mrs. Weinberg's house to the left. Across the street under the two old Big Leaf maples in front of the gate of the Crenshaws was a mid-'90s Buick and further down toward the Jefferson house was a red sports car of some sort with a large spoiler on the back. Both were empty.

"What are we looking for?" Rachel asked.

"I don't know."

Just then someone sat up abruptly in the Buick. Heart thudding in his chest, Sam strained to see the driver, but all he could see was a slumped figure as he pulled away from the curb.

"I don't recognize either one of those cars," Sam acknowledged, pointing to the red car with the spoiler and the departing Buick. "Come on, let's go."

"Go where?" Rachel asked.

"It's time for Barnaby's walk. I was going to take him to McDougal Park," he said when something caught his eye out the window.

The sun had pulled out from a veil of gray, wispy clouds, bathing the eastern part of High Street with patches of bright luminescence. Behind the Crenshaw's massive maples, Sam saw a spark of light. He leaned closer to the window. The light flashed again from the crystal of a wristwatch. Someone was hiding behind the tree, watching them.

"Did you see that?" he asked Rachel.

"Someone is behind the tree," she breathed.

For Sam, all fear suddenly evaporated. He was furious his privacy and sense of sanctity of the home had been violated. He spun on his heel, charging down the stairs. Barnaby took off like a fired bullet behind him, yapping loudly.

"Sam!" Rachel shouted, running down after him.

Sam threw open the front door and marched down the front steps bellowing, "I see you, you—psycho idiot!"

"You know Sam, it *is* occasionally appropriate to swear," Rachel whispered.

The man behind the tree ran frantically out from his cover toward the red car. Sam grabbed a decorative rock from the flower bed on the porch and hurled it toward the fleeing figure. The man grunted as the rock smacked him in the back of the head and he fell. In a flash, he was back on his feet and plowing headfirst into the red car. With a squeal of tires the red Subaru sped down High Street and through the stop sign, out of sight.

Rachel couldn't help but burst out laughing. "Oh, Sam, that was brilliant!" she said.

"Well," he said, blushing, "I was a bit perturbed."

"Great shot," she said. "I had no idea you had such a good arm."

Sam looked at Rachel with a crooked grin and said, "Neither did I."

❖

Jake drove the Cruiser home to the sounds of Lisa Gerrard's haunting music. It seemed to calm him and helped while cogitating on something. He kept thinking he'd overlooked something. Simplicity, as Thoreau yammered incessantly about, was genuinely the key.

Three things needed to be answered in order to solve who killed Susan Crane: who had motive, who had the opportunity to do it, and who had the power to cover it up.

Motive was easy to come by. It seemed half the populace of Seattle, several different lawyers, and a few politicians certainly had reason to kill her. It was then merely just a case of finding out who was where when Crane had been killed. According to the autopsy report uncovered by the reporter, she'd been dead for no more than twelve hours. That put it somewhere around three a.m. Friday. Where was Crane staying? Why San Juan Island?

Something was missing from that photograph, Jake thought. He knew what he had to do next. It was time to talk to Dennis Crane. And maybe Lila Beyers, too, if he could get hold of her. According to Rachel, she *seemed* genuinely shaken by her sister's death. He wondered if Alex had her number.

Alex. Jake was still angry with him for lying, but upon reflection, he also understood Alex's motive. He knew all along Alex had a past he wasn't proud of. Over the years, though, he'd seen Alex's struggle to better himself. His long struggle to metamorphose into a compassionate human being was perhaps finally coming to fruition.

The sky shifted to the color of slate, the clouds low and threatening. Fat drops of rain laden with sleet smacked the windshield heavily as Jake turned from 33rd onto High Street. It wasn't even four p.m. yet, and darkness was already falling over the land, sneaking forth with deepening patches of gray fog and shadow. Jake found himself yet again disliking the winter. While no fan of the heat of summer, he did love the hours of daylight that seemed to stretch on and on. Somehow the longer hours of light made him feel more alive, whereas the ever-earlier darkness made him feel closer and closer to death.

Stop it, God damn it, he thought, as the friendly face of 100 High appeared, the house ablaze in light. Jake pulled up behind Rachel's rented car, locked the Cruiser, and sprinted toward the front porch, still managing to get soaked in the process. Entering the house, he was greeted by Barnaby and the two cats while he set his gym bag down. He shut the door and locked it behind him, calling out, "Sam?"

"Up here," came Sam's voice, trailing down the stairs.

Jake trudged up the stairs to the spare bedroom, which was completely dark. He stepped into the room and tripped over Sam's outstretched form on the floor, barking his shin on something heavy and wooden, then landing headfirst in the easy chair.

"Dammit! O'Conner, what the hell are you up to?!" Jake cried, rubbing his shin.

"Shh!" Sam hissed. "You'll set them off."

"Set *whom* off?" he asked, annoyed, stepping back and treading upon something soft and pliable.

"Ow! Watch it, Gobo!"

"Rachel?" he asked, surprised. "What the hell are you two doing on the floor in the dark?"

"We're laying new carpet," Rachel shot back. "Care to join us?"

"Come down here!" whispered Sam.

"Where?"

"Here! Oof!" said Sam as Jake trod upon him again.

"At least he got you that time," Rachel said. "Are those steel-toed boots you're wearing, Jake?"

"Yes," he said, finally giving up. He crawled on his hands and knees toward Sam, who was lying facedown toward the window, and he snuggled in between the two of them.

"Aren't séances supposed to be held at tables?" he asked.

"Someone is watching us," said Rachel.

"What?"

"Here," Sam said, placing binoculars in Jake's hands. His eyes now adjusted to the light, he could see Sam's bearded face ever so slightly in the dim light. The blinds on the window had been drawn up just enough to poke the binoculars through.

"Where's Jason?" asked Jake, peering through the street at the Crenshaws' front door. Al Crenshaw was just getting home. He stood on his front porch shaking out his umbrella, only to be knocked flat by their rambunctious sheepdog, Greta. Jake found himself chuckling.

"What's so funny?" Sam demanded.

"Nothing. What am I looking for?"

"Down from Crenshaw's. Just past Halliyard's."

"Looks like a Buick," said Jake.

"It is. It's been there for hours. It's been up and down our street all day."

"Oh damn," said Jake, cursing himself. "McEvoy. Hand me the phone."

Sam placed the cordless into his hand. Jake dialed up Alex's number and got him on the third ring. "Blackburn."

"Hello, Alex," Jake said quietly.

"Hey, Jake."

"What's he got to do with it?" Rachel whispered harshly.

"Alex," Jake said, "what's McEvoy driving these days?"

"I'm not sure. He changes cars every other day to make sure no one gets a fix on him."

"Can you call him on your cell?"

"Yes. Is something wrong?"

"I don't think so," said Jake, smiling. "When you get him, have him flash his lights just once, please."

"All right."

A moment or two passed. Then suddenly the Buick flashed its lights very briefly.

"Thanks, Alex. And thank McEvoy," Jake said.

"Hang on a minute," said Sam.

"Just a sec, Alex," Jake said into the receiver. "What's up, Sam?"

"Have Alex ask this guy if he knows of anyone who owns a red Subaru. The sporty ones. Impreza! That's it. A red one with a big spoiler."

"Just a second, I'll check." Jake relayed the information to Alex. He felt himself go cold. "When did you see it, Sam?"

"Just before we took Barnaby on his walk. About one, I guess, before the weather got crappy."

"Did you see the driver?" Jake asked.

"Just the back of his head after I beaned him with a rock."

"*What?*" Jake shouted. "Oh, sorry, Alex."

"He was hiding behind one of the maples in front of the Crenshaws' house," Sam explained patiently. "I—" He paused, not wanting to explain his lapse in temper. "I saw him and yelled. He took off like a shot. I threw a rock at him and smacked him in the back of the head with it."

"Hell of a throw," Rachel chimed in. "It was rather gallant."

Jake looked at his partner with growing admiration. "Nice aim, Sam! What's that, Alex? No? Okay. No, no. We'll be all right. Thanks. You too. Good night."

"What's up?" Sam asked.

"As you've surmised by now, Alex has some of the security people from his company keeping an eye on us. Alex has complete faith in them, particularly McEvoy, the guy who heads up the team."

"The fellow in the Buick," Sam stated.

"Yes. He regrettably missed the incident that happened to you this afternoon. He…well, was answering a call of nature. He was sure the street was deserted, although the red Subaru *had* caught his eye as it looked out of place in the neighborhood."

"Which is why I noticed it," Sam said.

"In any event, McEvoy didn't get a look at anyone in the car, but he did take the plate number down."

"Let me guess. It was stolen."

"Yes, it was," Jake replied, feeling a sense of dread growing in the pit of his stomach.

"And let me guess! Description of the thief: heavy-set, black hair, pockmarked man," Rachel said.

"Got it in one," Jake said.

Sam hugged him. "This sucks, kiddo. I don't mind telling you I'm a bit frightened."

"Me too," said Jake softly, thinking of Lopez. "Me too."

❖

The next morning Jake and Sam made plans to set off for Bellingham.

"Are you sure you don't want to go with us?" Jake asked Rachel as they all sat down for coffee in the kitchen.

Rachel shook her head. "I'm going to take some things I got for Christmas back and exchange them. As much as I love my brother, he has appalling taste."

"I'm not sure I like the idea of going off and leaving you alone," Sam said.

"I'll be fine. I'll park close, and I'll be surrounded by a lot of people. Besides, I'm sure Alex will have some of his people on my tail the whole time."

"She's right," Jake said. He took her hand from across the table and gave it a reassuring squeeze. "You sure?"

"Go. And tell me everything when you get back."

After sharing a quick breakfast, they watched Rachel back out of the driveway in her rental before pulling out in the PT Cruiser themselves. He and Sam drove mostly in silence, Jake watching the familiar scenery around Lake Samish out the windshield. The sky was stone gray and unbroken, with low-hanging fog and steady drizzle. Jake hated late December and January when it wasn't cold enough to snow or freeze. It was unendingly wet, with a dampness that crept into the bones.

He shook his head, looking at Sam, who was staring contently at the falling rain as they raced past Lake Samish. He was thinking negatively, something that genuinely irritated him when he got into such a rut.

It was the continuing fear that was poisoning his outlook. He knew once this mess was over with, he'd go back to being his usual "cynical but sunny self," as Sam had pegged him. He hoped this trip would put a few pieces of the puzzle together, and they could clear it up at last. The first visit on their list was Dennis Crane.

Crane had been easy enough to locate. He was a professor at Western Washington University, Jake's old alma mater. He taught geology, and Jake wondered if he'd recognize Crane, possibly having passed him in Red Square.

Jake turned off Harris Street and toward Edgemoor, where some of the more affluent homes in Bellingham were located. He watched the streets go by until he located Acacia Place, pulling into the driveway of 1717, a house no different from the others in style but with a dark green paint job, white trim, and numerous potted plants lining the front walk. A large cedar tree grew at the edge of the yard, which was bordered by hedges and neighbors on either side. A white Lexus was parked in the driveway, soaked in the cold rain. Christmas lights were still in the hedge and around the trim of the house. Jake and Sam got out of the Cruiser, walking slowly up to the front door.

"What are you going to say to him?" Sam asked.

"I'm not sure. I'd just like to understand Susan Crane better. I think maybe if I did, I might be able to figure out who killed her."

"Ten to one, it's our pockmarked thug," said Sam disgustedly.

"No, I don't think so. The way she was killed, it was personal. Our thug may have been the triggerman, but someone else was behind it."

"True," Sam agreed.

Jake rang the bell, standing close to the door under the eave to keep dry. When no one answered right away, he pushed the brass button again.

The door swung open to reveal a short, balding man with salt-and-pepper hair and a thick beard. He was clad in a green sweatshirt and sweatpants. A pair of reading glasses was perched on his nose, and, unbelievably, a pipe smoldered in the corner of his mouth. *The stereotypical college professor*, Jake thought.

"Um…Professor Crane?"

"The same. You must be Mr. Finnigan and Mr. O'Conner. Won't you come in, please," he said, motioning them to step inside.

Professor Crane led them through the foyer and down a hall peppered with family photos to a comfortable room that had to have been Professor Crane's study. The walls were lined with books, rock samples, and photos of volcanoes. He sat down behind a cluttered desk, looked at something briefly on his computer terminal, and then shut the screen down. Piles of papers littered the top, most of them school papers, along with pens, paper clips, the odd coffee mug, and CDs for the computer.

"Well, Mr. Finnigan, what is it I can do for you? Susan and I have been divorced for a good many years. I'm not exactly sure what it is that you think I can help you with," he said sternly.

"Why did you marry her?" Jake blurted, before he could stop himself.

Crane arched an eyebrow, then looked at Jake curiously for a moment. "You know something, Mr. O'Conner—"

"Sorry, I'm Mr. Finnigan. Jake," he said, realizing he'd never properly introduced himself.

"Ah. Well then, Jake, that is something I've been asking myself for many years." He sat back in his chair, puffing methodically on his pipe. "I met her when I was forty, and she was just twenty-four. That should have set warning bells off right away. Everyone said she was after my money, but I knew she had plenty of her own." He shook his head. "Exactly *why* do you want to know? Is it important?"

"I don't know," Jake conceded. "What I do know is that since she—ah—appeared in my life, I've had no peace." He looked over at Sam and smiled. "Very nearly, anyway." He turned back to Professor Crane. "I know she's *dead*, but it doesn't seem to have stopped her from insinuating herself into every facet of my being. Since this incident has happened, there have been attempts on my life, there's been at least one other death, and now the whole law enforcement network in Kulshan County is crumbling."

"Yes, I read about that. Sheriff Danvers. He was a good friend of Susan's father, you know," Professor Crane said distantly. "I can't help but think no matter where Susan ended up, she's having a good laugh over this."

"Everyone we've talked to," Sam interjected, "speaks about her like she was plutonium. Everything she touched seemed to have some sort of grief attached to it."

"She was rather like that," Crane agreed, tamping out his pipe and gently removing the tobacco from it. "I always thought of her as the Hope Diamond. Beautiful, brilliant, and cold. So very, very cold."

"Cursed?" Jake offered, his mind echoing the phrase about Sheriff Danvers that Dennis Crane had just spoken over and over again in his mind.

Again the eyebrow shot up. "Perhaps that as well."

❖

Rachel turned down Arrow Bay Avenue and headed out Highway 22 to Mount Burlington. She'd felt bad for not having gone with Jake and Sam, but she had wanted some time alone to think—and for once it was not about Susan Crane.

She was a little frightened at the rapid way she was making such long-reaching decisions. Putting her condo up for sale, deciding to end her career in Washington D.C.—she wondered if she wasn't suffering from an early midlife crisis.

She knew one thing for certain. She was *not* happy. She was tired of the life back East and wanted desperately to come back to the Northwest. This was *home*, and driving through the gloomy, wet December weather reassured her of that.

Long lines of headlights stretched up Mount Burlington Way clear to the mall, making Rachel groan. She followed the stop-and-go traffic for a short while, turning off into the mall as quickly as she could. She parked the rental close to the mall and hopped out with the packages she intended to exchange, thinking she might get Jake and Sam something to help cheer them up. She knew they had to be feeling the oppressive atmosphere weighing on them as much as she did.

❖

"Susan, when I met her, was not the person she became much later. Though don't get me wrong, the blueprint was clearly there." Professor Crane looked at Jake with a steely eye. "No one likes to be made a fool of. I have to admit for the record she made one of me, though given what became of some of her later victims, I ended up much less worse for the wear. She didn't ruin my reputation or my bank account," he said. "But she did trample all over my heart," he added softly. He looked up and smiled. "I like to think of myself as Susan's test case. On me, she learned how to manipulate and expose people's weaknesses. She knew that once she had an in, nothing could stop her from getting what she wanted.

"By age twenty-four, she was already on her way to becoming a brilliant reporter. She was very intelligent, as I've said. She worked tirelessly, constantly reading, doing articles, preparing herself. I've never seen anyone as driven. It impressed me. I didn't realize until much, much later it was for all the wrong reasons."

"How so?" Sam asked.

"She was preparing herself for battle," said Professor Crane simply. "She kept a list of people she felt had done her wrong and, one by one, she was going to get back at them."

"You actually saw the list?"

"By accident," Crane conceded. "It was around the holidays. We'd been married only a month. I thought it was a Christmas card list. When she found out I'd seen it, she was furious."

"Do you remember who was on it?"

"No. Though the one at the top of the list I do remember. It was her father. You know about that?"

"Yes," said Jake, somewhat uncomfortably.

"I wish I knew who gave her those papers. Without them, her father would have been untouchable." He considered for a moment. "Not that her father was any prize himself. I only met the man once. He accused me of being an old pervert out to corrupt his daughter. Ha! If only he'd known how things would end up for him!"

"You still haven't said why you married her."

"No, no I haven't." Crane took a deep breath. "She was, when I knew her, one of the loveliest women you could look at. She had the clearest blue eyes. She was small, delicate...almost gnome-like. She had a way of making you feel she needed to be protected, when nothing could have been further from the truth." He looked at them over his reading glasses. "I'd like to blame it all on the fact that I'd lost my wife of nearly twenty years the winter before. And I'm sure it had something to do with it. When friends of mine introduced me to her, she was the first woman who really seemed to have a genuine interest in me. I've since found out there was no truth to that. But back then she was the one who seemed to hang on every word I said." He laughed. "I was so stupid. From introduction to marriage was six weeks."

"How long were you married?" asked Sam.

"Till she landed her first real job. Two years and three months later. The day she got the job, she handed me divorce papers."

"That's just..." Jake fumbled.

"Cold?" Crane smiled bitterly. "That was Susan. Cold and brilliant. And possibly cursed, as you suggested. To be perfectly frank with you fellows, I'm surprised no one killed her sooner."

"Do you have any idea who might have done it?" asked Sam.

"Take a number. I could give you a list of about thirty."

"Including you?"

Professor Crane smiled. "No, Mr. Finnigan. You see, after Susan divorced me, she really began to display her plumage. I was happy to be as far away from her as I possibly could be." He packed his pipe, lit it, and puffed for a moment. "She hated the smell of my pipe. Went without it for nearly three years. First thing I did when she left was break out the briar."

"I've always liked the smell of a pipe," Jake confessed.

"Susan hated the smell of anything sweet. She never wore perfume, never had fresh flowers in the house. Couldn't even stand to be around anything baking that was sweet."

Jake felt like they hadn't accomplished anything, but at least they could cross Dennis Crane off his list of suspects. He'd clearly spent the last ten years keeping away from his ex-wife.

"Well, I thank you for seeing us," Jake said, rising. Sam gave him a perplexed look, shrugged, rising from the chair.

"Certainly," said the professor, showing them to the door.

They were about to leave when Jake stopped. He turned to Professor Crane and said, "What was it that put her father at the top of the list?"

"You know, I've never quite figured that out. Oh, I have a few suspicions. None of them provable. When it comes right down to it, no one can piss you off like family. I suspect in Susan's case, it probably wasn't anything much. She could carry a grudge like nobody's business," Crane said, a wry grin crossing his face.

"Thanks again," Jake said, as the front door closed behind him. He didn't say anything to Sam until they were inside the Cruiser.

"Well that was a big waste of time," said Sam crossly. "All the way up here to find out zero."

"I don't think Crane was telling us everything," Jake reflected, starting the car. "On the other hand, I don't think there was much more to tell us." He pulled out of the driveway, smiling. "Plutonium?"

"You're not the only one who reads, you know. Besides, in her case I'd say it was pretty apt."

"Definitely toxic," Jake agreed. "And you didn't have to be very close to her to be brushed by it. Alex found that out the hard way."

"So you've said," Sam said. "Are you still angry at him?"

Jake shook his head. "No. I was at first. But…well, Rachel was right about him being ashamed about his past. God knows if I had had anything to do with Susan Crane, I wouldn't be admitting it. He was really trying to protect us." He shook his head again.

"That is a rather large skeleton in the old cupboard," Sam agreed.

"Although he should know you well enough to know you would probably forgive a friend of anything short of murder."

"Alex was too afraid of destroying the respect of two people he really values."

"Yeah, I'm realizing that now," Sam said. "And also that I haven't been exactly fair when it comes to Alex. Rachel nailed me on that one."

"She's good at that," Jake said.

"She is," Sam said. He watched the buildings glide past in the gray, wet air, the fog slowly moving in from Bellingham Bay. It dawned on him that they were still moving north, into the center of downtown. "Where are you going?"

"Jennings's law firm on State Street."

"What on earth for?"

"We've got an appointment."

"For what? You planning on suing someone?" asked Sam.

"No. We need to speak to the fellow who was sued. A Jeremy Young."

Sam's eyes glazed over in thought. "What…why does that sound so familiar? Oh, now I remember. We're back to little Miss Goody Two Shoes."

"The idea was to knock out two cardinals with one rock," said Jake.

"So long as they don't fall on your head and clock you one," Sam said, grumbling again. "What if this cat doesn't want to talk to you?"

"I'll let him charge me a consultations fee. Ever known a lawyer not to talk if you wave a dollar bill in front of him?" asked Jake.

"Ha," said Sam. "I would *not* say that in front of Rachel if I were you."

❖

Rachel emerged from the mall holding twice as many packages as she had gone in with. The sales, she had soon discovered, were incredible. Aside from exchanging everything she hadn't wanted for things she did, she had purchased gifts for Sam, Jake, and Jason, her parents, and her sister.

She was about to get into the rental car when her cell phone rang.

"Marcy, hi," she said, digging her keys out of her purse. "Can you hold on for a moment? No. I see. Okay. No, I won't be back until after the first. Well I don't care what Beiterhoff says, I won't be. No," she said, having found the keys. She pointed the remote at the rental to start it up and unlock the doors.

"No, Marcy, I will not—" She heard a muted *whump* followed by a billow of black smoke from the engine. Rachel watched stunned as the flames engulfed the car.

"I gotta go, Marcy," she said into the phone as the car continued to burn. Patrons of the mall had come out into the parking lot, watching the fire. In the distance she could hear sirens wailing. "Marcy, I've got to go. No! No! My car just burst into flames."

CHAPTER NINETEEN

Jake squirmed uncomfortably in his seat as Jeremy Young stared directly through him.

"Give me one reason why I shouldn't throw you two out of my office right now," he growled.

"Because you've got an office full of people out there," Sam said calmly.

"Mr. Young, I don't mean to offend you or bring back any unpleasant memories," Jake said sympathetically, annoyed as his cell phone vibrated in his pocket.

"You sure have a hell of a way of going about it," he spat. "That—that *cow*. She…" He growled again in his throat, slumping back into his chair. He was a slight man, with a neatly trimmed beard, round granny glasses, and unkempt hair. He was clearly trying for something of a hippie look canceled out by his tailored suit and thick layer of Drakkar Noir.

"The allegations were baseless," Jake said flatly.

"Of course they were! And we could have proved that in court, but Bradbury—the senior editor before he retired—didn't want to risk it. We settled. I never had a chance to clear my name in the press, never had a chance to refute her in court, and all the while she's stealing stories out from under me!"

"I wondered how an unproven reporter ended up covering Inez Cookson," Jake mused.

"That was what started it. Started saying I grabbed her in the lunchroom. She was supposed to keep quiet about it if we handed her that story. Just what the heck is your interest in her anyway, Finnigan?"

"Her body was dumped on my boat."

Young chuffed, looking at the window. "Stupid move. There are hundreds of places around here to dump a body. Why the hell leave it on the ferry?"

Jake shrugged, having had the same question echoed through his mind many times before. He was about to ask Young another question when the scent of Drakkar Noir made him sneeze.

"Bless you," said Young.

"Thanks," said Jake, taking a tissue from the dispenser on Young's tidy desk. As he did so, something clanged in his brain. He was missing something important, but he couldn't figure out what. "Dammit," he said aloud.

"Jake…?" Sam asked.

"You're right, this is getting us nowhere," he said, getting up. "Thank you, Mr. Young. I'm sorry to have brought this up. C'mon, Sam."

"Wait!" Young shouted after them. "Wait just a minute. *Please.*"

Sam looked at Jake, his eyebrows raised. Jake sat back down.

"I'm sorry I snapped at you," Young said, suddenly looking much older. "Just that name—that woman—what she cost me, I still haven't recovered. My wife nearly left me, my reputation was ruined. I've had to change careers completely, regain my credibility because of that witch."

Jake found himself wondering if Jeremy Young struck his finger with a hammer he would shout out, "Ow-diddley-ouch!" instead of cursing blue blazes like the rest of humanity would. The man was distinctly non-threatening, even effeminate. Young was very, very delicate in movement and structure, looking as if he might shatter if he fell over. Jake mentally scratched him off the suspect list, though he knew looks could certainly be deceiving. Feeling sympathetic, Jake asked, "Have things gotten better for you?"

"Moderately," said Young glumly. "You have to understand that despite all the support I had, settling with her made a lot of people presume my guilt. I had a lot of lean years, and then the paper folded. My employers stood by me. That made a lot of difference when I chose to switch careers. I've slowly built up my practice, but I handle pretty mundane stuff. Wills, powers of attorney, partnership agreements. It's not at all like reporting was."

"Did you think about relocating?" Sam blurted, having mulled the idea over in his head for several minutes.

"My whole family is here. My mother was ill at the time. I couldn't leave."

Jake felt they'd covered enough ground. His cell phone buzzed again in his pocket, annoying him once more. "Well, thank you for taking the time to talk to us, Mr. Young."

"I'm sorry if I was upset earlier," said the wispy lawyer. "It's still a very sore subject with me."

"We understand. In the limited time I've been researching Susan Crane, I've come to understand she was a bit like…" Jake faltered.

"Plutonium," Sam offered again cheerfully.

"That's about it," Young agreed.

They turned to leave, something finally clicking in the back of Jake's mind. He stopped abruptly, Sam running into him. "Can you think of any reason she might have gone to San Juan Island?"

Young shook his head. "No. Well, wait, possibly. Years ago, the family had a summer house there, near Friday Harbor. I thought it had been sold or seized by the bank. When her father killed himself, he left a lot of debt. The insurance companies wouldn't pay up on the claim because he took his own life."

"Can they do that?" Sam asked, incredulous.

"They can if there is a clause in the policy. The family had to sell off most of their assets, and the rest were repossessed. I can't imagine how it must have felt to have the heart of the family ripped out like that. Not that Old Man Gordon was any saint. He had his fingers in more crooked deals than any ten politicians in the state," said Young. "Still, I would never have wished anything like that on him."

"No, me either," said Jake. "Thank you again for your time," he said, more certain of his hunch now than he had been.

"You're welcome. And if you need any legal work done, please remember me," said Young, almost pleadingly.

Back in the car and heading down the highway, Sam again looked out the window, an ironic curl to his lip. "Well, that landed us a big fat zero," he said.

"That's the second time you've said that," Jake said, getting back onto I-5.

"Well, the net result was the same, *n'est ce pas*? At least stop at Bob's so we can get lunch."

"Not a bad idea," he said, as the phone in his pocket buzzed again. Giving an annoyed grunt, he pulled it out of his pocket and handed it to Sam. "Check that, would you please? There's at least two messages," he said.

Sam dialed and said, "What's your code?"

"2001."

"Message one. It's Rachel. It—oh no!"

"What is it? Is Rachel okay?"

"She…yes, she's fine. I'm going to call her."

"Not before you tell me what's going on!"

"Her car caught on fire."

Jake felt as if he'd been doused with ice water. "Was it an accident?"

"She doesn't know."

Jake found himself wishing he had called dispatch and taken a sick day. He knew it was too late now to try and replace him, and his sense of duty wouldn't allow him to leave his captain and coworkers in a bind. They drove back to 100 High Street as quickly as they could, finding Rachel sitting on the couch, Manhattan in hand.

"What happened?"

"I'm not entirely sure," she said. "I think maybe someone tried to kill me. God, that sounded melodramatic didn't it? *Someone tried to kill me.* I feel like Myra Hudson!"

"Myra Hudson?" asked Sam, confused.

"*Sudden Fear*," said Jake. "Joan Crawford, Jack Palance, Gloria Grahame. 1952. Crawford plays a writer whose husband—Palance—is plotting to bump her off."

"I have that same white camel hair coat," Rachel said.

"How many of these have you had?" Jake asked as she finished off her Manhattan.

"Just the one," she said.

"Sadie," Jake said with reproach in his voice. "What happened?"

"I pushed the little clicker thing and *whoosh*. Up it went."

"Clicker?"

"The remote start," said Sam.

"The rental agency is *not* amused. They were most reluctant to loan me another car."

"What did you need another car for?" Jake asked.

"I'm going to Port Jefferson tonight to say good-bye to the folks. I didn't tell you guys how much I love you before you left today," said Rachel, tears spilling down her cheeks. "Don't ever let me do that again."

"Oh, Sadie," said Jake, giving her a hug. Rachel was one of the strongest people he knew. Her breakdown could only be attributed to the stress over Susan Crane and the rental car.

"I don't think I can take much more of this," she said.

"It'll be over soon," Jake said, looking at Sam. He hoped for all of their sakes it was true.

"I'll get you something to drink," said Sam.

"Better make it juice, Sammy," Rachel sniffed. "I'm driving later."

"Yes, take it easy, Myra," Jake replied, making her laugh. "I have to go to work. I can't get out of it, it's too close to sailing time. Take it easy tonight, okay? Both you and Sam. I'll see you tomorrow afternoon."

"Okay, Gobo," she said, sniffling again. "Thanks."

Jake stepped into the kitchen, pulling aside Sam, goosing him to get his attention. He kissed him softly on the lips.

"Accident?" Sam offered.

"You think?"

"No, not really," Sam stated.

"Dammit!" Jake cursed, looking at his watch. "I've got to get going. Take care tonight, okay?" Jake said, feeling uneasy.

"Wouldn't do anything but, love."

Jake slipped out of the house and into the Cruiser, heading for the Arrow Bay dock as darkness folded in over the landscape. The steady drizzle was continuing unabated, but the fog that had clung tenaciously to the evergreens had dissipated into a leaden ceiling of oppressive rain clouds. The wind was up to nearly twenty-five knots by Jake's estimation, and he hoped it would dwindle. He was never fond of navigating any vessels in heavy wind.

Sitting ablaze in light, the *Elwha* awaited him, his mind was as far from work as it could possibly get. Questions still lingered, circling over his head like smoke rings.

Why would *anyone* in their right mind haul a body onto any boat, let alone the international one where every passenger would be subject to Customs inspection and possibly searches? The passengers that got on at Friday Harbor were given a card before boarding indicating they were domestic traffic only and, in general, Customs tended to wave them through a little more quickly. Still, someone not accustomed to that might have only become aware of it once they were already on the boat. It happened frequently enough, much to his annoyance.

He left the Cruiser in the parking lot and crossed over to the ferry, thinking about a second possibility. Perhaps it was entirely intentional. Perhaps someone had been set up to take the fall. Perhaps a certain pock-faced man was supposed to go down with an impromptu inspection at Customs.

Why had he been so dumb? He'd been focusing so much on the *why* he'd forgotten the basic simplicity of *how*. The answers had been there all along.

He greeted Captain Trelawney as he stepped into the wheelhouse. "Where's Fred?" Jake asked, seeing a relief mate at the helm.

"Seattle," Rhoda Trelawney said. "Remember, he had this day scheduled off for that concert."

"Right."

The *Elwha* loaded cars without incident and departed for Friday Harbor on schedule, the wind and rain lashing the boat, rocking it none too gently in swells that were three feet in the strait and getting higher.

"Dirty night," Captain Trelawney commented. "And bound to get worse. We've got a classic howler coming in from the north."

"I hadn't caught the forecast before I left," Jake replied, feeling remiss in his duty.

"Well, we'll get out to the harbor and see what it's like. If this thing follows the path they say it will, we could be up to well over fifty knots and some pretty heavy swells. If we start facing anything more than that, I'm tying up for the night."

"Understand that," said Jake as the boat dropped into a trough. He held tight and brought them through.

The next hour slipped by with little event other than the wind, as predicted, picking up in speed. Even the sheltered waters around the Islands were starting to get rough, and Jake was relieved to see the friendly lights of Friday Harbor burning in the distance.

They docked and unloaded traffic, taking note of the gusts. The wind was now blowing steadily between thirty-five and forty knots and gusting higher. Captain Trelawney decided they'd make a run back to Arrow Bay and see how conditions were at that point. Picking up a total of twenty cars, they immediately headed out for Lopez Island.

It was Jake's time off the wheel, and he happily went to his cabin, taking the opportunity to lie flat on his bunk, his eyes closed, thinking some things through. His mind was wedged in a groove about the car being left on the boat to possibly set someone up. It didn't gel. Whoever had hired Mr. Pock-Face had continued to use him. Lopez had found that out the hard way. He and Sam had nearly found out themselves. And now of course Rachel...

Possible motives fluttered around his head like moths. He thought about what Dennis Crane had said. *No one can piss you off like family.*

Jake sat bolt upright, his heart hammering in his chest. A shiver ran through his body. He suddenly knew they were in a lot more danger than he thought. Dennis Crane had also said, *She hated the smell of anything sweet. She never wore perfume.*

"Sam!" he whispered harshly. "Oh no, Sam!" He shot up from the bed and tore to the wheelhouse, fighting against the continued rolling of the boat. He had to get back to Arrow Bay as quickly as possible, and he'd shake the damn boat apart if he had to.

Jason wasn't surprised the lights went out. He'd been anticipating it all evening as soon as he'd left Seattle. He'd come home and started lighting the candles. Jake, in all impracticality, had vanilla-scented emergency candles. The house was now completely aglow with them, smelling like a waffle cone.

He assumed Dorothy and Sophia were hiding upstairs, but he couldn't find Barnaby. As he entered the kitchen, he heard a scratching at the basement door. Frowning, he walked over to the door and opened it, Barnaby rushing out at once. Still frowning, Jason said, "Whatcha doing in the basement, Barnaby?" Looking down the steps, he called out, "Sam? Rachel?" Nothing.

Shrugging, he closed the door, his thoughts drifting to his brother on the *Elwha* out on the waters of the Rosario Strait, which he knew could be incredibly brutal. What he'd heard on the car radio hadn't made him feel any better, either. Swells of up to nine feet had been reported, and gusts were now up to over sixty miles an hour. Service at Keystone had already been halted, as well as at Mukilteo. There were concerns over the 520 bridge in Seattle, as was usually the case. No mention of Arrow Bay or the San Juan Islands had been made.

Unable to concentrate on one of the innumerable crossword puzzles Jake had left around the house, he grabbed a book from a shelf in the living room and sat down, packing his briar pipe with cherry tobacco. He lit it, puffing on it in an attempt to distract himself. He was just deciding he couldn't read by candlelight when he heard a large thud coming from the garage. Barnaby let out a low growl and pointed toward the front door. Groaning, he stood up, wondering if the doors on the garage had blown open.

The front door banged violently open in the wind, and Rachel stepped in, soaked from her quick trip from the garage to the front of the house. She shook off her coat and flung it onto the coat rack, stepping into the living room.

"When do services begin?" she asked, looking around at all the candles.

"Power's out," Jason replied between puffs. "Where were you?"

"I had been planning on going over to Port Jefferson, but they canceled the run," she said. "And I'm not surprised. It's truly foul out there."

"I know, I was just thinking about Jake," Jason said, looking past Rachel into the foyer. "Sam with you?"

"No," she said. "I assumed he was here. He was when I left for the ferry."

Another loud thump from outside made them jump.

"Something's out there," Jason said, setting his pipe in an ashtray.

He and Rachel crossed into the kitchen. Jason took the Mag-Lite from a shelf in the pantry and went out into the kitchen. He threw the side door open and flashed the light out into the darkness toward the garage, but the boxwood blocked his view.

"Can you see anything?" Rachel asked.

"No," he said. I'll have to go out."

Jason stepped out the kitchen door and out into the night. Rain pelted him in the face as the wind howled around the house, the Crenshaws' maples across the street groaning under the strain. Rounding the boxwood, he saw the garage doors had been blown full open in the wind. With a grunt he pulled the door on his right shut, then held it with his foot as he reached over to tug the other door shut. He had just managed to secure the two when a hand fell on his shoulders.

"What the hell are you doing out here!?" Jake demanded.

"Holy Christ, you scared the hell out of me!" Jason shouted back, only to have Jake all but pick him up and squeeze him in a rough bear hug.

"God, am I glad to see you!" Jake said.

"Well, so it seems," said Jason, taken aback. "What's up? And can we go inside? We're getting soaked."

"Of course we can go inside," said Jake, relieved.

They trudged back into the house, where Barnaby stood awaiting in the kitchen, looking expectant. Jake made sure the kitchen door was locked tightly behind them.

"Your captain cancel the run?" Jason asked.

"Yes, but I requested emergency leave anyway. I was worried."

"So I gathered. What's wrong?"

Jake was relieved to see his brother, and even more so to see Rachel, standing in the kitchen surrounded by the glow of candlelight.

"Sadie! I thought you were—ah, they canceled the ferry."

She nodded. "Jake, something's wrong."

Jake closed his eyes slowly, feeling his legs grow weak from under him. "Sam's not here, is he?"

"No," said Jason. "But his car isn't in the garage…"

"He doesn't *have* a car, Jason. His Subaru isn't getting in until next week," he said, trying to control himself. He looked at Rachel and said, "I need you to confirm something for me, Rachel."

"Yes?"

"When Lila Beyers accosted you in the parking lot, you said you smelled cloves. Could you have been wrong?"

"I—I guess."

"Could it have been patchouli?"

"Yes," she said at once. "Yes, it could have."

Jake nodded. "I know who killed Susan Crane."

Alex watched the waves lash the shoreline outside his condo in the dark, illuminated by the lights of the Essex bio-fuel refinery operating on backup generators. The refinery was never dark, always casting an orange glow on the clouds above, always looking like a city in miniature on the eastern horizon.

He jumped when the phone rang, nervous because the condo was abnormally silent in the darkness. He'd forgotten that even if the power was out, the phone seldom went with it. He eschewed cell phones, finding them not only a nuisance, but too susceptible to being intercepted. He insisted that everyone he did business with have at least one grounded phone to talk on.

He picked it up on the second ring, his eyes not leaving the tempest outside. The clouds overhead were streaking across the sky, the sound of the wind buffeting the sides of the condo, rattling the glass. Rain pelted the windows while fifty yards below, waves of over eight feet smashed into the shore, tossing up driftwood and beach logs. The normally placid waters of the bay were a frothing fury of whitecaps, pushing steadily in from the northeast on the rising tide, which Alex knew to be one of the highest of the year. Had the power been on, he'd have still been sitting in the dark, playing Richard Strauss or Rachmaninoff, something that would be an adequate accompaniment to the tempest furiously pounding outside.

"Blackburn," he said into the phone.

"Alex! Craig here."

"I was hoping to hear from you. What have you got?"

"It's a go. New Year's Day, just as planned."

"That's great."

"Your friend at the *Examiner* will have the documents delivered to him in time to go to press."

"Wonderful. You're a miracle worker, Craig."

"You did all the work, buddy. We're all very hopeful and excited."

"I couldn't have done it without you. Or Susanne."

"Well, just hang in there. The ink will be dry soon."

"I can't wait until this is over," Alex said, surprised at the force in his voice.

"Hang in there, boss, we're nearly into the light."

"Thanks again, Craig. Happy New Year."

"You too, boss."

He rang off, leaving Alex to contemplate the furious storm outside the window. Abruptly the condo flooded with light as the power came back, leaving Alex bathed in the glow of the Tiffany desk lamp on his right. He stared at it for a moment, thinking of how good it was to be out of the darkness, then wondered if he could handle everything about to come down.

He knew at least he could rely on his friends and that they would never let him down. He just hoped that over time, Sam would be able to see he wasn't a threat to him or his relationship with Jake. He silently wished them his best, then, exhausted, he shut off the light and went to bed.

❖

"For crying out loud, Jake, who?" Jason shouted, just as the power came back on. The house was instantly awash in light.

"For too long, I was looking in all the wrong directions. I kept thinking, *who could have done it, who had the motive* and I kept focusing on her work, which seemed like a natural thing to do."

"Well, yes…oh wait, I think I know where you're going with this," said Rachel.

Jake nodded.

"Jake, what's wrong?"

"Sam," said Jake, tears in his eyes.

"What about Sam?" Jason said, a growing sense of dread creeping over him.

"Lila Beyers, Jason. I'm *positive* she killed her sister," said Jake, starting to pace. "I've been so stupid! All the political factors, all the enemies she made, I think it comes down to the simple fact that Lila hated her sister for the death of her father and ruining the family.

"Two things clicked today. The first thing was when Susan Crane's ex-husband said she never wore perfume." He looked at Rachel and his brother. "When that trunk was opened, Jason, it *reeked* of the perfume Diana." He shook his head. "I didn't think anything of it. Lots of women wear perfume. Hell, Crane even had a statue of the goddess Diana in her office, so it all fit, or so I thought."

"What else?" Jason asked.

"Jeremy Young said the family had a place out on San Juan Island. That could be the only reason she'd be out here. I think Lila got her up here on some pretext and then…" He shrugged. "Shot her."

"Then she got the stout, pockmarked man to haul off the body," Rachel said.

"Who she may or may not have been setting up. I can't say for sure, but I'm convinced this guy isn't too bright. He may not have known he was boarding the international sailing and would have been subject to Customs inspection. He probably got in line, didn't realize it until it was too late, then just walked off the ferry."

"You're sure about this?" Jason asked.

"I am," Rachel said. "I thought it was a clove cigarette I smelled on Lila Beyers when I met her in the parking lot, but I bet it was Diana. The two aren't all that dissimilar," she said.

Jake said, sitting down shakily. "Sam's not here," he said, panicking. "Sam's not here! He hasn't got a car, where can he be?"

"Jake," Jason said. "Calm down."

"I can't! I don't know where he is, there's no message, there's nothing!"

"I'm sure he's fine! Maybe he's gone out, or something—" Jason stopped short, the memory of Barnaby bounding up from the basement. "Oh, God."

"I've been so stupid! Why did I have to get involved with this?" Jake yelled. "Why couldn't I have left well enough alone? It was covered up and nobody cared!"

"How did—" Rachel started.

"Danvers was a personal friend of Richard Gordon. I wouldn't be at all surprised if he was more than happy to bury this as a suicide and be done with Susan Crane altogether." Jake sighed, sinking into the living room sofa. "I'm sure Lila Beyers had something on him to force his hand," he said, dialing Sam's cell phone number. "Given what kind of evil person she was, I'm not sure I did such a good thing by digging into all of this."

"You said it yourself, Gobo," Rachel said, sitting next to Jake. "No one deserves to have done to them what Susan Crane had happen to her."

"You're right," he said, wiping away a tear. "Why won't he answer?"

"Jake, let's call the police," said Jason.

"Why? He hasn't been missing that long. The police won't do anything until he's gone twenty-four hours. He could be dead by then!"

"Don't say that!" Rachel moaned.

The phone rang, breaking Jake out of his thoughts. He felt an ugly clamminess weighing down on him. He picked up the receiver saying, "Hello."

"Jake! Is that you?"

"Sam! Sam, where are you?"

"I—I'm in trouble, Jake. I was at home when—he got in through the dog door, Jake. He'd been in before. It's—you have to come get me, Jake. He says he'll kill me if you don't come."

"Where are you?"

"I don't know! He doesn't want you here...he says..."

Jake heard muffled grunting in the background, the sound of rain splattering and echoing through a hollow room, and an uncomfortable groaning sound.

"Meet him at mile marker 89 on Highway 22 just north of

Concrete. There's a side road. He says if you want to see me alive again, be there in four hours."

Jake could tell Sam was terrified. "Sam, are you okay?"

"Pray for me, Jake. Use Mom's *rosary.* Please come!"

The line went dead.

"Jake! What is it?" Rachel asked. "You're white as a sheet!"

He looked into Jason's eyes. "He's got Sam. He says he'll kill him if we don't meet him in four hours."

"Jesus Christ! Call the police!!"

Jake shook his head, an odd feeling of calm descending upon him. "He'll kill him anyway, Jason. I've got to think..." he said, sinking down into the couch.

"What did you *hear*, Gobo," Rachel said, slipping into cross-examination mode.

"A hollow sound," Jake said. "Rain splattering in the background. Hollow..."

"Was it the kind of splatter you hear on a roof?" she persisted.

"No, a floor," Jake said. "And something creaking. Groaning."

"Trees?" Jason suggested. "Like in the wind?"

"No, but wood. Straining wood..."

"And what did Sam *last* say to you," Rachel pressed.

"'Pray for me. Use Mom's rosary.'"

"What? Sam's Catholic, isn't he?" Jason asked.

"His mother burned her rosary years ago. Why would he...?" Jake's eyes widened at the sudden realization the word *rosary* clanging through his head over and over again like a ringing bell, mixing with the sound of groaning wood.

Rachel caught his look and said excitedly, "You know where he is!"

"Sam, you brilliant son of a bitch!" Jake shouted. "He's on the *Rosario!*"

CHAPTER TWENTY

"This is stupid, you know. You're violating every one of Spievens's rules," Rachel said as Jason guided the car up Highway 22 toward the *Rosario*.

"And every bad horror movie I've ever seen always ends with the guy refusing to call the police and confronting the killer on his own," Jason said, squealing around a corner.

"It isn't my fault," Jake insisted. "*They* started it. *They* were the ones that chased us down the mountain in a living cliché. *They're* the ones that blew up Rachel's car."

"Technically it didn't blow up," Rachel said. "It merely became the main attraction at a one-car barbecue roast."

"This is *Sam*, you guys. I can't just…" He found himself unable to argue. "Just let me get up there. Give me exactly fifteen minutes. I *know* that boat. Sam does, too. I'm betting the goon hasn't a clue as to what he's doing."

"That's a cliché, too," said Jason as the Cruiser screamed around another corner. Jason nearly lost control of the car, but the antilock brakes kept them from careening down the hillside.

"For Chrissakes, don't kill us before we even get there!" Jake shouted. He'd had Jason drive as he was too on edge, despite the eerie calm that had overtaken his thinking.

"Sorry," Jason said. "When all this is over, we'll take that vacation to Alaska we always were going to but never did."

"Quit saying stuff like that!" Rachel snapped. "Haven't you ever seen *Love Story* or any one of those god-awful made-for-TV Lifetime movies! The characters say shit like that and ten minutes later they're wracked with Ebola and making beautiful corpses!"

Please, whatever higher power is out there, let him be okay, thought Jake. *I'll continue to hog the sheets and snore and Sam can continue to spike me with those dragon toenails of his and we'll lead a humdrum dreary life in Arrow Bay where the most entertaining thing will be the arrival of the electric bill, and I'll never, ever get involved in something like this again.*

"Slow down, Jason. It's just ahead. If you go too fast you'll miss it."

Jason slowed down to make the turn onto the road. Halfway in, he killed the engine and shut off the lights, not wanting to attract attention.

The sound of the rain pounding on the roof of the car was all they could hear. Nothing could be seen outside in the swirling darkness. Jake reached over to embrace his brother and collided with him in the dark instead.

"Ow! Oh, my nose!" yelled Jason.

"I think mine is bloody," said Jake.

"Will you two try not to kill one another before Jake even gets out of the car?" Rachel asked, exasperated.

"Oh hell," said Jason, hugging him. "Fifteen goddamn minutes, Jake. You know you're making me furious by leaving me here."

"You'd only get yourself killed," Jake said, already halfway out of the car. He popped on his Mag-Lite. "You don't know that boat like Sam and I do. Lock the doors. I'll be back. Promise," he said. Then catching Jason's expression and the tears running down Rachel's face, said, "Bad pennies always turn up, you two."

He turned and began tromping down the pathway. The rain was slackening a bit, but he was already half soaked through his coat and work pants. His shoes were wet and squishy, and he felt chilled. He wasn't sure if this was his actual state or if it was shock of some sort. He kept telling himself over and over that Jason and Rachel were absolutely correct. He was walking into a death trap and *was* violating at least Rule One of Kent C. Spievens: *never* go into the killer's lair.

In the distance, he could see a light flickering inside the cabin of the derelict ferry. He quickly extinguished the Mag-Lite and stepped toward the vessel, tripping over the gnarled root of a Western hemlock. Landing face first in the muck, Jake spat out a mouthful of foul-tasting earth, cursing Susan Crane's name again. He stood up and fumbled the rest of the way to the *Rosario*.

The gangplank to the upper promenade deck stretched out before him. He paused with one foot on it. Stepping back, he crouched down, looking in through the mostly shattered windows into the cabin where the light was emanating from. He couldn't see anyone. Jake knew the thug probably had Sam on the other side of the cabin, away from the road.

Jake dropped down to the side of the gangplank, looking down the embankment the *Rosario* was next to. A gap of about ten feet separated the shore from where the ferry was silted in. He risked a peek with his Mag-lite, shining it through his cupped hands. The bank was mainly bare, a portion of it having come away only last spring. The river hadn't carved through it yet, but Jake suspected it wasn't entirely solid. Knowing his other option was no good, he dropped down, sliding on his heels down the steep bank until he was level with the side of the boat.

His intuition on the solidity of ground was correct; instantly his foot was sucked into the saturated earth. He held on to the rotten planks of the ferry's siding, yanking his foot out with a hideous sucking noise, until he missed a step and dropped four feet into the steadily rising, ice-cold Skagit River. Still gripping the ferry's wooden guard, he managed to pull himself onto the lip of the half-collapsed forward car deck. He turned on the Mag-Lite again, groaning at what he saw.

The Skagit River had risen and was running full-tilt through the car deck. The water was the color of coffee, moving languidly around the center staircase leading up from the car deck. Light was filtering down in small pools from the cabin above. For the first time he heard voices—one female, one male, possibly Sam.

He had no idea how long it had been since he left Jason and Rachel back in the cruiser. Perhaps five minutes, perhaps not. His heart was thudding in his chest, and he knew he had to do *something* because hypothermia was a reality that was beginning to sink in with every breath.

"Oh, to hell with it!" he said, stepping onto the submerged car deck. The water rose up to his knees, and he was thankful it wasn't any deeper than that. He could tell he was no longer standing on wood, and with each careful step, he figured the entire engine room was filled with thick Skagit River silt.

The staircase was a tantalizing fifteen feet in front of him when he encountered the first hole. He sank down on his left leg, pitching forward into the water with a splash. His hand found solid planking under it and he quickly pulled himself forward, yanking his left leg out of the chasm and cutting it on splintered wood.

Totally soaked to the skin now, Jake saw the staircase was a mere six feet off, surrounded by a small island of silt. Carefully but rapidly moving toward it, Jake pulled himself out of the water and onto the platform, now able to clearly hear his partner and a woman talking.

Panting, he twisted the top of the Mag-Lite again, igniting the beam. At one time, a set of doors shielded the staircase from the air of the car deck. One was gone entirely, but the other, its bottom half rotted away, hung askew from brass hinges that still glittered dully in the light. Jake played the beam up the stairs, encountering a hole near the top where the last six stairs should have been.

He shook his head. *Heroics should be left to the James Bond types,* he thought. *You're an English major, what the hell are you doing?*

"Saving my husband's ass," he whispered to himself as he started up the stairs.

The last stair splintered, but held as he reached it. Looking down the hole, he could see the car deck below still strewn with the jagged, rusting remains of the cannery equipment. He knew if he slipped, it would be a fast, but highly painful and unpleasant death.

The door was too far to jump for. As quietly as he could, he tested both the remaining handrails. They remained fastened tight to the wall. Using them like balancing beams, he dropped his legs into the hole, then a few inches at a time, pulled himself up. His biceps were burning by the time he reached the top. With a grunt, he rested one leg on the cabin floor, and pulling up the other, rolled over onto his stomach.

He found himself staring into the eyes of a bloodstained corpse.

Jake nearly screamed. All that came out was a sound of escaping air as he quickly snapped his jaw shut. Like a crab, he scurried backward away from the bloodied body, someone he recognized all too quickly: the pockmarked thug. He'd been shot between the eyes at close range.

What is it with these people? he thought wildly. *Can't they come up with anything more creative than a shot between the eyes?*

Rising, Jake heard footsteps, then a voice call out, "Why don't you join us, Mr. Finnigan? We've been listening to you thumping around for the last ten minutes."

❖

Jason looked at his watch. Three minutes, four minutes, five minutes. Seven minutes. It seemed like each sweep of the minute hand on his watch was taking hours.

"How long?" Rachel asked.

"Nine minutes."

"This is stupid, why did we agree to this?" she barked.

"You ever try to talk Jake out of something?"

"Yes."

"You have your answer," Jason replied.

The rain appeared to be letting up. The sound lessened on the roof of the Cruiser. Rachel was aware of a pounding and realized it was her heart.

"Time?"

"Fifteen minutes!" Jason said. "Call!"

Rachel reached into her purse, pulled out her cell phone, and flicked it open. She had just hit the 9 on the keypad when a flashlight beam burst into the car.

"You might have said something earlier and saved me some effort!" Jake shouted. "Sam?" he called, moving around to the opposite side of the staircase. "Are you there?"

"He's here, Mr. Finnigan," said Lila Beyers.

"I want to hear him say something."

"Go on, say something," said the woman.

"Here, Jake. I'm here."

"Are you okay?"

"No, I'm—" His words cut off abruptly.

"There was a bit of an accident, I'm afraid. Your friend needs medical attention, and I'd say the sooner the better," said Lila Beyers.

"What have you done to him?" Jake asked, keeping his voice level.

"I did nothing. My late associate, Mr. Monrovia, was a little rough with him. Against my *express* wishes," she said. For the first time, Jake noted the fury in her voice.

"Let him go."

"I'd be happy to, but you seem to have complicated things, Mr. Finnigan. And quit moving around. Come out where I can see you."

"No," Jake said simply.

"Fine. This vessel isn't exactly large. You'll come out sooner or later, particularly if you feel compelled to," she said.

Sam's scream filled the cabin. Jake immediately rushed forward and cut over to the port side, slowing to move around the railing of the stairs. "Cut it out, God damn it!" hee screamed, turning his head toward the stairs so his voice would go upward.

"You couldn't leave it alone, could you? You had to keep poking into things that were none of your business! Why couldn't you let her be dead, Finnigan? Why couldn't you just let it go?"

"Because no one deserves to die that way," he said, inching around the stairs. He slowly made his way around to the port side. No one was there. He glanced over at the light of an old battery-operated Coleman lantern. He had sworn she was right on the other side of—

He spun around, looking back toward the dining room. She *had* been there. She was doubling back behind him. He reached down, pulled up a loose tile, and threw it toward the back of the ferry. Instantly the pop of a .22 pistol went off.

"Son of a bitch!" Lila Beyers screamed. "You bastard. You *knew* what my sister was, and you *still* kept after me? Why?"

"I didn't even know it was you until a few hours ago," said Jake honestly. "Why'd you do it?" he shouted down the deck, hoping the police were well on their way. "Was it your father? Were you getting revenge?"

"Isn't that enough? Do you know what it is like to lose everything? Do you know what it is like to have everything you've ever loved and cherished ripped out from under you? Do you? She *deserved* to die! She destroyed my family, she destroyed other people's lives, and she was going to destroy *me*."

"I don't care!" he shouted back angrily. "Just leave me and my partner and get the hell out of here!" Jake looked up the stairs, a thought flashing though his head. *Fourteen, four, two. Fourteen...*

"You've totally screwed that up, you asshole! If you'd left it alone, I'd be out of the country by now! But thanks to your private sleuthing, you've got the feds involved! You think they're going to stop until I'm caught? Do you?" she shouted into the gloom. In front of her lay the rotten remains of the *Rosario*'s dining room. A few tables remained upright, one even with the remnants of a decaying tablecloth that fluttered like a moth's wings. Shining the small penlight downward, she could see the spatters of blood trailing over the tile floor.

Grinning to herself, she followed the trail from the dining room along the inside passage to the forward observation room. To her right, the bench seats along the passageway sent things scurrying in the beam of her light. Dust motes obscured the beam as she made her way forward. The sound of the rain on the roof and the steady drip of water seeping into the cabin were all she could hear. The wood of the vessel groaned in the wind.

Lila cursed aloud as she tripped over a fallen Philco radio, its glass face smashed. *He* hadn't tripped. She'd have heard that a few minutes ago. The floor creaked uneasily under her feet. In front of her, thick with the smell of decay and moldering upholstery, the chairs fell over one another like a mass of tin soldiers gathered around the stairs leading up to the promenade deck. She could see drops of blood and fresh footprints in the beam of her failing light.

They trailed up the staircase.

"Give it up, Finnigan! I know you're up there! You can't hide! I know you're bleeding!" *To death with any luck*, she thought bitterly. "Don't be stupid!"

Something above her thudded heavily. Dust sifted from the support beams and a light fixture fell from the ceiling, shattering on the tile floor. Had he fallen, unable to walk anymore from lack of blood? Had hypothermia set in?

She smacked the flashlight, the beam cutting through the thick tide of dust long enough to illuminate her first few steps onto the creaking staircase. Something popped unpleasantly under her foot. A second later, her penlight flickered out.

"Damn!" She took the next step, crying out as her foot went through the wood. The brass kicker plate caught her cuff, tearing it and slicing into her leg. She jerked it out with a yelp, steadying herself on the balustrade, which shuddered but held. Catching her breath, she ignored the pain in her leg. She closed her eyes. *Think, dammit, think!*

She waited until her breathing calmed, keeping her eyes shut the entire time. When she opened her eyes, they'd adjusted to the inky darkness. She could see the fourth step was missing a board. She carefully stepped over it, and up the next one, which was surprisingly solid. She continued her way upward.

"I know you're up here!"

❖

Yeah, so do I, thought Jake. He was starting to get cold, shivering in great heaves, but he fought it off. Sweat poured into his eyes and stung, but he ignored it. Just a few more steps.

Jake heard her fire a shot into the night. The sound of the bullet and the clanging of metal somewhere on the *Rosario*'s deck reported back, echoing into the blackness of the river valley.

"God damn it, come out here! You can't get away from me!"

"*Here,*" he tried to shout, but it came out as a hoarse whisper. Jake felt himself struggling with consciousness.

Lila whirled. "You think I'm that stupid? You think I'm just going to come running over to you because I hear a little *noise*?"

And then she was on the deck. Jake gasped. How the hell had she gotten over step fourteen? The son of a bitching step had nearly taken him out... He cursed into the rain. Lila Beyers didn't weigh even half of what he did. The stair had been strong enough to hold her.

Better come up with Plan B quickly, dammit, he thought, crouching down behind the funnel casing. He thought he saw lights approaching through the rain, but he dismissed the thought. The police couldn't have reached them that quickly. It hadn't been more than a few moments since he'd come up from the car deck.

"I know you're here, I know you're hiding behind the...the *thing,*" she shouted.

"Smokestack, you idiot," Jake said automatically.

Lila Beyers whirled around from the head of the stairs to where she'd heard his voice, and instead of taking the *port* side where Jake sat crouched, she charged down the *starboard* side.

In spite of himself, Jake nearly shouted a warning.

The moment she stepped past the funnel, the sound of groaning wood screamed into the night. Jake heard a roar as the partially collapsed ceiling in the dining room gave way in a snap of rotten timbers. With a metallic wail, the casing around the funnel sheared, sending the red-hued stack careering over onto Lila Beyers, cutting off her voice in mid-scream.

Lila Beyers plummeted through to the deck below, the smokestack of the once jaunty little *Rosario* trailing after her. With a thunderous roar the starboard side of the cabin gave way, carrying with it several tons of rotted lumber and rusted steel. The deck below was unable to withstand the weight; Lila Beyers and the funnel assembly roared down through the floor of the passenger cabin, coming to rest in the silt-filled water on the car deck.

The *Rosario* gave an unearthly groan, sinking farther to starboard. A large plume of dust and rotten wood erupted from the side of the cabin, shifting the ferry deeper into the mud. And then it was silent.

Jake sat down with a thud, looking into the gigantic hole in the side of the vessel. Fully one third of the cabin below him was gone, a tangle of crushed wood, shattered glass, and twisted steel. As the dust settled, he looked carefully downward, trying to catch a glimpse of what lay below.

There was nothing but darkness.

"SAM!" he shouted. A sudden burst of adrenaline shot through him, and he sped toward the stairs. Jumping over the fourteenth step that had annoyingly supported Lila Beyers, and skipping over numbers four and two, Jake burst into the cabin, looking toward the light of the lantern now shining from a gaping hole through the floor from a mass of rubble on the car deck below.

"Oh no," he whispered.

"Jake?" came a tentative voice.

"Sam?"

Stumbling slightly, his eye blackened and lip split, Sam O'Conner emerged from the intact port side of the ferry. His arms were still tied to the rotted back of a chair.

"I was going to come help you," he said. "Once she left all I had to do was stand up. Damn chair fell apart. What kind of moron ties someone to a rotten chair?"

"I don't know," Jake said, laughing through tears as he untied Sam. "Let's get the hell out of here, the whole thing may go."

Carefully they made their way back up the stairs, onto the boat deck, and down the gangplank to shore. Just as they did, the lights of McEvoy and three of his men surrounded them.

"You know something, Mr. Finnigan, I think my boss underestimates you," McEvoy said.

Something had changed, making Jake stop and look up.

"Hey," he said simply. "The rain's stopped." And then he passed out.

CHAPTER TWENTY-ONE

Sam sipped his coffee watching the ferry *Chelan* pull into the dock from the window of Lassen's Restaurant. Keeping an eye on Jake, Rachel, and Jason, he watched them all sigh in unison as the *Elwha* pulled out for annual maintenance and dry-docking. In spite of himself, he smiled.

"Happy New Year," said Jason.

"Amen," said Rachel.

"How's your leg, Jake?" Jason asked.

"Sore still, but no troubles. I was lucky."

Jake and Sam had both spent several days in bed recovering, having been thoroughly looked over by Alex's private physician. The doctor, a striking African American woman with very expressive eyes, hadn't seemed the least bit curious about Sam and Jake's wounds. Jake had figured it was one of the reasons she was Alex's *private* doctor in the first place.

The memories of what had happened after the nightmare on the *Rosario* were fleeting. He remembered seeing McEvoy talking animatedly on the phone to Alex. He'd only caught part of the conversation, but clearly remembered McEvoy saying, "It's such a goddamn mess in there I doubt *anyone* will know what really happened, boss. I think if we stick to our story, it'll all wrap up nice and neat, and that'll be the end of it."

Much to Jake and Sam's relief, that was exactly what happened. McEvoy had gone to the FBI first, notifying an agent who Jake later learned was a buddy of McEvoy's.

The official story was that Lila Beyers had become a "person of interest" to Blackburn's security when she requested some old documents the company had on her father's business dealings with

Alexander Blackburn Junior. McEvoy suspected blackmail, but had been "startled" to discover that Beyers was likely responsible for her sister's death—revenge, it would seem, for destroying the family, causing her father's death, and confining their mother to a mental institution.

McEvoy, through Lopez, discovered Susan Crane went to San Juan Island on what had been her sister's request. Lila Beyers killed her and stuffed her in the trunk, dousing the corpse with the heady perfume Diana to help mask the smell. The ultimate plan had been to dispose of the body in a place where it would never be discovered. Instead, she and her pock-faced henchman had gotten on the wrong ferry. When the man, Monrovia, realized he was going to be subject to an inspection by U.S. Customs, he'd panicked and left the car on the boat.

Marlon Monrovia was known to the FBI as a felon and possible murderer. His brother had been working for Sheriff Danvers as a gardener, and the brother had likely put Monrovia in touch with Beyers, to Monrovia's peril. When an official investigation into Susan's death had been opened, Lila Beyers had Monrovia threaten and blackmail Sheriff Danvers. She had a number of her father's old files that showed exactly *how* Danvers had been able to raise the funds for his first campaign for Kulshan County Sheriff. His fear of exposure had caused him to lean on the coroner, who'd fled in terror.

When McEvoy found the real autopsy report and gave it to the press, Beyers and Monrovia knew it was only a matter of time before they would be caught. They'd gone out to the *Rosario*—where Sheriff Danvers had set up the first meeting between Monrovia and Beyers— and gotten into an argument. Beyers had killed Monrovia, then, while fleeing the decrepit vessel, had accidentally killed herself falling through the floor, where she had been crushed by the collapsed ceiling and impaled on submerged cannery equipment on the car deck of the rotting vessel.

Jake and Sam were perfectly happy to go along with that. It was *essentially* the truth, after all. It just removed Sam from the scene and covered up what Jake considered his own idiotic heroic attempt at rescue that had nearly gotten them both killed. Nowhere were the names "O'Conner" or "Finnigan" in any of the official reports, which suited both of them fine. Jake knew Alex would accept nothing more than thank you. It was his way of atoning for the lie he'd told Jake about Susan Crane in the first place.

One thing still puzzled Jake, and he supposed he'd never have the answer to it. Something Lila Beyers had shouted at him continued to plague him. He knew that the revenge motive, while certainly part of it, had not been the entire story. The motive was the one question mark in the reports appearing in the special editions of the *Arrow Bay Examiner* and in the official FBI reports. In his mind, he knew he'd always be able to hear Lila Beyers screaming at him, "She destroyed my family, she destroyed other people's lives, and she was going to destroy *me!*"

He suspected he *did* know a little bit of what that meant, if Susan Crane's pattern of destruction was any indication. Crane was likely going to pad her bank account extorting her sister, though Jake had no idea what information Crane had on her or where it had gone. He couldn't help feel a little bit sorry for Lila Beyers, then the cold, dead face of Monrovia would float before his eyes and any sympathy, no matter how remote, would flit away. His desire to know what exactly Susan Crane had on her sister evaporated. She was dead, Monrovia was dead, and as far as he was concerned, the ghost and stigma of Susan Crane attached to the *Elwha* was exorcised. As he watched the ferry round the curve of McDougal Point, he wished the ferry well.

The *Rosario* was going to be demolished later that week. After the bodies had been extricated, it was decided the derelict vessel was a menace and would be reduced to kindling by a large backhoe.

"Apparently Sheriff Danvers is cooperating to get a reduced sentence. The whole department is now under investigation. They're going to root out all the corruption, though most of it begins and ends with Danvers," said Rachel. "And I'm happy the coroner returned from hiding in California," she added, shaking her head. "Who knew Lila Beyers had such clout?"

"Her sister," said Jake. "That's what she was counting on, anyway. In a sick way, I think Lila Beyers did do the world a favor by bumping her sister off. Susan Crane was a—"

"Nasty piece of work," said Sam, Jason, and Rachel in unison. They'd heard this rant many times over the last two days.

"At least some good is coming out of it," Sam said thoughtfully.

"The sheriff's department is going to get a long-needed cleaning out," observed Jason, "a trio of truly nasty people can't hurt anyone anymore, and justice has been served."

"You sound like Kent C. Spievens," said Rachel with a chuckle. Jake stared out across the water. She took his hand and gave it a squeeze. "I know what you're thinking."

Sam looked at Jake, then at Rachel, and nodded. Jason did the same and said, "If only it had been the same for Chris."

After a few minutes of silence, Jason broke it. "I see I'm going to have to start reading these books. I feel out of the loop the way you all keep referring to them."

"I've got them all. Start with *Death of the Dowager*," said Sam.

"Why kill the guy in Seattle, though?" Rachel asked. "I still don't understand that."

"He let it slip about where she went. Very few people knew about the place on San Juan Island. I suspect they also felt he might carry out Crane's plans for her sister, whatever they may have been," said Jake.

"I think if we hadn't stuck our nose in, Dennis Crane and Jeremy Young might have met untimely ends as well," said Sam quietly.

"I hadn't thought of that," said Jake, squeezing Sam's hand under the table.

"We fell into the same trap as the authorities," said Rachel. "They all felt it had something to do with her stories, her work. She hadn't had contact with her sister or family in so long, who'd have thought anything about them?"

"That's a long time to harbor a grudge," said Jason.

"You can say that with a straight face with Ingrid Finnigan as our mother?" asked Jake. "She's still pissed at people from thirty years ago."

"Good point, little brother," said Jason with a wink. "Now, can we all agree on something?"

"What's that?" Rachel asked.

"No more sleuthing for you, eh, Jacob?" said Jason.

"Hear hear," said Rachel, raising her glass of Pepsi. "Here's to a long, fruitful, and hopefully decidedly dull career as a writer."

"I'll drink to that," said Sam, raising his glass.

"Me too," said Jake.

"That's settled then," said Jason, and they tapped their glasses together.

"'I think I shall retire to Devenport, my dear Henry,'" said Jake, quoting Harvey Wallace Claypoole's often-repeated line in the mystery series.

Their food arrived, and they tucked in with considerable vigor. Jake felt as if he hadn't had a proper meal in days and ate his eggs Benedict with particular relish. Sam and Rachel both wolfed down their corned beef hash while Jason tackled a chicken fried steak half the size of his plate. After they'd consumed their food, Jake enjoyed sipping coffee and chatting, feeling relief wash over him like waves hitting the beach outside.

"I still don't see how your friend's death—the man on the *Rosario*..." Rachel said.

"Arden," Sam supplied.

"How does Arden's death fit in with everything?" asked Rachel.

"It doesn't," said Sam, looking sadly into his cup. "Any more than the engine fire with your rental car, which was an unchecked recall issue on that model."

"What?" Rachel exclaimed. "Those bastards! I'll sue!"

"Calm down, Sadie," said Jake. "It's not important, is it? Really?"

"No," she said. "Now what about your friend, Alvin?"

"Arden," corrected Jake. "We asked about it."

"They'd just gotten the results in from the autopsy. Arden was riddled with cancer. He killed himself, probably to avoid the pain, which according to the coroner had to have been excruciating," said Sam. "There was so much debris around the body, I didn't see he still had a gun in his hand."

"I feel bad about that," Jake said. "We should have seen him more often."

"Jake, there was nothing we could have done," Sam reminded him. "Arden did everything his own way, right up to the end."

Jake nodded, looking out at the water. The sun had just burst through the low clouds, a widening patch of blue stretching out toward Mount Baker. A flock of seagulls took flight as the venerable ferry *Yakima* departed for Orcas Island, turning wide to avoid an incoming tug.

Sam's phone rang, making him jump. He looked at it, read the caller ID, smiled quizzically, and answered the phone. "O'Conner." He looked at Jake. "Yeah, Alex. Happy New Year to you. No, we're fine. Mr. McEvoy was very nice. Thank you. Did you want to talk to Jake? Oh. I see." He held the phone away from his mouth and said, "Jason, can you get a *Times* from the stand out front?" He turned back to the phone. "Okay. You want to join us? No, I understand. Sure. Soon. Okay, you too. By—Oh? Tell Jake 'It's over.' He'll understand? Okay. Yeah, you too, Alex. Bye."

"I don't see anything," said Jason, returning with the paper.

"He said to turn to the business section," said Sam.

"Ah," said Rachel knowingly.

"Sadie McKee," said Jake with a suspicious grin. "You *know* something, don't you?"

"*Absolutely Fabulous*," said Rachel. "Bubble remembering Patsy had a sister."

"Full points," said Jake, winking at Rachel. "Are you sure you have to go back to D.C.?"

"For a little while. Not long, I promise," she said. "Now, turn to the business section."

"He just said to tell Jake 'It's over' and that we'll all talk 'brass tacks soon.' He also said there should be a surprise out the window any minute."

"Well, here's the paper," said Jason, flopping it down.

Jake looked down. Suddenly all the air left his lungs.

BLACKBURN INDUSTRIES SHAKEUP
OLD GUARD FIRED WHILE COMPANY REORGANIZES
BLACKBURN JUNIOR OUSTED FROM OWN COMPANY

"Alex, you dog!" Sam said.

"So *that* is what he meant when he kept saying 'it'll be over soon,'" said Jake, grinning. "The sneaky little S.O.B. took over his father's company!"

Jake and Sam sat back and laughed until tears ran out of their eyes. Jake was still laughing when he noticed Sam had suddenly grown quiet, his eyes wide.

"I don't believe it!" he breathed.

"Sam, what is it?" burst Rachel frantically, fearing a heart attack. "Are you okay?"

"I'm fine! Just tell me what I'm seeing is real! Jake, do you see her?"

Jake's eyes were now riveted to the water as well. The tug, which had previously rounded the point, causing the *Yakima* to avoid it, was now completely in view, its tow behind it.

Sailing into a patch of sunlit water was the streamlined form of a ship, rust streaking her sides. Her ill-fitting funnel, though not her original, had been repainted a magnificent crimson. Her name was clearly painted on her bow.

Names, Jake quickly amended, for there were, in fact, two of them painted on the bow. The much older *S E C H E L T Q U E E N* was preceded by the name *C H I N O O K* painted in black.

"So *that's* who bought her," Sam said, grinning. "I don't believe it."

"I don't either," said Jake, slinging his arm around his partner. "But maybe you'll get to realize your dream of restoring the old girl."

"You think?" asked Sam excitedly.

"You think Alex would go to anyone else?"

The *Sechelt Queen*, once known as the *Chinook*, still managed to look elegant. Her arrow-like profile, rudely shorn of its proper bow, still held a dignity. Her clean lines, designed by William Gibbs, still looked graceful despite the rust streaking her sides. As she sailed into the sunlit waters toward Sutherland Shipyards, Jake found himself wishing her well and wondered just what Alex had up his sleeve.

"I hope not," said Sam.

"I'd say New Year's is off to an interesting start," said Rachel.

"Well," said Sam, grinning and squeezing Jake's hand as he looked at his family gathered around the table. "We'll just have to wait and see."

About the Author

Steve Pickens was born in Seattle, Washington. He has spent his entire life in the land of Bigfoot, strong coffee, ferryboats, heavy rain, and active volcanoes, all of which have influenced his work.

When not writing, he can be found tending and photographing flowers in the garden, taking trips into the Cascades, or wandering along the shores of Puget Sound. He and his husband live in northwestern Washington in a town that bears more than a passing resemblance to the one in his mysteries with far too much ferry ephemera and two spoiled cats.

Steve can be contacted at StevePickens37@gmail.com
www.steve--pickens.blogspot.com

Books Available From Bold Strokes Books

Final Departure by Steve Pickens. What do you do when an unexpected body interrupts the worst day of your life? (978-1-62639-536-7)

Love on the Jersey Shore by Richard Natale. Two working-class cousins help one another navigate the choppy waters of sexual chemistry and true love. (978-1-62639-550-3)

Night Sweats by Tom Cardamone. These stories are as gripping as the hand on your throat. (978-1-62639-572-5)

Soul's Blood by Stephen Graham King. After receiving a summons from a love long past, Keene and his associates, Lexa-Blue and the sentient ship Maverick Heart, are plunged into turmoil on a planet poised for war. (978-1-62639-508-4)

Corpus Calvin by David Swatling. Cloverkist Inn may be haunted, but a ghost materializes from Jason Dekker's past and Calvin's canine instinct kicks in to protect a young boy from mortal danger. (978-1-62639-428-5)

Brothers by Ralph Josiah Bardsley. Blood is thicker than water, but you can drown in either. Jamus Cork and Sean Malloy struggle against tradition to find love in the Irish enclave of South Boston. (978-1-62639-538-1)

Every Unworthy Thing by Jon Wilson. Gang wars, racial tensions, a kidnapped girl, and a lone PI! What could go wrong? (978-1-62639-514-5)

Puppet Boy by Christian Baines. Budding filmmaker Eric can't stop thinking about the handsome young actor that's transferred to his class. Could Julien be his muse? Even his first boyfriend? Or something far more sinister? (978-1-62639-510-7)

The Prophecy by Jerry Rabushka. Religion and revolution threaten to bring an ancient civilization to its knees…unless love does it first. (978-1-62639-440-7)

Heart of the Liliko'i by Dena Hankins. Secrets, sabotage, and grisly human remains stall construction on an ancient Hawaiian burial ground, but the sexual connection between Kerala and Ravi keeps building toward a volcanic explosion. (978-1-62639-556-5)

Lethal Elements by Joel Gomez-Dossi. When geologist Tom Burrell is hired to perform mineral studies in the Adirondack Mountains, he finds himself lost in the wilderness and being chased by a hired gun. (978-1-62639-368-4)

The Heart's Eternal Desire by David Holly. Sinister conspiracies threaten Seaton French and his lover, Dusty Marley, and only by tracking the source of the conspiracy can Seaton and Dusty hold true to the heart's eternal desire. (978-1-62639-412-4)

The Orion Mask by Greg Herren. After his father's death, Heath comes to Louisiana to meet his mother's family and learn the truth about her death—but some secrets can prove deadly. (978-1-62639-355-4)

The Strange Case of the Big Sur Benefactor by Jess Faraday. Billiwack, CA, 1884. All Rosetta Stein wanted to do was test her new invention. Now she has a mystery, a stalker, and worst of all, a partner. (978-1-62639-516-9)

One Hot Summer Month by Donald Webb. Damien, an avid cockhound, flits from one sexual encounter to the next until he finally meets someone who assuages his sexual libido. (978-1-62639-409-4)

The Indivisible Heart by Patrick Roscoe. An investigation into a gruesome psycho-sexual murder and an account of the victim's final days are interwoven in this dark detective story of the human heart. (978-1-62639-341-7)

Fool's Gold by Jess Faraday. 1895. Overworked secretary Ira Adler thinks a trip to America will be relaxing. But rattlesnakes, train robbers, and the U.S. Marshals Service have other ideas. (978-1-62639-340-0)

Big Hair and a Little Honey by Russ Gregory. Boyfriend troubles abound as Willa and Grandmother land new ones and Greg tries to hold on to Matt while chasing down a shipment of stolen hair extensions. (978-1-62639-331-8)

Death by Sin by Lyle Blake Smythers. Two supernatural private detectives in Washington, D.C., battle a psychotic supervillain spreading a new sex drug that only works on gay men, increasing the male orgasm and killing them. (978-1-62639-332-5)

Buddha's Bad Boys by Alan Chin. Six stories, six gay men trudging down the road to enlightenment. What they each find is the last thing in the world they expected. (978-1-62639-244-1)

Play It Forward by Frederick Smith. When the worlds of a community activist and a pro basketball player collide, little do they know that their dirty little secrets can lead to a public scandal…and an unexpected love affair. (978-1-62639-235-9)

GingerDead Man by Logan Zachary. Paavo Wolfe sells horror but isn't prepared for what he finds in the oven or the bathhouse; he's in hot water again, and the killer is turning up the heat. (978-1-62639-236-6)

Myth and Magic: Queer Fairy Tales, edited by Radclyffe and Stacia Seaman. Myth, magic, and monsters—the stuff of childhood dreams (or nightmares) and adult fantasies. (978-1-62639-225-0)

Balls & Chain by Eric Andrews-Katz. In protest of the marriage equality bill, the son of Florida's governor has been kidnapped. Agent Buck 98 is back, and the alligators aren't the only things biting. (978-1-62639-218-2)

Blackthorn by Simon Hawk. Rian Blackthorn, Master of the Hall of Swords, vowed he would not give in to the advances of Prince Corin, but he finds himself dueling with more than swords as Corin pursues him with determined passion. (978-1-62639-226-7)

Café Eisenhower by Richard Natale. A grieving young man who travels to Eastern Europe to claim an inheritance finds friendship, romance, and betrayal, as well as a moving document relating a secret lifelong love affair. (978-1-62639-217-5)

Murder in the Arts District by Greg Herren. An investigation into a new and possibly shady art gallery in New Orleans' fabled Arts District soon leads Chanse into a dangerous world of forgery, theft…and murder. A Chanse MacLeod mystery. (978-1-62639-206-9)

Calvin's Head by David Swatling. Jason Dekker and his dog, Calvin, are homeless in Amsterdam when they stumble on the victim of a grisly murder—and become targets for the calculating killer, Gadget. (978-1-62639-193-2)

The Return of Jake Slater by Zavo. Jake Slater mistakenly believes his lover, Ben Masters, is dead. Now a wanted man in Abilene, Jake rides to Mexico to begin a new life and heal his broken heart. (978-1-62639-194-9)

Rise of the Thing Down Below by Daniel W. Kelly. Nothing kills sex on the beach like a fishman out of water… Third in the Comfort Cove Series. (978-1-62639-207-6)

First Exposure by Alan Chin. Navy Petty Officer Skyler Thompson battles homophobia from his shipmates, the military, and his wife when he takes a second job at a gay-owned florist. Rather than yield to pressure to quit, he battles homophobia in order to nurture his artistic talents. (978-1-62639-082-9)

The Fall of the Gay King by Simon Hawk. Investigative journalist Logan Walker receives a mysterious erotic journal that details the sexual relations of a corporate giant known in the business world as the "Gay King of Kings." (978-1-62639-076-8)

Backstrokes by Dylan Madrid. When pianist Crawford Paul meets lifeguard Armando Leon, he accepts Armando's offer to help him overcome his fear of water by way of private lessons. As friendship turns into a summer affair, their lust for one another turns to love. (978-1-62639-069-0)

The Raptures of Time by David Holly. Mack Frost and his friends journey across an alien realm, through homoerotic adventures, suffering humiliation and rapture, making friends and enemies, always seeking a gateway back home to Oregon. (978-1-62639-068-3)